W9-BYF-486

DISCARD

Lewis & Clark Library

3 1159 00 513 5360

120 S. Last Chance Gulch
Helena, MT 59601
lewisandclarklibrary.org

DISCARD

Bridge to Happiness

Center Point
Large Print

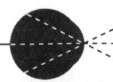

**This Large Print Book carries the
Seal of Approval of N.A.V.H.**

Bridge to Happiness

Jill Barnett

LEWIS & CLARK LIBRARY
120 S. LAST CHANCE GULCH
HELENA, MONTANA 59601

CENTER POINT LARGE PRINT
THORNDIKE, MAINE

This Center Point Large Print edition
is published in the year 2013 by arrangement with
BelleBooks, Inc.

Copyright © 2011 by Jill Barnett.

All rights reserved.

This is a work of fiction.
Names, characters, places and incidents are either
the products of the author's imagination or are used
fictitiously. Any resemblance to actual persons (living
or dead,) events or locations is entirely coincidental.

The text of this Large Print edition is unabridged.
In other aspects, this book may vary
from the original edition.
Printed in the United States of America
on permanent paper.
Set in 16-point Times New Roman type.

ISBN: 978-1-61173-936-7

Library of Congress Cataloging-in-Publication Data

Barnett, Jill.
Bridge to Happiness / Jill Barnett. — Center Point Large Print edition.
pages cm
ISBN 978-1-61173-936-7 (Library binding : alk. paper)
1. Large type books. I. Title.
PS3552.A6983B75 2013
813′.54—dc23

2013028198

Dedication

March is not us, nor are her experiences ours. This story is fiction. But we know her world, because we have traveled down the same kind of unfamiliar, muddied roads, because we had to overcome the past to find a future, because of this, and so much more, *Bridge To Happiness* is for Jane, Meryl, Cathy, JJ, Deb, Betina, and me.

What is this really like? Never mind the conventions and the decisions we've all made together. What is it *really* like?

—Mike Nichols, *Inside the Actor's Studio*

PART ONE

San Francisco is a mad city—inhabited for
the most part by perfectly insane people
whose women are of a remarkable beauty.

—*Rudyard Kipling*

Chapter One

The month of March is a time of lions and lambs, and in California, the time of four-leafed mustard blooms some claim are luckier than clover. Certainly they are more resilient. No matter what the weather: freak snow and ice, brush fires, crackling drought or Pineapple-Express-rains that drive homes down crumbling hillsides, despite everything that Mother Nature can cast down from the heavens, each spring the mustard grows back.

March Randolph Cantrell was named for the time of year she came into the world, and had lived all of her life in a golden state. Native Californians are immanent beings who can recognize instinctively the color and stillness of earthquake weather, and are never divided by that invisible latitude/attitude that separates Northern from Southern; they understand the human geography of one whose first breath of air was in a land of gold rushes, gold hillsides, and golden bridges.

A native can stand on the sandy spot where the biggest and deepest blue ocean in the world touches land and know there are more hungry sharks behind them than in front of them.

California native was just one of many things

that defined March: woman, daughter, artist, wife, mother, friend, businesswoman, now grandmother, a title that sounded too decrepit for a baby boomer who still wore string-bikini underwear and listened to rock music.

Growing up on the West Coast in the 1950's and 60's, March and her sister May were known as those Randolph girls with the strange names. Back in Connecticut, where the Randolph family had deep roots, names like March and May were simple tradition, as appropriate as Birch and Rebecca, and not uncommon to girls with a great aunt named Hester, who had pointed out during one family holiday, "California is a fine place to live if you happen to be an orange."

One bright blue day when March was eight, someone called the Randolph girls California natives. So with the peacock feathers from her mother's vase sticking out of her ponytail, March stood at the medicine cabinet mirror and war-painted her face with blue and white tempera paint left over from vacation bible school.

For those few weeks during an incalescent and sullen August, she ran around with a rubber *Cochise* tomahawk tucked into the waist of her seersucker shorts, speaking to everyone in bad Indian dialogue from an old black and white western.

At night, in those deep, still, blue hours, the Randolph girls lay in bed with thoughts of secret crushes and dreams of grown-up lives. Her sister May had a passion for heart throbs like Tab Hunter and James Dean. March dreamt about falling in love with someone like *Cochise*, a noble man with a big dream. That was 1958. Ten years later, she met him.

A year after the Summer of Love, 1968 San Francisco was filled with youthful dreamers fast becoming disillusioned. The sweet legacy of Haight had suddenly become hate. Every night the broadcast news about Viet Nam was too bleak to watch and too important to miss. In a single year both Martin Luther King Jr. and Bobby Kennedy were gone. Coffee house talk and the underground presses compared recent events to history's anarchies. The city's street-corner disciples railed at the establishment, shaking their fists as they cried over the injustice of men killed here and overseas.

At home, where it was supposed to be free and safe, someone was assassinating the country's heroes. Most people carried a silent, dark dread down to their bones, and the youth of city sought anything available to pull away from a world so out of control they had to shout at it.

March's father was only a single generation away, yet a continent stood between their ideas. He taught math and geography, was logical, conservative, a genius, a veteran. Her mother was a housewife who sewed from Butterick patterns, played bridge and the organ at church, and served dinner at six o'clock. March was raised to be standardized and conventional, the perfect round peg to fit in the perfectly round hole.

Her sister May fit precisely into the Randolph mold. She was stockings and white shoes. May was the one who went off to Smith and was picked as one of Glamour's college girls, modeling in the magazine in her plaid skirt and cashmere sweater, her hair cut in precise angles and her smile as perfect as piano keys, even without braces.

March, however, was bare feet and Bernardo sandals. She regularly forgot to wear her retainer and lost it often enough that she had to get mouth molds for new ones at least three times a year. Right after graduation, she was out of her parents' house and living on her own near the Haight in a room cut out of the attic in an old Victorian. She worked a part-time shift in a coffee house bookstore and attended the Art Institute, where thought was free, ungendered, and where those East Coast kinds of traditions her sister May wrote home about were nowhere to be found.

San Francisco's artists worked in loud, in-your-face-you-can't-ignore-us colors that defined the place and time. At the Institute, among so many unique individuals, March didn't have to be exactly like her family.

A close friend from a graphics class created psychedelic posters advertising local rock shows at the Fillmore and Avalon ballrooms. Another designed velvet, lace, and leather clothing, fringed sweaters and beaded tops for a trendy boutique frequented by local rock singers. Some poster work came to March via her graphics friend, and by connection, she was soon part of the San Francisco music scene most weekends.

It was dark inside the Fillmore that night in mid-June, one of those down moments between music sets. The place was filled with three times more people than city hall permitted, because Joplin and Santana were on the bill. The cloying, sweet scent of hashish floated above the crowd in foggy clouds of contact highs, and crudely-rolled cigarettes were passed from hand to hand, glowing like red fireflies through small, compact circles of people.

As one of her friends dragged her through the crowd, she spotted a stranger a few feet away, standing alone, wearing a Nehru jacket, faded jeans and sandals. His hair was thick and dark and almost to his shoulders. His profile was noble, even the lack of light. His close-clipped black beard couldn't hide his dark, intense looks, the kind of guy girls noticed but only the bravest or silliest would ever approach. Within seconds, the music started again and she lost sight of him as he was engulfed by a flood of half-stoned people making for the stage.

By midnight the Fillmore's light show rose up from behind the band in those vibrant, poster-colored hues, pulsing with the ragged voice of Janis singing a spiritual song turned into hard rock by Big Brother and the Holding Company. Near the stage rim, March danced in a circle, barefooted, her sandals stashed in the deep pockets of her long velvet dress, her arms raised high in the air and five inches of mismatched bangle bracelets rattled down her arms.

Freedom rang through the notes of the music and the words of songs: there was nothing left to lose, something that felt more true lately. Her loose, uncut hair hung freely, and beneath the heavy velvet dress she wore nothing—free after being held captive by elastic garter and Kotex belts. Even the apples in a copper pot by the Fillmore stage were free for the taking, but often laced with something to make your mood too free.

When she looked up, he was standing in front of her, his hand out as if they'd known each other forever. But she kept dancing, shouting over the music. "What do you want?"

"You."

His eyes weren't drug-shot, but clear, his manner too confident and too knowing for her. He'd caught her off-guard and she didn't know how to react, so she shook her head and turned her back to him, cutting him dead and feeling surprisingly calm about doing so.

Earlier, in a ballroom filled with people, she had looked at him and felt something she couldn't name, followed by an odd sense of regret when he'd melted into the crowd. She had thought about it a little later and told herself the moment had been silly and Hollywood, the kind of moment that called for elevator music playing in the background.

A numb second or two passed before she felt his breath above her, the heat of his body as he came closer. Guys came onto girls all the time. Three, four, or more times a night someone would hit on her. But they gave up easily when she always hesitated. You couldn't go two blocks without seeing a sign that said, Make Love Not War. Love was as free as thought, as free as speech, and as free as most girls nowadays.

But he hadn't moved on to some other girl who would give him what he wanted. He stayed by her, but didn't touch her, a good thing since she might have incinerated right there.

The music stopped with a loud end note from the band. In that first heartbeat of silence, he leaned in and said in her ear, "You're a fraud."

She faced him. "What?"

"I see a barefoot girl, dancing alone, dressed in velvet, and with ribbons in her hair. If I stand close enough, when she moves, her jewelry sounds like tambourines." He touched the necklace she wore. "Tell me those are love beads."

She stepped back and pulled the necklace with her. "Do I know you?"

"No. But I'm trying to fix that mistake."

"Who are you?" she asked.

"You didn't answer my question."

"You called me a fraud first. Let's stay strangers for now and deal with that."

He shrugged. "You disappointed me, Sunshine."

"March. My name is March."

"That's different." He sounded surprised. "I like the name March."

"My mother will be thrilled."

"Good. You can take me home to meet her. Mothers love me. My own can talk about me for hours."

"I don't live at home."

"Even better. Where do you live?"

"I'm not going to tell you where I live." She laughed then. "I don't even know your name."

"I'm Michael Cantrell. Don't disappoint me, Sunshine."

Sunshine? The truth was she liked that he called her Sunshine; it gave her a light case of butterflies. But out of self-protection, she ignored that. "Okay, Michael. Look, you don't know me so how can I disappoint you?"

He didn't answer immediately, but studied her thoughtfully, seeming to find his words with care.

She knew she was giving him a hard time, and she had the awful thought that the next word he might say next would be "Goodbye." He could easily turn around and leave, when secretly that was the last thing she wanted him to do.

"You look to me like the kind of girl who chooses to walk in the rain. Who stands on the breakwater, arms spread wide and laughing as a storm rages in. A girl who sings even when there's no music playing. And quotes poetry. Who'll eat raw oysters and drink Ouzo. The rare girl who will easily jump out of a plane or into my arms. Someone who'll love me so long and hard I can't stand up in the morning."

It took a minute for his words to sink in. His words? Oh . . . his words. So far from what she'd expected. She had always thought in a visual sense, the natural artist in her, believing life was most powerful if spoken through the eyes. Through vision, life had volume and depth, color and impression. The things you saw, you could always remember in color.

But his words came with more feeling than any first visual impression she could ever paint in her mind. She understood clearly at that moment the color of words.

What he said to her was so different from anything anyone had ever said to her. Until that moment, standing in front of this one guy, she would have never believed a minute of conversation could affect her so completely.

She heard his voice over again in her head

saying those things about her. Is that who she was? A free spirit. Or was that only who she wanted to be?

This stranger standing before her was suddenly something else altogether, and he watched her as if her reaction were the most important in his life. He was perfectly serious, waiting, and a little on edge. The way he looked at her made her feel exposed, film out in the noonday sun; vulnerable, like he could see her past and into her future; and sexually charged, naked and out of control.

The music started again, loud and vibrant, and the crowd closed in. She had moved back as far as she could and felt the hard edge of the stage against her shoulder. Still, only a few inches separated her from him—they were breathing each other's air—like a helium balloon she felt as if she needed to be anchored to earth. The poetry of what he had just said to her, the images it created, his honesty, all deserved more than her usual smart comebacks and flip comments.

Clearly this was one of those seminal times in her life when a new door opened wide. She could choose to walk right by it, or through it. There was still enough of the good girl in her to make her pause. Her sister May would not understand and would run in the other direction. Her friends might see open possibility. But did anyone else really matter?

In a crowd of almost a thousand, at that single moment, there was only the two of them. Michael Cantrell stood in front of her and asked her to love him. So without a word, she took his hand and left.

Chapter Two

For the six months after that night at the Fillmore, Mike Cantrell had kept a secret part of himself from March. Some days more than others, it was easier to believe the right time to tell her just never came. He told himself she was worried about making her rent when her shift at the bookstore was cut; about a difficult project for a final exam; a friend from school who couldn't find his muse without psychedelic drugs. She had too much on her plate.

And those times when they were having fun—so often now—he would think, why screw it up? Other times, in his head, he couldn't find the exact right words he could say aloud. Funny that he could find the words for justification. He could find the words for his excuses.

To hide one passion while another consumed him was not an easy existence, like straddling life between two worlds. His life was great with her in it. So great he wanted to stand on a mountain and shout. Amazing! Righteous!

But the truth was that March was fast becoming the best part of him. Yet she didn't know one of the biggest parts of who he was. She didn't know his dream. Some wounds just ran deeper than love and trust, and got all mixed up in his head when he tried to believe. What he did believe was families could so simply and unknowingly cut the deepest wounds in one another.

Don Cantrell, his father, was an executive with Spreckles, the sugar company, a success, a man of few words and many expectations. Mike and his older brother Brad had grown up at a dinner table with only their mother on most nights. Except Sundays. The one night when his dad would sit at the head of the table set with fine china and dominated by a standing rib roast, smoked ham or leg of lamb, a knife in one hand as he tried and failed to carve some kind of relationship with his sons during an awkward, too-formal meal. Being a father was the single thing at which Don Cantrell failed.

His father's success was a matter of pride, driven by some hungry, innate gene that battled with the few cells his dad inherited that were gentle and understanding. He was self-made, the son of a farmer, grandson of a Swiss immigrant who relocated to America near the turn of the century to save his sons from being conscripted.

Last year Brad had torn up his draft card, stuck the pieces to the refrigerator along with his draft notice, and was now somewhere in Canada, a subject handled in whispers by the family and friends and anyone who knew the truth about his older brother. That their ancestors had come here to escape the draft was almost as ironic to Mike as the idea that his father worked for a company that produced sugar.

Since the day Brad ran, everything Don Cantrell had expected from both of his sons fell on Mike's shoulders. In a moment of foolish idealism, Mike had made the mistake of telling his dad about his grand idea, and what he wanted to do with it and his future.

His father laughed, until he realized Mike was perfectly serious. Don told him he was a fool who needed to grow up and stop thinking life was only about fun and games and things that weren't important. What Mike needed was to think straight, be a man, find something he could do to make an honest living for himself or for a family, that was . . . if he ever chose to become responsible enough to think of someone other than himself.

Because the most important man in Mike's life called him a failure, Mike thought everyone else might believe that, too. He went to college since that was what the world expected, and he didn't want to find himself in Dah Nang any more than the next guy.

But one of his buddies once joked if there had

been six feet of snow in the jungle, Mike would have signed the enlistment papers and taken the oath. The joke was too close to the truth. Mike would crawl through jungle, through desert, through nails to get to the perfect hill, to find the perfect conditions, to experience perfect packed snow.

For almost a week straight it had been snowing in the Sierras, a sign it was time to test March, or himself, or what they were together, so with some measure of hope and false courage he walked into her place at five thirty on a Saturday morning, fell on her bed, swatted her on the nicest backside he'd ever seen and said, "Pack some warm clothes. I'm taking you to the mountains."

They had to chain up on Interstate 80, but came into the Tahoe Basin as the snow stopped and patches of blue grew into a huge bowl of a Sierra sky, the lake shimmering as silver as the ore mined by all those barons from the last century. Mike left the main road circling the lake and soon pulled his old car into the parking lot at a small North Shore ski area.

March turned in the seat. "What's this? You told me not to bring my skis. Ugh. I hate to rent."

"We're not going skiing."

"I hate surprises more than renting equipment."

"No, you don't. What you hate is not knowing the surprise."

"I must be doing something wrong in this

relationship because you understand me. I'm supposed to be the mystery woman, capable of shocking. To be an enigma. To keep you constantly on your toes. A true paradox. I want you to look at me and see fine wine, hundred year old scotch. Smooth and unexpected." She frowned at him. "Instead I've become boring. Like milk."

"I like milk, and you'll never be boring. Let's go."

He pulled gear from the back of the wagon, slung the large bag over his shoulder and carried the rest. She took one canvas duffel bag from him, then locked her cold fingers through his and trudged alongside.

In the complete silence of freshly fallen snow, the slick fabric of their winter wear rubbed together and made a scratching sound. The air was cold and tasted pure. Mike was quiet, a million things running through his head and all of them centered on the fact that now it was too late to go back.

After a few minutes she said, "This better be good."

"Are you warm enough?"

"Depends on what for. I won't know until I see where you're taking me."

"It's a surprise," was all her single-minded questioning would get out of him. He took her to the maintenance building—a trio of oversized metal garages where the snow had already been packed down. From behind came the sound of a snow plow engine and a big yellow Cat chugged and coughed around the corner, stopping in front of them.

The engine died and Rob Cantrell jumped down into the soft powder. He pulled off his ice-crusted ski mask, sending his black frizzy hair in every direction, and walked toward them, ski vest open over a flannel shirt, a leather bota bag with a red plastic cap hanging from his waist. "Mike! Hey, cousin. You made it. Great."

"Rob. This is March."

Rob stared at March for longer than a couple of deep breaths and said, "I think I'm in love."

She laughed and Mike punched him in the arm. "Back off. I saw her first."

"You always were a lucky stiff. Although I'll tell you something, March. He's the blackest sheep in the family."

"Really?" March threaded her arm through his in a way that said everything Mike didn't have to. "The family's black sheep? I'm glad to hear it. I would hate to think I ruined one of the good ones."

One thing about March, she wasn't easy to fluster. She seldom lost a word battle, seldom missed a beat.

"I like her," Rob said, recovering well for a first meeting with March Randolph. "And, I guess I was wrong. Your brother Big Brad earned the blackest sheep distinction. Any word from the family draft dodger?"

"Last I heard he was hitchhiking through British Columbia. But that was a few months back."

"And Uncle Don?"

"Still a jerk."

"That's my father's brother," Rob said. "Same gene pool. Same personality pool. The war hero in my dad still can't forgive me for being 4-F. Look. Put your gear in the cab and climb on board. I'll help March up."

"Just keep your hands where I can see them," Mike said.

Minutes passed as they rode the Cat around the base of the mountain, and Rob told March every stupid when-Mike-and-I-were-kids story he could muster up: the time they stole penny candy from the neighborhood market and were picked up by a squad car and brought home with sirens blaring; a Sunday when they put Milk of Magnesia in their grandmother's famous butter cake; how loud Mike had screamed the day their grandfather chopped the head off a chicken and the headless bird came right at him; and the day they were fishing for snapping turtles and were cornered by their grandfather's prized bull, an animal Rob swore was the size of Godzilla.

Mike tossed out some terrible Rob-tormenting-his-younger-sister stories, until, shaking her head, March said, "You both have no idea how glad I am I never had any brothers."

The Cat took a sharp turn and easily rumbled down through the trees and into a clearing where there was a short steep run with a rope tow, chained off with a "Closed" sign. His cousin killed the engine and hopped down. "Here, pretty baby. Jump into my arms and run off with me. Leave this weird geek. I swear I'll be sweet to you."

"Sweet like you were when you locked your poor sister in that trunk?" March jumped down on her own and gave Rob a quick pat on the shoulder. "Thanks, but I don't think so."

"Don't think I'm terrible. She only cried for an hour. Hell, I couldn't sit down for days." He raised his hand to Mike. "Give me a minute. I'll unlock that chain and start the rope tow. Then the run is all yours."

Mike dropped the bags. "I brought three boards. You staying?"

Rob turned around, walking backwards and grinning. "Absolutely."

"What boards?" March looked over his shoulder as Mike dug through the gear, grabbed his goggles, and pulled on his ski gloves. She leaned closer. "Are you going to tell me what we're doing now?"

"No." He unzipped a long ski bag and pulled out three of the latest and best skiboards he'd made in his garage during the summer. The skiboards were wide and formed like a skateboard without the skates. They had foot plates and buckled straps to hold regular leather snow boots, and he'd crafted the edges of each board as close as he could to the metal edges on his Rossignol skis.

"Mike?" March asked, frowning. "What are you doing?"

He slung a board over his shoulder. "We'll show you. Watch us." When she started to argue he added, "Stay here, woman, and watch."

She saluted him irreverently, then gave him the finger.

The rope tow was glacier-slow and seemed to take forever to get to the top of the run. But once there and poised at its crest, a wide chute of white before him, the air like fresh laundry, the sun gleaming almost too white on the powder below, Mike adjusted his goggles and looked over at Rob. "Ten bucks says it takes us twenty passes to the bottom, and you fall first."

"You're on." Rob pulled down his own goggles and they took off a heartbeat apart.

The snow was perfect, the new board design much improved, and better than his skis in deep powder, which showered up and over them. It was something to be on the mountain again. He shouted out, unable to keep his excitement inside, and shook his fists, crossing Rob twice and edging ahead down the run.

The new board turned more easily, cut well, and gave him more control than on these same slopes last spring, when he'd ridden so often his old board felt like he was skiing on a cloud, a natural extension, floating on the snow, almost like flying.

Years ago, for only a short time, there had been a ride at Disneyland called the Flying Saucers. Contained inside a huge, circular pit in Tomorrowland, the saucers were big, flat, round and rubber. They hovered off the ground just a few inches and could race across the pit when you leaned into the direction you wanted to fly. That is, if you had a clear path. Without one, you bounced off the other saucers like buoyant bumper cars.

That one summer trip, he and Brad had spent half the day and into the night chasing each other around the pit and crashing into each other and the walls, bouncing away, and really flying. It had been the best ride at Disneyland, a true E-ticket, though the park hadn't been using old fashioned ticket books much anymore. When the amusement park first opened, they sold ticket booklets for their rides and each ticket class was A, B, C, D, E, E being the best rides in the park and the fewest tickets in the booklet. That was how he felt on this hill, at that moment, on that board. All he had to do was lean into the direction he wanted to fly. His newest skiboard was an E-ticket.

He cut across the hill and flip-turned, then flew past his cousin. Rob tried the same maneuver and went down. "Ten bucks!" Mike hollered as he passed him, whipped down to the bottom and skidded to a stop right in front of March. Snow coated his lenses and he could only see part of her smile, so he raised his goggles and kissed her before she could speak, then lifted her off the ground, spinning around. "God . . . It doesn't get any better than this."

"Yes, it does. I need to be on that hill with you. Let's go." She picked up the other board and ran toward the rope tow ahead of him.

"March, wait!"

But all too fast she was on the board, hanging onto the rope and heading up the hill. About twenty feet up, he said, "Get off now and we'll take a short test run first."

"No guts, no glory!"

"Come on. Get off."

She looked back at him, probably planning to flip him off again, but she lost her balance and slipped off the rope, swearing. So he stepped off and helped her up. "Don't be so quick. Let me tell you what to do."

"There's a man for you," she said. "Always wanting to tell a woman what to do." For just a moment she looked irritated.

"I don't want to bring you home with a broken leg, Sunshine."

"I've been skiing since I was three."

"This is different than skiing. More like a skateboard. Have you ever ridden one?"

"Yes." But the way she said it told him March and a skateboard weren't close friends. Her stance was unyielding. "So come on, big man. Tell me what to do. Time's a-wasting."

"I'm waiting for you to tell me what happened on the skateboard."

"This snow is a lot softer than concrete."

"Break anything?"

"Nothing important." She turned away and looked up the hill.

"I have all day."

"Okay, okay. I only wore a cast on my wrist for six weeks. I can do this. Really. I can." Then she relaxed long enough for him to tell her how to turn and most important: to dig in her heels to stop.

"You should be good at that," he said.

"Funny man." She patted him on the cheek.

"I'll go first. You can follow, but not until after I stop at the bottom. Agreed?"

"Yes. Yes. Yes . . . come on."

"Watch me and don't go until I tell you. Got it?"

"Yes, master."

Laughing, he took off down the short, flatter section of the run, stopped and turned back toward her.

"Can I go now, master? Please? Please?"

"Someday your mouth is going to get you in deep trouble."

"It already has," she called down to him. "Just ask my father. Although he's not talking to me this week." She took off.

To his complete amazement she made three perfect turns—not even a wobble—stopped a few feet from him grinning and cocky. Rob was at the top of the run, whistling loudly. Typical March, she made an exaggerated bow, her hand gesturing from her forehead like a Swami. But she bent too far, lost her balance and fell on her face in the powder.

It took a minute for her to look up at him, snow hiding her expression, her voice a little muffled, "*Now* will you let me go all the way to the top?"

The first thing out of Rob's mouth when they came off the rope tow at the top of the run was, "Wow. She's a natural."

"Why do you men always talk about us as if we're not here?"

"Sorry," Rob said. "But hell, I skidded down the hill on my face the first time I tried this. Tell her, Mike. My nose was bleeding everywhere. Look. No blood. She went down that hill like she'd been doing this for years."

Mike expected a smart comeback, but March wasn't paying attention. She stood right at the edge of the run looking down. "You know . . . if

I had poles," she said thoughtfully, "I could really shove off. Maybe get a little air."

"You can get air. Just jump," Rob said. "Like this." He pulled his knees up and was off.

"No!" Mike reached for her. "Don't do it."

But it was too late. She was already in the air, board pulled up to her chest so tightly she looked like a big, dark human fist, sailing through the air, the fur-trimmed hood on her parka hanging behind her.

He stopped breathing until she landed on the steepest part of the hill. The board flew out from under her and she tumbled head over heels for a good ten feet. When he reached her, she was already sitting up, hands resting on her knees. All she said to him after she spit the snow from her mouth was, "I need poles."

"No you don't. It's called balance," he said and took off.

She cupped her hands and called out. "It's called unfair advantage. Cheater!" She stepped back into the board and came after him full speed, yelling at him. He stopped at the bottom of the run, turned just as she sat down low on the board and came right at him.

She took him out, both of them tumbling together in the snow, her laughter muffled until they lay still and dusted in powder. She raised her head and said, "Gotcha. Master."

"I hate surprises," he spit snow.

"No, you don't. What you hate is not knowing the surprise."

"Funny."

"I know," she said.

"I don't get it. Have you ever surfed?"

"No."

"Slalom waterskied?"

"A few times. I wasn't very good. Why?"

"How the hell did you come down that mountain so fast without falling?"

"Talent, my dear. My innate skill. The ability to learn on my feet. With my feet. Ha!" She picked up the board. "Besides, I'm a woman." Then she began to sing a Maria Muldaur hit about all the things a woman could do.

She stood above him, dancing, singing, and grinning as if the world were hers. He rested his arms on his knees. "What does being a woman have to do with it?"

"Old Russian proverb. Women can do everything; men can do the rest." She held out her hand. "Get up, pokey. Let's do it again."

So that was how Mike spent only an hour teaching March to board, instead of the whole weekend he'd expected. When he thought about it later, driving to his cousin's cabin near Tahoe City to drop off their stuff, exhausted, high on the day and her, he realized he shouldn't have been surprised. Nothing about March was expected. How nuts it was that she wanted to be special and thought she was ordinary. She was better than one of his father's expensive wines, better than any hundred year old Scotch.

Sunshine. The name just came out of his mouth at the Fillmore that night, along with everything else he was thinking and feeling. Enter brain, exit mouth. He'd spilled his guts and said exactly what he thought, all the while expecting her to turn and run. But here she was, now the brightest part of his life. His luckiest hunch.

At dinner that evening with his cousin over draft beer and thick sirloin burgers covered in onion rings, served in red plastic baskets at his favorite place, a small shack near the water packed with locals every night, they sat on metal chairs and ate on an old, mismatched dinette table in front of a huge fire. She quizzed him about everything, how he made the boards, where his idea for them had come from.

"It all started with a sled you could stand on and slide down the hill, a Snurfer. But before I ever saw one, I'd spent plenty of years on a skateboard. And Brad and I surfed summers in Santa Cruz."

"We all got Snurfers one year for Christmas from our grandfather," Rob told her. "Gramps said they reminded him of when he was a kid and they used to ride down hills standing on barrel slats tied together with clothesline." Rob nodded at Mike. "Genius here was the one who after one Snurfing season wanted to improve the design."

"I got tired of face-planting."

"You always were an over-achieving jerk."

"Better than just being a jerk."

"You're jealous because Gramps liked me best."

"No. He worried about you the most. It was that IQ test you failed."

"Screw you, Mike." Rob laughed, finishing off his beer.

Rob and Mike were the same age, personality, and shared the same fire in the heart, both forced to survive in a conservative family run by men who demanded they be anything but what they were. In each other they found the strength to hang onto their fire when others kept trying to extinguish it.

"We had to do a project in my shop class," Mike went on. "I figured I could combine the idea of a Snurfer with something like a skateboard, a surfboard and skis. That first skiboard was made out of wood and a piece of carpet and aluminum."

"Man, was it fast." Rob shook his head. "If you could stay on and if you could control it, you could book it down a hill."

"We started racing each other on those." Mike pulled out his wallet to pay the bill. "I'm still trying to find the right material for the board's bottom. The aluminum facing isn't right. Still, these boards are so much more controllable than last year's. But there's got to be something better."

March had one of those contemplative looks on her face again, and for a tough, doubtful moment he wondered if she was thinking like his dad. He worried that he'd just bored her senseless talking about board construction. Rob was right. He was a weird geek.

She tapped the tabletop. "Have you thought about this stuff? Formica? I remember seeing my dad install it in our kitchen. Don't you laminate it onto a wood base?"

Mike exchanged a look with Rob, who was shaking his head. It was so simple.

"What?" she asked, looking back and forth between them. "You don't think it's a good idea?"

"Sunshine . . . it's the perfect idea."

By the time they were scraping the snow off the car, she was talking to him about how he needed to apply for a patent. Back at the cabin they walked inside and she turned around, walking backwards, her hands moving in time with her mouth. "I think you should try to sell your boards, Mike."

With those few words from her, everything his father had said to him evaporated. March Randolph was the smartest girl he'd ever known and she believed in him. Until then, he hadn't actually admitted to himself how badly he wanted to be important in her eyes.

Later that night, after they were lying in the

dark, legs tangled, March in the crook of his arm, he told her how proud he was when she came down that hill. That he was surprised. Amazed. And his cousin was right. She was a natural.

She told him she loved him and was quiet for a long time, but awake, fiddling with his chest hair. He was almost asleep when she asked, "Mike? Are you awake?"

He looked over at her. Something about her tone said trouble. "Yeah. Why?"

"I have something to tell you."

"What?"

"When I was about thirteen," She paused. "Maybe I shouldn't admit this." Her voice gave her away. She was trying not to laugh.

He rolled over with her and pinned her to the bed. "Spill it."

"My dad bought me a Snurfer for Christmas."

After a heartbeat of silence, he was the one laughing. And he knew then he wanted to live the rest of his life drinking only milk.

"Sweetheart? Can't you and Mike just have a normal wedding? In a church?"

With those words, March realized that Beatrice Randolph, her mired-in-tradition and old-fashioned mother, didn't remember there was supposed to be romance in a wedding. Clearly her parents could never possibly under-stand the open, unfettered appeal of marrying the man you loved outside of a church, on rolling lawns, surrounded by the freedom of open blue skies and cypress trees twisted by the wind. How could marrying on a San Francisco hillside not be the perfect wedding venue, surrounded by nature's honest realism?

In the time March had lived away from home, nothing had really changed there. Her parents could never see her unique place in the world, as least not in the way she did.

"It's a religious ceremony," her mother said, standing in the family kitchen, a large eat-in room with off-white painted cabinets, copper pots hanging alongside fish-shaped aspic molds, and those classic blue and white dishes that had been around for more than a few hundred years displayed on crisp ivy papered walls. "We belong to a perfectly lovely church. The whole congregation has known you since you were baptized."

"It's not their wedding," March said simply. "It's mine. And Michael's." In her heart, she wanted no traditional trappings. She was acutely aware of that fact while standing inside her parents' home, which only reinforced her determination to make their wedding about the two people taking the vows.

"The wedding is about the bride, dear, not the groom," her mother corrected her.

"It's his wedding, too. It's our marriage. This is important to both of us."

"Of course it is."

"We're only going to do this once, Mother."

"Then I don't understand why you want your only wedding to be in the woods."

"It's not the woods. It's a park. You've lived here long enough. You know the city. The view from that hillside is spectacular. When you stand up there, you can see from the ocean to the bay, you can see the bridge and all those blue skies."

"March. Please . . ." Beatrice Randolph sat down hard on a kitchen chair, a sure sign she was disgusted. Littered across the painted table-top were bridal magazines and old-fashioned etiquette books with gingham covers her mother borrowed from the neighborhood library, along with printers' samples of engraved invitations on heavy cream-colored stationary with vellum inserts and embossed tissue. Her mother must have brought them home and called March after the very first flush of wedding news.

"The park is closer to Heaven than inside any stuffy church," March told her.

"And so windy you'll blow away. Think of your veil."

March snapped her fingers. "Not a problem, Mom. I'm not wearing a veil."

Beatrice sank her head into her hands and groaned.

"No white lace gown with a train either."

"You need to think about this. It's outside, March."

"I know."

After a too long silence her mother said, "The seagulls will poop everywhere."

"Oh, Mom . . ." March burst out laughing. "If we were Greek, that would be good luck."

"If we were Greek, you'd still live at home and we wouldn't be having this argument."

March sat down across from her mother and took her hand, looking her straight in the eye. "Are we really arguing about my wedding?"

Her mother swallowed, clearly uncomfortable, then looked down at her hands, thoughtful. Her nails were manicured into perfect ovals, cuticles pushed back, and painted with her immutable Coty red. The familiar pale skin of her mother's hands didn't have a single mark, not even a freckle. Her mother had the ivory complexion of a natural redhead. For as long as March could remember a bottle of Jergen's that smelled exactly like maraschino cherries sat next to the kitchen faucet. Her mother's hands had always been one of the softest things in her life.

Harsh paint cleaners and hard city water purified with bleach made her own hands a mess, split her impossibly short nails. Her cuticles were hopelessly snagged and often bloody. The engagement ring Mike gave her was lovely, perfect really: white gold and a row of small baguette diamonds around an oval aquamarine, her birthstone. Just looking at it made her unbelievably happy. But her hands were god-awful, and she said as much.

Her mother laughed, took March's hand and looked at the ring for a long time, her expression slowly changing. "I suppose a church can be stuffy," she said after a minute.

At that moment March knew she had won. Her wedding would be exactly the way she had envisioned: majestic views and green grass, kites in the air and a hundred wind chimes in the trees. Tomorrow, those gingham covered etiquette books would go back to the library, the bridal magazines to the waiting room of her uncle's dental practice, the invitations in the trash, or even better, in a folder kept for her sister May.

Beatrice took her other peeling, dry, ugly hand. "The beauty is inside your hands, not outside; it spills out onto blank paper and canvas. You have the creative hands of an artist." Not even on her most cynical day, could March miss the pride in her mom's voice.

Funny how the small and irritating things in a day could evaporate in the face of a moment of honest emotion. Her conservative family, all of them, would wear whatever she asked, hike up a grassy hill and stand in the Pacific wind to witness the moment she promised life's most important things to the man who loved her.

She'd grown up in this house. For all its

unappealing and stodgy tradition, the kitchen was the heart of their home and had only been changed once, when her parents put in all electric appliances like in all the suburb tract homes built in nearby neighborhoods.

Her own place in the Haight had a tiny kitchen with one of those old gas stoves you had to lean into the oven and light with a match. She always expected it to blow up in her face. She'd come back home today to tell her mother the latest, most important news, fully prepared for the same kind of reaction.

"I want to show you something." March put her portfolio on the table and pulled out her initial sketches and samples. "These are my hand-designed wedding invitations. Each one is a little different. See? No printer could create these for us."

Her mother took each one, studying it before spreading them all out before her. The paper March had used was raw with frayed edges, soft and fibrous, hand-printed with pen and ink like old scrolls or music from the Middle Ages. Birds and stars, music notes and snowflakes were in free-form designs and patterns, some done as borders. Another had a very small pattern of the male and female symbol on each side of a scale, at equal levels. Her mother looked at them for a very long time. "They're lovely, and very much like you."

"Take a look at these, too." March slid two folded note cards across the tabletop, holding her breath for a few counts, and she waited.

Her mother looked confused by the soft colors and design.

"They're both very traditional," March said. "I thought you'd like that. See the colors? Pink or blue. We'll have to send them sometime in October. The baby's due around October 10th."

For a few heartbeats her mother said nothing at all. Then Beatrice sank her shaking head in her hands all over again. "Oh my God, March."

So the wedding was briskly-planned and Renaissance-styled, outdoors in a lush park high on a breezy San Francisco hillside, and the best of days, the way March wanted it to be. The wind was a participant; it kept the bright silk kites flying high in the air and rang the many wind chimes they'd hung in all the trees; it ruffled the sleeves of Mike's white shirt and blew at their long hair, hers topped with a flower wreath and trailed with candy-colored ribbons.

The wind billowed and flowed against her embroidered peasant dress, made of cotton the color of kite string, and whatever direction that wind blew, it outlined the softest beginnings of the change in her once youthful and free life, the rounded bulge of her first pregnancy and a future: motherhood.

Chapter Three

Mike had been working at Spreckles for a while when his son Scott made his long, difficult entrance into the world, at exactly three thirty in the morning. Labor for March lasted more than twenty four hours, much of that time with her acting uncharacteristically irrational, banishing him from the room one minute and the next, calling out for him to never leave her.

By the time he first held his son, looking like a small red face swamped by a blue-striped blanket, Mike was blurry-eyed, over-emotional, numb, his hands crushed by hours at her bedside, and he was sapped dry of everything, especially sleep. When asked to, he dutifully counted the fingers and toes and came up with nineteen the first time, then twenty two.

"Count again, Mike," March insisted.

"Look. He has one head. I'm not worried." But Mike was worried. Nothing would ever be the same for them again.

The baby became the center of their world. Everyone's world. He would come home from work to their apartment in Redwood City and meet his mother or mother-in-law, both who were there so often it seemed as if they were living with them. Both women handed out advice that often contradicted each other's.

Already he spent a third of his life on a crusade of germ warfare, boiling everything that came into contact with anything "baby." (He had read all the baby books himself. On occasion, March had even accused him of memorizing some of them.)

To go anywhere they needed a moving van for all the child paraphernalia. March was determined to breast-feed and had a frustrating and uncomfortable time. She cried as much as the baby at first.

All of those changes he could handle. What scared him was something else altogether. He was a father, a word that held roiling meaning for him and caused him plenty of internal anguish and self-doubt. He was responsible for his son, for his child's life and future and happiness.

Ahead lay a world of strangers who could easily swallow his child whole if given the opportunity. Life, people, took big bites out of you. Mike felt this immense, overwhelming responsibility to protect his son from everything he knew awaited his child, and it scared the hell out of him.

Finally one night, when he paced the room with the baby so March could sleep, he made a promise to his son, and to the world in that room, and mostly to himself: he would never be distant and demanding. He wouldn't be the thing that stood between his kids, the way his father had often put himself between Brad and him. He would definitely not come into the house one day a week to rule the roost, carve some meat, and expect those slim, atavistic moments to stand for fatherhood.

Still, every morning, Mike got up at five a.m., just as his father had for so many years, and he went to work at a job he hated because the paycheck was good and the insurance even better. He had a family, so he did what was expected, everything Don Cantrell had said to him.

March accepted the news that she was pregnant for a second time without too much terror. Scott wasn't even a year yet, and honestly, she was too tired to summon up any negative emotion. Again, the pregnancy was an accident, one that happened during an exhausted night when Scott was barely four months old.

A few months into her new pregnancy, Mike came to her one night. (He'd been reading the latest books again.) One of the things she had always adored about him was his ability to see even a small modicum of possibility, and to embrace it with his own Cantrell enthusiasm.

But her pregnancy was now his sudden obsession. Any day she expected him to double over with Braxton-Hicks contractions. On that night, after he had read somewhere that infants inside the womb could hear, Mike had come to her with a grand idea to start their baby's education early.

"If a child can hear, what if he can learn?"

"Just what are you thinking?"

"Let's teach him to count."

"Great. He can help us during the contractions. I can hear him now, calling out of my uterus, One! Two! Three! Breathe . . . Push!"

"March. This is serious. What if it's true? We have to try this."

She snapped her fingers. "I have an idea. Let's teach him algebra. Geometry? Trig? You took calculus, didn't you? Or we could always call my dad over to teach him. Maybe by the time the baby is a toddler he will do polynomial equations with rational coefficients and even draw sketches of the seven continents."

But despite all of her sarcasm and teasing, Mike had been undaunted. At night he read to her belly, which was fine because he often read some kind of classic literature, *Call of the Wild*, *David Copperfield*, *The Grapes of Wrath*, which made her fall asleep more easily. For the first trimester she could have easily slept twenty hours a day without being read to.

She loved it when he read poetry. Mike's deep voice reading the Metaphysical poets, or beat poets like Cohen and Ferlinghetti. It was sexy as hell. The only real argument they'd had was when Mike decided to read a popular contemporary fiction novel and for some unknown reason picked *Rosemary's Baby*.

Every day there was something new. He moved the radio by the bed and played the classical station, old standards, musical soundtracks and the Beatles. The eight track tape player in the car had everything from Bach to Bob Dylan, the Smothers Brothers to Hair. One night she awoke to him hovering above her protracted stomach, counting in Spanish.

About three weeks before Phillip was born, Mike was sound asleep after one Spanish lesson, two Wagner arias, Peter, Paul, and Mary and multiplying the sevens. She was wide awake at two-thirty in the morning, the baby tumbling and kicking her ribs like crazy.

Since it was partially her husband's fault she was sleepless, she leaned over and punched him in the arm. "Quick. Mike. Wake up."

"What?" He sat up, disoriented. "Is it the baby? Don't move. I'll call the doctor."

"No. No. It's not the baby. I want you to get the protractor, honey, and draw an isosceles triangle on my stomach, then later we can go over to the Castro District and I'll get pi, 3.1416, tattooed right here."

Groaning, Mike flopped back on the bed, "Funny. You wake me up for jokes." He stretched and yawned. "You can't sleep again, right? What time is it?" He glanced at the clock, turned and faced her. "You laugh at me, Sunshine, but wait and see. This kid's going to be Nobel Prize material."

Months and months later, when their wonderful son Phillip finally spoke something other than baby gibberish (much later than Scott since Scott spoke for him most of the time, a fact that drove Mike crazy) Phillip's first word was 'Mama.'

For two long and wickedly hilarious months he called Mike 'Mama.' To March, the only way it would have been even funnier was if the baby had called Mike '*mamacita*.'

Eventually, from their Nobel prodigy came his second word: "shit." His first sentence? "You idiot," which he shouted after March had honked the car horn and waved at a neighbor. Yes, Mike had educated Phillip. Their Pavlovian child had learned from his father that whenever you honked the horn, you had to holler out *you idiot!*

Mike had always made his skiboards in his parents' garage. At March's insistence, he'd applied for a patent not long after that winter so long ago, when he'd first taken her skiboarding and long before they ever got married. But with marriage and family and work, he hadn't made a skiboard in too long for him to remember.

After Phillip was born, Mike went over to his folks place one day to find his dad had put all of his board materials and equipment into the shed

51

because "Son, you have more responsibility now. You aren't a teenager anymore."

No one argued with Don Cantrell, so whenever March asked Mike about his boards, he blew her off with some lie.

He came home from the job he hated one night, stepping over baby toys into an apartment that smelled like spaghetti sauce and baby powder. He tossed his tie and sport coat on the sofa in the living room and headed for the kitchen.

March met him with an icy beer in one hand, waving a letter from the Department of Commerce in the other. "We have something to celebrate. The patent came through."

He took a sip of the beer, sat down and read the letter with mixed emotions.

"I have more news. I weaned Phillip early and took a job today."

That got his attention. He set down the beer. "Why? I make good money. You don't need to work."

"Yes. I need to work, not only for me. For you, Mike."

"You don't have to work for me. I thought we decided that we didn't want to farm out the kids."

"We don't have to. I can work from home. Dave Williamson, you remember him from when I was still at the Art Institute? He called last week. Would you believe he's with the biggest ad agency in the city? Stone-Morgan and they want me to do some of their graphics. Most of the time, I can work from home, but they have day care on-site—the company's run by a woman—so when I have to go to the office, it won't be a problem. The pay is less than you make, but it comes with full benefits and it's enough for us to get by."

She knelt down in front of him and put her hands on his knees. "Quit your job. You hate what you're doing. I don't want it sapping all the joy from you. It kills me to see you give up on the skiboards. I know you have, by the way. I can't get you to talk about them. You're trying to hide it. What you can't hide is that giving up your dreams is slowly killing you.

"I talked to your mom. She told me your dad packed up all your boards and tools months and months back. You never told me, Mike. You're supposed to talk to me. You don't have to protect me."

"I'm fine," he said. "Dad was right. Chasing after some dream doesn't make practical sense with the boys."

"It makes more sense with the boys. It's their future. The pregnancies, the marriage and babies, all of it got in the way of what we wanted. The kids are gifts. They are certainly not a reason to turn our lives into our parents' lives." She gave a short laugh. "It's not just you who is changing." She lowered her voice. "A month ago I actually bought three Butterick patterns."

"You? Sew?"

"Happy-Hands-At-Home March. If I start to play bridge it's all over for me."

He wanted to believe they could shuck everything practical and shoot for the moon. He wanted to work at a job that made him want to set the alarm clock, that made him want to work long hours and take pride in what money he made. But he was a father with two young sons. To chase his dreams felt irresponsible.

"Look, honey," March went on. "I believe this letter is a sign. It's telling us something. Let's move back to the city. Get a place with space for you to work on your boards. I've been thinking all day. Maybe a warehouse or a place where we can live above a shop? It's only two hours up to the mountains. We can go up to the ski resorts on weekends and you can try to sell your boards. The boys are young now. They're not in school yet. When they are in school, that's when we will be tied down.

"Look. I'd be willing to bet we can get some kind of exhibition meet organized with Rob and his local connections. I can see if we can get support for some kind of race, a special run. Maybe at Northstar? The resort is new. They need publicity. I can get ad sponsors. What if I could get some good sponsors through my new job? This is our time. Our chance." She took his hands. "This may be our only chance. Do you really want to look back and think if only?"

He was acutely aware that his wife knew exactly what to say to him. She knew which buttons to push.

"We'll do this together," she said so easily and confidently. "You can make the boards and I'll design the graphics for them."

Inside he was warring with himself, what he wanted to do with what he should do. What was right, what was wrong. Could it all be so easy?

"You're too quiet. You know you want to. Say yes."

"I don't know, Sunshine."

"Say yes. What have we got to lose? We don't own a house. We aren't tied down financially. If we fail, what's the worst that can happen? We start over. But at least you'll have a chance to be happy, even for a while."

"Happy with you supporting the family?"

She stood up so fast, hands on her hips, glaring. "Since when are you Mister Macho-I-Must-Be-the-Breadwinner? Why is this any different than if I were putting you through med school or law school? That's pretty small-minded of you, Mike. Are you planning on keeping me barefoot and pregnant too?"

"Not a bad idea. We had a good time making those two."

"Both accidents." She grabbed the letter and waved it under his nose. "Are you, a smart and talented man with honest vision, really going to ignore fate and probably ruin our destiny?"

"Destiny? Hell, I don't want to ruin our lives."

"You won't. I've always believed in you. Don't tell me you can't believe in yourself, too." She paused and leaned very close to him. "Let's do it."

Of everything that streamed through his head in those few moments, the most frightening was her complete and absolute faith in him. This whole thing wasn't a lark to her. For one brief moment he wondered if he would lose her if he failed, but then thinking that way meant he didn't have the same strength of faith in her she had in him.

Maybe because she believed in him he could let go of all of his dad's hauntingly defeatist phrases. But then self-doubt was the worse kind of weak-ness, worse than anything his father had ever said.

There it all was: his dream laid out before him, door open—come this way—with all the possibilities flashing through his mind in neon letters. Races. Skiboard runs. Sports shops. Endorsements. TV. The Olympics?

He almost laughed at that last one and couldn't even say that improbable pipe-dream aloud, so he took a drink and lifted the beer in the air. "What the hell. Let's do it."

Chapter Four

A year after champion board racer Hank Knowles appeared in a national beer commercial on a Cantrell board, and twenty eight months after *Sports Illustrated*, *Good Morning America*, and *Entertainment and Sports Program Network* covered the first National Snowsurfing Championship, March and Mike moved from the first house they owned in the Marina District to a large place on Russian Hill with a hundred and eighty degree view of San Francisco and the bay. Both homes were a huge change from the crumbling, drafty, three-room Eleventh Street apartment over a warehouse, that first place in the City they'd moved back to after Mike had quit his job at Spreckles.

In that old building, near a knot of San Francisco's freeway interchanges, was where March chased two small and energetic little boys while her husband worked long hours producing the skiboards he sold in the local mountains on winter weekends.

One tired and impossible-to-keep-clean-apartment was where both she and Mike took turns cooking dinners in an oven that burned the edges of every casserole they struggled to make, and where they had scraped by on graphics work she did on mornings so early it was still dark out, and during the kids' nap times.

As bad as that apartment had been, in retrospect, it was where the Cantrell family really began, and being there brought them all into a time when the boys didn't need naps, a place where the oven worked perfectly and a job where March oversaw the graphics end of Cantrell Sports, Inc.

Skiboarding had morphed into snowsurfing, and into snowboarding, a new sport which bred almost simultaneously on both sides of the country—on the West Coast by Mike, and the East Coast by Jake Burton. Both called visionaries, kindred in their love and creation of snowboards, who along with some other enthusiasts from surfing and skateboarding promoted and pushed the sport, met then raced each other at events in Colorado, Vermont, Lake Tahoe and Mt. Baker. The *Entertainment and Sports Program Network* desperately needed to fill 24 hours a day of air time and began to televise the meets and races on cable TV.

By the time the Cantrell boys were nine and ten, snowboarding parks were successful at some of the major ski areas and the family move to the Russian Hill came about because of an absurd need for a much larger tax write-off.

But the truth was: March loved the house from the first moment they walked inside. They were lucky to live in such a romantic, red-blooded city, and certain landmark homes were natural to that terrain. The classic old glorious houses she had driven past so many times began to sneak into her wildest dreams.

Like some foreshadowing of what was to come, over the years March had felt some odd sense of joy just sitting at the red light and merely looking at that same house. *Living there would make life perfect.*

It was a big beauty of a home on a famous corner near the crookedest street in the world, with views that went from foggy bridges and city lights, to glimmering water and all those blue skies. Wrapped in California stucco the color of butter, with a terra-cotta tiled roof and dark-timbered doors and window frames, it spoke of the homes on coastal hillsides along the Mediterranean and had once belonged to an infamous Spanish opera singer.

Shortly after they moved in, March redid the second floor master bedroom in Chinese red, because she'd read enough history of the place to believe the room needed color—passionate color. The night after painting the room red, she and Mike drank a rich bottle of Sonoma County cabernet, listened to Carmen, fed each other fruit and imported cheese and made love three times on a three hundred year old antique silk rug.

Not long afterward March was sick every

morning and sound asleep by seven o'clock every night, signs she knew all too well from her previous two pregnancies. Nine months and three days later, Molly was born, to the instant delight and future dismay of her two older brothers, Scott and Phillip.

One look at her and Mike had laughed—their own intimate joke—because their daughter had bright red hair. From that day on they always associated her with red, a color of high emotion. More often than not, Molly lived up to that association.

She came into the family like an earthquake, and shook it up, so different was she from Scott and Phillip. March could gauge her boys and understand when something was wrong, see trouble coming with a mother's sharp and innately-tuned instinct.

But unlike the boys, Molly didn't cling to March even as a toddler. The outside fascinated her. From the sight of her first butterfly to the crowds in Union Square during Christmas, Molly believed the whole wide world was all hers.

March had come from a family of three women and one lone male, her father, while Molly was born in a family of men, with March the only other woman. Instead of combining feminine forces, they were always at opposite sides, like knights on a jousting field and ready to knock the other one off the horse.

While March's strength and control was the fulcrum on which the family pivoted, Molly was the family princess, with an amazing ability to get her way and make everyone circle around her like footmen.

March and women like her were products of a generation that straddled two feminine cultures, raised to be good girls, like their mothers, yet they ended up rallying for their independence and their individual rights in a society that for all its touting of freedoms and liberties was dismally patriarchal.

Most women back in the Sixties and Seventies had to have male co-signers for anything financial. Early in their marriage, when March called the credit card company, they wouldn't talk to her, even though she made most of the income and paid the bills. They had to speak to Mister Cantrell.

But her daughter Molly was born into a world of men changed by women like March. Almost as if with that first breath of post-feminist air, Molly innately understood how to work inside her world, and it was very different from how March's world worked.

Mother and daughter could look out the same window at completely different scenes. Mothering Molly was like some kind of grand game of *Where's Waldo*. There was an undeniable sense of irony in that March had wanted a daughter so badly, only to give birth to a diva instead.

Beatrice's only answer was, "You were a difficult child. She takes after you, dear. Your father and I always felt your name was perfect. March, in like a lion."

"Daddy said that all the time. Funny I don't feel like a lion." March was exhausted. "Molly and I are polar opposites. My daughter is nothing like me."

"She will be," was all her mother had said.

Mike set her straight in terms more clear, the way men could see the world in black and white while women saw nothing but a confusing mass of passionate colors. "You are and always have been an independent woman and never afraid to tell the world what you think. Look, you're a strong woman with strong emotions. Why on earth would you want a daughter who is any less?"

March was quiet for a long time, knowing he was right. "Because my life would be easier if she were a little more malleable."

"And our marriage might have been calmer if you had been that way."

She punched him in the arm. "You know you love to argue with me. Makes your life colorful and interesting."

"So look at it this way, Sunshine. Our little red Molly is the color in your day. She will never bore you. I was reading on the plane, a book about how we parents make the mistake of looking for pieces of ourselves in our kids. The psychologist said it's natural, narcissistic and necessary, that we think if we can catch a glimpse of ourselves in our kids then perhaps we will understand how their minds work. But it's a scientific fact that traits skip generations. So in the same way our own parents didn't have a clue about us, neither do we about our own kids."

"God cannot possibly be so cruel." March sank down into a club chair, hugging its pillow to her chest. "And Mother Nature wouldn't do that to another woman."

"Women are toughest on other women. You've said that yourself. Motherhood is an emotional extreme for a woman—"

At that moment she wanted to zip his mouth shut. He was a man who couldn't pick up his shoes, shirt, or tie, who regularly lost the remote control but like magic could always find her car keys, and he was suddenly quoting some new self-help book about the differences between women and men and telling her about mother-hood? If only one of their babies had been born through his penis.

"—Manhood and womanhood are forced on us by chromosomal serendipity, but we actually choose to be parents. Fascinating stuff. Our choices become some of our biggest mistakes and the hardest to live down. Basically, the point this doctor made was: we can never live down our kids." Mike took off his tie and hung it on the closet's doorknob—the tie rack was a foot from his nose—then he kicked his shoes off near the bed and walked away from them.

If she didn't pick them up, she would trip on them in the middle of the night on her way to the bathroom.

He pitched his shirt across the dressing room and missed the laundry basket, then faced her, hands on his belt.

"Mike?"

"What?" His belt buckle banged the door as he hung it from the bathroom doorknob.

"You really have to start reading fiction." And she threw the pillow at him.

The month Mike appeared on the cover of *BusinessWeek* with the caption "It Only Looks Easy," (it referring to the rise of the sport of snowboarding) Mickey, their fourth child, tried to ride his Transformer car down the stairs and had to have seventeen stitches in his forehead. Behind the accident were Scott and Phillip, caught standing in the corner of the upstairs landing and whispering sworn vows to not tell Dad what they did.

Mike had grown up with an older brother and clearly understood sibling dynamics. Brad duped him enough times to make him remember all the bruises and challenges and dirty tricks.

The antics between his older brother and him were a rite in natural family order.

But it was his father's reaction that changed the dynamic from brotherly prank to damage. Every time Brad got the better of him, Mike could see he became more and more of a fool in his dad's eyes. Sometimes the darkest legacy between brothers was more about emotional scars than the physical ones.

Through the coming years his own kids made his life fuller, even though they fought over Monopoly money, the biggest slice of cake, who would sit in the middle, which bedroom was better, often with Scott and Phillip so involved arguing with each other they never realized Molly just waltzed in and took what she wanted when they weren't looking.

Occasionally they managed to get even with her, like when they taught her to snap her fingers backwards or filled her bed with ants. But for Mike she was a butterfly who seemed to light upon the ordinary things in his world, making them seem rare and special. Her Mollyisms could paint the unexpected into a regular day.

"Dad? Do you know where rainbows come from?"

"Ireland?" he'd asked.

"No, silly."

"Leprechauns?"

She had giggled in that way little girls did, a

simple sound that gave him a great sense of joy.

"Light refracts through the water droplets," she'd said. "And because water droplets are round, they cause the light to bend. A rainbow is really a full circle of colored light but the ground stops you from seeing the other half of the circle."

"Where are the pots of gold?" he asked to tease her. But he knew the real pot of gold was walking alongside him, her red hair in long braids, the little girl who snapped her fingers backwards, explained scientific facts, got even with her brothers by rolling their boxer shorts in itching powder—payback for the ants—and constantly reminded him what a wonderful thing the imagination was.

They were walking toward Alioto's for oysters that day she told him about the rainbows and he stopped for a second. "Look at that, Shortcake." He pointed to a white seagull feather on the ground. "Do you know what that is?"

She reached down and picked up it up. "This is a feather."

"It's also a message. A white feather is a gift from someone who loves you. Someone in Heaven. When I was about your age, not too long after Poppy, my grandfather, your great grandfather, died, I began to find white feathers in my shoes, my school notebook, stuck to my bicycle handle. One day my grandmother saw me pick up one and she was the one who told me they were from him. Signs that he missed me, she'd said."

He didn't tell his daughter, looking up at him with her wide-eyed expression and wonder at a perfect white feather, that his father had told him to forget all that rubbish. Poppy was dead and the feather was only some seagull molting.

For Mike, watching his children grow up, when the boys pulled funny but awful pranks on each other, or his imaginative daughter and her stories, and Mickey the fearless, who would try anything because his brothers did, made Mike understand what his own father has missed.

Early on Mike made his decision about what kind of father he wanted to be: a father who kept the peace and used bargaining chips, who went out of his way to make everything even for his children as much as possible.

He gave the older ones both the same bike on the same Christmas. Each child always had the same number of gifts, even the same dollar amount spent; it was a pattern which lasted until the two oldest boys were teenagers, when work ethic came into play and he made Scott and Phillip earn the right to use the car or boat keys.

But for most of their lives, he had chosen to be a father who measured the cake into even sections before anyone ever cut it. Unlike March, who from the time when the kids were young, would let them battle it out or choose to make her life easier by picking the winner with some trumped up reason the boys always bought into without a lick of resentment.

But then along came Mickey, the youngest and his namesake, who grew up trying to find a place amid all the strong Cantrell personalities. He was close to his mother in a way lost to Mike. To his sister Molly, he was half-pet and half annoying little brother, the one who chanted stupid kissing rhymes out the window during her teenaged years whenever a boy came to pick her up for a date. He was challenged by a pair of brothers who were more than a decade older, and who he worshipped at the same time he constantly tried to keep up with them.

To level the playing field full of powerful 9.75 siblings, Mickey had to be a 10.0. He learned to throw caution and thought and fear out the window and "just do it." Following his brothers boarding down the toughest mountain faces made him fearless before he ever started school, and eventually turned him into a hotshot, the Cantrell who sought the limelight. In almost every moment of family video, Mickey's antics dominated most of the camera time.

Being the youngest he had to work hard to fight for a place in his family. It wasn't easy to come after a sister like Molly and his older, dynamic brothers, who taught him he could only earn their attention by breaking all the rules.

Suddenly there was no way Mike could even the playing field for his youngest son. Mickey spent more moments in the emergency room than all the other kids combined, was suspended from kindergarten, held back a year, but then went on to skip the third grade. In junior high, he was the only honor roll student suspended, after he managed to sneak into the administration building and change the school bell system so the bells rang every two minutes. The limelight was important to Mickey, whether the light was positive or negative.

Mike had never been or wanted to be the kind of father who inspired fear in his kids, but Mickey tested his well-thought-out father plan to the limits. There wasn't a book on parenting or child psychology in existence to help him prepare for raising his youngest son, or to make him understand Mickey's surprises that were always waiting around the corner for him.

Chapter Five

March gave Molly her old Brownie camera when she was barely ten and bought her a good thirty five millimeter when she was in junior high and planning a trip to Washington DC with her class. By high school, Mike had built a darkroom for Molly in the back corner of one of the garages and she was chronicling Cantrell life moments in both black and white and color.

One Sunday afternoon, post Forty-Niners' football, Molly dragged Mike and her out with the excuse that she had an assignment to do a family portrait for a photography project in school.

Indian summer burned through most of California in early October, days where the temperature in the city was still seventy five degrees at four in the afternoon and the later sunsets would turn the western skies red and purple. It was that warm when Molly insisted they travel across town to the hillside where March and Mike were married, and she took a couple rolls of film of them all over that hillside.

There were moments that afternoon, sitting on a rock or leaning against a twisted cypress tree when March looked up and caught a certain look in Mike's eye.

He squeezed her shoulder. "I think this was where we were standing when May dumped that Singapore Sling on Rob."

March began to laugh and ruined their pose.

"Mother! I can't get a good shot with you bent over."

"Sorry. Your father's making trouble."

"Daddy . . . please."

"Okay, Shortcake." Mike leaned in and said, "I can still see your mother swatting bees with that huge straw hat."

March tried not to laugh again but failed at the image of her mother hitting Mike's dad in the back of his bald head. "Your father looked pretty dumbfounded when he turned around and saw it was her. I felt sorry for her, standing there embarrassed. She was just so scared of bees."

"After your mother smacked him a good one, my first thought was to find some way to paint honey all over his head. Figured your mother could get even for the crap he'd put me through."

March looked at him and patted his hand. "I know. I don't think he knew how to be any other way."

"Hel-lo. Earth to parents." Molly stood in front of them, clearly annoyed. "Would you two please pay attention to me? I need you to look at the camera before I lose the perfect light."

Mike looked at her. "You need to stop making jokes, Sunshine. You heard your daughter. We need to look in the camera before she loses the perfect light."

March jabbed him in the ribs.

Molly walked back, muttering, "You two are such a problem."

Mike looked at her. "We're a problem."

"Good," March whispered.

So they spent a Sunday on a hillside, smiling into a camera lens, Mike goosing her or poking her, and annoying their daughter when they laughed too hard. Later, whenever March asked to see the shots Molly was always too busy. She showed them one or two shots that were not as good as March knew Molly could produce. When March said as much, Molly told her she had turned her only good prints into her teacher and she would make more copies when she had time.

They spent Christmas that year at their house in Lake Tahoe. On Christmas morning under the tree was the best gift March could ever remember. The photo Molly took of Mike and her was amazing. Their daughter had caught all the love and humor between them as they looked at each other, the best they could each be because they were together, and Molly had captured that look forever in celluloid.

Chapter Six

March had started her official life as a Cantrell on a San Francisco hillside, and four kids and almost thirty four years later she was still on a San Francisco hillside. Though her generation had once sung about the sounds of silence, the sounds of the city were what she loved: those white mornings when the plaintive notes of foghorns floated above the bay, the deep water and moisture-thick air magnifying every sound so that whispering wasn't really secretive at all.

At noon, there was the chatter of people at the

corner deli on short lunch hours ordering salami and Jack cheese on fresh sourdough (Dijon mustard and pepperoncini, no pickles). Muni trams rattled regularly on tracks over the Avenues, and freeway traffic during rush hours hummed like distant swarms of bees. Horns honking, voices and air brakes, close to home the distant clanging of a cable car bell at Leavenworth & Hyde and the soft rumble of an automobile changing into low gear to power up the hill were merely single moments in a day where the constant din of life was going on around her.

For her, there was something incredibly grounding about a place where she'd taught her children to ride a bike to the ringing of a cable car bell and the applause of tourists, and where the call of gulls was as much a part of the air she breathed as oxygen.

The noise of the city was most noticeable in the old brick courtyard at the center of their home. Mike called it March Country—an oasis where on temperate mornings she drank her coffee surrounded by raised planters and huge stone pots spilling over with flowers the color of a fall sunset. Some of the wind chimes from their wedding hung from courtyard posts, ringing out occasionally in the October wind.

March looked up from the kitchen sink when she heard her grandson cry. Sixteen month old

Tyler was out in the courtyard trying to scale the seven foot brick wall and not one bit happy that he was failing. She dropped the pasta strainer, and wiping her hands on her shirttail, she was through the French doors in a heartbeat. "Hey there, sweetie. What are you doing out here alone? Escaping?" She scooped him up and headed inside. A minute later she stood in the door of the media room, Tyler hooked on her hip while a good minute and a half of Sunday afternoon, Forty-Niner's football passed without a single male in the room noticing them. "I think you lost something, Scott."

Her oldest son looked at her, then quickly glanced at the corner where a five foot square rainbow of bright Fisher Price toys lay abandoned.

"Daddy!" Tyler shouted. Her grandson had great timing.

Scott was up and made a beeline for her. "Damn, Mom. Sorry." He took his son. "You okay, buddy?"

"Daddy!" Tyler rubbed his hands on Scott's cheeks.

Scott groaned. "What's all over his mouth and hands?"

"Dirt. He was trying to climb the courtyard wall." She held out an open container of baby wipes.

"One play," Scott muttered. "I only looked away to watch one play." He cleaned up his son and wiped his own face. "He fell off the back of the toilet last week when I was watching him. Renee will kill me."

"Then you're lucky she's out with Molly and Keely," she told him.

Her eldest son looked at her over his son's head, thickly-covered in his same black curly hair, and Scott grinned at her, knowing she wouldn't say anything to his wife.

For just one second, one small heartbeat of memory, there stood Mike in another time and place holding Scott and giving her that same grin. Those moments were why she wouldn't want to be twenty five again. The future was always a blank, out of control; it lay out there as unclear as morning fog on the horizon. But the past was familiar and kept coming around and around in tender, special moments that gave her some measure of contentment about her choices in life.

Looking back was the best way to understand destiny—something she'd always believed in because how could life and all its complications be completely accidental? There had to be a master plan, a book somewhere, like something out of an episode of the *Twilight Zone*, that foretold who, why and where everyone existed.

"Tyler's part monkey. Takes after you, big brother." Phillip set down his beer and grabbed a handful of chips. "You've always been the live and hairy proof that Darwin was right."

"You're just pissed because I actually have hair."

"I have hair. See?" Phillip bent over and rubbed his dark-stubbled scalp. "Keely loves this. Women go for men with the confidence to shave their heads. Think Willis. Think Agassi."

"Think MiniMe," Scott finished.

Mike set a box of Wheat Thins on the table and stood, stretching. "Remember the time Scott disappeared, Sunshine? You were a climber, too, son," he said to Scott. "We looked for you for almost an hour. Your mother was frantic, crying like crazy, certain you had somehow gotten out in the street and been kidnapped. Eventually we found you sitting on a ceiling beam watching us."

"I was just glad you were safe," March told him.

"So I guess that means I'm not going to get much sympathy from either of you."

"Payback is hell," she and Mike said at the same time.

"See?" Phil said laughing. "I keep telling you. I'm the perfect son. That's why they like me best."

Scott looked at Tyler. "Do you want to go to Uncle Phil?"

"Yes!" (Tyler's favorite word.)

Scott set his son in Phillip's lap, sat down in a club chair and picked up his beer. "Daddy is smarter than Uncle Phil, isn't he?"

"Yes!"

He took a swig of beer. "And Daddy is more handsome than Uncle Phil, isn't he?"

"Yes!"

Phil just shook his head and turned to Scott, who said, "Uncle Phil has big, ugly, jug-handle ears, right?"

"Yes!"

Phillip smiled, familiar, a little wicked, the same way he had as a kid when he just passed *Go*, collected two hundred dollars and owned Broadway with a hotel. He glanced at Scott, then held up Tyler in front of him and said, "Your daddy likes to dress up in your mommy's clothes, doesn't he?"

"Yes!" Tyler said in perfect toddler Pavlovian.

"I'll get the kid gate," Mike said, laughing.

"It's in the laundry room," March told him.

Mike swatted her on the butt as he walked by. "I know."

On the third Sunday of every month, like today, March cooked for the entire Cantrell clan, kids, wives, grandkids. Most of the year they met in the house in the city, except during the winter season, when they spent weekends at their place in Tahoe. Years back, Cantrell, Inc created the roving three day week during the months of snowboarding season, so everyone from the top down could take advantage of the Sierra snow. They worked longer hours, a little harder in late summer and early fall to get ready for the new

77

season, but when the lifts were running, at least one week a month the whole company worked three days and took off four.

Already into late fall, the past week had been crazy with Mike working fourteen hour days, Mickey in the beginning of his senior year with college selection on the horizon, and an auction and benefit March was chairing coming in mid-October, all pre-snow season.

While she was still intimately involved in the family company, she didn't spend the time there she used to. Other than the board meetings, and there was one this coming week, she had hired good managers for the graphics side of the business. The graphic designs for the new season had been selected months ago, so she had home time now, time for some charity work, her grandkids, and a gourmet cooking class she took from one of the top chefs in the city.

Tonight the menu wasn't gourmet, just the kind of food her family liked on these evenings: salad, hot bread, lasagna and anything chocolate and gooey for dessert.

March was spinning lettuce dry when she heard her granddaughter Miranda chattering even before she heard the sound of the electric garage door closing.

"G-Mo! G-Mo! Look what I made for you!" Miranda came running across the courtyard from the open door to the garage, followed by her daughters-in-law Renee and Keely, then her own Molly.

The kitchen was suddenly chaos, all of them talking at once, shopping bags on the counters, a couple of long loaves of fresh Boudin's bread and two bottles of Chianti suddenly in her arms, her granddaughter jumping up and down and tugging on her shirt, trying to tell her everything they had done in the last three hours.

"I think we got everything from the list," Renee said. "Let's see . . . You have the wine. I gave you the bread." She looked up. "Did we forget the garlic?"

"No. I put it in the cart. It's there somewhere. Here it is." Keely handed it to her.

"Oh. We couldn't find the nine-layer cake so we got chocolate banana from Henshaw's." Renee closed the refrigerator door. "Was the baby okay?"

"He's fine."

"Neiman's has the most beautiful suede jackets, mom. You have to get one. Look at Keely's shoes," Molly insisted. "They are to-die-for."

March glanced at Molly. "What did you do to your hair?"

There was utter silence. The words had slipped out of her mouth before she could stop them.

"I had it layered last week, Mother." Molly shook her head defiantly and her deep auburn hair, once sleek and gorgeous, went every which way possible.

Keely checked her watch. "Two minutes," she said to Molly and Renee. "You owe me lunch."

March was at the kitchen island . . . feeling like one. The girls had bet on her reaction, which really should have been funny. She should have been laughing, but it stung a little instead. "It looks nice," March lied, thinking her daughter looked as if she had a run-in with a lawnmower. "Change is good."

For a few seconds no one spoke, so March opened a nearby drawer and took out the foil, which she would have rather chewed on than stand there in the telling, heavy silence of generation gaps between women.

Miranda sidled up to her and tugged on her shirt. "I made this for you in art class, G-Mo. It's a birdfeeder. Look. Look."

For one brief moment March wished Molly were still six and their relationship were simpler. She squatted down eye-level with Scott's daughter. The birdfeeder she held was large, made from a milk jug, and awkwardly covered with silk leaves and sparkles. "Wow. Did you really make this?"

Miranda nodded.

"Let's go fill it." On the backside of the feeder, written in sparkles, was *G-MO*. In a strange new world reduced to initials J-Lo and BFF, grandmother simply became G-Mo.

"I really didn't do everything," Miranda

admitted quietly. "Mrs. Burke helped me with the sparkles." She looked up to March for approval. "But I did all the leaves."

"You know, I think I love the leaves the very best."

Miranda's whole face brightened. March could encourage her granddaughter and not feel as if something she said opened wounds or created new ones. She wondered if Molly would take a bet on what she said to Miranda. Somewhere in their mother-daughter lifetime, she and Molly had become real adversaries. "Come along. You can help me find the perfect spot for this most wonderful of birdfeeders."

A ten foot ficus tree she had grown from only knee high dominated one corner of the courtyard. There were other birdfeeders in different shapes, along with all those old wedding wind chimes hanging from the painted beams and lathe. March hung the birdfeeder on one of the ficus branches. "What do you think? Here?"

"It's perfectly perfect, G-Mo."

March stepped down from the brick planter and stood back. "I believe this is my favorite gift ever."

Miranda melted against her and they stood there like that, the fugal sounds of the city outside, overhead, the tinkling of a few wind chimes with a whisper of a breeze that skirted the courtyard, young women's laughter coming through the slightly open French door, one of her sons shouting about a play in the back room, and through her cotton slacks, against her thigh, March could feel the flutter of her granddaughter's heartbeat.

"Look! Look!" Miranda broke away, jumping and pointing at a hummingbird that flitted from a giant fuchsia in a hanging basket right to the lip of the feeder. "It works! I'm gonna go tell Daddy!"

And her little hummingbird of a granddaughter flew into the house. The next sound March heard was the phone ringing.

Mike followed his youngest son down the front steps of the juvenile wing of the San Francisco Police Department in tense silence. Mickey and his friends were brought in for stealing a local icon, the brightly painted grinning cow sculpture from the neighborhood drive-thru dairy, then hoisting it up their high school flagpole. All because stooge Mickey Cantrell and his clown buddies had thought it would be fun to concoct a little surprise for the student body on Monday.

Mickey stopped at street level. Since his son didn't know where to go from there he was forced to wait, his back to Mike, his hands shoved into the kangaroo pockets of a dark hoodie emblazoned with the new season's slogan *Elevate! Eliminate Snowboredom* and the Cantrell logo.

"The car's this way," Mike said, walking to

where he'd parked. They would laugh about this some day, but there was little room for family jokes inside the tight confines of Mike's German sports car. Mickey needed to get the message that getting arrested wasn't okay. His son hadn't looked him in the eye again since he'd first walked into the detention room, and somewhere in the release process had taken on that typical boy-in-trouble attitude, mumbling or grunting responses. Behind his act and I-don't-give-a-damn demeanor, the truth was: his fearless son was scared to death.

Mike didn't start the car. He called March on his cell, told her they were on the way home, then rested his arms on the steering wheel, still searching for what he could say that would make an impression on a bullheaded teenager without yelling at him like his own dad would have done. A couple of deep breaths and the best he could do was "What the hell were you thinking?"

"It was a joke. We wouldn't have even gotten caught if Gabe would have moved the car like we told him."

"This discussion isn't about getting caught. It's about doing something stupid. Really stupid." Mike started the car and headed home. "Where was your judgment?"

"Okay. I'm sorry."

But his tone wasn't the least bit apologetic, which really pissed Mike off. "You're off to college in less than a year. A dumb prank like this one could keep you from getting into the school you want. Your grades are high and your SATs are amazing, better than anyone else in the family. You can get into the best schools in the nation. We're proud of that, son. Those kinds of grades don't come easily. So why would you blow all that work for a few laughs from a bunch of your buddies?"

Mickey was staring out the window.

"Trust me. It's not worth it. Your education is your future." No matter how hard he tried to be different, there was an echo of Don Cantrell in what he'd just said.

After a few miles of prolonged silence, Mickey said quietly, "Maybe education is not my future."

"What's that supposed to mean?"

"I've been thinking." He paused. "I might not go to college."

That got Mike's attention. "Since when?"

"I'm not going to be a doctor, so what good is a degree? I keep hearing how few graduates actually get jobs in the field they study. Why should I do all that work for a degree I won't use?"

"Not an option. You're going to school." Mike punched the button on the garage door opener and pulled into the driveway. There he was again. *Hello, Don.*

"I've been thinking that I want to make the switch to professional boarding."

84

Mike killed the engine and held up his hands. "No way." He was mad at himself. Madder at Mickey. Mad that this wasn't going well.

"You don't think I'm good enough," Mickey shot back, his voice high and angry. "But I am. I can outboard every person in this family. Just because you're the big man who invented it, you think you can judge me? That's not right."

Mike took a deep breath, then another, and said calmly, "What's not right, sport, is you not going to college."

"You don't think I can get sponsors for the circuit?" It was clearly a challenge.

Mike laughed at him, the sound loud and abrasive in the small sports car. "I know you can get sponsors." He lowered his voice to an even tone. "Nice try. You want me to get pissed off and tell you I can stop everyone in the business from sponsoring you. Even if I could, I don't work that way."

"You can't make me go to school."

"And you can't get me to fight with you over this. There is no discussion. Your mother and I raised you to make decisions for yourself. You're a damned smart kid. Sometimes too smart for your own good. You know what you need to do. Picking a fight with me isn't going to change the fact that you need an education in this world. It gives you a step up and the brains to make solid choices."

Mike turned in his seat, giving Mickey a square look, so there would be no doubt he meant what he said. "Yes, we're lucky. Our business has done well, but that business didn't appear overnight. Your mom and I worked our butts off. You don't get to skate inside because you're my son and Scott and Phil's brother."

"I've worked in the factory and warehouses every summer since I was thirteen."

All of four years, Mike wanted to say but didn't. "So that's the kind of work you want to do for the next forty or fifty years? You will need more than a last name to move into any good job out there without education and experience."

"I can get experience on the circuit."

"And you think school is hard work?" Mike laughed again and shook his head. "Be pissed off all you want. Try to pick a fight with me about college and change the focus of why we are even in this car and talking right now. We are here because you were arrested for blind stupidity and you're in deep trouble. Here's the payback, sport. No car to drive until I see a big change." Mike reached up to the visor and punched the garage door closed, then got out of the car. They faced off over the top of the Porsche as the garage door slowly went down.

"How am I supposed to get to practice?" Mickey said, his voice distinctly whining. "How am I supposed to get to school?"

"We live in a great city with public transportation. Use Muni. Use your friends. Your mom and I will drive you, when it's convenient for us. You can walk. Ride a bike. But your idiotic decision just cost you a big chunk of your freedom. Get it?"

"Yeah. Great. I got it." Mickey headed for the door but not before Mike heard him swear.

"You boys stop it," March said, half annoyed and half laughing. Scott and Phillip had invaded her kitchen and were tossing a wooden pepper grinder back and forth like a football, first over her head, then holding it out to her, acting contrite, only to snatch it back when she reached for it, crowing and using the granite island to block her from getting to them.

"Aw, Mom," Phillip pitched the grinder to Scott and scooted around the island. "What happened? You used to be quicker."

"She's getting older."

"Scott!" She stopped where she was, hands on her hips. "Give me the grinder."

"Nah."

"I'll tell Renee you let Tyler eat dirt."

"Don't believe her, big brother. Mom never breaks a promise. Over here." Phillip stood behind her, all six feet two of him, his shaved head shining from the recessed lighting, his long arms in the air waving like an open receiver."

March jammed her elbow into his ribs.

"Ouch! Ma . . ." Phillip waved a yellow dish towel. "That's a foul."

"You knucklehead. I guess that's what I get for saying hand me the pepper."

"Is that what you said? We thought you said hand-off the pepper."

"You always were a lousy liar." She pulled out a small pepper bottle from the spice drawer. "You boys can have your toy. I'll use this." She hammered a bottle of seasoned pepper over the Caesar salad a couple of times, then looked up just as Mickey came out of the garage and stalked toward the kitchen, head down, looking guilty and sullen and angry. Her stomach sank.

Mike followed on his heels and paused in the kitchen doorway. One quick, pointed exchange and a nod told her everything with the police was okay.

She put her hand around Mickey's neck and kissed his cheek. "Hey. Rough day."

"Yeah."

"Good work, numb nuts," Phillip said, then turned to Scott. "Look at that. He gets himself arrested wearing a company sweatshirt. Next time you're going to do something stupid, wear Burton."

"Phillip!" March said.

"I was only joking. Trying to lighten things up for him. The kid looks like he's going to cry."

Mickey spun around, the skin on his neck and face instantly bright red, eyes still moist, and pinned his brother with a hard look. "Good thing I'm not wearing your SkiStar logo, Phil, since everyone says your part of the company isn't doing so hot."

For the longest, stunned few heartbeats, the room was dead quiet, the unspoken just spoken, and the family itself suddenly cracked in half. Two of her sons looked like junkyard dogs, facing each other and ready to pounce.

Scott grabbed Phillip's right arm as he pulled it back, hand in a fist. "Don't."

Mickey started to move toward his brother.

"That's enough, you two," Mike said, stepping in between them.

March couldn't move. Yes, the SkiStar division had been losing money for the past three years, but there was a long-standing, solemn rule that the family only discussed company business together at the office and in the board room. Mickey might be seventeen, but he knew the rules.

In family business, lines had to be drawn to separate family from profit and loss, especially when the company and the strong-minded, strong-willed Cantrells were all tied so tightly together, with every one of them having a stake in the business, in its red and black, and its future.

"The table's ready, Mom." Renee walked in

with Tyler, started to give him to Scott, then stopped, looking around. "What's going on?"

March handed her the salad. "Put this on the table for me, dear, and get the girls to come eat."

Renee left, but not without exchanging a questioning look with Scott who said, "Come on, Phil. Get your wife and let's eat."

Mickey stood in the middle of the room, alone on his battlefield after trying to cause a war when no one else wanted one. He was confused, angry, embarrassed, full of young male emotions that needed blowing off. "Go wash up, Mickey," Mike said, talking to him as if he were ten years old without realizing it.

Mickey scowled at Mike, turned away and walked toward the heart of the house. "I'm not hungry."

Mike started to go after him but March placed a hand on his shoulder. "Let him go. He needs to work things through and get the salt out of those wounds of his." Through the wide kitchen archway, she watched her youngest run up the stairs.

"He's trying to pick a fight with anyone he can," Mike said.

"Did it work?"

"Close, but not quite. Not with me, anyway. Phil almost took the bait, though."

"Mickey's embarrassed. He can't control his emotions."

"He'd better control his impulses pretty damn quick or I'll show him what a jerk I can be."

"Mike. Come on. That's not how you do things."

"I took the car away. No driving till he changes his attitude."

She had seen the tears glistening in her youngest son's eyes. Times like this were when she remembered that not even for a reflection without a wrinkle would she want to be seventeen again. March picked up the dish of lasagna. "Come on. Let's eat."

Chapter Seven

Four hours later, Mike flipped the light on in his wine cellar carved into the bowels of the three story house, found the bottle he wanted from the racks and headed upstairs to their bedroom. In the corner of the sitting area, near an original slate fireplace flanked by mahogany bookcases, he'd had a private bar installed. Over the years, for birthdays, Father's Days, Christmases, his kids made certain it was stocked with any and all the high-end wine paraphernalia.

He was just pouring the red wine into stemmed bubble glasses from a Baccarat decanter etched with his initials when March came out of the bathroom, freshly showered, hair slightly damp, makeupless, creamed up and wearing something black and lacy and barely there, with a tiny pair of matching panties.

It seemed almost another lifetime ago, and perhaps only yesterday, when he'd first spotted her dancing to music loud enough to shatter the pricy wine decanter in his hand, under the flash of a Sixties' psychedelic light show that captured every movement of her incredible body.

He had been raw, kind of half-finished in the way all young men were at some point, a kid in the Sixties, still hampered and driven by dark and uncertain coming of age edges, with a free heart and a ton of baggage, even more bravado that hid the fact that his father had killed any natural belief he had in himself.

Saved by a golden girl in a Golden State, Sunshine, amazing and dancing in a rapid squall of colored light that night. She captured his heart and became the woman who believed he could do anything, gave him his family and pride and would grow old with him, always still the single most beautiful thing in his lucky life.

She took the glass of wine he offered her and sat down on the sofa by the fireplace, settled back, her long legs drawn up beside her. All golden skin and black lace in the firelight, she patted the sofa pillow. "Come sit."

He set the carafe on the coffee table as she took a sip of wine. She frowned slightly at the glass and looked at him first, frowning, then at the bottle sitting on the bar. "Is that Opus? What's the occasion?"

"A really crummy day." He sat down and put an arm around her, then added, "And those panties."

A car horn honked in the distance. A truck changed gears up a nearby hill. But those were the only sounds around them after a day filled with noise: football, his sons, a sleepy, cranky toddler of a grandson and chattering grand-daughter he adored, even though she could talk the ear off of an elephant. The family all talking at once. The sour words and fights started by his youngest and the empty place at the table that said more than stern words could.

At that moment, it felt so damned good to sit there next to March, saying nothing at all and not feeling like he had to. One of the things about a marriage of over thirty three years was you could live in long silences without either of you feeling like you had to fill them. "Our anniversary this year," he paused. "It's thirty four years, right?"

"Thirty five."

"Is that one of those important ones?"

March started laughing. "What?"

"You know, tenth, twenty-fifth, thirtieth—the ones that mark some irrational, special numbers— the ones you get in really deep trouble for forgetting. Is thirty five important?"

"Every anniversary is important, you stupid fool," she said. "You've never forgotten our anniversary."

"That's right. It was your birthday I kept forgetting. How many years was it before I realized it wasn't in July?"

"About five. But I didn't care. I always made out like a bandit those years, with two birthday gifts. The makeup present was a really, really good one. You should forget again, honey. I want that Cartier bracelet."

"What bracelet?"

"The one I've been dropping large hints over for a good five years."

"Oh, yeah. I'm waiting to surprise you."

"I hate surprises."

"No you don't. You just hate not knowing the surprise." He rested his head back and took a deep breath, staring up at the ceiling, the vagaries of his business running through his head after Mickey's words to Phillip.

After a few minutes he said what was bugging him out loud. "I wonder now if buying SkiStar was such a great idea."

"Don't let what Mickey said get to you. He's seventeen. He thinks he knows everything. He was embarrassed and angry at Phillip for pointing out he was going to cry, probably even more angry at himself."

"Pissed at me, too, for taking the car away."

Mike poured some more wine. "He's right, though. There's a lot of talk."

"I know SkiStar is struggling. But the brand was already failing when you bought it. No man can make a business turn around overnight."

"Three years and counting isn't overnight. Orders for the new line are in the toilet. Scott's been making noises about all the money we've been pouring into Phillip's side of the company." Mike paused, staring at the dark color in his wine. "Just the other day Scott said something to me about how Phil is always just skating by. He was complaining that because he's older, he's had to pave the way and take harder knocks."

"That's not true and you know it."

"But he thinks it's true."

"Children always think we ruined their lives. Those two operate so differently. Scott analyzes everything, thinks it through. He's methodical. Risk adverse. Phillip makes his decision and that's it. He'll decide whether the risk is worth it quickly, then jump on it or walk away. He has a quick mind. He's you."

"But he doesn't suffer fools and says exactly what he thinks, like someone else I know."

She laughed. "Some of my better points."

"I know Scott's frustrated and I understand that," Mike said. "SkiStar's pulling a hell of a lot of money every year out of the board business, and with no sign of any gain at all." He paused.

"I wonder sometimes if I'm beating a dead horse."

"Is it Phillip? Is he screwing up?"

"No. He told me tonight he has some kind of plan to present to the board Wednesday. I know he's doing the best he can. But Scott isn't happy about it. I think the financial draw and constant losses are starting to create friction between the two of them, which is exactly what I was trying to avoid when I bought SkiStar."

"You have always tried too hard to keep things fair and even for them. I know why you do it and I love you for it, but they're brothers. They're going to compete. It's perfectly natural. Look at them on the slopes. Look at how they've always fought for our attention. They need to work out their own status in life and in business. Each of them needs to find his place. As much as you'd like to, you can't make their worlds perfect."

"Well, that's good because I haven't. Things are far from perfect."

"Don't beat yourself up over it. Listen to what Phillip has to say."

"Whatever it is, it's going to cost money and Scott isn't going to be happy."

"Too bad for Scott. Don't let them put you in the middle because your father was a jerk with you and Brad. It's your company, Mike. You make the decisions. I'll support you. The boys will have to accept your decisions."

Mike set this empty glass down. "Has Mickey said anything to you about joining the professional boarding circuit?"

March laughed. "Only constantly since his sophomore year. He's looking for a reaction whenever he says it."

"Well, I gave him one."

"I won't," she said stubbornly. "You know what the real problem is?"

"Enlighten me. You've got a better handle on him nowadays than I do."

"He's just unsure of himself and looking for an easy out. These kids today have so much pressure on them and they're greener and even less ready to choose their futures than we were. They have so many more choices. College selection is coming up. The truth is he's scared he won't get accepted at his first choice. It's important for him to shine in this family. Look at Scott and Phil. He's afraid to want it too much and be let down. Or worse, he's afraid to let you down."

"Hell, I don't care where he goes to school as long as he goes and gets a decent education." Mike drank some more wine, then added, "And I do care that he doesn't become a convicted felon in the next nine months."

March laughed. "I know as a parent I should be concerned about what happened today." She paused. "But Mike, really . . . The purple cow?" She began to giggle.

"When Mickey was still in the detention room with his idiot buddies, even the cops were laughing about it. This is all your fault. He gets that wicked mind of his from you, Sunshine." He winked at her and relaxed.

Soon he was aware that all his problems from a few minutes before didn't seem too bad. He wouldn't trade places with anyone. He lived in a marriage where he could say aloud what was bothering him and March could make him feel better for it. He took the glass out of her hand, placed it on the table. "I think it's time to talk about something else."

"What?"

"Something much more important." Mike leaned toward her. "Come here, and let's do something about these panties."

Wednesday morning dawned bright and clear and easy, no big local news, no trucking strikes, no traffic jams or bridge problems. You could scan the horizon from north to east and see Marin, Angel Island and the East Bay's gray-green foothills. The water in the bay was crystalline and mythical, like a panoramic image from a Peter Jackson film, its edges still tinted gold in the rising sunlight. The city, its streets, public transportation and sidewalks, had all settled into a continuous, routine system of mid-week order.

March leaned over and placed her hand on her

husband's knee as he downshifted the sports car. "It's only 8:15. We have time. Take Eleventh Street."

He made a quick right turn and in a few more minutes they were in front of the old apartment. A huge square brick building covering most of a weedy city lot, it was flanked by a small gas station without automated pumps, a tire shop and an Hispanic market, all set against a gray tower of cement freeway pillars.

The building's roof was flat, with broken black gutters in the corners, but some of the mortar looked new and lighter, and the sliding windows had finally been replaced. For years, left over from the turbulent Sixties, there had been a huge peace sign and a big blue eyeball painted on the south side of the building.

"They've repainted the brick."

"The eye's gone. No one's done a thing to the roof, though." Mike paused. "Man . . . Listen to that freeway noise."

"I hear it."

"I don't remember the noise being that bad."

"It wasn't. At least I don't think it was. The boys were so young. They could never be quiet for more than two minutes straight and you were working downstairs in the shop most of the time."

"You used to play your music so damned loud," Mike laughed at her. "I could hear it over the grinder. The bass was turned up so high sawdust shook onto the floor. Even the commercial neighbors complained."

"I'll have you know the boys loved my loud music."

"We're lucky our children don't have hearing problems." He leaned on the steering wheel, looking up at the old place. "With the price of property now, I'm surprised this place is still here and no one's converted it. Looks just like what it was: an apartment over a warehouse."

"I'm glad it's the same, proof of our history together." She was quiet for a moment. "Maybe we can sneak down here some night and paint Cantrell Museum on the side."

"See. There's proof. Mickey and the purple cow was all your fault." He put his hand on her leg. "I never knew underneath the graphic artist I married is a hidden graffitist."

"I love it when you start a sentence out with 'I never knew.' I'm still an enigma." She glanced at Mike's profile as he drove, loving that this man was hers, then she looked out the window. She was pretty certain her little silly secret was safe and he didn't know she foolishly drove by the old apartment whenever she was alone and nearby, or on her way to the office. The old place was only a few blocks out of her way, and she always justified her drive-bys with the idea that seeing where you came from never hurt where you were going.

The executive offices of Cantrell Sports Incorporated took up five floors of the Sutter Building, along a grand canyon of steel and glass monoliths on Montgomery Street in the center of the financial district. They got off the elevator into the bold, graphics-painted lobby she had designed, filled with clean-lined, European-styled furniture from an upscale importer and large blown-up images of the latest Cantrell boards in every kind of snow and air action, along with the latest ad slogans.

Mike headed for his office and March, who hadn't been to the offices officially in a few months, spent some time visiting the departments, especially the art and graphics floor, saying hello and asking about families and kids and parents.

At nine thirty she walked into the boardroom, passed by the box of hot Krispy Kremes, a stack of five-hundred-calorie-each croissants, and collection of fruit Danish and grabbed a non-fat fruit yogurt and black coffee.

Her tall, slim and athletic sons joined her, the boys she had raised on organic baby food she made herself in a blender, painful breast feedings and then organic whole milk for their growing bones, and years of healthful, well-planned and balanced meals.

They each grabbed donuts and croissants and Danish—all plural—stacked high on their small white plates, along with creamy lattes, juice and milk. Phillip, aged thirty-two, actually carried a bottle of chocolate milk.

Scott had already eaten two donuts by the time he sat down, drank the milk and was starting on a croissant with butter, then looked up at her. "What?"

"There isn't enough butter already cooked into that for you?"

"Nah. Hand me the jam, will you?" He grinned at her.

"The fact that neither of you have an ounce of fat on you is proof to me that God is a man," she said.

Phillip sat down across from her. "Of course He's a man. That's why we run the world. Hoo-yah!"

"Stop beating your chest, son, and try to remember we *women* give birth to you." She took a bite of yogurt and pointed at him with her spoon. "Your tie doesn't match."

Phillip frowned down at his clothes. "Yes it does."

"You're wearing the wrong tie again, Phil." His wife Keely walked in and poured herself some coffee. "I can't let you leave the house after me."

"You should pin notes on his clothes," Scott said. "That's what mom did all through high school. He looked like crap in college. Purple shirt. Brown pants. Red hightops."

Color blind, her daughter-in-law silently mouthed to March over Phillip's bald head.

Looking at Keely it was hard to believe she had been through so much just a year ago, when after struggling to get pregnant for two years, she'd had an ectopic pregnancy that put her in the hospital, left her with one ovary and tube, and put Phillip through hell. It was not easy on either of them, but Keely was well now and March knew she was still longing for a baby. They were trying again, but no luck. March gave her a quick kiss. "I didn't know you'd be here today."

"She's presenting the new ad proposal for SkiStar," Phil explained then looked at his wife. "Get me another milk, baby, would you? Chocolate."

"Only if you promise to pour it on that tie," Keely shot back. She was a good match for Phillip.

When Molly graduated from UCLA with an award winning portfolio and the beginnings of a great reputation, she was hired as a commercial photographer for one of San Francisco's largest advertising firms, the same firm March had done graphics for years back, then Molly quickly met and bonded with Keely Robinson, a tall, blonde, super-smart junior ad consultant. Before long, Molly had played matchmaker between her irrepressibly-fun, completely helpless bachelor of a brother and her friend. The rest was Cantrell family history.

Within a few minutes the board had settled in, and for more than an hour, they completed regular board business before Phillip opened the discussion of SkiStar's losses and failing position in the industry, then led into Keely's ideas, which she pitched as she handed out her proposal folders. "The time-proven, best publicity tool for increasing the sports industry positioning and sales is celebrity endorsement. The statistics and historical percentages of growth and profits, some done in colored graphs, are in your folders. They start on page four."

Her facts and research were impressive, but that wasn't surprising. What was impressive were the projections and goals for SkiStar, which looked too good to be true, if the company followed advertising history.

Scott closed his folder. "I thought we decided endorsement was too expensive and risky." He paused, then added, "When? Two years ago?"

"The risk was in the celebrity list we were considering then," Phil said.

"So what's changed?"

"One name," Keely looked at Phillip, who gave her a wink.

"Who?"

"Spider Olsen."

Olsen was the only industry name that could make every person in the room stop and believe. And March understood why. Spider Olsen. She glanced at Mike. He wasn't saying anything. His expression was one she knew: thoughtful, a listen and wait look.

The top winter sports broadcaster for almost two decades, working for ABC, NBC and ESPN, Spider Olsen was a household name, the only American skier to win three Olympic gold medals for downhill and two consecutive for slalom. Spider Olsen's name was synonymous with United States skiing.

A five-time World Champion, Olsen had refused all endorsement offers since he left the sport almost twenty years ago. But the networks had gone to Spider for every winter Olympics coverage since, for the world championships, and he anchored and mediated network winter sport commentary.

Blond, tall, aggressive and intelligent, with a deep and distinctive voice, he was also just as often in the entertainment headlines, married and divorced from an ice skater, an actress who starred in a long-running Emmy-winning sitcom, and, most recently divorced from the grand-daughter of a United States vice president. He was everything March had thought the first time she'd ever met him. Spider Olsen was a hound. Pure trouble.

"What makes you think we can get Olsen?" Scott asked, laughing slightly at the idea. "No one else has. He's turned down every endorsement offer for years."

"He won his medals on SkiStars."

"In the 80's."

"He likes Dad," Phillip said.

"Yeah, right," Scott said. "He likes the millions a year he thinks we'll pay him."

Phil looked at Mike. "I didn't know you knew him, Dad, until Keely introduced him to me. He said he knew you from years back."

"I know Olsen," Mike said without emotion.

"All our conversations indicate he's open to an endorsement for SkiStar . . . especially now that it's part of Cantrell." Keely set the folder down.

Mike laughed, shaking his head slightly, his hands steepled as he rubbed his chin.

As far as March knew, Mike's contact with Spider Olsen was limited to his fist to Olsen's jaw in a bar in Calgary.

No one at the table really needed convincing. An endorsement from Olsen was exactly what SkiStar needed. There wasn't a person there who didn't understand Olsen's appeal. Olsen was bigger than life. March had already promised Mike she'd follow his lead on this. Her smart-as-a-whip daughter-in-law understood the power of the carrot she'd just dangled in front of them.

Phillip looked up at his dad every few seconds, tapping his pen on the arm of his chair with his usual energetic lack of patience, waiting for Mike to say something, and Scott was silent and not particularly receptive, even when he glanced at her and gave a slight smile. She knew he was worried about the amount of money a contract with Olsen would cost the company, money that would come directly from Cantrell's profits, on Scott's side of the business.

Mike sat back, his decision clearly made. "Okay." He looked at Phil and Keely. "You got it. Let's start negotiating."

Chapter Eight

The odometer had broken at one hundred and eighteen thousand miles, and the front bumper stayed on thanks to an old coat hanger and half a roll of electrical tape. Years of sea and road salt had turned the car's paint the same dull color of concrete, and the stained interior smelled like dried apple juice, Arrowroot biscuits, and struggle.

Between San Francisco and Lake Tahoe, along the snakelike miles of Highway 50, the history of Cantrell Sports Inc. had evolved inside a stinking, broken Chevelle Malibu wagon.

In those early years, Mike had made his living from the back of that Chevy station wagon, selling his first snowboards on weekends and holidays in the parking lot below the face of Heavenly Valley, back when there was still a T-bar on the bunny slope and calling his first board *The Cannabis* had helped grab the attention of most skiers.

But now it was a lifetime later, and the rental car he had parked at the Stateline casino valet was a luxury SUV with electronic aroma dispensers, GPS, and satellite radio. Behind the casino, up on the mountain, high-speed quads and a six-pac chair carried skiers and boarders to the summit of Heavenly, and board lingo like "smoking a fatty" was no longer a reference to recreational drugs.

From the long windows of a luxury casino penthouse used by ESPN for event after-parties, a majestic view of Heavenly filled an indigo panorama. Dark drifts of plowed snow framed the perimeter of the parking lot, shadowed gondolas dangled from their cables like bats, and steep, pristinely-groomed slopes appeared blue from the February night sky, where every star above the Sierras flickered like distant, approaching headlights and a thin sliver of a winter moon rose above hostile, black diamond trails.

Tonight was a lifetime away from those days of that rusted station wagon, when he had been a young husband and father of two baby boys born fifteen months apart, living with March on little but his pie-in-the-sky dreams, and his absolute belief in the possibility of a new kind of sport.

He remembered one night standing down at the foot of Stateline in the dead of winter, the smelly old Chevy parked somewhere down by the lake, on a Saturday when he hadn't sold a single board. The streets and sky had been illuminated from the bright lights of the hotel-casinos, Harrah's, Harvey's and the old Sahara.

You couldn't see the stars over Heavenly when you stood in the bold lightshade of the casinos, just stacked floors of lit hotel rooms and the dotted lights of the wide-windowed restaurants topping them. Whenever an electric door opened, the discordant ringing of slot machines would break up any moments of winter silence, just like they still did if you stood there in the winter night air, even with nothing but dreams to bet on. He didn't gamble his money in those days. His sure thing was an idea, not an endorsement contract with a hotshot skier who lived a life of completely different values.

When he first met with Spider Olsen again, a few months back and after the board's decision to shoot for the endorsement contract, he and Olsen had laughed about Calgary, where Olsen's comments about snowboarding and his drunken attention on March made Mike lose his temper and punch his lights out.

They were still two completely different men.

March had asked him once when they were first dating if he believed in destiny and fate. One of the things that separated her from the other girls he had known was the way she asked him questions about things he hadn't thought of.

Mike understood that a man thought alone, his dreams and plans were often his secret life. Men acted on their ideas. Women talked about them. He'd told her back then he believed every person had some kind of blueprint. But he would never believe his life was completely in someone else's hands. Somewhere in his bones he knew he had to make his life what it would become.

That dismal night long ago when he was standing on the California and Nevada state line might have been the first time he really understood he could chisel his life out of the great unknown because he had her at his back.

One of the things he remembered being aware of in the days when he was struggling and things were not good was that life carried with it a subdued sense of lost time. The job at Spreckles had been gone, with no regrets. He had a family, but March stood by his side. She had always been there, something that allowed him to take risks because he wouldn't want to die and be in that last instant of life and regret something he'd never done.

So he didn't carry the kind of regrets he figured Olsen carried, if the man actually had any kind of a moral compass. Now, tonight, looking down from the ESPN party inside a high-priced Stateline casino, Mike felt disconnected from those years of history which seemed as if they had happened to some other man.

The noise level in the too-slick, too-crowded, too-warm suite grew higher and irritating from the strident sound of young women laughing too loud, while others danced alone, provocatively, to lure the attention of downhill racers, celebrities, and Spider Olsen, who was one of those men who held some strange kind of magnetism for immature and needy young women.

Olsen, barely dwarfed by a towering marble fireplace, stood across the room surrounded by women half his age. Mike spotted a redhead in her early twenties, close to his own daughter Molly's age, and he had the fatherly urge to tell her to run home and stay far away from Olsen.

As ideal as the man was for a SkiStar endorsement, he was close to fifty years old and the human equivalent of a tomcat. Spider Olsen was the kind of man who was hard on women.

But Mike's business was boards and skis, not Olsen's love life. Inside his briefcase was what he came for: his signed endorsement contract. For the next three years, Olsen and SkiStar were one. Those freezing hours of standing on the street below with his empty pockets were another lifetime ago.

Mike turned away from the window wondering what he was still doing there. He'd made his necessary appearance.

Earlier, after the race Olsen commentated, Mike had left the mountain, packed up his stuff and locked up the Tahoe house. Now he had a plane to catch. He wanted to get home tonight. Standing at the window, a looking glass into the world of his past, had merely killed time inside a room he didn't want to be in.

A quick glance at his watch and he waded through a Heffneresque crowd of ski groupies, uncomfortable when he was followed by too many, too-young and too-hungry female looks.

"Mike." Olsen shook his hand.

"I need to get to the airport."

"My offer still stands. Wait until tomorrow and the network jet will take you back in the morning. It's still early."

Mike shook his head. "Mickey has a game tomorrow. I promised March I'd be home yesterday. I'm already pushing it." Olsen gave him a look they both understood, so Mike clapped Spider on the shoulder. "With the right woman, marriage works." Leaning closer, he added, "But I can guarantee the right woman is not in this room."

"You're probably right." Olsen laughed. "But there's more fun here than in any of my marriages, so I'll suffer through."

Twenty minutes later, Mike drove down the steep hairpin turns of Kingsbury Grade, a shortcut that would put him in the flatlands of Gardnerville and take at least twenty minutes off his trip to the Reno airport. He sailed around one turn and the car went suddenly dead. No power. No lights. Zilch.

With no control and tight steering, he struggled to pull hard into a turnout and set the parking gear, then turned the key. Nothing happened, so he popped the hood. But even the engine compartment light was out.

He reached inside and hit the GPS call button on the headliner console and waited. No ring, no answer, no monotone voice wanting to give him movie times and make dinner reservations. He swore under his breath—it was cold as death outside—and shrugged into his jacket, leaned against the car and pulled out his cell, waiting impatiently for a signal. The words "no service" lit his blue screen.

With so little moon, the road was pitch black; overhead, just an unending bowl of night sky and the saw-like shadow of Ponderosa pines backed by crests of the snow-covered Sierra Mountains. From the valley below, small lights flickered from an occasional farm, a cold, long walk that could easily make him miss his plane.

For a day that had started out as the answer to SkiStar's problems, things were going into the toilet fast. Twenty two degrees had been the last outside temperature reading on the dead SUV. To make the plane, he didn't have time to screw around, so he grabbed his bag from the backseat and started walking down the mountain, checking his cell every few minutes for a signal.

Behind him, distant music and the growl of a big block engine sounded from up the road, so he turned just as the gleam of headlights came at him from around a sharp turn. He stepped into the road and headlights and waved his arms. A three quarter ton truck swerved and barreled past, country music blaring from inside the closed crew cab.

"Don't stop, whatever you do," Mike muttered. "I'm freezing out here."

Ahead a red flash of brake lights suddenly illuminated the road, and he ran toward the truck as the tinted, driver-side window hummed down.

The man inside wore an expensive Stetson low on his head. In the reflection of dashboard lights, he looked all clean-cut cowboy in that Tim McGraw way, and a little older than their oldest son, Scott, late thirties maybe. As the driver reached to turn down the radio, Mike spotted the dark silhouette of a guitar case on the passenger seat, hay on the floorboard, and a tattered leather briefcase with white sheets of music stuffed inside.

"I broke down a mile or so back," Mike told him. "I'm trying to catch a flight out of Reno."

"I saw the car." A soft Southern drawl coated the driver's deep voice and the door locks clicked. "Hop in." He shoved the guitar and music in the back of the crew cab.

"I appreciate this." Shaking hands, he said, "I'm Mike Cantrell."

"Rio Paxton."

Mike recognized the name from years back, when Rio Paxton had been chosen Country Singer of the Year, youngest in history, and his songs were all over the radio. There had been some kind of talk of burnout, cancelled concerts and the kind of wild behavior that could consume someone caught in the fires of instant fame. Rio Paxton and Olsen could have compared notes on screwing up life.

Paxton must have seen his recognition. "Yeah. That's me. *Wunderkind.* I incinerated pretty fast and very publicly. I still can't remember 1989."

"My youngest son was born in '89. He can incinerate a few things himself. Just dropped the bomb that he wants to can college and join the professional snowboard circuit."

"Cantrell?" Rio paused, then looked at him curiously. "Like Cantrell snowboards?"

"You got it."

"Is your son any good?"

"Yeah."

" '89? He's only a year or two younger than I was then. Keep him in school and out of the spotlight."

"I'm trying. It's hard to talk to a hardheaded teenager with no experience."

"He knows everything. Didn't we all?"

Within minutes they'd launched into natural male conversation—car engines (horsepower) and music business, snowboards and horse ranches near Sparks, talk that filled the time along the straight asphalt roads toward Reno.

The airport was on the town's southern outskirts, built and expanded on a desolate plain of Nevada's vast chaparral; it was easy, accessible, efficient and made for the kind of travel that after age fifty made Mike occasionally long for a life much simpler, in a place unlike ebullient San Francisco, and removed from the complicated lifestyle he'd carved out for himself and his family. A man's dreams could change.

They pulled right up to the airport curb. No cabs, no limos, no waiting in lines of people blocking the sidewalks and unloading carts full of luggage, no interminable drive into the city from the airport.

Mike took Rio's card. "I appreciate this. I'll send you some new equipment for the ride."

"You don't have to do that."

"Yeah, but I will." Mike grabbed his bag from the seat. "Thanks, again, man." He shook Rio's hand. "I would have missed this flight."

"Glad to help out."

Mike shut the truck door with more than enough time to deal with the rental car agency and easily make his flight. There was no need to rush through the automatic glass doors.

Behind him came the sudden rumble of a Ford big block and the truck pulled away, the mute, distant CD sound of Jerry Jeff Walker singing *Up Against the Wall You Redneck Mother.*

PART TWO

I used to think getting old was about
vanity—but actually it's about
losing people you love.

—*Joyce Carol Oates*

March

And how am I to face the odds
Of man's bedevilment and God's?
I, a stranger and afraid
In a world I never made.

—*A. E. Housman*

Chapter Nine

It was two a.m. when I awakened to the incessant ringing of the doorbell, and Mike's side of the bed was still empty. But he'd called me earlier to let me know he was coming home, late apparently. "March," he'd said, "I'll be there, but I've had one helluva a day, good and bad."

When he was out of town, I had this habit of chain-locking the kitchen doors, which drove him nuts. I climbed out of bed just as the phone began to ring. I guess he had lost his patience, and was now resorting to using his cell phone to wake me up.

Ignoring it, I stumbled out of the room and downstairs, muttering about the faults of men and husbands in particular. He had a set of damned keys. Where did he leave them this time?

Both the doorbell and the phone rang again and again. "I'm coming!" I pulled open the door, not exactly smart for a woman who locked the place up like Fort Knox. By the time the thought crossed my mind that it was two in the morning, the door was open and I was staring at a dark uniformed cop standing in what looked like parade stance, tall and straight, illuminated by a muted yellow bug light Mike had just replaced the Sunday before.

"Someone's home," he said into the black cell phone at his ear, and a few seconds later the house phone stopped ringing.

It was damp out and cold, and I was wearing only a thin sleep tank and drawstring bottoms, so I wrapped my arms over my chest.

He looked me in the eyes with an expression that was strained and serious. "Mrs. Cantrell? Mrs. Michael Cantrell?"

Like dense fog rolling in, an alien kind of emptiness settled over me, starting from the place where my heart had just stopped beating. I felt separated from the scene suddenly unraveling before me, and what was happening hit me with such clarity it took a moment to speak. "Is Mike alive?"

"I'm sorry." His look, his whole demeanor was one I would come to recognize over the coming months as an awkward mix of apprehension and pity. People don't know what to say to a widow, especially when you were the person who had to tell her she had just become one.

Mike Cantrell was dead because he was in the exact wrong place at the exact wrong moment. Just a few miles from home, a driver going the wrong way on one of San Francisco's one-way streets killed my husband of thirty four years and the father of our four kids.

My mind spun from thought to ironic thought. He had flown back home safely. He hadn't been driving his Porsche, the car most likely to kill him, because he refused to park it in the airport parking lot where people dented doors and banged bumpers. He was driving the sedan, a heavy, expensive, German car made of hard steel, with airbags and an engine that could reach top speed on the autobahn. A big engine and air bags, all those things that are supposed to protect you.

He had spent his adult lifetime driving in traffic and fog, those years driving that crappy old Chevy up to the mountains where the roads were snowy and slick and sometimes covered in deadly black ice. He'd flown in all kinds of planes all over the world. But a one way street just blocks from home brought his life, his glorious and wonderful life, to an end?

"I've had one helluva a day . . ."

My whole world changed inside of a mere second. You hear that expression, even say it sometimes, having no real idea of the horrific truth of it. Life changed with a few words, two of which sounded so cheap. *I'm sorry.* The officer was sorry. I couldn't do anything but stand there in front of that poor, apologetic messenger of death as tragedy punched me right in the face.

Crying felt impossible, because every human emotion spun around inside of me all at the same time. I turned away to see Mickey standing on the stairs, baggy pajamas hanging off his hips, watching, curious, his hair poking out like it had when he was three.

How do you tell your children the most important person in their lives was dead?

I found out how: You stand there, a phlegmatic shell in a zombie-like state, and say words you never think about saying, and then you watch some beautiful, innate part of your children evaporate right before your eyes. And that was only the beginning of one of the worst parts of life: dealing with death.

The numbness began to leave me a week after Mike's memorial service, when I had left the house for the first time and was hiding in the park where we had gotten married. I'd just had too much of everyone who wanted to be there for me, even my best girlfriends who, like everyone, watched me as if I were a vial of nitroglycerin.

Thank God for my kids. Because of them I couldn't disappear. I couldn't curl into an amoebic ball or drive off and never come back. The family had to stay a family come what may.

Day in and day out, we all watched each other, circling like beaten dogs with fearful and wary looks that had never been in our eyes before. Somehow, we needed desperately to find between us something other than our kindred pain or the complete and utter fear. We tiptoed around each other, awkward and silently bleeding until there was more meaning when we didn't talk than in anything we actually said.

A moment's impulse was what made me run from the house, away from friends calling to see how I was, from the business that had been my husband's life continuing on; from the tax forms needing to be signed; the bills that had to be paid; the mundane things that went on when everything inside of me screamed, Stop! Stop! Stop! The world had stopped.

My world had stopped.

So I sat in brittle isolation, high on a glorious hill in my beloved, heterogeneous city surrounded by bays spanned with bridges and the Great Pacific Ocean. There was a reason why crooners sang about her, and I believed I had run to that exact spot looking for my own heart.

A twisted cypress tree with thready bark was at my back, and the cool wind off the water hit me in the face. It was too early for spring. There were no lush velvet pansies in the beds and no scrabbly dandelions or the bright yellow mustard poking through the grass yet. But it was a blue-sky, blue-water California day, with the wind coming in off the Pacific to gently beat the bay into soft white peaks, like meringue pies and whipping cream.

Cookbook language. *Do not over beat.* I had been doing that lately, unconsciously hitting my leg with my fist when I sat still for too long. Molly was the one who pointed it out to me, with

127

a look that made me question how well I was doing at my big plan of not giving my children anything to worry over. Even as a child my daughter could zero in on the more obscure things in the landscape: the owl up in the tallest tree; a single whole sand dollar lost in a bed of broken ones; a satellite looking like a star moving across the clear Sierra mountain night sky. I knew early my daughter was destined to be behind a camera, something that could capture her view of the world.

She had told me once there were three hundred and sixty-four mistakes in *Buffy the Vampire Slayer*, and I suspect she watched every episode and found them all. She usually won the family film pool of who-could-find-the-most-movie-mistakes, a Cantrell family tradition, which said a lot about the kinds of films we went to. Her skill came directly from Mike, who was such a film buff he had walked around whistling for most of the day when they released *Star Wars* on DVD and had added a loud thump sound when a storm trooper accidentally hit his head on the doorway.

That Lucas could poke fun at his mistake made Mike's day—he could laugh at himself like that—but in a family of clowns, Molly took herself much too seriously. She was the one who had always sought something so much deeper than the rest of us. I like to think of myself as a smart woman. But my mind did not easily travel down the same thoughtlines as my daughter. We locked horns often, and to my great frustration I never could see our battles coming.

The Sunday before she had been talking to Phillip when they didn't know I could hear them from the next room. I'm a mother, of course I stopped outside the room and listened.

"Why?" Molly said.

"Why what?"

"How many times had Dad driven down that same street? Why then? Why him? Don't you ask yourself why?"

"No, Midget. And I don't want to know any more than we already do. He was driving home. Some truck jackknifes, turns over, a car turns the wrong way to miss it and Dad's dead." Phil paused and his voice dropped a little. "You can't keep rehashing what happened."

"I have to."

"Well, I can't go there." Phillip sounded upset.

"I need to find some sense in it. Some reason."

"There is no sense in death. There's probably none in life either," Phil said and I hated the bitterness I heard in my son's voice. He left Molly alone to go to his wife. I hoped Keely could give him what he needed at that moment.

I had my back to the wall and I waited, trying to decide if I could go in there. When I wasn't weak and grieving, Molly was not easy to talk to or confront. That day, I was shaky, so I chickened out and didn't go to her. Molly had sat there for the longest time, and I believe now it was a mistake for me to leave her alone then, because although I made an attempt to talk to her later—before she left and when I felt more in control—she wouldn't talk to me about her father. A dark cloak of despondency had settled over her. She'd brusquely changed the subject, and afterward I couldn't help feeling if because of my own weakness, I'd lost my only opportunity for the two of us to grieve together.

The night of Mike's death, the police told me he had died instantly, a clichéd choice of words that was supposed to give me some sense of peace. *He died instantly.* I never repeated those words to our children, true or not. The images they brought to mind were more cruel than the news itself.

So now, today, on this hillside, what answer was I looking for? I picked at the grass beneath me and looked out from the park at the water beyond, wondering why I had come there, why I had really run there?

Because it was a weekday (Tuesday? Wednesday? Whateverday) there were only as many boats in the bay as fingers on my left hand, where I wore a wedding ring that after more than three decades no longer had a matching one. "Now" had no relevance. The views from that hill were panoramic and unobstructed, but I couldn't see any future.

I was perfectly aware of one thing: I had just lived through a week and a half that would change the course of my life and even in one of my favorite places in the world, I found it difficult to hide. No matter how hard I tried, I still didn't feel much of anything, so I finally stood up, and the wind washed over me, cool, a little damper and at least *there*. And then the same wind was at my back, pushing me home, because there was really no place to hide.

It took time before I began to feel my skin again, days longer until I could taste or smell anything. I could have eaten a lemon without flinching, held a wild skunk in my arms, or opened my refrigerator door without even a whiff of what was rotting inside. After all I was only doing the same.

Days passed and I didn't remember much. My children had to repeat things to me. I watched them closely so I wouldn't have to look too closely at my own grief, moving forward in a semblance of normal living. I went through every day, every hour and minute like a character in a play written with invisible ink.

This wasn't happening to me. This wasn't reality.

But the truth was: this was my new reality. Michael David Cantrell was dead, and for a long time afterward I wanted to be.

Chapter Ten

As those passing days turned into weeks, I found myself comforting others when they called, Mike's friends and brother. It was amazing how easily I slipped into the role of pacifier, taking on the job to try to make their loss easier to cope with. Funny how I would be doing alright just before they called to check on me, then we would spiral into discussion of what Mike had meant to them, something they needed to tell me, and some part of me probably needed to hear what they said. But I did keep answering the phone.

But eventually I would say goodbye, hang up and find I felt lost all over again, swallowed by a bleak cloud that seemed to hover over me, and just when there had been some modicum of normalcy creeping back into the misery of the day.

Sometimes, I would hang up and get into my car and go shopping. But the only things I seemed to ever buy were expensive leather handbags. I had tired of trying to soothe those people who loved Mike, I had to escape, do something mindless, like shopping, because then for a little while I could ignore the dismal place where I kept trying to be normal when nothing would ever be normal again. I foolishly believed I could find something to make me happy.

Those who knew Mike, worked with him and respected him, wanted to have a commemoration ceremony at a major annual circuit event in Heavenly Valley. His business associates and the winter sports industry needed to do something for Michael Cantrell. So that was how I ended up outside the East Peak Lodge in Tahoe on a cold Friday afternoon in early February. None of us had been back up to the lake since Mike's death.

Traditionally, the south shore was where the family spent most weekends in the winter months. I can't explain why we hadn't gone to the mountains. Before this ceremony came up, we never talked about it. We just somehow knew. Maybe we each were afraid to mention Tahoe. But hanging over us was the knowledge that there was still something the kids and I needed to do for Mike. So because of the snowboarding event, a weekend trip seemed the right timing for the family to privately celebrate Mike's life, too.

Before me stood the lift and a whole mountain of snow and ice, with sharp dark peaks sawing across a brilliant but fading cyan sky, and I was reminded of my place now, too small and inconsequential in this big wide world that was suddenly so unfamiliar. I was facing the massive climb of life ahead of me, my first journey in decades without my husband.

I did not know the road ahead, and the unknown was treacherous and overwhelming. A real and horrific fear had seeded itself deep down into my bones. Mike didn't have my back anymore. To hide that fear, I had cultivated a fragile mask of normalcy. I had become paper-thin crystal, and with the wrong touch or right note I could easily shatter into a million pieces.

Today I felt no thrill or excitement in the sport that was so much a part of our lives. Yet I did love this sport. Mike had loved this sport. I couldn't bear to lose my love of it. But the last time any of us had been on boards was over the holidays, and Mike had been there.

Rationally, I told myself I had stood in this same spot and boarded down that same mountain ahead of me too many times to count over the years, sometimes with my kids or grandkids cradled in my arms. This time I carried a wood box that contained all that was left of my husband.

The wooden box. I laughed then, because our choice of that wooden box had been just the kind of thing Mike would have found pretty damned funny. In the somber days after his death, the kids and I had to go to the funeral home (a family necessity that really should be performed by anyone but the family). A tall man dressed in a crisp white shirt, a dark suit and dull matching tie handled all the details, then placed a couple of thick plastic notebooks in front of us and asked in a deep and gentle voice if we would please select a crematory ash container. He left us to our decision, and the door clicked shut loudly in the room's heavy silence, trapping us, a family who normally couldn't shut up and talked all over each other.

None of us wanted to be there. It was almost as if we collectively forgot to breathe. Then Phillip had turned in his chair, picked up a photo of the man and his wife that was sitting on the desk. He examined it for a few seconds and held it up. "Look at this. Did any of you notice that he looks like Lurch?"

The other two boys laughed quietly.

"Phillip!" I said.

"Well, hell, Mom. What is he? Six foot eight?"

"What if he hears you?" I said in a hushed voice.

"He left us alone. If he hears me, he shouldn't be listening."

"You're such a jerk, Phil," Molly said. "This is no time for your stupid jokes. Please don't upset Mom."

But I wasn't upset. I realized I needed Phil's humor right then. I understood that we all desperately needed to laugh again, because for those few silly seconds we didn't hurt so much.

"Here." I handed Phil the other book. "Make yourself useful and look through this one."

We leaned over the heavy binders, Scott and Molly and I with one, Phil and Mickey with the other, turning the plastic pages and having no idea what we were looking for.

"This one has a dog on top of it," Mickey said, clearly baffled.

"You're in the pet section, numb nuts," Phil said. "That's why you start from front to back. How did you score so high on the SATs?"

Mickey's expression was priceless. "They have urns for dogs?"

"And cats and birds and horses." Phil went back to the catalog. "Hey, look at the size of these horse containers."

Mickey frowned down at the page. "It says at the bottom you can add a music box to any container. There's even a song list. And here's a whole section called 'motorcycles.'"

"You're kidding?"

Mickey looked up at me, uneasy and protective, then said, "Let's skip it."

"No. Wait. I want to see them." Phil flipped through the pages and mumbled something about gas tanks and orange flames.

"Keep turning the pages, Scott," I said, hating the choices in our book. It was like looking at cast bronze Hummel figurines.

"Sorry, Mom. These bronze angels are pretty bad. There are pages and pages of them." Scott looked up at me. "Do you really think they sell that many? Who buys these? This one has an angel holding an American flag."

Phillip leaned over. "Look at the one next to it. The angel's holding a Confederate flag. Might as well put a white hood on it."

I sank my head in my hand and groaned. "Oh my God . . ."

"See? You upset Mom," Molly said testily.

Phil leaned over. "Are you crying, Mom?"

"Of course she's crying," Molly said, disgusted. "You are such a toad."

Scott slipped his arm around me. "Mom?"

I tried to keep control, but I wanted to laugh and was afraid if I started laughing it would be hysterical, flooding out of me, uncontrolled and unnatural. I was afraid Molly would get even more upset. When I thought I wouldn't break into laughter or tears, I took a deep breath and looked up at Molly. "I'm okay."

"Here's one that looks just like the lamp in the TV room," Mickey said brightly, turning the book sideways so we could see it.

"Let's get that one, Mom," Phil said, running with it. "It's better than that bronze angel with the flag. We'll put a fancy shade on it and keep dad in front of the big screen."

Scott burst out laughing. "Then he won't miss a game."

"Maybe we can get one of those leather flap things for it to hold the remote. You know, those things they sell in the airline magazines? Dad was always losing the remote."

My husband was infamous for ordering gadgets from the airline magazines: portable clothing steamers; gadgets that held CDs onto your car visor; digital recorders; and even an electrical outlet device that shut on and off when you clapped your hands together.

"Maybe we can get a clapper to turn it off and on."

I put my hand over my mouth. I had to stop myself. Even during the worst moments, my sons' banter could make me laugh.

"I hate you all," Molly said, turning to the book indignantly and thumbing through the pages with a too-serious look, while my sons made faces at each other and commented on containers shaped like golf bags, airplanes and train engines.

"Oh my God . . ." She slammed the book shut and turned away.

"Molly?" I said, placing my hand on her shoulder. It was shaking.

Scott leaned over. "What is it?"

"Let me see it, Midget," Phillip said.

"This." Molly opened the book. Elvis' profile was carved out of pinkish skin-toned alabaster and his hair and features were painted in glossy black.

Phil looked up at us, straight-faced. "Wanna bet it plays *In the Ghetto*?"

We all lost it, and from the expression on the funeral director's face when he came back in, he must have thought we were crazy, unholy, and completely irreverent.

So Mike ended up in a highly polished rosewood box with a rich grain that flowed across the top like rivers of time and life. It was perfect.

I ran my hand over the top of it now and hugged it a little tighter to my chest. Behind me, my children were gathered near the base of the run, dressed for the trail, setting their gear, and stepping into their boards. I turned back to the face of the mountain and leaned down close to the box. "I know you wanted this, my darling. And we'll do it for you. I know I have to let go. But please don't blame me if I don't let go easily."

"Hey, Mom. You okay?" Scott skidded his board to a stop next to me.

"Just talking to myself."

"Rob's on his way. He was waiting for the mountain to clear out. It closed down fifteen minutes ago."

"Good. We won't have to wait much longer then." It was cold but I wasn't certain if I was shivering from the air or my state of mind.

"There he is," Scott said. "I'll go get the others together."

I turned around and watched Rob jump off the lift and board over to me. He was now Vice President and Director of Operations for Heavenly

Valley, a far cry from his days of running a grooming machine on a small ski area between Truckee and Tahoe City.

Where had the time gone? As I watched him walk toward me, I longed to be back there, to that first day on the slopes, back when we all were young and free and believed in the impossible.

His wild Abby Hoffman black hair was now clipped short and his face was tanned and lined from the weather, but his smile was the same. When Rob Cantrell turned his attention on you, you appreciated the manner of the man.

"Hey, Gorgeous." He gave me a huge hug and then pulled back and looked down at me. "You okay?"

"I am. Thank you so much for this."

"There isn't anything I wouldn't do for Mike and for you. You know that."

"Even let us on the mountain to do something completely illegal?"

"Illegal? What're you talking about?" He laughed, his arm still slung around my shoulders. "What could you possibly do that's illegal? Besides, sweetheart, when illegal battles with moral humanity, humanity's gonna win in my book. And I don't know of anything illegal. We opened the mountain for private skiing after hours." He stepped back as Scott, Mickey, Phil and Molly joined us. "Take the quad up to the top. I can open the gates on the bowl runs, but this

140

time of day it's hard to see and probably icy on that side of the hill. You decide."

"We won't need the bowl runs," I told him and looked at Scott, who nodded.

"We'll stay on the main face," he assured Rob, then turned to me. "You and Molly ride with Phil, and Mickey and I will take the next chair. Right, Squirt?" Scott patted Mickey on the head like a pet dog, something Mickey usually hated but today he just laughed Scott off.

It had not missed my notice that my youngest had grown closer to his older brothers lately and less willing to pick fights with them or let their teasing affect him. But he was too quiet sometimes. We all were.

"Come on, kids," I said to Phil and Molly. "We'll meet you at the top." We boarded over to the lift, stepped out of our back bindings, and sat down as it took off.

From the chair, I could see the open horizon, the vast landscape for hundreds of miles. Home was out there somewhere, but far beyond the slight scope of my human eye. The sun was lowering into the west and outlining the rim of land in the distance orange, and the edges of sky were beginning to turn bright colors. Behind us, the lake was an enormous glasslike sea of fresh blue water surrounded by cold mountain peaks fading into lavender in the waning light, and ahead of us was an almost indefinable wall of stark, blindingly white snow and steep runs. The air had grown colder, but there was no wind, and I felt my daughter shiver, so I rested my hand on her thigh.

We, who always had so much to say about anything and everything, said nothing for a few minutes, but seemed to collectively watch our breath fog into the cold air as we climbed to the top on a high-speed quad . . . then Phillip began to hum. *In the Ghetto.*

I laughed. Before I could tell him how awful he was, Molly was singing about a cold Chicago morn. I joined in, and we sang at the very tops of our lungs, loud and obnoxious and mostly out of tune, trying to either out-sing or keep up with each other. Soon I heard Scott's deep voice, off-key just like his dad's in the shower, and Mickey, too, singing as loudly as we all were, butchering the melody, forgetting the words and half laughing.

I believe we sang with the hope that the air above us would somehow carry our voices up higher than the sky and more reverberant than a mountain echo. In the sheer stupidness of what we were doing, I was overcome by the oddest sense of joy. There was no show of strength now, no façade or convention or need to act like we were completely sane. It was one of those "who cared?" moments that Mike would have loved.

Somewhere close to ten thousand feet, where a

blue net spread out from the sides of the chair platform and over the sharp and deadly drop straight down, we slid off, our boards on icy ground again, still singing verses we didn't really know, though our voices were hoarse and fading. But we still laughed, stumbling into our boards and circling around each other in a ring of flat and final notes, smiles that had been lost to us suddenly creasing our faces.

At the end of my life, when I am almost gone from this earth, I know I will remember that moment of absolute joy as I stood with my children, high on a mountain that divided two states. The awkwardness I'd been feeling for days waned, and a strange sense of peace seemed to hold me in its arms.

Scott squatted down and pulled a bottle of Mike's favorite wine from his backpack, stood and opened it, then said, "Here's to Dad." He took a swig and passed it around.

"I gave you paper cups," Molly said. "Where are they?"

"I left them in the car. Hell, we're family. We have the same cooties."

"Cooties? God, Scott. How old are you?" Molly asked sarcastically.

"I have a six year old. She affects my vocabulary." He looked at his brother. "What's your excuse, Phil?"

"Brain damage. You beat me up too much when

I was a kid and there was that time you punched me in the head and I had to get stitches." Phil handed the bottle to Molly. "Here, *I* don't have any communicable diseases. Is there something you want to tell us, Midget?"

She rolled her eyes and shook her head, stepping out of any bantering with her brothers and raising the wine bottle, and as she did so, her face grew serious and her emotion was raw and open for us to see. Since she had lost her father, my daughter the photographer had a constant case of red-eye. "To Daddy."

We were quiet again when she finished, and it was then that I noticed Mickey standing awkwardly outside our circle. "Come here, love." I held out my arm and he moved close. I put my hand around his thin waist and handed him the bottle. "Here. It's okay."

"No backwash, kid," Phil warned. "That's not a bottle of Orange Crush."

"Bite me," Mickey said. "To Dad." He took a long swig of wine that brought tears to his eyes and a flush to his cheeks when he lowered the bottle. He was seventeen, and had no palate yet, though we'd served him wine during holiday dinners. He'd always left most of it in the glass and Mike usually finished it off. "I'm not going to waste that wine," he'd say. "Why do you pour it for him?"

"Because he doesn't need to feel ostracized."

"But he doesn't drink it!"

"You'll drink it. Besides, I don't really care. I won't make him feel left out. You're the parent. You should be happy he doesn't drink it."

"That logic doesn't fly with me. If it were beer, the kid would have chugged down the whole thing."

Mike seemed to have completely forgotten that back in 1968 he drank Red Mountain for a buck a bottle.

We finished the bottle, Phillip making more wisecracks so he wouldn't get emotional and lose it in front of us all. But he had a tough second or two when he toasted his "Pop" so I took his hand in mine as I saw my other children look down or away. There was something about seeing Phil hurting that struck each of us deeply. Maybe because he was the Cantrell who worked so hard to cover up what he was feeling.

I held out the wood box to Scott. "Here. Let's open it."

We all stared at the bottom of the sealed box.

"How do we open it?"

Phil removed the wine cork and handed the corkscrew to Scott.

As I watched him break the seal, something inside of me seemed to unwind. Maybe to strangers the irreverence of laughing over an Elvis urn and using a corkscrew to open an ash container would seem horrid and tacky and disrespectful. But Mike had the blackest sense of humor. He needed one to grow up with a man like Don Cantrell as his father. That black humor was one of Mike's most valuable legacies to us, so somehow what we had done and that we could laugh at our malediction seemed right.

Once open, we all looked into the box, uneasy, but morbidly curious. It was a wooden box filled with tan-gray ash that almost looked like sand.

"It's time to do this," I said, turning away with a rush of mixed emotions, and we moved over to the edge of the run.

Scott handed Mike to me. "You go first, Mom."

I touched the fine ash and closed my eyes. *I don't want to let go. . . . I don't want to let go. . . .* I could feel the tears burning up my throat, I could feel so intensely my love, my respect, and my need for that man swelling up from deep inside of me, so I just leaned over the edge of the run and jumped outward, pulling my knees up to my chest as I had done that first time on a snowboard so long, long ago, and I tilted the box behind me as I flew through the air.

South Lake Tahoe is a strange and beautiful mess of a place. Not much can bruise the grandeur of the lake or the magnificence of a Sierra mountain against a backdrop of those unending skies. Nature often revealed its most profound beauty there.

146

The television show *Bonanza* was partially filmed on the northeastern side of the lake, and the old set of the Ponderosa complete with a western town and a replicated ranch house was a tourist destination for over twenty five years, until the property became too valuable to leave undeveloped.

When the kids were young, for the price of admission you could see a medicine wagon show, take a walk through Hoss' mine, and buy a fancy black hat with a silver studded hatband just like Little Joe's. I read somewhere once that the original show was created by RCA to sell more TVs in the 1950s, and it went on to become one of the longest running television series in history. But it's gone now and lost to whole generations who have never heard of the Cartwrights.

Our family has a significant, almost innate history with the lake, and we bought our place there because Tahoe really was our second home—where Mike sold his first boards in the ski area parking lot long before snowboarding even had a name—and we loved it there.

Nestled into a private plot of wooded mountain with northwestern views of the lake and surrounding Sierras, the house is hidden from sight and doesn't corrupt the landscape. You would never know it was there until you turn off Kingsbury Grade onto a private road flanked by a statuesque forest of tamarack pines. Our home is made in the lodge style and constructed from recycled wood, glass, and stone, with four rock fireplaces and a two story wood-beamed great room supporting six-foot wide iron chandeliers salvaged from a silver baron's old hunting lodge, and has enough bedrooms and high-end energy efficient baths for everyone to have their own space.

When Mike first bought SkiStar, the brand name needed a boost after straddling the hurdles of bankruptcy restructure, so in the name of publicity, our privacy was compromised and the Tahoe house filled the pages of a winter issue of Architectural Digest. I remember opening the magazine to a huge glossy photo of our great room with me sitting on the sectional and Mike standing behind me, his hand on my shoulder. On the day the photos were taken, there had been photographers and assistants, light meters and reflective shades everywhere, and their makeup artist pasted enough pancake makeup on me to make my face crack if I smiled.

Our mountain home was and always has been a haven for us, and I never quite got rid of my urge to run out and burn every issue I could find. I never told Mike, but the day the magazine hit the stands I bought up every copy at the neighborhood market and tossed them in the recycler. (I think now I wish I had those magazines, just to see his hand on my shoulder again.)

But the truth is I'm just not a public person and never relished being in the spotlight. The artist in me is private and would prefer to be locked away in my garret.

My friend Ellie would say I'm an idiot. "Think of the exposure. It is perfect for company publicity." Which was just my point; in my mind exposure is not a positive word. But then Ellie was Bariella Crocker Hutcheonson, pedigreed, driven and smart, and over the years she'd made solidifying her position as one of San Francisco's leading socialites her own artistic endeavor.

On Saturday morning I was up early in the huge kitchen of the Tahoe house and making buck-wheat pancakes for my brood, who gobbled down breakfast and went off to the mountain to watch the day's qualifying runs. Renee had stayed home with the kids, who were all still asleep. Not long after my children took off, Miranda came downstairs in a flannel nightgown and bunny slippers and asked, "Is Daddy gone?"

"He just left, Sweetpea."

"Tyler's still asleep and Mama's sick again."

When Renee arrived the day before she looked gray and peaked, and she was quiet at dinner and went to bed right after the kids. So I set Miranda at the table with a Mickey Mouse shaped pancake, a bowl of berries to make his face, and a bottle of syrup and I went upstairs. Scott's family took up the suite of rooms at the north end of the house, and I knocked quietly on their door, then opened it. "Renee?"

The bed was empty, the covers thrown back. I could hear her vomiting in the bathroom. She came out, and I was sitting on the bed. The expression on her face was resigned.

"Well," I said, "that look tells me what I wanted to know. I was going to ask you if you wanted herb tea and toast, or ginger ale and crackers. I take it you want the ginger ale and crackers." She had that gray morning-sickness pallor any woman who's ever been pregnant can easily spot.

"Oh, God, Mom, I don't dare eat anything. I'm so sick this time." She was half crying.

I wanted to know the due date, but didn't press her. Being a grandmother had unveiled to me another whole dimension to life. A new grandbaby. I could feel a warm happiness bloom inside of me, and I had to resist the urge to dance a jig.

Happiness, what a strange feeling it was.

Right then, I would have given anything to hold a new baby. Babies were all about the future and love and life, and lately my life had been all about death. A secret part of me wanted to shout it from the mountain, but poor Renee was in no state to be joyous or for me to be shouting. "I think with the boys I was sick the morning after conception. For months I could barely brush my teeth past my bicuspids without gagging." I stood. "I'm sorry you're going through this. But I'm so very happy about another baby."

"The room is spinning." She flopped down on the bed and hugged the pillow to her chest, then moaned, "Right now I hate being pregnant."

She'd get past it. My china doll of a daughter-in-law was breathtakingly beautiful the two times she'd been pregnant. I went into the bath and came out with a cool washrag for her forehead.

"Oh . . . bless you." She flung her arm over her eyes and lay there. "I'll just sleep a little bit longer." Her voice began to drift off. "Then I'll get Tyler up."

"No. You stay there. I'll take the kids today. We'll go up on the mountain. You can have the whole place to yourself. Just get some sleep."

I stood up to leave and she said, "Mom? Don't tell Keely, okay? Last week she was so upset when she started her period."

"I won't say anything." Phil and Keely had been trying to get pregnant again.

"I know I'll have to tell her eventually, but I don't want to kick her while she's down. You know?"

"I understand you don't want to hurt her, but I don't think she'd want you tiptoeing around her about this either."

"They've been trying for so long. She's really stressed over it."

"Maybe Scott should tell Phil and let him break the news."

"That might be better, I guess, but please not this weekend. This weekend is about Mike. I'll be better tomorrow. I want to be there with the family."

So I spent the day on the lower slopes of the mountain with my grandkids, Tyler in my arms because he was still too young to put on a board and Miranda dressed in her Pepto Bismol-pink jacket and board pants, silver glitter goggles over a beanie with earflaps and white fuzzy pompoms, and riding the *Miranda*, a board I'd designed with pink and purple graphics, yellow shooting stars and her favorite white, lop-eared bunnies riding snowboards.

We ate corn dogs and fries for lunch and came back to the house mid-afternoon with the kids ready for naps and me looking forward to a half an hour in the steam room in our master, followed by a long hot bath, a glass of wine and a night in front of a roaring fire with a novel.

Instead, the evening was taken over by my kids, who probably needed to blow off steam. Renee was her old self and had cabin fever, so I went along with their plan to eat out. Mickey wanted to stay home with the kids. His ego was on the line because Miranda was beating him on one of the latest XBox games.

After steaks at the casino restaurant, we had split up, the others going off to the lounge shows or a craps table. I stood outside the high-end hotel boutique, eyeing a red Balenciaga handbag in the window before I walked away (the place was closed) and I ended up at a lucky five dollar blackjack table where there were no smokers. Behind me was the constant, distant moaning of Aztec slot machines. I preferred the loud ringing bells and the whirring and spinning noises of those old handle slots. The new digital slots talked to you: they screamed like peacocks and sang surfing songs.

When the casino lounge show started up, I could hear some cowboy singer performing a song about Texas that was popular years back, and I tapped my toes on the stool rail while I sat there wasting time I didn't care about, winning several hundred dollars from a dealer who loved me because I kept tipping her half my winnings.

Watching her reaction and the pit boss eying the tips stack up gave me more of a thrill than beating the house odds. I really hated blackjack. Close to eleven p.m., I was sipping a gimlet and had just split a pair of aces when the dealer paused. I felt someone standing behind me, then his hands on my shoulders, which was Phillip's normal way of getting my attention. I was long past ready to go home. I set the drink down, turned around, and came face to face with Spider Olsen.

Going to the Calgary Olympics in 1988 had been a first for us. A lifetime of watching the games on

TV had not prepared me for how the games actually worked. Television cameras and satellite transmissions made it easy to flash back and forth between venues, so at home you sat there with a bowl of popcorn in your lap and watched the world's top athletes compete. I was spoiled, because the drama and anticipation were brought straight into my living room. But I had no idea of the actual logistics, of the massive distances between events, the transportation nightmares, the individual planning and hours wasted trying to get from one event to another.

And if I was frustrated, Mike was ten times worse. It was hell, so everyone blew off steam at night in the Olympic Village bars. Mike and I were still young enough then to party late into the night, and the business was growing fast, the sport spreading like wildfire, so we had something to celebrate. While snowboarding remained an outlaw sport to some, many were finally acknowledging and embracing it. When Mike and I were alone, and sometimes after a little too much to drink, we talked then about our dreams: that maybe someday there would be an Olympic boarding event.

At night, the crowds in the bars were wild, an international mix of revelers celebrating, drinking, and dancing—line-dancing, since the music was top country hits. You would have thought you were in Texas, not Canada.

I'm not a Spider Olsen type. Back then, he was in his late twenties, and I wasn't. But he'd come on to me twice that night and Mike had jokingly told him to check out another run. But Spider kept drinking, and after a while the bar filled with rowdy, elated and drunk Italians. The gold medalist, Alberto Tomba, was gorgeous, but he was young and his ego was on par with Spider's. It was pretty ugly in that bar that night. I've always felt that the reason Mike and Spider came to blows was because Spider didn't take losing well or having his nose rubbed in it by Tomba's crowd. He'd already lost to Tomba in the World Cup prior to the Olympics. But putting his hand down the back pocket of my jeans while Mike's back was turned wasn't smart. I pushed him away, but Mike saw it and decked him. That was the last time I saw Olsen in person until Mike's memorial, which was a day I can barely remember and walked through zombie-like only because I had to.

"March," Spider said. "I was looking for you."

"Why?" It just slipped from my mouth.

He laughed and winked at the dealer, who was in the throes of being starstruck. Spider had a way of connecting with you, a look, that for me was unsettling and too intense. You weren't quite sure if he was really interested in talking to you or coming on to you, and he was helped by Nordic good looks and his reputation: famous or

155

infamous, depending on how you chose to look at his lifestyle.

As a woman of a certain age, I was fairly unimpressed with the type of men that dated women half their age. "I meant why would you even know I was here or be looking for me?"

"I was sent on a mission," he said confidently and waved to someone, his hand above me and pointing at my head. I looked across the casino and decided I was going to kill my son. Phillip and Keely were walking toward me.

"Hey, Mom, look who we ran into."

"We came to find you, because we've had a change of plans," Keely said. "We're holding tables in the lounge so all of us can go to the next show."

My son and daughter-in-law were wide awake, smiling and obviously having a great time. My mind flashed back to Renee that morning, almost begging me not to tell them she was pregnant. I loved my children and wanted their lives to be easier than mine. They needed a night out. But I knew I couldn't sit through a show. "You all go ahead." I made a point of turning to Spider. "My grandchildren wore me out today."

"Grandkids can be a handful," he said easily. "I've got two myself."

"You all go on," I said. "I can take a cab home."

"No cab," Spider said. "I'll take you."

"That would be great," Phil said.

"No." I put my hand on Spider's arm. "Really. You go to the show." I turned and pushed my stacks of chips toward the dealer and told her I wanted to cash in.

"I was at the earlier show already. I'll take you home. I insist. My car's in valet. After all, your company is paying me well enough that I can be your taxi for one night."

Great. Nice way to remind me we had an important business relationship, one Keely and Phil worked hard for and needed. What had Mike given up for that contract? I felt sick to my stomach, and suddenly, I had no energy left in me to argue. I just wanted to go home.

Five minutes later I was in a large silver SUV that smelled like lemon air freshener, and we were spiraling up the mountain road and away from the Stateline casinos.

"I had an ulterior motive for wanting to drive you home tonight. There's something I want to talk to you about."

"Okay," I said. The fact that he wanted to talk to me gave me mixed emotions. Good business or bad business or some other business.

"I'm not certain how you'll take it or whether you feel like discussing this."

"Try me," I said. "Take a right on the next private road. It's not too far. Just past the next mile marker."

"I remember," he said. At our private road,

Spider turned right and headed up the hill. "Mike and I spent time at the house away from all the attorneys. Actually, we talked a lot when we last met up here." He glanced at me to see my reaction.

Mike was with Spider that whole weekend just before he died.

"I really liked Mike. He was a good guy. I know there was that stupid thing in Calgary. I was a jerk, and I need to apologize to you for that. I told Mike he should have hit me. I would have hit me," he said, laughing without humor as he pulled the car to a stop in front of the house. He turned in his seat, arm resting on the back. "I'm sorry, March. I'd like you to forgive me for that."

I don't know what I expected from him, but the way he said it was sincere and I felt an acceptance of him I didn't really want to feel. That he seemed genuine bothered me, which says a lot about where my head was and my own judgment issues. I didn't really know this man, and I didn't really need an apology for something so many years ago. "It's forgotten, Spider. Really." I started to reach for the door handle.

"Wait. I needed to apologize, but that's not what I wanted to talk about. Mike mentioned that your youngest son had been fighting with him about going to college."

"Yes. Mickey was giving Mike a hard time, but I think that's over now."

"You do? Why?"

"He's been working really hard in school. His grades are strong. I think he feels guilty that he and Mike were not on the best terms when he died."

"Mickey tracked me down today on the mountain. He wanted to talk to me about the circuit. He said he wanted some advice and he couldn't talk to the family because they didn't get it. He felt I had more experience, and probably thinks I don't have a vested interest in him going to college. We're supposed to meet tomorrow. I wanted to talk to you first."

I was devastated, and my mind raced from thought to thought. I tried to think back but nothing I could remember gave me a clue that Mickey was serious about not going to college, especially when he knew Mike wanted him to go. It was only a matter of weeks before he'd hear from the colleges where he'd applied. I couldn't think clearly, feeling blindsided, and it was cold, barely twenty degrees out. "I'm freezing. Come on in with me. We'll talk inside."

He followed me up the front steps. "Is Mickey home?"

"It's a big house. He might be in bed already. He was planning to hit the mountain early."

"He wanted to meet me in the morning," Spider said. "He probably shouldn't see me here talking to you, March."

Spider was right. The upstairs hallways flanked the great room and from the basement you had to walk through the great room to get upstairs. I unlocked the door but didn't open it. "The master wing has a sitting room and complete privacy. He won't come in there." I quietly opened the door. "Take a left. There's a bar fridge in the room. Help yourself and I'll be there in a few minutes."

I dropped my purse and keys on the table, slipped off my shoes and went upstairs to check the kids and to look in on Mickey. My legs felt heavy, the muscles tight, and I wasn't sure if it was from boarding all day or from my disappointment. I was scared and didn't have Mike to turn to. We always talked over our decisions and how to handle the kids. He joked once if we ruined their lives, it was a group effort. But Mickey and his future were my responsibility alone now. I needed to guide him down the right paths. My fear was palpable, and I stood there feeling extremely lost in my own home.

God, Mike, why? How do I do this alone?

Upstairs, the little ones were sound asleep, Tyler in his crib and Miranda in a bed shaped like a bobsled and surrounded by stuffed bunnies, bears and kittens, and a very real looking stuffed collie she'd named Harold. I paused before I closed the door. Next year, we would have a new baby in there. Then my thoughts went to Keely, and I wondered when they would tell her. She was a strong girl and Phillip loved her. Having children had been all too easy for us, so I could only use my imagination to place myself in my daughter-in-law's shoes. However, I did know what it was like to want something very badly and know you cannot have it.

As I walked toward Mickey's room, I made a mental note to take Keely out for lunch and shopping or a spa day, just the two of us. I listened at Mickey's door and slowly turned the knob. It was dark inside, but a lava lamp was boiling red in the corner and the air was stuffy with boy funk. The smell of his shoes alone was enough to bring tears to my eyes from ten feet away. Once you've raised a teenaged boy, you never again cry at the odor of onions.

I watched him sleep; he was snoring softly, arms thrown over his head, looking like he didn't have a care in the world. I still thought he was just scared about college, and perhaps I needed to talk to him about going to school closer to home. But it was Mike who pointed out that Mickey didn't shy away from anything. Why would college send him running? Maybe Scott or Phil could corner him at some point.

What was I doing? When did I become so weak? So unsure? I never had to tiptoe around my sons. Molly was another story, but not with the boys. Mickey was seventeen, and we had always been close. I should just play the guilt card with him—wasn't it a mother's ace in the hole?

With so many questions eating at me, I left the room and joined Spider, to find he'd turned on the gas in the fireplace and was sitting on the sofa drinking from a green bottle of sparkling water.

"Mickey's sound asleep." I made myself a cup of green tea from the hot water dispenser and sat down on a chair opposite him, playing with the teabag string as I pulled my knees up. I cupped the hot mug in both hands. I wasn't certain what to say to him, but part of me wanted to beg him to please send my son running from the circuit with his hair on fire. Finally, I admitted, "This feels so awkward."

"Why? I don't bite."

"But I do." It just came out. My mouth has always been a problem for me, never for Mike. We had bantered like that for years. I couldn't look at Spider and instead just buried my head in my hand and groaned out an "I'm sorry."

He laughed, and I found myself staring at one of those sincere looks of his I didn't quite trust. "If you want Mickey to stay away from pro-fessional sports," he said, "I can paint a clear picture for him, one that's true and he'd believe if he talked to Seth or some of the others who have been around the sport for a while. You know he might also be talking to competitors, someone closer to his own age."

I took a sip of tea. "You'll leave out the thrills and glory and groupies?"

"And money." He smiled slightly. "I expect those things wouldn't help your cause with a boy his age."

"No, they wouldn't. He needs to finish his education. He's not nearly mature enough to handle that kind of life, let alone thrive in it, and frankly, I believe you have to have an innate passion for all that fame, as well as for winning to be successful in professional sports. He does like to win, and keeping up with his older brothers made him grow up incredibly fearless. On the slopes or half pipe, you should see him. He's amazing. When he was just a kid, Mike used to say he was in the air more than on the snow." I paused for a moment, then added, "But he doesn't understand what trouble there would be for him because of his last name."

"I'll point out the fact that I don't think his last name would help him or win him friends, no matter how great a kid or how good he is."

"For him to handle all that pressure, so soon after losing his dad . . . I don't know." I was terribly unsure of what to do and decided I had to trust Spider to try to help. "I have a really bad feeling about him doing this, and my instincts have always been strong. I think you have to discourage him. Someone has to."

"Okay." Spider downed the last of his water and stood. "I should get going."

I leaned forward to set my tea down on the coffee table, and he was next to my chair to give me a hand up. I come from a generation of women who remember how a gentleman showed his respect. Too many young women never expect and don't even know those gestures existed. Till the day he died, my father always stood when a woman left the table. Even now, years into a new millennium, I still hate having a man close a door in my face or run me down and elbow me aside for a cab or to get in a door first, and don't even get me started on men and grocery carts.

Frankly, since we didn't get the Equal Rights Amendment passed, I'll take anything I can get, including some old-fashioned male courtesy. I took Spider's hand automatically—Mike always helped me up—and found myself just a few inches away from him, a little unsteady from sitting on my leg for so long. His free hand went to my shoulder and I grabbed his arm.

"Mother!" Molly stood in the doorway. "What's going on here?"

Chapter Eleven

I actually laughed out loud at the ridiculousness of my daughter's shocked expression, but Spider wasn't laughing. His tanned face grew a little pink, and he quickly put some space between us.

The thought crossed my mind that he had just made us look guilty of something, and I suddenly felt less easy about his motives for being there. Very calmly I said, "Molly, this is Spider Olsen. Spider, my daughter, Molly."

"We've met," she said quickly, her fair skin flushing the same red color of her hair, which had grown out long again, and hung down to her shoulders in soft auburn waves. Even dressed in baggy plaid flannel sleep pants and a faded UCLA sweatshirt, my daughter was gorgeous. She held a glass of red wine in her hand. Clearly she had come home before me and been upstairs or in the basement. "I'm going to shoot him," she said none too sweetly. "For the SkiStar print ad campaign."

"Well, that's good. We'll keep everything in the family." My joke didn't clear any of the tension. You would think I would have learned over the years. "Your brother coerced poor Spider here into giving me a ride home from the casino while they all went to the late show. He was just leaving, so we can walk him to the door together." I threaded my arm through hers, which was still planted on her hip while she gave him a look that said he didn't belong here. I couldn't really get upset with her. All weekend she had been chiding her brothers about my feelings. Suddenly my fierce daughter was standing there, like a little dog, posturing and trying to protect me when there was nothing to protect.

Seeing Spider to the door was swift and uneventful, but I didn't let go of Molly's arm just in case—she'd thrown punches at her brothers over the years—and she closed the front door harder than was necessary, before pulling away from me. "You need to stay away from him, Mother."

"Just what did you think was going on in there?"

"I know what it looked like." She took a draw on her wine, set it on the table and headed up the stairs without looking back at me. "I'm going to bed. Tomorrow's a huge day. They're honoring Daddy, in case you'd forgotten."

It only took about a minute of standing there, staring at the empty spot where my daughter cast her parting shot, for me to pick up her wine and finish it off. I took the glass in the kitchen and put it in the dishwasher, annoyed, then changed my mind and refilled it from the bottle she'd left open on the counter. One look at the label when I corked it and the urge to strangle her hit me harder than it had a few seconds before.

You think by giving your kids the best, you are helping them . . . ha! In the name of parenting, you take perfectly naïve little Claymations and turn them into monsters who expect the best, rather than appreciating it. She was twenty three and she opens a two hundred and fifty dollar bottle of wine?

Then I realized I was thinking along the same lines as I had lectured Mike over, those silly times when he got so annoyed with Mickey over leaving the holiday wine untouched.

"And you accused me of being hard on Mickey for the same thing."

I could hear his voice as plainly as if he were standing next to me. I gripped the countertop until my knuckles turned white, hanging my head and looking down at the floor. Bottle in one hand and wine glass in the other, I escaped to our room. I wasn't going to waste the wine; instead, I would get wasted.

The bright morning sunshine at nine thousand feet didn't do a thing for my blinding headache. Of course Mickey was on my mind, but he hadn't said much since he'd joined us about a half an hour ago and now stood about thirty feet away talking with some of the professional boarders. I felt a distinct chill that had nothing to do with the weather and could only hope Spider had discouraged him.

I'd expected the cold shoulder from Molly, but she acted as if nothing had happened between us the night before, something for which I was grateful.

All of the Cantrells, my daughter, sons, their wives and kids, Rob and both generations of his family, were gathered at the top of the mountain,

Cantrell boards littered all over the snow, while we waited to descend *en masse* down the main run, which had been groomed and was closed to the public for the final events.

Starting ahead of us were some of the best known names in snowboarding and the winter sports business, along with international and Olympic champions from every freestyle event, carrying huge flags with the Cantrell logo, and behind them the family would board down the run together holding bundles of bright helium balloons that would float up into the sky.

From now on, the first of the most prestigious annual snowboard meets would be the Mike Cantrell Memorial Global Open. When I'd received the phone call to tell me what everyone in the snowboarding industry wanted to do for Mike, I cried. Not on the phone, but just as I hung up. I cried alone.

It was important to me to pretend I wasn't dying inside. It was important for me to look strong to everyone else. There was nothing I hated more than the image of me as a sniveling, weak widow who couldn't hold it together. And I was still new to the process of recreating myself.

Someone blew a whistle, and we dutifully stepped into our bindings and accepted the bouquets of balloons. Scott was going to carry Tyler down the mountain and was juggling him from arm to arm in order to secure the balloons, while his son giggled and batted at them so they bounced off his daddy's head.

One of the balloon girls tried to give Phil more than one bundle and laughing, he said, "No thanks." He slung his arm around Keely's shoulders and turned to us. "Hey, did any of you see that news story about the guy in Oregon who tied a bunch of heavy duty helium balloons to his lawn chair and flew up to thirteen thousand feet?"

"Tyler, stop hitting me in the head." Scott grabbed his son's hand and glanced at Phil. "You're kidding."

"No way. The guy had a GPS system, wind gauges, a camcorder, and used heavy water jugs for ballast. He'd turn on the water spigot or release helium from the balloons to raise and lower himself. Apparently he'd tried to fly via helium balloons once before, and when he let go of some of the balloons to adjust his altitude, he fell like a rock and had to use a parachute."

While my older sons were talking, my gaze drifted up to the sky and for one brief and fanciful moment, I wondered if I could gather every balloon on that mountain and fly right up to heaven.

"Where's Renee?" Scott was looking around the group.

"I don't know," Molly said, searching, too. "She was here a few moments ago."

"Mommy's sick again," Miranda said and

169

pointed toward a work shed behind the lift. "She's over there behind the building throwing up her breakfast. Like she did all the time with Tyler. Are we going to have another baby, Daddy? Another baby? Mommy said she'd talk to me about it later. I want a sister this time. A baby girl would be perfectly perfect."

Molly looked at me with wide eyes that said, oh no. . . . I didn't know until then she was in on the secret. She was very close to Keely. That Scott and Renee felt they had to hide their wonderful news was tough and not something either Phil or Keely would want, especially with so much loss. Suddenly we were standing in the midst of one of those family moments where you don't know what to say.

But I knew Keely must have been reeling inside. The blood had drained from her face and she stared off bleakly at the shed. Phillip dropped his arm and faced Scott. "Is Renee pregnant again?"

The word again said more about what he felt than any other, and I hoped no one but me caught it. Scott, however, looked completely uncomfortable. With guilt in his eyes, he glanced to me as if for help, then back at Keely and his brother. Resigned, he nodded.

"That's great, big bro." Phillip was genuinely happy for him and went to shake Scott's hand but between Tyler and the balloons, he had to clap him on the shoulder instead.

"I'll go check on Renee," Keely said hurriedly, her voice sounding higher-pitched than normal, and she took off toward the shed before anyone could stop her. Phillip watched her slide down the grade with a pensive look.

"I'll go, too." I started to step into my board and follow, but Phil grabbed my arm.

"No. Stay here, Mom."

"I don't think that's a good idea." My eyes were on Keely who leaned against the shed, clearly talking to Renee, who was still hidden from view.

"It's fine," Phil said. "Let her help Renee. She needs to help her. Renee needs to know we know."

With perfect twenty-twenty hindsight, I understood then that trying to protect Keely was the wrong approach. I couldn't blame Renee or Scott. Instinctively no one wanted to hurt Keely, but hiding the news so she found out this way was not fair to her.

I could only guess at what kind of conversation she would have with Phillip later. For all his jokes, and chatter, and clowning around, Phillip, with his vulnerable and gentle heart could be the kindest, most sensitive of all my boys. Often he was more tuned into the colors of my moods than anyone else in the family, certainly better than Mike was at gauging me.

With perfectly lousy timing, some official blew the damned whistle again and announced we had to follow the others down the mountain. Renee and Keely joined us together by then, but Renee's pallor was still grayish. "I'm sorry," she said, clearly out of sorts.

"Are you going to be okay?" Scott asked her before I could.

"Renee," I said. "You do not have to go down that mountain."

"I want to, Mom. I'm okay now. Really I am. Someone hand me some balloons. I won't get sick again." She laughed facetiously. "There's nothing left in my stomach."

"Except a baby," Miranda said brightly, tugging on her mother's jacket. "I want a girl, Mommy. One stupid brother is enough."

"Boy, isn't that the truth," Molly said to Miranda. "I'm plagued with stupid brothers. So is your Aunt Keely. Give me your hand, sweetie. You come down the hill with us and we'll tell you some of the tricks they played on us so you can be prepared for when Tyler gets bigger."

Across a sea of knitted beanies, I saw Mickey extract himself from a gaggle of balloon girls and plod across the packed snow in his boots. He had the biggest feet of all the Cantrell men, size thirteen, and was already six foot three.

"Glad to see you could pull yourself away from all the snow bunnies, Casanova," Phil said, teasing him.

"Jealous, old man?"

"I don't have to be jealous. I have the most gorgeous woman on the mountain," Phil said, and he rubbed Keely on the behind. The grateful look she gave him told me things would be okay for them. Phil would do what he needed to do to make things right for her.

"Here's my favorite snow bunny." Mickey pulled me into a hug, resting his chin on the top of my head the same way his father used to do. "You okay?" he asked quietly.

"I will be now," I said. For just that moment I let him hold me in his lanky arms the way his father had so many times, my cheek against his shoulder, thankful and trying not to get choked up and silly at my youngest son's moment of thoughtfulness. *Please go to college. Please don't be an idiot. Please . . . please . . . please . . .*

A little while later we released those balloons. Without a plan to do so, all of us stopped mid-run, and we linked arms, a daisy chain of Cantrells, as we watched all those huge and brightly colored balloons drift higher and higher. The crowds below us, the ones held back by the ropes along the run, cheered and whistled and applauded when balloons of every color filled the skies.

One of my favorite lines in the Nora Ephron film *You've Got Mail*, was when Meg Ryan's character told Tom Hanks she thought daisies were happy flowers. It was a simple truth: there were certain things in this world that were happy solely because they existed. In a tender moment of enlightenment, I realized that balloons were just happy, like Meg Ryan's daisies. And because Mike existed, both in my life and in this great confusing and impossible world, he made me incredibly happy for more years than I could count.

The official renaming of the annual winter event was announced from the network television box after we all reached the bottom of the run, and for a short while, we mingled together until the start of the boarding events drew close. My family had disbursed into the crowd when I caught Spider Olsen's eye and walked up to him.

"How did it go with Mickey?" I asked.

"We talked. I let him ask questions. But I had called Seth and some of the others late last night, after I left you, and told them what I needed from them. They met us this morning. I told Mickey he needed to talk to all of us to make a solid decision. I don't think you have anything to worry about. None of us painted the kind of glory and guts picture Mickey was dreaming about. Those boys were blunt. I think Mickey walked away believing half of them wanted to quit the circuit now. The last thing your son said to me was that he wasn't going to let his dad down."

Joy spread through me like warm sunshine. Everything would be okay. Mickey would be okay. My youngest was made for college, the smartest of the bunch, grades and studies came almost too easily for him. With his SATs and GPA, his apps letter, community service and outside activities, he was almost assured of getting into one of his top three picks, and there had been no more pranks involving the police.

"Thank you." I threw my arms around his neck and gave him a huge hug. Laughing with relief, I pulled back, but he loosely held my hands in his.

"I was glad to do it. For you and for Mike. He was a good guy." Spider paused and then said, "My biggest regret is that Mike didn't take me up on my offer that night—to fly home on the network jet the following day—but he was in a hurry to get home."

I stood there with my stomach somewhere near my feet. His words sank deeper into me, wounded me even more than I thought words could. I was bleeding inside. He was still holding my hands, but I was in shock and couldn't pull them away, and I couldn't believe what he had just said to me. His biggest regret?

A flash of familiar red hair stepped into my line of sight and Molly elbowed right between us, breaking contract. My hands felt scolded and I stared down at them.

"Scott's looking for you, Mother," she said sharply.

I didn't move.

"Mother!"

I looked up at her, frowning. What did she say?

His biggest regret was echoing in my head and I could barely hear anything else.

"Scott. He's over by the stands." Molly spun around, clearly dismissing me, but not before I caught her expression, a mulish one I knew all too well and had seen only the night before.

The network jet? The next day?

"I want to talk to you," she said and grabbed Spider's arm, pulling him away with her, but not before I heard her say, "You need to stay away from my mother."

"Whoa . . . Wait a second." Spider held up his hands. "You've got this all wrong."

"Mom!" I turned slowly at the sound of Scott's voice. He waved at me and was threading his way around the crowds toward the sideline ropes, and stepped under them. "I know we were supposed to go home tonight, but Renee's sick again and I think I need to get her home now. Mickey wants to stay for all the events and so does Phil."

"Okay," I said blankly.

"I need some help with the kids." Scott was usually my calm and thoughtful son. He seldom overreacted or let his emotions rule his decisions, but he sounded stressed.

"Of course I'll come with you now." I turned for a moment and saw Molly and Spider were still talking heatedly. I had this sudden urge to get my daughter away from Spider. What he had said to

176

me was unconscionable. "Maybe Molly will want to go with us."

Scott shook his head. "She's staying late, too."

I could barely stand to watch them without wanting to drag Molly away. What if he told her that? I took a protective step toward my daughter, but Scott stopped me.

"Leave her alone, Mom. Spider Olsen has plenty of experience dealing with hotheaded twenty three year olds. We need to leave. Now."

So I followed Scott instead, but in my head was the haunting question: if only Mike had stayed. If only he had taken that jet. If only . . .

Chapter Twelve

Time slogged by, the days and hours and minutes, and I spent much of that time in my bed. I lay there unable to move, my mind as blank as I could make it. I had stopped sleeping at night. Some days, though, I could sleep all day. God knows I understood why, I'd had psych classes, but understanding the ramifications of trauma didn't help me overcome my fear of falling asleep.

Intensely real dreams swept through my sleeping mind and I would awake with night terrors, something I have never experienced. In fact, in my lifetime I have seldom dreamt, or at least remembered any dreams. But now my mind played wicked games with me.

In those cruel dreams, I was in bed and I would wake up to discover Mike's death had only been a nightmare, that he was there sleeping next to me, or he'd walk out of the bathroom in a towel, laughing at me. These moments of illusion seemed so real that sometimes, right after I awoke, I couldn't stop my heart from racing as though it were trying to jump out of my chest. Other times, I would wake up already crying.

So instead of twisting and turning in bed, I tried to keep myself busy. There was a twenty-four hour market open a few miles away, and a twenty- four hour Starbucks drive thru. Grocery shopping around giant pallets of organic soup and dog food wasn't so bad, and I began to crave venti caramel macchiatos at three thirty in the morning.

The house had always been big but seemed hollow and cavernous now. So I cleaned all the time, even though I had a cleaning service that came twice a week.

It was a wide-awake Wednesday today, rather than troublesome Tuesday or frenzied Friday. (I had names for each insomnia-laced night of the week, now that I was better at knowing what day of the week it was.)

Around four a.m., I finished vacuuming, so I emptied the canister, took out the trash, did two loads of laundry, and wiped down the kitchen counters. Armed with a Pledge can in hand, I went from room to room, polishing the furniture, dusting lamps, newel posts, the wooden slats on the stairs, under the Louis XIV Bombay chest in the hallway. I cleaned the wedding silver I seldom used, my grandmother's tea service, and changed the toilet paper rolls in the three downstairs bathrooms so they were all dispensing from the bottom. That way, when you tore from right to left, the paper ripped along its perforations and didn't puddle down to the floor. Unless you were left-handed, like Scott and Molly.

These jobs were not important, except to me, but only because they were proof I was still functioning on some bizarre anal-retentive-toilet-paper-unrolling level.

Sometimes, when I looked up at a clock, I found time was belly-crawling by. I was born with a razor sharp internal clock and could look easily out a window or up at the sky and instinctively know what time it was. Now I lived within a skin and body where time had no reason to matter, and my instincts didn't seem to work anymore.

Across the room Mike's closet was empty, and if not for the three shirts the laundry had lost and delivered a month after his death, there wouldn't be a single piece of his clothing left in my world. You could look in the closet and never know he existed. The thought almost killed me, to think he was gone and so many people would never know him. The day the cleaners delivered those shirts, I unwrapped them and ran upstairs holding them to my chest. I hid them in our dresser like some survivor of a plane crash who hid her granola bars from everyone.

The kids had each taken what they wanted from Mike's things: Scott took shoes; Phil some ties; Mickey a leather jacket and Molly took a pair of blue sweats that were Mike's favorite. I was numb to it all. Everyone had been so anxious to get rid of his clothes for me as if what was inside his closet were more deadly than driving on a one-way street.

For some reason, in those first days and weeks, I had thought only in exchanges: *If I let them help me, they will leave. Give in, because they need to do something. What does it matter? Maybe then everyone will stop asking what I need.*

So I had let my well-meaning friends and family strip Mike from the house in the name of good sense and protection, and later regretted it terribly. I had completely lost the ability to say no and was wrapped up inside my own helplessness, which seemed to escalate the more I let everyone tell me what I should do.

For my own sanity, I knew I needed to find the courage to take control back from everyone I'd rolled over and given it to, those who only wanted the best for me. I needed to find out what was best for me. That was now the uncharted journey I faced.

Inside our bedroom where the king-sized bed was made perfectly; the Chinese lamps were on the nightstand; the damask bedding on the bed, the same throw pillows, the same striped sofa sat by the fireplace, and Mike's leather chair with an ottoman was parallel to mine—an old club chair that had belonged to my mother-in-law I'd had reupholstered—I realized most of my life had been parallel with Mike's. I had lived more years with him than without him.

Only last night I was reading the book that lay open on my chair. There was a woman wearing a dark dress and pearls on the cover, but for the life of me I couldn't remember what the story was about. What happened while I was reading that book was what hounded me.

While turning a page, I casually glanced up and saw Mike coming around the corner as he had a thousand times before. I sat forward so fast, afraid to breathe. For that one, heart-stopping instant, I really thought he was still alive. Struck almost frozen, I couldn't move or breathe or blink, because of the sudden, intense, almost blindingly exquisite joy that raced though me . . . until reality checked in. I was living a nightmare, not waking from one. Talk about your mind playing tricks on you.

Dear God in Heaven wasn't I pitiable enough? I felt crushed and mired in feelings and thoughts I couldn't control or stop. My life had become one that existed in another dimension to the chairs, to the sitting area, the bed, which all looked as if they belonged in someone else's world.

No matter how long I had looked in that same spot, nothing was there but proverbial thin air. Like some fairy tale character standing over a caldron and chanting, looking for a magic goblet or ring, I tried to bring Mike back to me. I turned on the lights. I turned off the lights. I carefully positioned myself in that exact spot again, holding the book just as I had been, and I glanced up, again and again. Before me was only the doorway, unchanged and empty.

Rational thought told me seeing Mike was impossible, but what I had seen was such a vibrant image. He'd been wearing his favorite aqua blue sweatshirt with the sleeves pushed up his arms, dark hair swirling around the scar on his forearm from an old board injury. Does a person hallucinate in color? You don't imagine images that sharp and real.

Human desire was a powerful emotion. When you wanted something with such need perhaps the mind could almost make it happen. Almost. Was I seeing him in some other place, halfway back into this life and coming back to me? I'd always been a spiritual person with a strong faith. I wanted to believe in Heaven, that Mike was safe and waiting for me, but I had this big beef with God now. We weren't on speaking terms.

No matter how desperately I wanted to conjure or wish or dream Mike back to me, he wasn't there. When a tree shadow from the window traveled over the carpet I had my rational answer. What I had seen was only a shadow of the tree outside the window. It was just a shadow.

So I had tried to go to sleep with the drapes closed, but woke up anyway. Now, there wasn't a single piece of furniture left in the house that wasn't polished into shining perfection. I set down my trusty Pledge can, my panacea to tormented moments of wakefulness, and I opened the drapes.

Looking around the room, I couldn't shake an odd feeling that I was a stranger in the one room that was most personal to me. I angled the Bose on my nightstand so the time read more easily from different spots in the room (I tested each angle myself), then adjusted the amber lamp cord so when you stood back, you had to really look closely to even notice it.

My mind flashed with the image of Jack Nicholson's M & Ms separated into jars by color in *As Good As It Gets*. I wondered if grief could make you OCD. I shoved the hair out of my face—when did I wash it last?—and caught a whiff of lemon oil in the air, which felt kinetic, like it could bend spoons.

For someone who couldn't feel anything for weeks and weeks, I was acutely aware of the hair on my arms and the back of my neck, and I sat down hard on the bed, hugging myself, looking around and feeling lost, then dragging my nails down my arms because my skin was so itchy.

Was it really possible? If he were there, maybe he could talk to me, like the Ghost and Mrs. Muir or Topper. "Mike?"

Nothing.

"Mike? If you're there, give me a sign."

I saw no floating pictures, no rattling of chains, or visions of my husband.

Those kind of things only happened in movies and books and TV, fiction from someone's vivid imagination. Deep down inside I had to believe the persons who wrote those stories had lost someone very close to them. You so desperately want another chance.

Outside the first morning sunlight was coming up in the eastern horizon, and the flower box hanging on the iron balcony spilled impatiens the same salmon, violet, and neon pink as the edges of the dawn sky. I heard Mickey's alarm go off down the hall, and a few moments later the rush of water from his shower.

For years at that time of the morning, when outside the city stood still, I would be sitting in bed, sipping coffee Mike had brought me, reading the paper or a book, my quiet time before I had to get up and make breakfast if Mike hadn't already. Now I would have given anything for some chaos and noise, for the sound of Mike on the treadmill in the next room or in the shower. He sang horribly.

I laughed out of a lost habit; it sounded as odd to me as speaking in tongues. My eyes burned with tears and my throat tightened. The reflection in the wall mirror was a pale image of me I barely recognized. Most days my skin held no color, as if my crying had drained it all away. I laid down to get away from what I saw, and there I was crying again, so I reached for the damned Kleenex box, one that was still embossed with gold Christmas ornaments.

Then I saw our photo was gone. It had been there last night. I was sure I remembered looking at it when I got into bed. For years I had looked at that photo of us before turning out the light.

Perhaps I knocked it off last night while tossing and turning and trying to find sleep, and sadly, another vision of my dead husband. I rolled over and looked on the floor beside the nightstand. Nothing was there.

Then I hung off the side of the bed and pushed back the dust ruffle and saw only a forgotten Ab machine that needed dusting. I slid to the floor, cheek pressed to the wool carpet, and looked under and behind the bed, opened the nightstand doors, but slammed them shut quickly to keep a shaky stack of out-of-date *Oprah* and *Coastal Living* magazines from falling out.

I had turned into a packrat who kept everything. Too much had been thrown out already in the name of good sense.

And I hated to admit it, but I had been doing strange things when I did sleep. I awoke in the bathtub once and honestly didn't remember getting into the water, and again in the kitchen, where one night I was standing in the pantry as if I were ready to cook something.

Every night I slept in the middle of our king-sized bed because I didn't have "a side" anymore. Sometimes I would wake up and believe I was somewhere else altogether, on good nights in a parallel universe where Mike was still alive and he laughed at me and told me everything had been a horrible mistake.

I got up off the floor and pulled open the nightstand drawer. Next to my hand cream was the photograph turned face down. When did I put it there? Why? Waking up in the bathtub, standing disoriented in the kitchen, hiding pictures? I was losing my mind. Widows did that.

I put the photograph back to its spot between the Bose and the lamp and walked out of the room without looking back. Mike's shoes weren't in the corner. His clothes weren't in a mess on the floor by the hamper. No wet towel was thrown carelessly on the bathroom floor. No scent of his shaving cream hung in the bathroom air when I first walked in, or toothpaste stuck on the side of the sink. His belt wasn't slung on the doorknob. But by God that picture would stay right where it belonged.

On a Tuesday afternoon in mid-February, I answered the door to two pounds of Belgium chocolates and a huge bouquet of gorgeous, blood-red South American roses the size of your fist, arranged in an extravagantly expensive crystal vase, along with a note from my dead husband.

> To my only Valentine,
>   Love always,
>   Mike

I sank down on the marble steps to our living room, hugging the vase at my side as the heady scent of red roses surrounded me, the chocolate box balanced on my knees. What I should have done was call the florist then and there and cancelled Mike's standing order. Instead, one by one, I ate the whole box of chocolates.

A few weeks later, on my birthday, a box needing a signature was delivered from Cartier in Union Square. Wrapped inside was the pave diamond panther bracelet I had been telling Mike about for so long. When had he done this? I wished I would have known the exact day he'd had me on his mind, because unlike the florist note, a standing order, this card was in his hand-writing.

Now you can't accuse me of never listening. . . . Happy Birthday, Sunshine.
Love,
Mike

Chapter Thirteen

I was in the kitchen making dinner around five o'clock one afternoon when Phillip walked in the back door. I glanced over my shoulder. "I didn't know you were coming over."

He closed the door and turned around, a brown grocery bag in his arm, but he took one look at me and stopped; the look he gave me was broken. "Mom . . ."

Now what had happened? I dropped the knife and faced him, bracing myself against the granite counter, my stomach sinking. "What's wrong?"

"You're crying."

The silence drew out between us before I understood, and relieved, I laughed then. "I'm cutting onions. Look." I stepped away from the island and swiped at my eyes with my forearm.

My face was damp and probably red and blotchy. The odds were high that I looked like hell anyway. My makeup drawer hadn't been touched in more than a week. I was dressed in old jeans and a sweatshirt, and early that morning I had pulled my hair into a ponytail in a lousy attempt at personal grooming. If anyone leaned too closely, my fragrance of late was *eau du* lemon oil, Comet, or in this instance, chopped onions.

He laughed, relieved, and set the grocery bag on the counter. "Keely's got a dinner meeting tonight, so I was winging it. I thought you could feed me."

"You mean it's your turn to check on the grieving mother." I turned back to the counter.

"That, too," he said without missing a beat. "Where's the punk?"

"Mickey had a team meeting after school and practice. He'll be home later."

"Good." Phil crossed to the fridge and took out a carton of milk. "He can give me a ride home."

"What's up? No car?"

He turned away from me. "I had a couple of drinks after work so I took the cable car."

"Take the Porsche if you want."

"Mickey can drive me," he said casually and drank the milk from the carton.

I said nothing about the milk carton. Telling the boys to use a glass hadn't done me any good over the years and I wasn't going to waste my breath now, but something about his tone bothered me. Last weekend Mickey had been with Phil and he had come home quieter than he'd been in a long time. I thought maybe something had happened between them, but I couldn't get him to talk to me about it. "Try not to push your brother, okay?"

"What? Me?"

"That innocent act didn't work when you were a kid and it isn't going to work now either."

"Hell, Mom, sometimes he's just so easy."

"Well, life isn't exactly easy for any of us right now. He needs your ear, maybe even your shoulder, not your teasing."

Phillip's cell phone rang and he flipped it open. "Hi, Babe." My son's expression grew tight as he listened. "I'm sorry." His voice was tense and his usually casual posture was stick-straight. "I don't know why it's so hard. I know." He paused, listening intently. "I know. We'll talk tonight." He flipped his cell phone closed and pocketed it. "Life isn't easy," he said quietly. "I would be happier right now if no one needed me."

If ever there was a cry for help, that was it. I pulled my hands out of a bowl of meatloaf and washed them, leaning against the counter as I used a dish towel. "Do you want to talk about it?"

"Another false alarm on the pregnancy front." His tone was more bitter than I'd heard from him in a long time. "She cries and I don't know what to say anymore. She keeps asking why it's so hard when this is supposed to be the most natural thing in the world, and I can't do anything but give her weak apologies. I know she needs to hear more from me, but there's nothing else to say that hasn't been said for too many months already." He faced me, his hands out in frustration, his color high. "I have no new words to take her disappointment away, nothing to encourage her, and every time she cries about it, I feel even more inadequate."

Phillip sat down at the kitchen table, resting his forehead on the heels of his hands, before his words came out in a flood, "I feel like nothing but a failure, and I think I resent it. Maybe that's why I can't summon the words to placate her anymore, Mom. I know I should say something, but it's all too much. Because of SkiStar, I have to prove myself at work, and to Scott, and I want to do well for Dad. He had such faith in me, and because of Keely, I have to prove myself in the bedroom. My life feels like it's all about performance."

I stood behind him and massaged his tense shoulders, waiting for him to get all his feelings out.

"I'm not even sure I want a kid anymore." He closed his eyes and let his head hang back against my hands.

Phillip was a grown man on the edge of fatherhood, and yet I could look at him and see him at every age, as a conglomerate being—all those stages of hurt over the years, suffering the meanness of other children, fights with his older brother, disappointments, tennis team loses, broken hearts, the loss of his grandparents, and the harsh consequences of the same kind of stupid mistakes we all make.

I brushed his forehead with my hand and he opened his eyes, staring up at me upside-down and looking for answers from me that I couldn't give him, because I wouldn't help him by picking sides in this. My kids were raised to think for themselves and thinking for him now wouldn't help him.

"You're frustrated and hurting," I told him. "It's hard to decide what you want when you're under pressure. I do know this. You've always made no bones about wanting a van full of kids. But even if you do change your mind at some point, I don't think that's the best thing to say to you wife right now, especially when what you're feeling is probably pressure."

"I know," he said with resignation.

I sat down next to him and took his hand in mine. "It wasn't all that long ago that you sat at this very table telling us how ready you were to start a family. Both of you were so excited."

"Then disaster hit. I was afraid I was going to lose her, Ma," Phillip said, the emotion still choking his voice more than a year later.

"I understand. It's perfectly natural to be afraid after what you both went through."

"But she wants a kid. It's like she's driven to do this, like she has something to prove. I don't know what's happening to us."

"She told me the doctor says she's fine now and that you can go on to have a normal pregnancy."

"It could happen again."

"Then you deal with that if it happens. If this pregnancy issue comes between you, then you need to think about some counseling, before you both crack under the pressure and say things you don't mean."

He was quiet for a long time, then he said, "I shouldn't have dumped this on you."

"Phillip, I would hate it if you were to stop coming to me to talk out your problems. I'm always here to listen. Don't you know that I cherish the knowledge that you feel you can come to me whenever you need to vent? I'm here, just like I've always been. Please don't tiptoe around me. I just hate being treated as if I'm going to shatter in a million pieces any moment. I haven't shattered yet."

"Life isn't easy right now for any of us," Phil admitted. "You're right about why I'm here. We all decided to take turns checking on you." Phil paused, looking thoughtful, then he shook his head. "It's pretty arrogant when you think about what we're doing. Scott, Molly, Mickey and I . . .

we think we can keep your life together just by our mere presence in it."

"I don't know what I would do without your presence in my life. Although there are days . . ." I teased him. "Honestly? I don't know what to do with you and I don't know what I'd do without you, and I love each of you, even when you all have some annoying and screwball master plan to protect me."

"Hell, Ma, we have to have something to do." When he called me Ma he was back to teasing. "We're your kids. We figure we can each take turns butting into your daily life, and then we can argue over who screwed up the most."

I laughed. That was probably one of the most truthful things to be said in the last five minutes. Our family either joked or argued over almost everything.

"Hey! Is that the radio I hear playing upstairs? And what's that sound droning from the media room? How many times over the years did you yell at us for leaving the stereo on and abandoning the TV?"

I raised my hand. "Guilty. You caught me." I didn't tell him that I needed sound around me because the utter and complete silence made me want to scream. The sound from electric appliances had become my new companions. "I just forgot to turn them off," I lied.

Lies seemed to roll so easily off my tongue

nowadays. We all lied now. Better to lie than live in the painful, if-only silence caused by the truth.

Dad is gone. What do I do now?

I'm falling apart. I think your father is a ghost.

Each of us chose to hide from the truth instead of looking too closely and deeply into the fact that we were all trying to stay afloat and clearly drowning. Yet somehow, we had to not tread on each other's fragile spirits.

Phillip watched me as if he could read the truth just looking at me, and for a second I thought he was going to call me on it, so I admitted, "I'm scattered a lot. Last month I sent the check for the power bill to the phone company. I sent the phone bill payment to VISA, and I forgot the American Express bill altogether. I expect my credit score is in the tank, and I don't give a damn."

"I can pay your bills for you if you want."

"No!" I snapped, then regretted it immediately when I saw my son's face. His offer was automatic. That he cared and was thoughtful was not something to shout at him for.

What was it that made me feel as if I had to protect myself from my own children who were trying to protect me? "I'm sorry. Thank you for offering, but I can handle the bills. I don't want you taking care of me. I just need for everything to be normal . . . to feel normal," I added, my voice drifting off. I wanted to spin my life backwards and relive my adult years and my marriage to Mike all over again, but I couldn't say that aloud, because I knew my children had their own regrets.

The temperature buzzer on the oven went off.

"What's for dinner?" Phil asked, clearly changing the subject.

"Meatloaf. Food of the gods. A gourmet specialty." I filled a loaf pan, topped it with a ketchup, dry mustard, and brown sugar sauce, and put it in the oven along with some roasted potatoes drizzled in garlic infused olive oil.

"You're fixing Mickey's favorites," Phil said.

"Had I known you were coming, I'd have made spaghetti and meatballs."

"My favorite."

"Your favorite." I smiled at him

"What's going on with him?"

"I think he's afraid to pick a college that's too far away." I washed my hands and dried them on a towel. "Would you talk to him when he takes you home? I want him to pick the school he wants, not the one he thinks is closest to home."

"Didn't he apply to Stanford?"

"He's waitlisted."

"Okay, I'll talk to him." He looked at me through wise eyes. "Tell me something."

"What?"

"Are you sleeping okay?"

My hands went to my bare face and then to my

hair, which was falling out of the rubber band. "I look like hell, don't I?"

"You look tired."

"I'll be fine," I said, certain I would never be fine again.

He placed the grocery sack in front of me. "I brought you a present."

"What's this?" I looked inside and there were four industrial sized cans of Pledge Lemon Oil Furniture Polish. My son's expression was half knowing, half sardonic. I burst out laughing.

"I didn't want you to run out. In the middle of the night . . ." he said dryly. "You know, when you're sleeping so well."

Other than a few lapses, I focused more diligently on hiding my grief from my kids. I stopped grocery shopping in the middle of the night and was cautiously quiet when I went out for lattes at an hour when most of the city was asleep in their warm beds. I certainly didn't run the vacuum at four in the morning anymore or else my youngest son—the mouth that roared— would have told the others like he did before.

I believed I was becoming pretty accomplished at being Wonder Widow whenever my children were around. I was certain I was showing them how well I was moving forward and powering through without their father.

Show was the right word. All for show. I came

from a generation who believed mothers were strong. Mothers shaped futures. But I wasn't exactly the 1950's prototype for the perfect mom. My job as a mother was important to me and certainly part of how I had identified myself for years, because I took the job seriously. My kids had been tantamount in my life. I'd spent years learning balance between my children and my husband. Now I was unbalanced.

Since Mike's death, I had worked very hard at making my time with them as normal as our lives could be now. They never saw me sobbing on my bed. They didn't see my red, swollen eyes when I woke up at three a.m., and they were in their own homes or at work and school during those times when I sat in a cotton field of wadded up Kleenexes.

But it was later that morning when I had another bone-chilling moment of seeing Mike in our bedroom. For that to happen twice was tough on my sanity and pretend-strength, especially when I was so unprepared.

This time I was coming out of the bathroom soaking wet and wrapped in a towel and thought I saw him walking across the room to our dresser. I screamed his name, as if screaming could make him stay. My towel slipped from my hand and I was standing half-wet and naked.

But he wasn't there. Another wavering shadow from the tree outside swept over the carpet, and

I swore I would cut that blasted tree down before I went completely mad. I was feeling so unhinged that I put on one of Mike shirts, buttoned it down the front like I had when we were first married. Perhaps I thought holding onto something of his would help me. But I just stood there until my hands weren't in tight fists and I could breathe evenly.

There is a solitude that comes with loss, an aloneness that wraps itself around you and makes you feel as if you are drifting through time like a helium balloon with no one left to hold the string.

I had been alone in our home for years, since Mike had always worked weekdays. But now, the house was my whole world and it was empty, even when people were there. That aloneness had settled into my bones and blood and I carried it with me all the time even though I didn't want to feel that way. I wanted to do the opposite of everything I was feeling. I wanted to laugh. I wanted to sing. I wanted to live.

I've always played music too loud, and not to cover up loneliness. I've known it was too loud but I was still a child of the Sixties who liked to feel the music and lose myself in it, so most days I kept the house sound system tuned to a local rock station as background.

But now a raspy-voice Mick Jagger was singing about shadows, so I turned the volume up until the wall speakers were throbbing and I couldn't stand still any longer. I sang as loud as my voice could sing about shadows and I danced in front of the French doors as if I were trying to exorcise Mike's ghost, the shadows of him haunting me. Right outside was the stupid damned tree that was trying to drive me insane. I turned around and around, arms in the air as I sang, spinning around the room until I was dizzy.

The song ended and I stopped, stumbled a few feet and fell onto the bed, hoarse, half laughing, half crying. I was curled around the Kleenex box when my sobs finally dropped to whimpers of self-pity.

"Mom? I just picked up the keys for Tahoe. I've got a photo shoot this weekend and I—"

I sat up, horrified, but was too late to hide. I was sitting in the middle of a hundred wadded up tissues, wearing Mike's shirt and still half-sobbing and trying to catch my breath.

Molly stood in the doorway of the bedroom. My daughter had never looked at me that way.

"Molly," I choked out her name. "Darling . . ."

She turned and ran away from me as if I were the devil incarnate. *Oh, God, what have I done?* By the time I was almost down the stairs, I heard the front door slam shut. Outside, on the front porch, I saw her car back up too fast, whip around as I chased after her, but she sped through the green light at the corner.

A cable car went rattling by. Someone let out a

catcall. A horn honked. I stood there on the sidewalk of the crookedest street in the world, wearing only Mike's shirt and telling myself it was not hatred I saw in my daughter's eyes.

Chapter Fourteen

I called Molly again and again, but there was no answer, and when I called Stone Morgan, I was told she had left to do a photo shoot in the mountains and wouldn't be back until early next week. Chasing her down was not an option, and again I wasn't really up to a confrontation. Frankly, I was afraid of what she would say to me after that look. When it comes to working things out with my daughter, I was a coward.

I decided I needed something to do besides hallucinating, shopping for purses (I'd bought two Gucci bags that week) and feeling sorry for myself, and I wanted to take charge of something and feel as if I were capable. Making my life appear as normal as possible became my single-minded goal.

Without warning anyone, I walked into Cantrell, Inc for the first time since the week we'd lost Mike and met head on those looks of pity and helplessness I hated. Everyone at the company loved him and had no idea what to say to me. Some famous philosopher once said that life doesn't exist without death, and without a moment of life, there can be no death. But the truth about death is: no one knows what to say.

There isn't anything you can say, really, except for the one sage friend who warned me people would say the stupidest things to me. While it seemed like odd advice at first, I found out pretty quickly that she was right. In their need to say something soothing or to be of help, people say the exact wrong thing.

Perhaps the clear knowledge I would be facing those looks and condolences was one of the reasons I decided to not let anyone know I was coming. From the house, I drove straight to the offices, lived up to my name and marched right in like a lion at eight a.m., and went to work in the graphics department, calling in my managers and assistants to schedule a meeting that afternoon, before I asked to see the final art concepts for the next season. I caused a bit of commotion, but that kept everyone's focus on work instead of what to say.

The number of image files on the computer was huge. Apparently, because in my absence, everyone had an opinion and no one wanted to make the final decisions, so the designs were not cohesive and we had some of everything. Still, all the new graphic designs for this winter's lines of boards and skis had to be ready and in place before the end of April.

A few years back, Mike and I had made the decision to keep the graphics department as it was—a single department within the company to work on all the lines, boards and skis, along with the clothing end of the company, which was expanding fast. So I spent most of the morning going through a computer slideshow of sample graphic images, before I printed out a stack of proof sheets, sipped my coffee and X'd out the weaker images with a black marker.

Because I was behind, it was imperative that I narrow down the number of images by almost eighty percent immediately, and I made some notes to discuss color changes and adjustments in imaging, before I met with the graphic designers that afternoon to hash out the top designs.

I had a real problem when I returned to the computer and called up the SkiStar art; it was dated in my opinion, and not as graphically dynamic as today's winter sports enthusiasts and youth demanded. I fully intended to send everyone back to the drawing board. The exception was a separate file I found with two of the most amazing image designs for the new *Spider O* line of high-tech alpine skis, and a really incredibly sharp logo—a bright orange O shadowed in silver gray with a stylized black spider inside of it.

"Wow . . ." I muttered and picked up the phone. "Phillip. This logo for Spider's line is amazing."

"Mom? What are you doing here?"

"Working. The same thing I've been doing for thirty years."

"I'll be right there." He hung up.

I stared at the phone in my hand, then quickly called the graphics manager for the SkiStar division, and told him I wanted to see more from the artist who designed the *Spider O* images.

"What *Spider O* images?"

"They're in a file under Olsen. I have them on my computer. I'll email them to you."

"I'll take care of it," he said and hung up, just as Phil came through the door.

"I don't think you should be here," my son said to me. "You don't have to do this, Mom. We can handle it."

"Sit, please. Based on the designs I've just seen for your next season, I do need to be here." I pushed the SkiStar proof sheets across my desk. "These are abysmal."

Phil agreed.

"But the new *Spider O* line is a winner, especially this logo. Whoever did this has the best eye I've seen in a long time. I want this logo on the tips of every ski in that line. And see how it's elongated in the face of the ski? Perfect. You don't have problem with them, do you?"

"No, I wouldn't question you on this. You'll just remind me I'm color blind." He laughed, but I still thought something was bothering him.

"As I remember it, Spider has approval in his contract," Phil said absently.

"Oh, he'll approve these. Trust me. He's not blind. These images are exactly what we need. They're night and day from the rest, which look too much like SkiStar's old designs, from a good decade ago. I want the colors amped up, at least two with some dark comic graphics, and completely different color combinations from our board lines. With this relaunch and the new sales and marketing campaign, I want to make certain your skis are the ones the buyer's eyes go to first. I'm going to have graphics redo everything, but this *Spider O* grouping."

Phil checked his watch. "It's almost noon. Let me steal you away. You can come to lunch with Scott and me. He doesn't know you're here, right?"

"I didn't tell him. He'd just try to discourage me, like you did," I said and walked over to my son who had the good sense to at least look embarrassed. "Let's go surprise him."

We passed by Mike's office on the way to Scott's. Part of me thought he should have moved in there by now, but I kept silent. Inside his own office, my oldest son was standing with his foot on a chair, while he buffed his shoes, his father's wooden shoe shine kit open next to him. I stopped because he looked so much like his dad just then. Phil was taller and lankier, and Mickey was the tallest and still trying to grow into his bony feet and hands, but my oldest son and his dad wore the same shoe size, carried the same kind of build, and were the same height and weight.

Not *were*. *Had been*. Among other things, death changed your verb tenses.

"Look what the cat dragged in," Phil said as he walked past me and helped himself to a chair.

"Mom? What are you doing here?"

How did I suddenly become such a pariah? I was one of the people who built this company. I had every right to be there. "I'll tell you the same thing I told your brother. I work here."

"Do you think you should be here?" Scott asked tentatively.

"She's been here working all morning," Phil said quickly and before I could say anything. "I figure you and I should kidnap her and take her to lunch. By the way, you're buying."

"The graphic designs have to get settled. Stop worrying about me, please. Both of you. I really need to be here." I paused, sitting down on Scott's desk as I had a moment's flashback of Mike holding that same shoe brush over the years and another image of Scott when he was six or seven. "I remember when your dad used to give you a dime to shine his shoes. You'd have thought he'd hung the moon."

Scott set down the horsehair brush. "A few

years ago I gave him a hard time about using me as child labor back then. And on being a cheap-skate." He laughed quietly. "Hell . . . you couldn't even buy a pack of gum for a dime."

"The money wasn't the point, although saving might have been. Your dad was determined not to be like his father, so that ritual became bonding time each weekday for just you and your dad. It was important to him that you felt you were special."

"We needed to feel special to someone. We were traumatized because we could never get you to pick a favorite," Phil said to me.

"Yes, I know. I was a cruel, cruel mother."

"And you were just a geeky, shoe-shining kid, Big Brother."

"You wouldn't understand, loser, since you can't shine canvas."

"I stopped wearing hightops after my wedding."

Scott laughed then. "Only because of your wife."

"What kind of little kid actually wants to shine shoes?" Phil said, showing as little interest now as he had all those years ago. Phil and Mike had had their bonding moments over washing the cars.

"Some little kid who isn't color blind," Scott said. "When you're wearing a pink shirt and a red tie with brown pants, Phil, everyone has to refocus their eyes again before they can even try to look down at your scuffed shoes."

Phillip swung his big feet up on Scott's desk. "Look at these. My shoes are brown. They're unscuffed and match my pants."

Scott pulled open a drawer to get his keys, and I placed my hand on his to stop him from closing it. "Is that your father's wallet?"

My son's face paled somewhat. I remembered that Scott had picked up Mike's belongings when he went to the morgue. "I kept it here because I needed to cut up his credit cards. I keep forgetting," he said, clearly not admitting the truth. He handed it to me.

Inside, Mike's face stared back at me from a holographic California driver's license. "Hand me the scissors, Scott, and we'll cut them up now." As I pulled out the credit cards, a hundred dollar bill Mike always carried behind his license fell out and there were smaller bills inside the billfold, along with the ticket stub from his flight to Reno and a business card from some ranch in Sparks, Nevada. Folded in half was a blue Post-it note and a yellow credit card receipt. I opened the Post-it to a list in Mike's handwriting:

Batteries
drill bit
¼ inch trim
2-penny nails
Bug lite

The receipt was from Ming's in Chinatown, dated the week before Mike went to Tahoe, and a small, thin green piece of paper was stuck in the crevice of the wallet; it was a fortune from a fortune cookie, and it read:

You will gain admiration from your pears.

There was a heartbeat of silence, and then I burst out laughing. "Look at this." Of course Mike would keep that fortune with his sense of humor. My boys each put their arm around me and we shared a good laugh.

I learned something important about death. You have to remember who and what the person was to you, and to others, and celebrate their uniqueness in this crazy and pain-filled world. Surprisingly, you could still grab something joyous about them even after they were gone, and maybe in that joy, came an instant of peace. I handed the wallet to Scott. "You can keep this."

"I don't know, Mom." He paused, then realizing he did want it, said, "You're sure?"

"I'm sure."

Phil winked at me. We both knew why Scott had the wallet in his desk.

"I'm hungry. Let's go eat," Phillip said, and he began to pull me toward the door.

"Wait. Where are we going?" I stopped in the hallway.

Phil looked at Scott and at the exact same time both my sons said, "I feel like Chinese food."

Out the blue, my grief hit me like a two-by-four when I was at Cummings' market, standing in the cracker aisle. How could a yellow box of Wheat Thins destroy you? One moment I was okay and the next I was crying so hard I couldn't catch my breath.

A woman stopped, reached across her cart, and handed me a Kleenex. I took it and when the woman asked if she could help, I shook my head and held up my hand, unable to say, No thank you. You're sweet but . . . Go away and just let me cry. The woman turned, unfortunately not before I caught that look, the one of pity and confusion and if-only-I-could-help-you. The look of "you poor thing."

The crying went on for a long time, the tectonic-deep sorrow that shuddered through me like a 7.0 earthquake, all because Mike could polish off a box of Wheat Thins in one sitting.

Some employees from the store stopped, talking quietly about twenty feet away, near the "Ten for Ten Dollars" end caps. Two women started down the aisle, took a look at me crying like crazy, and turned their carts around. It might have been funny if I could have stopped.

A young mother bravely powered down the aisle with a little boy and a toddler in the cart seat. She pulled down cereal and oatmeal boxes from the opposite shelves, tossing them in her cart as fast as she could and not looking at me.

"Why is that lady crying, Mommy?" The dark-haired little boy asked. He looked like he should be singing about his baloney first name.

"Shhh, Michael," she said.

The sound that came from me was the kind you made when someone hit you in the stomach. His name was Michael.

His small hand tugged on my shirttail the same way my boys used to do when they wanted my attention. "Why are you crying lady? Are you out of Froot Loops, too?"

I half-laughed, but it came out like a sob and I looked at the frazzled young mother whose shirt was buttoned wrong, (there were jelly finger-prints on it and it wasn't ironed) clearly embarrassed, both of us, and I tried in the poignant silence to plaster a smile on my hot, burning face, then I nodded to this little Michael.

As the mother hurried them away, the toddler began to whine and the little boy was looking worriedly over his shoulder.

I grabbed two huge boxes of Froot Loops, held them up so he could see, and dropped them in my cart.

I wasn't out of Froot Loops. I was Froot Loops.

Eventually I went to the small restroom behind the swinging gray doors in the back of the vegetable section, splashed cold water on my face, blew my red nose until I could smell the pine cleaner they'd used in the bathroom. How long could I stand there?

Someone knocked on the door. I quickly rummaged through my purse. Dark sunglasses on, I headed for the checkout, where an elderly woman was counting out her total grocery bill in coins, and the next woman in front of me decided to talk to the clerk about organic cantaloupe, before she actually stopped and handwrote a check, taking her time to thumb slowly through her check register and list the check amount.

Didn't everyone use debit cards nowadays? You just punch in a password and your groceries were paid.

So instead of the quick retreat I so desperately needed, I stood there, trapped, humiliated at what I felt was my complete lack of control, ashamed and embarrassed and trying to ignore the side-long looks I was getting. Apparently everyone had seen me. I was exposed, a fraud, broken in front of the world, and I wanted to hide. My sunglasses just didn't do it for me. What I needed was to go back to grocery shopping at three in the morning.

Once outside I closed the car door, buckled my seatbelt, but I didn't drive home. I closed my eyes and dropped my head back on the headrest. Who was this lost woman living inside of my skin?

Where was I going? How could I go anywhere for the rest of my entire life without Mike? I sat with my head back and my mind empty of answers. I needed guidelines, some kind of roadmap on how to go on living my life.

There was a huge, multi-story bookstore on the northwest corner of Union Square, not far away. I headed straight there and never stopped to look at a single handbag. Once inside the bookstore, I took the escalator to nonfiction and headed for the self-help section, Mike's favorite, where shelf after shelf were there to guide all the poor slobs like me into understanding and coping with life, with my inner self, and with those around me.

Poor slob, poor thing, poor lady, poor widow. The Widow Froot Loops. I had to find some way to help myself.

Kneeling down in front of the grief section, scanning the titles, it wasn't lost to me that I had been working in a bookstore when I met Mike. I opened a few books, sitting on the floor Indian style and skimming them, stopping to read the bold topics.

Recognize the loss. Acknowledge the death. Understand the death.

Understand the death? What a crock. I tossed the book over my shoulder and opened the next one. I was supposed to understand that the man I had loved most of my life was crushed to death inside a car.

Somewhere in this massive obelisk of the printed word, on one of the long shelves of hundreds of books with impossible demands and dismal titles like *Grieving Mindfully* and *The Loss That Is Forever*, there had to be what I needed . . . something easier, more contemporary. Something simple like . . . *Death for Dummies.*

I sat on the overstuffed sofa in the media room where it was fairly dark and pretty much impossible to read the three grief books gathering dust on the floor next to me. Around me the walls were lined with framed posters of Mike's favorite movies. *Jaws. The Godfather. Apocalypse Now. Star Trek. Last of the Mohicans.*

Last of the Mohicans. For three and a half decades I had loved a man who was never embarrassed about his romantic side. He'd played the sound track in his car for months after we saw the movie. I stuffed a handful of crackers in my mouth.

Barefooted, feet on an ottoman, a crushed box of Wheat Thins hugged to my chest, I sat there with the television on, wearing red sweats with the Cantrell campaign slogan from ten years ago, and the thought came to me that I might have slept in them. I sniffed my underarm. Baby powder. Maybe I had changed clothes today after all. The polish on my toenails was chipping off. I flexed my feet, toes splayed. One big toenail, once wearing a solid dark red coat of a color called *Not in Kansas Anymore*, was now polished in the shape of—I studied it for a minute—Idaho.

Once and always I was the daughter of a geography and math teacher. My father would have been proud that I could still, in my fifties, identify the states by shape alone.

I leaned my head back and stared at the green recessed ceiling. Idaho. The Gem State. Capital? Boise. Highest peak? Mount Borah. Lowest point? The Snake River. Home of the deepest gorge in North America: Hell's Canyon.

I'm there now.

Chewing on another handful of wheat crackers made me feel better. Mindless eating was like mindless living, like mindless existence. The thin foil liner inside the box tore. When did they stop using waxed paper? I felt suddenly older than dirt.

On the TV screen a man was walking across a pristine, stainless steel factory. They panned to a close-up of a conveyor belt spilling peanuts into a dark vat of caramelized sugar, making me hungry again.

Five boxes of Wheat Thins in three days. Staring into the dark recesses of box number six, I swallowed, thinking some honey-nut peanut butter (lately I kept a spoon near the jar) would be good to dip them in, maybe chase it all with a shot of Herradura.

But then I would have to get up, pull out the silver and blue tequila bottle from the bar cabinet across the room, get out the cutting board, find a lime, and the salt . . .

Way too much work. Besides, wasn't drinking alone supposed to be dangerous?

So I lost myself in afternoon programming, living inside the big screen, rectangular, HDTV (the one that in full screen mode made everyone look like dwarves.) "Sneezy, Happy, Grumpy, Sleepy, Doc, Droopy," I recited. "No . . . Droopy was a dog."

Flashing across the screen was a line of bright red words: *Attention women between the ages of 18 and 65.*

"Women over the age of fifty cannot remember the names of the Seven Dwarves," I said to the empty room.

"Are you feeling sad?" A woman's voice asked through the sound speakers in the kindest of tones.

"You bet I am," I said.

"Fatigued?"

"Bingo."

"Agitated? Experiencing a lack of confidence, a loss of interest in activities you once enjoyed? Are you having trouble sleeping?"

"Big Brother is watching me," I muttered to the television, cramming another handful of crackers in my mouth and wistfully thinking of peanut butter.

"Qualified participants may receive study-related medical care, medications and lab work at no additional cost. Please call this number."

I picked up the phone and had half the 800 number punched in when I heard the back door and a minute later Mickey came into the room, walking in his lanky style, slightly hunched over in that I'm-too-tall teenaged boy way. Cursed by their height, all my sons had walked that way for a few years, until manhood caught up with their long bones and their bodies filled out.

"I'm home." He dropped his backpack in the doorway where I could trip over it, pocketed the car keys, and flopped down beside me, slapping his size thirteens on the suede ottoman. "Whatcha watching?"

"The history of Cracker Jacks."

"The Food Channel again?"

I nodded. "How was your day?"

"Fine." He took the collapsed cracker box off of my lap. "Dinner?"

"No. I have Froot Loops."

"You okay?"

"I'm fine. You?"

"Yeah." He lifted the box to his lips and poured some into his mouth, chewed for a minute then said, "They put my name up for valedictorian."

It took a minute to sink in. He had been suspiciously devoted to his school work, not that I had to ever worry much about him. He was the only one of our children who was like me, the one who never missed a homework assignment and voluntarily took extra credit. I used to have to get after the others, making them take extra credit to make up for the stupidity of not turning in their homework.

I think perhaps that was why Mike was often so frustrated with Mickey. To not study for a degree would have been a sheer waste for our youngest. "That's wonderful." I gave him a huge hug, then laughed because he was hanging his head and trying to hide his grin. I punched him in the arm.

"Ouch!" he said and laughed.

"Now all you have to do is pick a college," I said to him, hoping in my heart he wouldn't argue for a career as a professional boarder.

"I'm down to Southern Cal or Colorado."

I breathed a sigh of relief. "Close to home or close to the mountains," I said, aware of how he was thinking.

He shrugged, looking somewhat distant.

"You can talk to me about your choices, you know."

"I need to tell you something. Ron Wilson called me."

"Our graphics manager?"

"Yeah. I was at the office with Phillip one weekend and he had a bunch of work to do, so I was playing with the Macs in the design department and just kind of came up with the logo."

"What?"

"It was me who did the images you liked. Ron wanted me to tell you. I heard everyone talking about the new line and I was just bored and did some art for fun."

I burst out laughing and didn't know if I should hug him or kick myself. "Those designs were spot-on."

"I guess I take after you," he said, grinning, and I smiled. It felt so good. Mickey . . . He was better than I was at his age. "That's why I'm thinking of picking UCLA," he explained.

"The graphic arts program," I said.

"Yeah."

I was so thankful he wasn't running off to become a professional snowboarder. Not with the potential I saw in those designs. Without any of us even knowing it, my youngest son was already primed to join the company and someday, with some time and experience and a degree, he would step into my job. I felt something I could only name happy pain, a cross between joy and anguish, because Mike would have loved this. He wouldn't have had to buy another sports division for his last son, just to make everything fair and equal between them.

"Well, dear." I ruffled his hair. "I'll tell you what. This summer you're working in graphics, not in the warehouses or having your talent wasted doing gofer work for your brothers."

"Really? You mean it?"

"Yes, I mean it. But you'll be doing things besides designing. You'll need to start at the bottom."

"That's great, Mom."

"And you can pick your school without any influence from me. You're right that your dad would have wanted it that way."

The look we exchanged said everything, good feelings, pride, some bit of confidence in my son doing what he thought he should, which wasn't a bad thing; he was almost eighteen—until enough time elapsed and the moment grew empty because we were alone, Mike didn't live in this wonderful moment. I lived it alone, and then I was left with another reality. My last child was leaving home.

Chapter Fifteen

"Get up, you lazy slug."

"Ellie! Don't talk to March that way."

"How am I supposed to talk to her? Look at her. She hasn't moved." Bariella Crocker Hutcheonson stood at the foot of my bed, hands on her socialite-slim hips, as bossy as she was back in 1964, and living up to the audaciousness of her name.

"See there. She's opened her eyes. Hello,

March. We came to save you." Mariclare Davis flanked Ellie looking the opposite: anxious and sweet and worried.

I pulled the covers over my head. Two of my best friends were standing in my bedroom and interrupting my morning nap. Harrie, Dr. Harriet Fortis, was MIA.

Though at this very minute I regretted our first meeting, we had, years back, all found each other at the start of our freshman year of high school and stayed friends in spite of boys, college, careers and family, divorce and now death. That first year, Sierra High School had been brand new, and public, and each of us had come from somewhere else: private school, Catholic school, out of state, from another district. The four of us didn't have friends we had known since our days in a sandbox, and couldn't walk onto the center of campus that first day in an estrogen pack of box-pleat skirted teens, gathering like everyone else around the flagpole for the pledge of allegiance.

The truth was we found each other because of shoes. We all had on the same ones: black patent-leather Capezio Baby Dolls, which had only been stocked in and sold out of every small boutique or ballet store in the Bay Area. So we bonded over our shoes and our loneliness, at an empty lunch table, and because of some kind of kindred serendipity that brings friends together.

We were Bariella, Mariclare, Harriet and

March. But minutes into our first sleepover that next weekend, we realized three of us would be called Bari, Mari and Harrie, which sounded like female versions of Donald Duck's nephews. After giggling ourselves silly and talking in duck voices for five minutes, we came up with new nicknames, something less like characters from Walt Disney.

Almost forty years later Ellie, MC, Harrie and I were still the same, older and maybe not always wiser, but with an enviable history of friendship together. Our last names changed over the years as men had come in and out of some of our lives, Ellie's three times and counting, but our nicknames hadn't ever changed.

"How did you two get in?" I lay on my back in bed, still sluggish.

"The back door was unlocked," MC told me. "You really should be more careful. They never did catch the Zodiac killer."

MC had been the sweet Catholic girl, who came to that first day of school so excited because she wouldn't have to wear uniform plaid and Peter Pan collars ever again. Except that later that fall, box-pleated skirts and Peter Pan collars became popular.

We had laughed about it just a few years ago, because in high school, most of us wore the same thing anyway: sleeveless sheath dresses with low cut flats, double-breasted houndstoothchecked coat dresses and squat heels, fuzzy white car coats and hip-hugger cords with thick belts and boots. For those four years, we all made our own uniforms.

"It's like a morgue in here." Ellie snapped open each of the shades on the French doors and front windows. "*You* didn't die, March. Mike did. Now get dressed. We're taking you out to lunch."

"You could talk to her a little more tactfully."

Ellie, a woman on a mission, walked past MC. "Why?"

I merely groaned. The sun was shining brightly, too brightly. I covered my eyes with my arm. "Go without me. I'm not hungry."

"You need to eat."

"I have all the Froot Loops anyone could ever want."

"And we need to feel like we're helping you—although Harrie couldn't get away today, too many patients—so don't give us any crap. I know you too well." Ellie's voice drifted off.

I slowly raised my head. MC stood alone by the bed, her expression apologetic. I looked around the empty room and whispered, "Where is she?"

"In the closet," MC mouthed.

"I'm picking out some clothes for you. If I can find any around all these handbags," Ellie called out. "Get up."

I flopped back on the pillow and yawned. "I can't. I have to make cookies for a bake sale at

Mickey's school. The school band needs to travel to DC. I signed up back in January. Before . . ." I stopped, searching for the words.

My new life was defined in befores and afters. Happiness and sorrow. Then and now. Pre-Mike and Post-Mike, like Sunday football commentary. "Before," I repeated understanding how a single word was more than enough. I sat up and shoved the hair out of my face.

"You get no say in this. We're doing an intervention." Ellie came strolling out of the closet carrying a red cashmere sweater and a pair of gray pinstriped slacks on one arm, a classic gray-plaid Burberry scarf slung over her shoulder and a pair of suede flats dangled from her other hand. "You'll have plenty of time to make cookies later this afternoon. Let's go. Chop. Chop." She dumped the clothes in my arms and pulled me up. "I don't have all day."

"You could just go away," I offered.

"Fat chance."

"What time is it?" I turned toward the clock.

"Eleven thirty." Ellie took me by the shoulders, studying me for all of three seconds, her normal attention span. "You look like hell."

"Thank you," I said with as much indignation as I could muster.

"Well, it's true. You're wallowing. Don't look at me like that, MC. I know she has a good reason, but enough is enough. And she doesn't

224

need everyone tiptoeing around her, especially us."

"You have never tiptoed around anything a day in your life," I groused. "And you don't have to talk around me. 'She' is in the room, you know."

"Could have fooled me. Honey, you aren't even in the same universe as the rest of us." Ellie walked me toward the bathroom. "Wash."

"But I—" I turned around but Ellie closed the door in my face.

"And put on some makeup," came the obnoxious voice of authority through the door.

A small storefront restaurant in San Francisco's Sunset District was the home of some of the best Mexican food north of Veracruz. The fresh menu, handwritten everydday on parchment and slid into a plastic and leather holder the color of jalapenos, touted chile rellenos dressed with succulent pork and dried fruits, and an unforgettable seafood paella of Guaymas shrimp, Manila clams and halibut swimming in a sweetly-herbed sea created from fresh tomatoes grown on vines in the small garden behind the building.

The day's special was baked sour cream and spinach enchiladas with lobster and red pepper sauce. Famous for its handmade tortillas, always served soft and blistered, the place also boasted crisply fried chips that cried out for a dip into a chunky pool of the house specialty: spicy, burnt-chile, mango, and avocado salsa.

In a city that was known for its amazing food establishments, competition and the constant influx of the finest of culinary artists made quality, nouveau California cuisine, and consistency the only surefire recipe for a restaurant's continued success. So things like parking, the little extras and hands-on service distinguished the locals' favored spots from the tourist traps.

Sitting to the right of each place setting were steaming plates of complimentary mini tamales made of sweet masa and prime meat. Just the smell of the air over the table could make the average person willing to forfeit fresh white bread (even Boudin's famous sourdough) and buttery potatoes for that golden grain ground out from a simple stalk of sweet corn.

For too many years to count, we had spent many long lunches here, and I found myself actually glad to be there. "Everything smells so good." I was instantly famished. Food had become my best friend.

"How long has it been since you've been out?"

"Out?" I unwrapped a tamale.

"Yes. You know. To a restaurant."

"I had lunch with my sons," I said, but that had been a few weeks back and both boys encouraged me to stay out of the office, which did horrific things to my ego as well as my plans to keep myself powering forward through life.

I knew what my friends would say if I admitted the truth: that I hadn't left the house for almost two weeks. I suspected Ellie knew that anyway. Probably one of my snitch children had called and tattled on me.

Evidently, I was becoming a drag. Molly hated me, my sons didn't want me around work, and my youngest wanted to be a man and choose his own college. No one needed me.

"In other words, you've been wallowing indoors too long," Ellie concluded with her maddening ability to know everything you wanted hidden. "All those times you blew us off. I knew you needed a lunch. You need a serious drinking lunch. I, your friend for almost forty years—God, that makes me sound old—am here to get you completely drunk."

With perfect timing the waiter placed three glasses in the center of the table and added a large wooden salt shaker and a blue and yellow pottery bowl filled with sliced limes, before he poured shots from an ornate silver and blue bottle.

"Well, looks like I'm going to drink today," I said dryly.

"You complaining?"

"No. But I didn't see you order these."

"I called ahead. Now bring us a pitcher of margaritas please Tomas, then we'll order." Ellie waited until our waiter left and raised her glass, looking at me without a lick of the pity that was in everyone else's eyes. Still, there was an empty pause before Ellie said, "To Mike."

It was 5:30 p.m. when I stumbled out of the back of Ellie's limo and grabbed onto the door, weaving a little, my hair hanging in my face, because it was so windblown from standing up through the sunroof and singing *We Built This City* at the top of my lungs as we drove through rush hour traffic.

I turned and leaned inside, where the car smelled like leather and tamales. "Thank you both for a lovely lunch." I straightened and turned to try to walk toward the house, but Ellie's driver, Eugene was there to help me.

Eugene had a great face, like Ernest Borgnine, kind of rough and fatherly at the same time. "I love my friends," I said to him.

MC was giggling like a teenager, tequila did that to her. Ellie turned down the volume and crawled across the seat like Catwoman. "Remember. Find something to do. You're living in a vacuum. Do *not* let your kids keep you from work. You don't need protecting. You need to keep busy."

"Your boss is way too bossy, Eugene."

"Let me help you, Mrs. Cantrell," he said gently.

I sagged back against his shoulder and looked up at him. "I'm not Mrs. anymore." *What am I?*

"I'm sorry, ma'am."

I'm a ma'am? Ugh. "God . . . I'm old," I said, disgusted.

"You're not old and even if you are, don't ever admit it, or worse yet, use the word 'old.' You're just sloshed," Ellie said. "Get her to the door, Eugene."

"I can walk," I insisted. My throat felt scratchy from singing so loudly. But I took two steps up the drive and had to grab his arm. "Maybe you can guide me, Eugene. You can be my personal GPS system." I laughed.

He took my keys from my newest purse, a pearl-gray leather Vuitton, and unlocked the front door, while I leaned against the side of the house and insisted I was just fine and could easily use the key and walk into my own house without falling face down. "I am a woman of a 'certain age' after all," I said.

I managed to get rid of him, closed the door and leaned back against it, holding onto the handle. The alarm system was beeping in my left ear. Thirty seconds to punch in the code. Squinting, I put in the numbers and turned too quickly, and the room spun. But I told myself I was fine, disoriented, but fine. It felt good to let go. It felt good to drink myself into inhibition, to sing like school girls as we drove through the city.

The stupid alarm began to tick again, the yellow warning light blinking. "What's wrong with this thing?" I entered the code again, the light changed to green again, so I walked across the limestone entry, surprisingly steady considering.

He was there . . . sitting in the living room, his head bent over a book, flecks of gray all through that dark, thick, familiar hair.

"Mike?" My blood began pulsing. My skin grew hot.

Behind me I heard the alarm begin to beep again. "Mike?" He didn't look up. I ran toward him. "Mike!" It had all been a mistake. It was a bad dream. A joke. "You're alive!" I was crying as I reached for him, expecting him to laugh at me. "Mike!"

I kept my eyes glued to his image, afraid to blink or look away.

The house alarm continued to go off.

"Mike!" I yelled, desperate and needing to touch him. Something stopped me, tripped me, was blocking my way to him, and suddenly I was falling.

As if he couldn't hear me shouting his name, he stayed in the chair, calmly reading, wearing his red polo shirt with the blue ink stain on the pocket.

I never could get that stain out.

My head hit the coffee table, and the image of my husband instantly turned to black.

Chapter Sixteen

It turned out that the alarm company called Molly, who met the police and paramedics at the house. Despite all the blood everywhere and my bruises and aches, I didn't need stitches or a trip to the local emergency room. The gash causing all the blood was in my hairline and head cuts always looked worse. But as the emergency crew packed up their duffels and gear, one of them mentioned that I shouldn't be left alone or allowed to sleep for a few hours.

While I knew what he meant, that I might have a concussion, his words said something else altogether. *She shouldn't be left alone.* Which appeared to be the singular truth about me. I was broken. I was a mess. I hated what I had become, but I couldn't seem to stop any more than I could stop seeing Mike all over the house.

I lay on the sofa, my head throbbing, trying to look as if I were fine, but alternating between embarrassment and frustration. Somehow I had managed to lose a shoe, and a bloody towel lay on the floor next to me.

Molly let the EMTs out and picked up the bloody towel. I searched her face for the hateful look I had seen before, but thankfully it wasn't there. She was staring down at the thick ivory guest towel; it was made of expensive imported cotton and trimmed in satin and lace with small seed pearl trim and came from an ultra-upscale Italian bedding shop off of Union Square.

I had forever scolded one or the other of her older brothers for using the guest bathroom to wipe their 'grubby' hands on the good towels. "Mom, you know I'm good," Phillip would tease me, or "I am a guest," Scott would argue. "I haven't lived here for over a decade."

"I'll take this to the laundry room," she said in a hurry and left me alone in the room.

I laid my head back and closed my eyes, and I could hear Molly in the other room.

"There's stain spray on the counter," I called out.

"I know, Mother."

When she came back in I tried to sit up and winced. At least I didn't feel drunk any longer. I just hurt and my hand went automatically to my head.

"Don't get up," Molly said. "Just lie there. What do you need?"

"A stronger ego. Good lord . . . Did you see the looks they gave me? They think I'm a drunk."

Molly laughed at me. "Well, actually, I wouldn't want to light a match within two feet of you."

"You're kidding?" I closed my eyes, suddenly embarrassed all over again. "Am I really that bad?"

"Do you want me to lie?"

"Yes. No. Ellie and MC took me to lunch. Oh Lord my head hurts."

"You must have fallen right on your head."

"I did fall on my head, and my knee and my hip. I hurt all over already. I can't imagine what tomorrow will be like." I was talking too loud and winced again. "You know," I lowered my voice. "I think I have a hangover already. The stupid alarm kept going off. I thought I saw—" I stopped, remembering Mike's image in my mind and I was afraid to tell my wounded and judgmental daughter the truth. "I saw something odd. I never knew tequila could make you hallucinate. I think I panicked." I sank further into the pillows, feeling smaller than I ever could remember.

I lay an arm across my eyes because the tears I could feel welling up would spill out and I would really humiliate myself and fall apart in front of Molly. With every ounce of stubbornness I still had left in me, I willed the tears away. "Any second my eyes are going to shoot right out of my head," I murmured.

"I'll get you something for your headache."

I waved a hand toward the other end of the house. "In the kitchen. The drawer by the sink. Two please. Excedrin." I paused. "And ice water. Crushed."

"I know, Mother."

When Molly came back in the room, I slowly

raised my head. "Thanks, sweetie. I'm sorry you had to rush over here. I feel like an idiot. I shouldn't have had that last margarita." I set down the water glass. My daughter had put a slice of cucumber and a wedge of lemon in the ice water. Back when she was in college, I had flown down to LA and taken her to a seaside spa for a mother-daughter weekend after her mid-terms. On all the tables in all the spa rooms were pitchers of water with crystal clear ice floating with lemon and cucumber slices. The flavor was enough to change the way I drank water forever after.

Of course she would do that—my daughter with her eye for detail. So what had her sharp eyes seen in mine that I wanted to hide?

"How many margaritas did you have?"

"I have no idea. They came in these . . ." I raised my hands about a foot apart ". . . big pitchers."

"I can make you some coffee." Molly checked her watch.

"I don't want to just lie here."

"You're supposed to rest."

"But I can't go to sleep," I said, parroting instructions for the keeping of March Cantrell, mad woman. Mad, drunken woman.

"Right. I'll be right back. Let the aspirin go to work. I'll get you some coffee." Molly made a beeline for the kitchen.

"The beans are in the freezer," I called out weakly.

"I used to live here, you know."

"Kona. I like the kona blend. Your father loved kona, too. Your Aunt May sent it when she was in Hawaii. It smells so good when you grind it. I wonder why coffee never tastes like it smells?"

No response.

"Did you find it?"

"Yes!" came the sharp reply and I heard the coffee grinder crunching away in the kitchen.

I waited a minute more, and then I stood up and was much more steady-on-my-feet than I had been when I came home.

In the doorway of the kitchen I stopped. Molly was on her cell phone, her back to me. "I might need to cancel tonight. I know. I'll try, but no matter what, I'm going to be late. I really need to stay here with my mother." She paused. "Okay. I'll call you."

I stepped back a few feet so it looked as if I had just walked into the room. She pocketed her phone and turned around, clearly surprised. "Mom. You're supposed to be lying down."

"I'm not dizzy. And I forgot I have to make cookies for Mickey's school."

"Cookies? He's a senior in high school. Isn't that too old for class parties?"

"The parents are selling them at a bake sale to help finance the band trip."

"Mickey's not in the band."

"Mickey has nothing to do with it. The school needed volunteers and I signed up months ago."

My daughter checked her watch. "When does he get home?"

"Not until nine. He has practice." I took down a mug and leaned against the counter, waiting for the coffee. "Look. You don't have to stay." The coffeemaker was gurgling and I turned around. The room spun so quickly I dropped the mug and heard it shatter.

"Mom!" My daughter's arms were around me. How very odd. That was never her role; it was always the other way around. Molly was holding me up and the room was a blur, my vision swimming like my head. "Come over to the table and sit down."

I felt frail and frightened and a little nauseated. I rested my head in one hand while I waited for the feeling to pass. When I could focus again without feeling like I would faint, I looked at her, hovering over me. I had really scared her. "I'm sorry."

"I'll make the cookies. You stay there." She set a mug of fresh coffee in front of me, swept up the broken china and then said, "Are you okay sitting there?"

"I'm fine. The coffee is helping. The ingredients are in the pantry. Chocolate chip pecan with the ground oatmeal base," I told her, but she knew.

They were the family's favorite. "The mixer's right there."

When we redid the kitchen some years back, we had added a whole line of mahogany small appliance garages along the marble counter. The upper cabinets had beveled glass panes and were lit underneath and inside, displaying all the brightly colored serving dishes Mike had bought me on our trips to Italy over the years. Copper pots and pans and bowls, well-used but polished, hung like monkeys from a heavy iron rack above the center island and Molly took down the largest bowl. She slid open one door; it held the blender, the next one held the food processor, the next the pasta machine. "The last one. On the right," I said.

Molly pulled out the mixer and rolled her eyes. "I keep Williams-Sonoma in business."

"I can see that."

And as I watched my daughter make the cookies we had made together so many times over the years, I saw that something was still off with her. Mike could always charm Molly back from whatever dark place her mind seemed to go to. My daughter had stood in this kitchen so many times and yet now I saw that she looked uncomfortable.

I had a crazy thought. All those years ago, when I had stood in my mother's kitchen, arguing over my wedding and scared to death because I had to tell her I was pregnant. That day I had realized my parents' house was home, but it wasn't my home. I wondered if I looked to my own mother then, like my Molly looked to me right now, as if a pair of shoes she had worn forever suddenly pinched her toes.

A few hours later I walked my daughter to the door. She grabbed her coat and purse while I was looking at the bump on my forehead in the hall mirror.

"Daddy?"

My heart stopped and my gaze flew to my daughter's reflection. She was standing behind me, alone.

"Molly?" I turned around.

She was holding a white feather in her open palm.

"The cat must have brought a bird in," I said. "Twice in the last week I found feathers in the house."

She tore her eyes away and frowned at me. "What?"

"The feather," I explained. "From the cat."

"Oh. Right."

"You said, 'Daddy.' A minute ago." Should I tell her the truth? Should I tell her I saw him all over the house? Did she see him, too? I wanted to ask her. But how would she react? "Did you think you saw your dad?"

"See him? No. No. I was just thinking out

loud." Her look told me to back off. No confession for me tonight. Her cell phone rang again, shattering the moment.

"I've got to run," she said hurriedly and gave me a quick kiss on the cheek.

"Thanks for making those cookies, and for taking care for me." But she looked about a million miles away. "Molly?"

"What?"

"I'm sorry if coming here ruined your plans tonight."

"I'll call tomorrow, Mom, and see how you're doing." As she walked down the front steps, she'd already pulled out her cell phone.

Chapter Seventeen

Californians, the men and the women, seldom miss their regular hair appointments. Like clockwork I went to the salon every seven weeks, to the same stylist, for the same cut, year after year. As I sat in the chair, staring at my reflection in the mirror, I saw the same woman I had always been.

"March," Rico said, fingering my shoulder length dishwater colored hair. "I wish you would let me cut your hair."

"You say that every time." It was looking dull.

"I know. And every time you say no. You never change."

"You're right. I never change. But today I am. Cut it short and color it. You wanted to make it blonde. Go for it."

Two hours later, after a head full of foils, and some instruction on the use of molding mud and gel application, I came away with an abundance of light blonde streaks and a messy short hair-style Rico had wanted to do for years.

And I walked out of there for the first time in ages feeling like a different woman.

I told myself that now I was the blonde who could cope with her life. Walking down the city street toward Union Square, where Neiman Marcus and Saks Fifth Avenue displayed their purses behind glass, I felt like I was in one of those old Clairol commercials, except I didn't have enough hair to flip and bounce, and I wasn't wearing a pixie band.

Still, even when I arrived home with a luscious bronze leather Gucci handbag, I didn't regret the loss of my hair or the change, but I noticed that really short hair made me look more . . . *zaftig*.

Two weeks later I discovered it was not my haircut when I was standing on the professional scale in the doctor's office as my friend, Dr. Harriet Fortis, scribbled on my chart.

"March, you've gained some weight."

I stared at the silver metal marks on the scale bar and at the square black weight in horror and hopped down, kicked off my shoes and said to her, "Doctor's scales always weigh you heavier. I believe it's a plot by the American Medical Association so you can lecture us about our health. How old is this thing? Let me try again."

"Okay. Get back on, especially if you think your shoes weigh twenty five pounds."

"Ha. Ha. You're supposed to be my friend, Harrie."

"I like your hair," she said. "Not many straight women can get away with wearing their hair that short."

"Funny." I flipped her off, and then played with the balance weights, but no matter how much I adjusted it, or even after I lifted one foot a bit, I still had to use the heavier black weight that read 150 pounds and then move the smaller weight up and up from there.

"The truth is I'm jealous," she said.

"Why?"

"That haircut looks really good on you."

"Thanks," I said distractedly. Shoeless, the horrific number only went down a pound. "I wonder how much more my long hair would have made me weigh. Ugh." I tousled my stubby, shag carpet hairdo with one hand and could feel the product in it. There wasn't much to tousle. It was rather like patting your son on the head after his summer buzz cut was growing out. "At least now I know why I thought the haircut made me look fat," I said. "And why I thought the cleaners shrunk my slacks."

Apparently the easiest way to put on twenty five pounds in two months was living on a diet of Belgian chocolates, Wheat Thins, Froot Loops, margaritas, and the five dozen chocolate chip cookies Molly made but I ate. I had become a carbohydrate junkie.

To my chagrin, the day after my head collision with the coffee table, and after Molly had made all those cookies for me, I discovered I had missed the bake sale by three weeks. Weakly, I had trudged out of the school office in organizational shame, carrying a box layered with waxed paper and dozens of double-sized, really chewy, chocolate chip pecan cookies.

I had options. I could have taken them to the company office, which would have given me another excuse to show up there, but then I would have to admit to my sons that I screwed up . . . just one more thing their mother couldn't handle. And what if they told Molly?

Scott had given me the third degree about my hair during my last family dinner at their house, and I could tell from the looks they exchanged that all my children were certain I was falling apart.

"Mom! What did you do? Your hair is gone," Scott said.

"Scott! It looks fabulous, Mom," Renee said and she elbowed my son in the ribs.

"It's awfully short," Molly said. Clearly she hated it.

"I love it," Keely said.

Phillip frowned and walked in a circle, eyeing me like one did melons at the market. "Didn't Indian women used to cut their hair as a sign of grief?"

I believe at that moment I regretted that Phillip took history classes. Why couldn't he have been like those young people Jay Leno randomly interviewed on TV, the ones who don't know who the President or Vice President are and who think cyclamen is a venereal disease.

My hair was a pointed topic of discussion during the entire dinner, and I left Scott's feeling less good about myself than I had when I arrived. I didn't know what people wanted from me, especially my children, and worse yet, I didn't know what I wanted from myself.

Devouring the cookies became my home remedy, a chocolate and carbohydrate asylum I had committed myself to when I was all alone at home, when the loneliness I felt for my husband was more than I could bear and I, too, began to question my sanity. Right at that moment, standing in Harrie's office and looking at the scale, I wasn't certain there was even one aspect of my life that was under my own control.

Harrie shoved her tortoise rimmed glasses up her nose. I always wanted Harrie's nose. It was one of those lovely European noses, longer and pointed down just a little at the end, the kind that made her face look like it belonged to one of those great De Havilland or Fontaine beauties of the past. "When did you stop exercising?" she asked me.

"Around 1984."

She laughed. "At your age—"

"Our age," I said.

"I stand corrected. Bone and aging studies have proven that women over fifty need strength training. You're behind, March. Hire a trainer. Add cardio, walk more, and buy some weights."

"And here I thought lifting those cookies to my mouth was enough."

"I'm serious."

"I know, I know . . . But I hate exercise," I muttered quite petulantly.

"Next time we'll need to do a bone density check on you. You're probably fine, but make strength training part of your routine."

What routine was that? Self-pity, I thought sourly.

"Start with some yoga."

"I'd rather start with some yogurt . . . frozen, with hot fudge." I held up my hand before she said something. "Okay, I know that was bad."

Harrie did the exam and I got dressed and went into her office, where she closed the door and sat down at her desk.

"Am I going to live?" I said, joking.

"Do you want to?" She wasn't joking.

"Some days, no," I said truthfully.

"Scott called me, which is why I had the office call you about an appointment. Your kids are worried about you."

"My kids think I'm nuts because I cut and colored my hair," I paused, then added, "And got drunk. And had a little fall. But I didn't need stitches," I said too brightly.

"Scott said John Cummings told him you had some kind of breakdown in the market."

I groaned. "Scott knows about that, too? Damn. . . ."

"It sounds to me as if you're having a tough time. And you certainly have a right to, March. I cannot even imagine. Grief is a terrible thing to deal with. It's really okay if you need something to help you emotionally, at least something other than Ellie's deadly margarita lunches. I can give you something. Some Zoloft."

"You gave that to Ellie for her last two divorces."

"And she got through them both without killing her exes."

I laughed because Ellie was a pistol even when she wasn't spurned or angry. Her divorces thoroughly pissed her off. "But I'm not angry," I said defensively.

"Are you sure?"

"You think I'm mad at Mike? Oh that's right. Denial and isolation, anger, bargaining, depression, and acceptance. It's part of the grief process. Yes, I did buy some books. Why would I be mad at him? Believe me, I am absolutely certain Mike would have rather kept right on living. However, I don't want to ever *accept* his death," I said vehemently.

"And there are days when I feel as if my life is spinning out of control." I was quiet and thought about what I had just said. Harrie wasn't condemning me or judging me. She was my friend. "Well," I said more quietly. "I'm a little pissed off at God. I wouldn't mind doing a few rounds with Him."

"Oh, March. I'm sorry. That can't be easy to admit."

"Actually, I'm so angry, it's not all that diffiult," I said and was surprised by the bitterness in my voice.

Harrie shook her head. "No one, least of all me, has a right to tell you how to feel. What you decide to do about dealing with all this is up to you. You do what you want to do. I just want you to think about the options, especially when you're feeling lost and out of control. There are resources to help you."

I stared down at my clenched hands for a long time.

"Look, if you try them and they don't help you,

you don't have to stay on the pills, but if they can help why not at least give them a try? That's why these drugs were created."

"Our Prozac nation?" I said sarcastically, but she merely stared at me. "I don't know . . ."

"Grief counseling isn't a crutch. For some people, it helps to talk to someone, privately or in a group. I have some names here." She handed me some business cards. "I think you should consider getting some help. I'm talking to you because I love you. You know that."

I didn't want to hear this. I closed my eyes and leaned back in the chair. "I'm not sure medication is for me. And I'm certain group speak is not." Sitting in a room and telling strangers how I was feeling? I shuddered. "I'd like to think I can be stronger than that. And if I take the meds, doesn't that mean I'm giving in to this abysmal state I'm in and admitting I can't go on?"

"Is that such a bad thing to admit?"

"It is when it might mean I'm even a worse mess than my children believe I am."

"It doesn't make you a weaker person because you might choose to take an antidepressant. This medication is not addictive. The risks are minimal. If you don't like it, you don't have to take it. But it takes about six weeks for them to start to have an effect. I'm going to give you this prescription. You'll have it if you need it."

So I left her office more confused than when I

went in, and headed for my car, but I stopped and turned, looking up and down the street. Figuring I needed the exercise, I might as well start immediately. After checking my watch—as if I actually had something to do—I walked up the hill, and down another, and another, stopped at a toy shop and bought some puzzles for my grandchildren, then left and went down along Market Street to Nordstrom's.

I tried on dresses for Mickey's graduation; the size fourteens were tight and the few size sixteens that even existed in this new world where a size ten/twelve was an extra large, fit in the hips, but gapped in the arms and bust. The size-two saleswoman suggested I check out the plus size department.

Though I had always been a twelve, sometimes a ten, even in maternity clothes, I wasn't any longer. Eventually I found a black, boat-necked, cotton designer sheath with five percent spandex in size fourteen and a black Spanx that pretty much went from neck to knee.

My mother would have laughed and called it a full body girdle. I could hear her goofy laughter in my mind. She cackled like a chicken when she laughed. We all teased her about it, but my father was the worst. He used to say, "Beatrice. You're going to lay an egg any minute."

She had died five years ago, gone quietly one night just about six months after my father. You hear about those couples who grow old together and one dies first and other soon after. Both quietly. I had thought Mike and I would be one of those couples. Still I missed my mother, especially now without Mike. She would have been my rock. I made a mental note to call my sister May tonight. There were only the two of us Randolphs left, and I hadn't been very good about calling her back lately, and still she called regularly from back east. She knew how lost I was.

I sat in the Café, eyeing the fifty-grams-of-fat, six hundred calorie muffins—chocolate and carrot, both with pecan-crusted tops—the thick cheese and meat paninis, and wedges of bacon quiche, but only ordered two big glasses of iced tea with extra lemon. When I finished them off, I gathered my shopping bags and took one of the silver, snaking escalators up to a beautifully displayed, truly yummy, designer handbag department. I had decided to have leather for lunch.

I understood I was not in a healthy state, that Harrie had a point, so I took up exercising. Powerwalking to be exact, which was actually better than running over all the city's steep hills and curving streets. I wasn't certain I should even start running in my fifties, and since that sounded like a really good excuse, I used it.

I had hated track and field in high school and tried to ditch the class as often as I could. Back in the seventies, when jogging overtook the nation and health came to the forefront of our social culture, there was this great Henny Youngman joke: "Everyone's jogging. I can't jog. My cigarette goes out and the ice cubes fall out of my drink."

Even now it made me smile. To make Harrie happy, I bought a set of weights—an excuse to also get a cute little pink and black Prada gym bag—and a couple of books and DVDs on strength training, and learned I had muscles in places I didn't know could be sore. I took pictures of myself lifting weights, then contorted on the floor in mock pain with a digital camera and emailed them to Harrie.

I ate grapefruit for breakfast and more lettuce and cottage cheese than anyone without long ears and a cottontail should. I snacked on frozen grapes, and if I ate any more fish, especially tuna, I would eventually have so much mercury in my system I'd be as mad as a hatter and run through the streets yanking out my hair. Then I remembered I didn't have much hair left to yank out.

The whole idea of hiring a trainer didn't appeal to me. The word trainer brought to mind the image of a man with a whip. But my goal was set: no Spanx. So I took up powerwalking through the streets of San Francisco . . . mornings or afternoons, and I even bought a bathroom scale and set it to match the weight on Harrie's vile professional scale, which I still think was wrong.

After the first few days of exercising, I made good friends with eight hundred milligram ibuprofen. By the second week, I found I enjoyed walking all over the city, as long as I stayed off congested streets where you could smell the exhaust, and I stayed away from the cable car line because of the temptation to hop onboard.

I was sleeping better. Soon, my cleaning service actually had some work to do when they came. As I slowly powered and lifted and starved away the pounds, my mood changed and I started to laugh more.

Mike only appeared twice more, once in the kitchen and again in our bedroom, and both times I put on my athletic shoes and walked away. When I came home and flopped on the bed, sweaty and exhausted, I was more concerned about a long shower than my fear of what I might see when I came out.

By Mickey's graduation, I could wear the black dress without the body girdle, and the family made it through the event with only a few tears.

Publicly, the Cantrells stood together, and the pride we had for Mickey and his valedictorian speech superseded anything else. That day, I came home thinking that we had each taken on the role of standing in for Mike instead of

251

mourning his absence. Both Scott and Phillip had done overtime trying to make up for Mike's absence and by the end of the day, their jokes were a little harsher than normal and I thought Scott was annoyed with Phillip's mouth.

It did seem that we were changing how we dealt with life, and for the first time I wondered if we could ever truly heal.

Summer came in and Mickey was working at the company five days a week. I dropped by in spite of the fact that Scott thought I needed protecting, and I began to have our Sunday dinners again. But now I seldom served lasagna, because I had lost the extra weight and was almost hooked on exercise.

One sunny afternoon I was out for a long power-walk, and I took the route past the old apartment. I hadn't driven past it for a couple of weeks. I had just picked up my pace and was trying to get my heart rate up, when I rounded the corner.

Across the street, a large area was sectioned off with construction tape and big yellow barricades. Behind them were a group of giant orange construction machines. A couple of workers in hardhats were smoking on the corner.

"Hey guys," I said, waving away the smoke. "What's going on here?"

"That old brick warehouse is coming down."

My stomach was instantly somewhere around my ankles. I didn't say anything, but could feel something inside of me just snap, and I turned back around.

A crane was shifting position and I could read the side. *Golden State Demolition Co, Inc.*

Before me, covered in graffiti, was the beginning of my life with Mike. Somehow, in my mind over the years, this building had stood for us, where we'd been and from where we'd come. That it was still there, unchanged, fooled me into making it a symbol of us. Had this hap+pened before Mike died, I might have only been disappointed. But now I wanted to scream hysterically.

Instead, I casually made my way around the barricades, went under the construction tape, and powerwalked straight toward our old apartment.

Chapter Eighteen

Jail was a new experience for me. Somehow I expected it to look different in real life from all those television cop shows, but I was wrong. It looked the same: all gray; cement and metal, along with extremely questionable janitorial services.

The biggest difference between television jail and real-life jail was sensory. Sight and sound were the only senses you used to watch TV. Smell was not part of the equation. As long as I live, I will never forget the smell of jail. It is uniquely vile.

Pine-Sol and Clorox would have done wonders for San Francisco's slammer, which I was told was only a holding cell, a large square, barred, fifteen by fifteen foot windowless box, where I sat incarcerated with an interesting collection of other female misdemeanants. If I hadn't attacked the poor police officer who tried to pull me off the building, I would have only been ticketed for misdemeanor and let go. Various officers told me this at least seven different times.

There were six of us in the cell. However I was the only one with an embroidered designer logo on my sports clothes. When they first locked me away and I turned around and faced the others, I was a little nervous. That was the only moment when I honestly might have regretted my actions. (Well, biting the cop wasn't good either because when they first took me in, hand-cuffed, I had to get a blood test. It hadn't been much of a bite. They didn't think I was very funny when I told them I'd had my rabies shot.)

From the corner of my eye, I caught one of my cellmates eyeing my navy jacket with the gold charms on the zippers and matching striped track pants. Her name was Suki, and she wasn't young, in her forties, and had long wavy hair shot with gray that hung halfway down her back.

She wore a 1980's multi-colored Michael

Jackson jacket with big padded shoulders, and when we talked she explained she could wear two or three cashmere sweaters under it and no one at Saks or Neiman's could tell she was stealing. Suki was a professional shoplifter. And an eBay Power Seller. She was also a single mom of three.

The cell's youngest occupant was Danica, a law student overloaded with student loans and who was arrested on a warrant for twenty seven unpaid parking tickets. She was facing three days in jail and fines she couldn't pay.

Cherry and Lola were streetwalkers; neither looked like Julia Roberts, though they both could snap their chewing gum like champions. My children would have considered that as my punishment, since listening to someone pop their gum was one of my pet peeves.

Willow was the saddest specimen among us. Willow was her adopted name, one she'd taken to using in 1963. She was born Agnes Willamenia Gunther, and she was a drunk and a street person, beaten and abused over a lifetime, a woman who started off protesting the war and did too many drugs in the sixties.

With her wild and dirty gray hair and skin like Genoa sausage, she was the kind of crazy old woman who stood on a corner and shouted, or slowly pushed a grocery cart with all her worldly belongings up the city's streets. She reeked of unwashed skin and cheap liquor, but she talked constantly, slurring her words and asking questions with a lisp, because one bad man years back had knocked her front teeth out.

She told us stories that were probably not even near the truth. If she wrote a book about her life, she could go on Oprah.

When she heard why I was there, she stood up and banged on the bars and chanted over and over, "Death to the Establishment! Save that building!" I had a feeling she had said those same words decades back, perhaps when she had barely begun her downhill journey to the bleak place she was now.

I didn't know how long I'd been locked up, because when I first arrived the officers took my watch, jewelry and keys. But we were all sitting around the cell, playing three truths and a lie, when a female officer came to let me out.

As I walked out of the cell, all the women gathered at the bars, looking at me like children on the Kindertransport.

" 'Bye, March!"

"Remember! Sunflower Boutique on eBay!"

Pop! "Hang in there, girl."

"You tell those kids of yours Cherry says to back off!"

"Don't you get your*th*elf thrown in here again, mi*thy*," Willow said.

The door closed on their collective voices and I

walked down the barren hallway where another somber guard let us out.

Scott, Phillip and Molly stood across a large room with dull green paint and dirty windows, waiting, my judges and jurists. It looked to me as if they had already decided the verdict.

Molly was holding my Chanel tote to her chest, so she must have gone by the house and picked it up for me. When I was walking, I didn't take anything with me but a few bills and my keys.

"Hey, Mom." Phillip slipped his arm around me and gave me a hug.

"Are you all right?" Scott asked and he sounded just like his dad, concerned, not critical.

"I'm fine," I said more sharply than I meant to. I expected them to assume I was a mess and I was defensive.

At a small counter I picked up a manila envelope with my personal items. I put on my watch, but not my gold hoops.

"I stopped and picked up your purse and the spare car keys," Molly said more kindly than she had spoken to me in a long time.

With mixed emotions I took my purse. "Thanks."

My kids turned and started to walk away, assuming I would follow behind.

"Wait a second would you?" I dumped the contents of my purse on the counter and picked up my wallet and checkbook.

"What are you doing?" Molly asked.

"None of your business," I said calmly, looking through my wallet. "Please wait over there."

Since I hadn't bitten or punched or kicked the cop behind the window, he was willing to give me some of those large envelopes, and I left a gift for each woman, scribbling their name on the outside of an envelope before I sealed it. For Willow, a grocery card for a hundred dollars that I'd won at the checkout a few weeks back. I was afraid to give her money and hoped maybe she would get some food with it instead of booze. What I really wanted to give her was a lifetime of baths.

My gold hoops went to Cherry, and my makeup bag filled with Chanel makeup for Lola. I wrote a check to Danica for her twenty-seven hundred dollar fine, and I checked my purse to make certain the black Chanel authenticity card was in the zipper pocket, handed my tote to the officer and told him it was to go to Suki Collins. I would watch for it on the Internet under the eBay listing of Sunflower Boutique, and maybe bid on it.

Some new fire was lit inside of me, something I hadn't felt in months. I owed those women for my short time in that cell. My struggles, my pain were something I could overcome. Mired in my great grief, I was all tied up in my head and my heart, and I let all that stay there, held it close to me and refused to let it go, and it made me into someone I didn't like. In their shoes, what would I have done? Perhaps made the same bad choices they had made?

I crammed the rest of my stuff in my pockets and walked right over to my kids. "Let's go." Once outside, I asked, "Who's taking me home?"

Molly said, "Scott."

And at the same time Scott said, "Me."

"Great. Here's the deal. I made a mistake. We're going to drop this whole thing. Right now. It might take me some time, but I will be fine. I loved your father and I will always love your father, but now I have to love me." I stopped and faced them. "Got it?"

They nodded like obedient children, or those little plastic standing dachshunds people line up on their Impala dashboards.

"Good. I need you to stop by the pharmacy on the way home, Scott. I have a prescription to fill."

And, I thought, a life to figure out.

PART THREE

A single event can awaken in us a stranger
totally unknown to us.

—*Antoine de Saint-Exupery*

Chapter Nineteen

Thanksgiving was only a week away and Mickey would be coming home for the first time since late August, when we drove his car down to get him settled in at the UCLA campus. In October, Phillip, Scott, Molly and I went to see him for parents' weekend, my older children feeling as if they needed to fill in for Mike. Any concern I had over his adjustment to college life was put to rest once I saw him. He was happy and had adapted so well, and he was still only a short flight away from us. He had a good group of roommates and his grades were great.

That Mike missed this was tough, and the thought took me back to my elder kids' parents' weekends, those times when Mickey had gone with Mike and me.

I wondered if being away from home now that his dad was gone was not, in truth, the best thing for him, and perhaps had some part in his choice of a university. I had worried about him living away from home, but maybe he was running away like I had been for a long while, not too far away, but still running away.

I did feel as if I had some control of myself again, and perhaps I owed it all to Harric. I took a little pill that numbed me enough, and to my surprise I now had a size eight body with muscle definition. Weights were a good thing, and I was working pretty diligently toward a great six-pack. My friends were amazed at the changes in me. Ellie spent a fortune turning one of her many guest suites into a full gym, and she often met me for my walks. Lately, she could even keep up. MC was still making excuses.

A couple of weeks ago, I'd emailed Suki on eBay and sent her that size fourteen black dress along with some of my old size ten and twelve designer clothes. My friends, on my advice, did the same. I was on a mission to keep Suki out of jail and away from shoplifting.

Between all of us, I had hoped she could make enough on eBay to support her kids and even keep her daughters in ballet classes.

But now, in the last two weeks, I had the feeling things around me were starting to go on the rocks again. For some reason, Molly wasn't calling me back—nothing new in our relationship—and it used to bug the heck out of me, which was why she probably did it. I never did that to my own mother. I had always called home every single week.

I wondered what I had done now, but since I'd been taking Harrie's prescription, I didn't care as much. No doubt I had done something really horrific, like giving birth to her.

Still, I left repeated messages at Molly's apartment, on her work voicemail, and on her cell. The clock had finally slogged its way to seven a.m. when I felt I could call and maybe reach her. I picked up the cordless phone and punched in my daughter's home number as I walked out the French doors and onto the brick courtyard.

We'd had an Indian summer, so the planters were still lush with ferns and fichus trees, a couple of good-sized gardenia bushes, some hanging fuchsias and impatiens, which were finally starting to turn. I picked off the brown flowers and leaves as I listened the to the phone ring, one, two, three, four, five times until I heard the familiar click of the answering machine.

"This is Molly. I can't come to the phone right now. Leave a message and I'll call you back."

"This is Molly's mother, who has left six messages on this machine. Remember me? The woman who in spite of the AMA's nutritional guidelines on nitrates—and your grandmother's incessant harping—fed you Kraft macaroni and cheese, hot dogs, and grilled cheese and bacon sandwiches for the first seven years of your life?"

I paused, suddenly frustrated. Hurt, really. "Molly, please . . . Call me." Great, I thought, now I sounded needy and desperate.

"Look," I snapped out of nowhere. "I want to know if you're coming for Thanksgiving. Call me or I'll send the police out to find you!" I hung up and stared at the phone.

Lovely, a ticked off Molly wouldn't call me back.

Ever hopeful, though, I waited an antsy hour for a return phone call before I finally put on my athletic shoes and walked to the neighborhood gym. I had a trainer now named Rodney, who had a body like Mr. Universe.

One of the better things about Thanksgiving was how the whole house smelled like generations of family recipes—apples and cinnamon, sage and thyme, sausage and onions; the strong scent of bourbon in my grandmother's sweet potato soufflé, and from the large cocktail glass in my hand.

I added some Diet Coke and a fresh lime wedge to the mix and walked into the dining room.

When they built these manses back in the late 19th century, the dining room was the single room most used for entertaining, so it was enormous by modern American standards. Ours was thirty-five feet long and had a five-tiered crystal chandelier that had come to San Francisco around Cape Horn, and a hand-painted, twelve-foot coffered ceiling.

It had taken the decorator a good year and a half to find a table that would work in the room. I hadn't wanted one with seating for twenty or more, so she had to search for a substantial table where our family could sit down and not have to shout at each other from opposite ends of the room.

She was a smart cookie. Her answer was to divide the room and it became part sitting room, with a set of settees and matching chairs for conversation seating, along with a huge built-in antique mahogany bar and service area, flanked by a set of mirrored French cabinets filled with glimmering crystal. The rest of the room was formal dining, dominated by a Venetian table with four inlaid leaves and big, high-backed Scalamandré-upholstered armchairs.

I had to admit, as I adjusted the place settings and moved the chairs and Tyler's toddler chair, that the room was probably the most elegant in the whole house. But other than the occasional business or dinner party, we used it more casually set for our monthly Sunday dinners, and then once a year at Thanksgiving.

Thanksgiving was tomorrow. I had changed the place settings because Molly had finally left a message with some excuse about being too busy to call, and to let me know she was bringing someone to dinner. I reset the table for ten.

Molly was bringing someone. I hoped she was bringing a date and not a girlfriend. It had been a long time since she brought a boyfriend home, since her junior year of college. I thought perhaps my daughter could use a good man in her life. I wanted for her what Mike and I had. I was a lucky woman when it came to men. I had found the best one.

I have never loved Thanksgiving, other than it's a good excuse to drink my coffee from a mug shaped like a turkey. (I should have put my bourbon in the turkey mug.) Mike, on the other hand, lived for the Thanksgiving holiday. He played the *Friends* Thanksgiving DVDs and laughed every time Monica or Joey ended up with a turkey on their heads, and we owned three copies of the movie *Home For the Holidays*, where a turkey ended up in someone's lap.

Turkey was his thing. Every year he ordered fresh turkeys for all his employees and handed each of them out like reborn Scrooge. This year, Scott and Phillip gave away the turkeys, but I suspected it wasn't quite the same.

Over the years, the things my husband had done to our poor turkeys in the name of a Thanksgiving dinner was the kind of stuff that made "remember-that-year-Dad" jokes as much a part of our dinner ritual as giving thanks.

He had split and barbequed them, smoked them, spitted them, doused them in bottles of German beer, deep fried them, injected them with Cajun seasoning and fried them, and brined them. I found myself smiling. I had been a very lucky woman for a long, long time.

This year, Scott would be sitting in Mike's chair. I made out the place cards and adjusted what had been our traditional seating. I hadn't fallen apart while doing either. When I thought of

Mike now, I did so with a wistfulness or snippet of joy at some funny moment I cherished or wanted to remember. Doing so made me feel as if part of him was still part of me.

I didn't sob anymore—Harrie's little pills—but I admit there was an element of happiness completely missing from me. Somewhere deep inside me was numb.

I sprinkled the small copper foil leaves and corn candy my granddaughter loved around the clusters of glass candles and floral centerpiece, picked up my drink, and turned out the lights.

Mickey was out tonight with his high school buddies, who were home for the holiday and they hadn't seen each other since they all went off to their respective colleges. I expected him home pretty late.

The house was quiet again, the new normal—a silence that was natural to me nowadays and didn't scare me like it used to. In the kitchen, I cleaned up and set the coffeemaker to start brewing early, then turned down the lights and headed for the stairs.

The doorbell rang so I checked my watch; it was almost midnight. I padded to the door, my hand automatically on the doorknob, but I stopped and looked outside. My head swum and I almost vomited.

A cop was standing at the door.

Chapter Twenty

"You gave Mickey the keys to a hundred thousand dollar car?" Scott was standing in the driveway and yelling at me. "What were you thinking?"

"He wasn't hurt badly, Scott," I said to him. I was still not completely over the horrific, dizzying dread I felt the night before, when I opened that front door. Just thinking about it shook me up. "The accident was not his fault."

"But it was Dad's Porsche." Scott was frustrated. "The car's a mess."

"It's insured. So is the driver who's at fault. But what matters is your brother is okay. He has a black eye, a sore shoulder from the seatbelt, and a small cut on his forehead. That's it."

He muttered something again about a hundred thousand dollar car, which made me angry.

"Ask yourself this: if he were hurt, or worse, would you be standing here talking about the damned car?"

Scott closed his eyes and took a long breath. "You're right." His shoulders sagged and he walked over and put his arms around me. His aftershave smelled light and spicy. "I'm sorry, Mom."

Scott was stressed. I knew he and Phillip were

still having problems and Renee was three weeks late and looked like she was ready to explode. Her doctor wanted to take the baby by C-section yesterday, but Renee had begged her to please let her go through the holiday weekend, and after some monitoring, her doctor had agreed.

However, I remembered how tough that last month of pregnancy was. I expect that Scott had already been standing in for much of the parenting with the other two, along with the business and his troubles there, although there seemed to be a holiday truce between Phil and him. I decided I needed to give my son some slack. However, he was right. Why had I given Mickey the keys to Mike's Porsche? Where was my head? I frowned. Perhaps Harriet's little pills and their numbing effects were affecting my common sense.

"The car will be repaired, and I will not give Mickey the keys again. I made a mistake. It's Thanksgiving." I stepped out of his arms. "Come inside, and be sure to tell your brother every-thing's okay. He's still shaken up."

Scott's breath came out in an almost indiscernible moan of pain.

"Last night we were really lucky." I cupped his face in my hands like I had when he was young. "It's just a car. A machine. Not a person. Remember that when you're talking to him." I linked my arm with his and we went inside together.

An hour later when everyone was there but Molly, the kitchen buzzed with chattering and my boys were cheering on a football game in the other room, sometimes coming out to sneak a bite of something.

I basted the turkey, closed the oven, and poured myself a glass of good wine. I had remembered to open the bottles so they could breathe. Mike would have been happy. I leaned against the counter with a dishtowel over my shoulder and took a minute to relax.

Renee and Keely were sitting at the kitchen table while Tyler napped in my room and Miranda did ballet leaps out in the courtyard before she dressed the poor cat up in a holiday outfit made of orange kitchen towels, bag clips, and a pumpkin shaped oven mitt.

"Hi, Auntie Molly!" Miranda shouted.

I turned around just as Molly walked in through the back doors, laughing and holding hands with a stunningly handsome, and way-too-old for her Spider Olsen.

I finished off the wine in my glass as if it were Evian.

"We're here!" Molly called out. Within minutes everyone was in the room talking at once, my sons welcoming Olsen like an old friend and no one seeming to question the two of them being together.

I had been had.

Spider looked at me over my daughter's red head and smiled charmingly. He pulled himself away from her and crossed the room "March," he said and handed me two dozen amazing tangerine colored roses I so badly wanted to hate. "Thanks for inviting me."

It took everything I had in me not to say "I didn't invite you." I smiled instead, but it felt brittle. "Well, this is a surprise."

Molly shot me a look that almost dared me to say something, which I knew now explained exactly why she had been avoiding me.

"Happy Thanksgiving," I said to him as sweetly as I could, not wanting to ruin the day.

Molly had just lost the father she adored, and now suddenly she's dating this older man? A man who I knew was hard on women? At the casino he'd said he was a grandfather. My daughter was only twenty four.

I turned away, feeling sick, as they headed for the TV room and walked over to the sink and stood there, gripping the sides. My prescription bottle sat next to the soap dish so I opened the bottle, went over to the island, refilled my glass and washed the medication down with another glass of Mike's best wine.

Nothing would help me. I understood all too well what had been happening when I was self-absorbed by my grief. There wasn't enough Zoloft in the world to numb me to the fact that

Molly had not been watching out for me that night in our house in Tahoe. She had been watching Spider.

Everyone was sitting at the table, hungry and expectant, when I walked into the dining room carrying a big platter of turkey. Phil got up quickly and took it from me. "Wow, look at this," he said, holding the heavy platter up.

"Yeah, amazing," Scott said. "It's not smoked, fried, or pickled."

The kids laughed and I said, "Your father would love this bird." I had to admit that sitting on that huge silver platter, this turkey looked to be the most golden brown, perfectly-roasted bird I'd ever seen. Even with half of it sliced, it looked like the November cover of *Bon Appetite*.

Phillip set the platter on the table and the serving fork fell on the floor, so I went down to pick it up, and saw Spider's hand resting halfway up my daughter's thigh.

When I straightened, I could feel the imaginary red horns sprout on my head. I was already holding the long meat fork in my fist, ready to leap across the table and stab him in his black heart. But someone suggested we needed to say grace, so I had to sit down and behave. I couldn't murder him during a prayer, even though the Good Lord and I had been on shaky ground for a while.

So I tried for a rare second or two to actually speak to God. *Save my daughter, save my daughter, save my daughter* I mentally chanted. After all, He had saved my son last night.

But the moment was gone with an "amen" and it was immediately chaos with wine bottles and serving bowls passing hand over hand, while gravy boats and butter plates and bread baskets all made the rounds of the table, everyone talking at once.

"This is the best." Phil held the serving bowl and dumped half of it on his plate. "Sausage stuffing."

"Oh, Phillip, don't eat it all," Keely said. She took the bowl and went out to the kitchen to refill it.

"Oh my God . . . no!" Renee stood up quickly.

"Renee? What are you doing? You don't even like stuffing." Scott said, frowning at his wife. He looked up at her. "What's wrong with you?"

"My water broke." Renee looked down, helpless, then up, her face showing she was ready to cry. "Oh, Mom, I ruined your good chair."

"It's fine," I said, moving quickly to her side. "Are you having contractions?"

She nodded. "Since last night."

"What?" Scott burst out, and Renee nodded, then burst into tears.

Tyler looked at his mother, then at his father, and his small face turned bright red and he started wailing. "It's okay sweetheart," I said, trying to calm him.

"Since last *night?*" Scott was not happy. "Why the hell didn't you tell me?"

"Because it's Thanksgiving," Renee said sobbing.

I turned away from Tyler and said, "Stop shouting at her, Scott." Then I took a deep breath and added more calmly, "Take it easy. We'll time her contractions and then call her doctor."

Renee moaned and doubled over, gripping the back of the chair.

"There's a good one." Scott looked at his watch but forgot about his wife.

"For heaven's sakes, don't leave her standing there. Help her onto that sofa."

Tyler screamed again and Miranda told him to shut up and danced around the table plucking up the candy corn she'd been eating all afternoon, and spinning around the room in circles from all the sugar.

Renee grabbed her belly and I could see the contraction writhe across her bulging stomach. I remembered that pain even all those years later.

"One minute apart," Scott said. "Can that be right?" He looked up from his watch while Renee dug her nails into his hand.

"Mickey," I said quickly. "Go call 911."

"Okay." He dropped his bread roll and got up, but stopped suddenly and squinted at me from his good eye. "What for?"

"Renee's baby!" I shouted at him. "It's okay, Tyler. It's okay. Your mommy's fine. G-Mo didn't mean to yell. Phillip, stop shoveling food in your mouth and go see about your wife. And you, Molly, tear your goo-goo eyes away from Spider, who is old enough to be your father, by the way, and pay attention to what's going on in here." Miranda was spinning toward her parents. "Will someone *please* take these kids?"

Everyone sprang into action at once. But when Molly sent Spider over to take Miranda out of the room, I shouted, "No! She's too young." And I handed him Tyler.

"Mother!" My daughter gave me a horrified look.

But Spider laughed at me.

"I'm sorry," I said distractedly, waving my hand in the air. But I wasn't.

Keely had walked back into the room before Phil could go find her and she looked at Renee, took in her contracting belly, red face, and pain-filled moans, and the blood drained from Keely's face.

I knew that look. "Catch your wife, Phillip. She's going to faint."

"I need to push!" Renee cried.

"No!" everyone shouted at her at once.

I could hear the ambulance sirens so close. Thank God the fire station was only a few blocks away. Within minutes the paramedics were

277

inside, bags on the floor as they hovered over Renee and I just stood there, having a private conversation with God. I figured He just might have had something to do with the fact that on my husband's favorite holiday, at four twenty-two p.m., Michael David Cantrell the Third came into the world.

Chapter Twenty One

"You have got to help me do something about your sister." I paced the floor in front of Phillip's desk.

"If you'll remember, Ma, I tried to sell her to the neighbor when I was ten."

"I'm serious." My voice sounded strident. It was the Monday after Thanksgiving and I'd kept my grandkids over the weekend to help out Renee and Scott, and on top of everything, I hadn't slept much. I'd been panicking about Molly and waking up at three a.m., and I'd seen Mike again. My nerves were shot.

"I don't get involved in her love life," Phillip looked away and shuffled some papers. "She'd eat me alive."

"You can't possibly be afraid of your little sister."

"Oh, and you aren't? She's run the family since she came home from the hospital. Besides, she's a big girl. She can make her own mistakes."

"See? You think it's a mistake, too. Spider's way too old for her, and she's vulnerable, after just losing your dad, and the fact that she hasn't had a relationship in a while. I'm really worried about this."

"Spider's a good guy."

I ignored him. "She would have listened to your dad, so she might listen to you or Scott."

"No. She won't listen to us because we're not talking to her about Spider Olsen."

"I haven't even talked to Scott yet."

"He and I already talked. Mom, sit down. You're making me dizzy. Scott and I agreed not to get involved. Besides, as grandpa used to say, the horse is out of that barn."

I sat and crossed my legs. I knew what Phillip was saying. Molly was already sleeping with Spider. "I know. I could tell."

"How could you tell?"

"Besides the fact that he was groping her under the dinner table? Mothers just know these things."

"If that's true, then how come you didn't know they were together in Tahoe?"

"I'd be willing to bet she hadn't slept with him when we were in Tahoe."

Phillip frowned at me and asked, "You can actually tell when she's slept with someone?"

"I can usually tell when all my children are sleeping with someone."

His face was priceless.

"You and Julie Gardner after the prom. Angela Winston. Jennifer Wasinski. Scott and Crystal McCafferty." I didn't mention Molly.

She had been a freshman in high school and fallen hard for a boy who broke her heart, and she would never talk to me about it. She talked to Mike, not about sex, but about being in love and being so hurt when the boy dumped her for a blonde cheerleader.

Mike told me he was certain the punk who broke Molly's heart dropped her for a girl who would give out. I never told him Molly was the one who had given out. I had no proof, just instinct and a certain look, but I knew.

For a long time I would broach the subject of boys when Molly and I had some time alone, but she always changed the subject, as if talking to me about dating or sex broke some kind of teenaged taboo.

Before she was twelve, I gave her the mother-daughter sex explanation and risk talk, and later again the one about self-respect and owning your body and your choices. Because I wanted her to understand the value and power a woman had, and that she didn't have to bargain with her body. That she heard about the facts of life from me was important, to understand what I wanted her to know about love and sex, and love versus sex.

But I tried to make her understand she could

always come to me about her problems, about boys or men or heartaches. But she never did. The fact that she wouldn't talk to me was painful and made me feel like somehow, unknowingly, I had failed my daughter.

Phillip came around from his desk and settled his hands on my shoulders and massaged them. "You look a million miles away."

I leaned my head back and looked up at him and just sighed.

"She'll be okay, Mom. She will. They're probably not serious. Just let it go."

I didn't say anything more. My sons were not going to help me on this. They didn't even agree with me that there was a problem. I felt as if I were fighting some kind of unwritten sexist code, something genetic that came in the male chromosome. Except that I know Mike would have agreed with me.

Phillip was only half right. I was certain Spider wasn't serious, but I was worried Molly was.

The whole family went to Tahoe five days before Christmas, all staying together and boarding every day like we always had. But this was the first time without Mike.

Back when the company was beginning to see stronger and stronger profits, Mike made the decision to close the company, warehouses and factory from December twentieth until after the

New Year, with full pay for all employees. It was his bonus to them and their families.

Our holiday routine was pretty much the same, and we planned to drive home on January second. But this year we had Trey, officially Michael the Third, the newest Cantrell. His Uncle Phil had taken to calling him Turkey, and at first Renee looked horrified, as if she were afraid the nickname would stick. Until Scott warned, "Payback is hell, little bro. You're going to be a father at some point. You'd better watch out."

But when it came to teasing, nothing stopped Phil. I had a hunch poor Trey was going to be called Turkey for many, many years to come.

And Spider was seemingly inseparable from Molly. I kept wishing it were an Olympic year so he'd be gone commentating half a world away. Instead, he was included in everything we did, including Christmas Eve and morning. My sons continued to welcome him, perhaps even more than before, but I liked to think that was because his ski line and endorsements had sent our profits higher than anyone had predicted.

Scott admitted at the year-end board meeting that Mike had been smart to sign Spider to a longer term deal than Scott had originally wanted. They had argued over it at one point because of the huge amount of money. Now, compared to sales and orders, it looked like we'd stolen him for peanuts.

And Spider seemed determined to be accepted.

But there was still tension between my two older sons, though they both spoke of the company with pride and of its future with enthusiasm. I wondered if they could find a way to a true partnership, or if there would always be differences, just because they were so different.

Thanks to my grandkids and kids, Christmas worked. My family was raucous and challenging and fun when we were together. We laughed, played silly games or watched movies at night, and the days of celebration passed for me with only fleeting dark moments, late at night when I was alone in our bed. The rest of the time I was able to assuage the black hole of my loneliness by spending a lot of time on the mountain.

Chapter Twenty Two

A light snow was beginning to fall when I came to the bottom of a run and booked it toward the lift, which was almost empty. I figured I had plenty of time for a few more runs. The conditions were close to perfect; there was no wind and it was snowing. I loved this kind of snow—big, lightly floating flakes that made me want to catch them with my mouth like pieces of popcorn.

It was New Year's Eve and the crowds were leaving the mountain early. When the next chair came around, there was no one else but a guy in the singles line, so the two of us took one quad chair up toward the top trails.

We sat with just a few inches between us, surrounded by the utter quiet of snow falling on a mountain top. The snowflakes were drifting like feathers down through the air.

"It's so quiet when it snows like this," I said aloud. "Almost as if the snow makes everything it covers breathless." The words just came into my head and out of my mouth; it was the kind of thing I would have said to Mike, but never to a stranger. I was instantly embarrassed and could feel my flush. "I'm sorry," I mumbled and couldn't look at him.

"I read somewhere that snow can absorb at least twenty five percent of sound," he said to me in an amazing voice that made me have to look at him. "So you're right, snow makes the land breathless." His voice surprised me; it was slow and Southern, the kind of cowboy drawl you expected to call you "Sugar."

I was thankful to him for not making me feel like more of a fool, so I smiled.

He was decked out all in blue and wearing a knit hat over dark hair. He looked oddly familiar in the way some strangers do, that kind of déjà vu thing that has you scanning back in your mind for some kind of concrete recollection.

He had pale blue eyes with laugh lines in the

corners, dark stubble over a strong jaw, great nose, and was really, really good-looking in that edgy, outdoor-rough, Marlboro Man ad kind of way. He looked to be a good decade younger than Spider, and I idly thought that based on looks and age, I wished this guy had met my daughter first.

"The snow is perfect," I said for conversation, perhaps because I just wanted to hear his voice again.

"Sure is, but not too many of those folks down there seem to care."

Behind us, way down in the parking lot, people were gathering in dark clusters, packing up gear and driving away, and there were very few skiers and boarders coming down the top runs.

"Let the fools leave," I said. "I'd rather take a few more great runs than start partying. Been there, done that."

"I hear ya," he said. "Back when I was twenty two, I celebrated New Year's and completely lost the rest of 1989."

I laughed and did the math. He was forty one. Molly was almost twenty five. Sixteen years older? Before Spider Olsen, I might have thought that was too old for her. Now, compared to a tomcat player who was twenty five years older, and a grandfather, this guy was a kid. And frankly, I could listen to him talk for days.

"I'm here with my family," I offered, looking

for wife and girlfriend information. The trouble with winter sports was that gloves hid the ring finger.

"I'm all by my lonesome," he said, dragging out that last word as if it was part of a song.

I looked at him for a second—he really had the most incredible eyes—and said, "You know, I have a really good-looking twenty-four, almost twenty-five year old daughter."

"I just bet you do."

I leaned back a bit as I looked at him, gauging him. "Seriously."

"Seriously?" he repeated, looking me in the eye. "Then thanks, but I like my women a little less fresh and just out of the gate."

"Oh, I get it." I laughed. "You like the stale, barn-sour older types, probably what? Thirty?"

With a soft, knowing grin he said, "Tell me why you're trying to set up your daughter with a stranger who could be big trouble."

"Are you big trouble?"

"There are a lot of folks who would swear I was. But they don't know me now. I got over causing trouble a long time ago."

I liked his honesty, until he said, "You evaded the question about your poor daughter."

"My poor daughter is dating an older man, older than dirt." I couldn't keep the disgust from my voice.

He laughed. "So you're desperate."

"You have no idea. It gets worse. He's been divorced three times."

"Some folks just keep trying, thinking eventually they'll get marriage right with someone new. Usually the problem most likely isn't the need for someone new." From the way he said it, I knew he wasn't talking about the world at large; this was a man who owned up to the failures in his past. "What does her father have to say about it?" he asked.

"I'm a widow." I could say it without aching pain now. I'd had enough practice.

To his credit, he didn't give me that look I hated. "Then it can't be easy to sit back alone and watch," he said kindly.

I stared down at my hands. "You must think I'm nuts. Here I assume you're not attached. I try to set you up with my daughter. I don't even know why I'm telling you all this."

"Because you wanted to use me to save your daughter, who I'm sure would be real delighted to know about this conversation we're having."

I laughed out loud. "She would kill me." I liked him. I held out my hand. "I'm March Cantrell."

His grin faded and he frowned slightly, but took my hand, then slowly scanned the Cantrell logos on everything from the knit beanie on my head to the neon graphics on the board I rode. I was a poster child for the company that carried our name.

"Cantrell Sports?"

I held up my hand. "Guilty."

"Your husband was Mike Cantrell," he said flatly.

Before I could say anything, the chair stopped with a sudden jerk and I grabbed his arm instead of the bar.

"Whoa."

We hung there, slightly rocking. Lift chairs had glitches and stopped, and until they could get them running again, you were stuck there. We dangled above one of the steepest, rockiest parts of the mountain.

I bent slightly over the side and looked at the small strip of soft snow below us and the jagged gray rocks on either side. "That's a long way down. At least there's no wind."

He started talking to me, quietly at first, easily. He raised horses, which didn't surprise me, considering the way he spoke. I wondered if he had been on the rodeo circuit at some point, roping or riding. He was in board clothes, not jeans, but I expected off the mountain he wore boots and a belt with a buckle you couldn't miss.

He told me about his son, a twenty two year old musician and a guitarist, who had studied music abroad and was touring Europe with a country band. I did the math over again. He had been a young father.

"What made him go overseas?"

288

"The Royal Academy of Music. His mother is British. He calls me when he can, but . . ." he laughed slightly, "he's twenty two. I'm not at the top of the list. He spent summers at the ranch—I own a place outside of Sparks—but I usually have to track him down to see him for holidays."

"I would hate to be without my kids at Christmas," I said. "Although this year we're without Mike, and it isn't the same. There's that empty spot to remind you someone's missing."

"Your husband," he stopped for a moment as if he couldn't find the right words. He looked at me for a long moment and then said, "There was something in the Reno paper about him passing. It was tied to an article about the boarding event last winter."

"It was a horrible car accident. He was in the exact wrong place at the exact wrong moment. That haunts me sometimes, you know? I wonder if only his plane had been earlier or later, or if only he'd hit a couple of red lights along the way." I didn't say anything more, but turned and looked at him.

I wondered what he was thinking about because his look was distant and painful, almost grieving, as if what I said opened some old wounds for him, too.

I studied him, and he finally looked at me, and I thought an understanding passed between us. He got where I was coming from. I didn't have to say anything and neither did he.

"My son preferred his mother's people for Christmas." He changed the subject back on topic and shrugged. "I understood that. They're good folks."

"Your ex-in-laws?"

"I wasn't married to his mother."

"Oh," I said flatly and wanted to bite back the words. I didn't want to sound old-fashioned and judgmental and wasn't sure how I had come across.

"I suspect your daughter's out of the offering now." He laughed, clearly teasing me.

"That depends," I said. "On how you treat your women."

He said he learned that hard lesson a long time ago, and he sounded honest about it. He told me who his son's mother was, a name instantly recognizable because she was a supermodel who graced the covers of top magazines for fifteen years and was the famous face of a high end cosmetic campaign.

"I saw her once when we were in Aspen," I told him. "She's lovely. Didn't she marry some British rocker?"

He nodded, laughing. "I have access to good concert tickets for life."

"Why do you not hit me as the rock concert type?"

"You got me," he said with that honeyed accent. "I'm a country boy all the way."

The chairlift was still stalled and we had been dangling there for a long time while the temperature was dropping. Ahead of us, the top of the mountain was covered in a misty white cloud, and the snow had been falling more heavily for the last few minutes. I shook some of it off me and tapped my foot against my board to knock off the accumulating snow.

A shiver ran through me and I wrapped my arms around myself and rubbed my hands together. "I'm beginning to think those last few runs I wanted to take were not such a good idea."

"Are you cold?" he asked. "Here." He wrapped his cashmere scarf around me and moved closer, his arm pulling me against his shoulder. I didn't know whether the instant warmth I felt was from his body or from my embarrassment, but I was less cold, and my flush faded.

He smelled like cinnamon and man. Other than Mike, I hadn't been close enough to a man to notice a scent for longer than I could remember; it felt strange and provocative at the same time, and I was somewhat uncomfortable with my reaction.

"Better?" he asked me, and I was again aware of the timbre and lilt of that voice, the warmth of him next to me, and the awkwardness I felt or maybe thought I should feel. I wasn't certain how I was reacting. But I was reacting on some elemental, butterflies-in-the-stomach level.

I looked everywhere but at him. "I wonder how long they're going to leave us here."

"I read somewhere once about a ski area on the East Coast where the lift operators went home and left two people on a chair all night."

"Nice." I punched his arm. "How very comforting. Luckily I know someone in operations and the ski patrol here checks every chair and gondola on this mountain before they close it down."

He laughed, and we sat there huddled together in silence, the snow falling now in white sheets and the mountain trail only visible for about fifty feet.

I spotted a skier in a red patrol jacket burst out of the snow cloud and stop below us. "The lift's broken." He called up to us. "We're doing evacs." He then spoke into a radio for a minute.

"Great," I said looking down. "An evac. All these years riding and I've never been evac'ed. Lucky us, we're at the lift's highest point."

"I was evac'ed once years back. They threw a tennis ball with some twine over the cable—"

"Twine? I don't think so. I weigh more than that."

"You don't have anything to worry about. And let me finish . . ." he said and I could hear the smile in his voice. "They used the twine to pull a heavy duty rope over the cable with a t-bar seat attached to it. We crawled on and they lowered us down. A piece of cake."

My ego kicked in and I had the horrid thought that it might take a team of men to lower me down. I could hear Phillip now. Remember when they had to use half the ski patrol to lower Mom from that broken down chair lift? I'd be the butt of his joking for a good month, butt being the most telling word.

I looked down toward the ground again.

"Aunt March? Is that you?"

"Jared?" Rob's son was one of the ski patrol. He was actually my second cousin once removed, only by marriage. But family is family, and age and Cantrell custom dictated we were Uncle Mike and Aunt March since the time our kids could speak, and we had all spent so much time and endless vacations together over the years. "It's me."

"Want me to radio Dad?"

"God, no! I'm fine. Just get me out of this chair. It's cold up here." Within minutes the patrol was ready for me, so I kicked off my board.

"Look," my Southern friend said to me with the easy confidence you'd expect from a cowboy. "It's not going to be so bad."

Before me was a cable with a strapped seat like on a children's swing. I lifted the bar and immediately felt his arm around me.

"I've got you." His mouth was next to my ear and his breath was warm.

I grabbed the rope and crawled into the seat

and buckled up. As they lowered me to the trail, I waved up at him and realized he had told me about his son and about some of his life, but he hadn't told me his name.

They lowered me down rather smoothly considering. I was very thankful for both men standing below me as I stepped on solid ground and gave Jared a hug. "Thank you. I don't want to do that again for a while."

"How long were you up there?"

I checked my watch. "Over an hour." I watched as they sent the rope seat back up.

"You need to sign a release," Jared told me. "Laurie has it over there."

I wanted to talk to my cowboy friend, but I went over to the girl holding a clipboard, signed the release and she handed me a free pass.

By the time I returned, he was picking up his board. I held out the pass. "We have season passes. You want this?"

He looked at me and flicked his season pass clipped to the pocket of his jacket.

"Maybe for a friend," I said.

He took it. "Thanks."

"Can I buy you a drink? To thank you," I added, lamely.

He checked his watch and dropped his board on the snow. "I've got to be somewhere. New Year's Eve," he said, stepping into his bindings. "If I take you up on that drink I'm gonna be late."

"Okay," I said brightly and held out my hand. "Thanks."

He took my hand and held it for longer than normal. "Any other time I would have taken that drink in a heartbeat," he said and winked at me. He lowered his goggles and took off down the run.

After a second or two I called out, "Wait!"

He skidded to a stop at the berm of the run and looked back up at me, not lifting his goggles.

"I don't know your name."

"Rio," he said, and waved before he took off down the run, his voice echoing back to me with that Texas lilt. "Rio Paxton."

I watched him disappear around a curve and just stood there frozen like an idiot, board tucked under my arm, my hand on his scarf still around my neck. Rio Paxton. No wonder he looked familiar.

Chapter Twenty Three

Rio Paxton wrote his first number one country hit at age seventeen. At eighteen, he was performing on stage at the Grand Ole Opry. When he was twenty, the Country Music Association gave coveted awards to five different country star performers, duos, and groups for recording the songs Rio Paxton wrote. Just in time to celebrate his twenty third birthday, he wrapped up an extended tour of the US and most of Europe, playing to packed venues and sell-out shows.

Stardom reached out and locked him in vertiginous arms, and after a few more riotous years passed by in a blur, the booze, the drugs and women all caught up with him—along with a few nights in jail after public brawls and some talk of tax problems. His career was badly damaged from a trail of wanna-bes and bootlickers who stuck around him only for the prestige and free drugs, using him to create their own identities, until his reputation had crumbled into nothing but dust as fine as the dry red clay of West Texas.

Rio Paxton had been too young to see it all coming, too green to read insincerity in the bright lights, star shine and hypnotic lures of fame, and the demands of a wolverine industry that devoured the naïve and sucked the talent from the pith of their bones, leaving behind scorched and hollow human beings.

Before he was close to thirty, he was already washed up—a fallen star that burned out fast, barely a man—just that same thirteen year old kid from West Texas, who picked up an old guitar one lonely day and discovered he loved to sing.

His downfall had been public enough for me to remember it even now with some sense of pity and waste, like standing there and watching a tornado rip through a town. A disaster was happening and there was nothing you could do to stop it.

The charming innocence he had when he first hit it big disappeared painfully fast. Once his songs had crossed over into pop music and were played on all the radio stations, he won Grammys and American Music Awards along with his string of CMA awards.

Mike and I had seen Rio perform at one of the old casino showrooms at the peak of his popularity, and I remembered him walking on stage with a guitar strapped over his shoulder, dressed in cowboy boots and tight jeans, a simple plaid shirt with the sleeves rolled up, and a black hat low over his eyes as if he had something to hide.

But unlike so many other singers, the hat didn't stay hiding his eyes from the audience. For the first few songs, before he was joined by his band, he sat on a wooden stool in the center of the stage, one boot heel caught on the rung and he pushed the hat back, exposed to everyone in that crowded room.

On stage he had been a humble young man with a voice like melted butter and brown sugar, who talked to the audience between songs and could make you cry when he sang about Texas or his mother.

But that had been a lifetime ago.

Later that night, as I sat with my family taking

up three tables in the casino lounge, waiting for the ten o'clock show, Rio Paxton and what I knew of his history was on my mind. I honestly hadn't known he was playing at the casino tonight. The idea for us to hit a show belonged to my sons, after we all had a late dinner at *Ciera*, and like a lamb to slaughter I followed them to another casino, and the room behind the lounge bar, where to my surprise a big sign out front of velvet ropes showed Rio's picture and listed the special show times for New Year's Eve. There had been an early show, and then a three hour break, so I understood then why he'd left the mountain.

A cocktail waitress placed our drinks in front of us just as the house lights dimmed and the stage lights grew brighter. One set of red curtains opened to reveal a single wooden stool, and he walked on stage, guitar slung on a shoulder, wearing boots and dark jeans, shirtsleeves rolled up, an older more weathered version of the man I had seen perform that night so many years back.

Maybe it was the board clothes that made me not recognize him. No cowboy hat or jeans, but then my first thought when he spoke to me was that he should have been dressed the way he was.

Maybe it was senility. But he sang in those rich caramel tones I remembered, a song about bright city lights and a young cowboy. That song had shot to number one, broken chart records, and made Rio Paxton a name everyone recognized.

As he sang, his gaze scanned across the audience before he looked back down at his guitar resting on a bent knee, then hit another verse and raised his eyes to look in our direction. I knew the moment he saw me because his gaze didn't move on. I smiled. He didn't.

My heart jumped to my throat. Oh . . . no. . . . what if he thought I was stalking him? I wasn't quite old enough to be his mother, but I was an older woman who he had happen-chanced to sit with on a chair lift, a whack job who tried to set him up with her daughter and didn't have the good sense or memory to recognize who he was.

I felt like I was getting into a bad place mentally, so I sipped my drink and tried to listen to the music and let go of my feelings and my thoughts and concerns about how I had looked to him. He was merely someone who had been kind to me, but who I didn't know. A sweet man. Frankly, I was really getting too old to care about what people thought of me.

The music went on and eventually the back curtain parted and revealed his band playing along with him. Molly and Keely and Renee were clapping along to the music as the songs grew faster and more upbeat, and soon the place was rocking and I just joined in and had fun, though it took another couple of drinks to properly loosen me up.

After a short break, the next set of songs started

with ballads, and the songs built and the band rocked on until Rio and his guitar players were extending the songs with instrumental challenges, as he moved from rhythm guitarist, to the bass guitarist, to the drummer and to the keyboard player; one rocking song led into a well-known heel-kicker about lowdown bars and wild women. The crowd went nuts when they finished and left the stage.

Everyone was on their feet, clapping and waiting for the encore. They came back out and the crowd applauded and sat down again. I noticed Rio made some kind of gesture to the band before they played the intro to his biggest hit, *It Feels Like Crazy Sometimes*.

He started singing as he came down the front steps into the audience, walked in our direction before I could realize what was happening. He kicked the chair next to me around and straddled it, his arms resting on the back, holding the mike and singing to me.

Stunned, I stared down at the dark hair on his forearms, and when I braved a look at his face, those eyes had me and I couldn't look anywhere else as he sang:

It feels like crazy sometimes,
To have loved someone so long.
You wrapped yourself around me,
I can't breathe now that you're gone.

It feels like crazy sometimes,
This life I'm livin' now,
Gettin' through this world without you,
Some days I don't know how.
It feels like crazy sometimes,
To wake up and find you missing.
And I walk the floors and wonder,
What other man you're kissin'.
It feels like crazy sometimes,
When I think back so long ago,
To the days before I met you
When my heart had nothing to show.
It feels like crazy sometimes,
To know what my mistakes cost.
I have no one else to blame but me,
Because now I'm a man who's lost.
It feels like crazy sometimes,
Knowin' there's nothing I can do,
I can't go back and replay time,
And find my way home to you.
It feels like crazy . . .
Living life alone
It feels like crazy . . .
Knowing that you're gone.
It feels like crazy,
It feels like crazy,
Sometimes, it's just crazy.

Rio finished the last, long note and got up from
the chair, but he took my hand and brought it to

his lips. When he let go, he winked at me, then turned and loped back up on stage, "Goodnight, folks!" He picked up his guitar and left the stage to the audience's enthusiastic applause, and the curtains closed and the lights came up.

The audience was on their feet, along with my kids, who were laughing and cheering, Scott and Phil elbowing each other and getting a big ha-ha of the whole serenade to their old mother.

I, on the other hand, was still trying to get my head on straight and my feet back down to earth, but after a minute I realized I was smiling.

"I can't believe he sang to you," Molly said, sitting down again. "Wow!" She sounded impressed, but I wasn't as I watched Spider's arm crawl back around her. I wondered if there was some way I could switch him out for Rio.

But Rio was not the man for my daughter, either. I just wanted to think of her with someone other than Spider. Someone safer, I told myself, and Rio Paxton was definitely not safe.

"Can you believe those eyes?" Renee said in a dreamy voice.

"And that voice," Keely added in the same tone.

Renee sighed. "I'm melting . . ."

"Hey," Scott groused.

"Oh, stop it!" she said disgusted. "I give birth to your children. Let me fantasize about something, here, will you? This is the first time in months

I'm not waddling around or exhausted, first time in weeks when I'm not pacing the floor and nursing the baby, or covered in baby powder and spit-up."

"Yeah, jerkface," Phil said, giving him a hard time. "Let your wife dream."

"My dream is that you could sing like that," Keely said.

"Phil?" Scott laughed. "Oh, he can sing, but all the dogs in town would start howling along with him."

"I wonder why he picked you to sing to?" Molly speculated.

"She's a beautiful woman," Spider said, which almost endeared him to me, until I considered the source.

"Mom's safe," Scott said. "She's an older woman. She's not a groupie. She won't be waiting for him at the back door."

"Or throwing her panties on stage," Phil added.

My mouth dropped and I looked at my sons and asked myself when they had become so insensitive, and counted to three. "Please leave my age and my underwear out of this, boys," I said and finished off my last cocktail, popping the cherry in my mouth so I wouldn't say anything more.

Little did they know what was really going on. Although, truthfully, I wasn't sure what, if anything, was going on.

I'd been back home only a few days when I discovered Mike was back, or my visions of Mike were back, or my grief madness was back. Something was back. I came home late from Tahoe, took a long bath, and flopped into bed. As I reached over to turn out the light, I saw the photo was gone again. I closed my eyes in frustration, and in fear, because I actually thought I had been doing better the past few months.

Was I lapsing back into mental disorder?

It didn't seem possible, since I'd been sleeping and healthy and feeling as if each approaching day actually held promise. In the morning I could get out of bed and do what I had to do and not want to roll over and pull the covers over my head like I had for so long. I had thought my mind was actually under control again.

Because the photo and the visions had to be in my mind—there were no such things as ghosts— who else other than the housekeepers could possibly hide the photo? And they had no reason. I'd questioned them months ago about it, back when he was first appearing. These women had worked for me for years and would never play games like that with me. They were crushed when we lost Mike.

I stared at the nightstand drawer for a long time. I almost didn't want to open it. But I did. The photo wasn't there. It wasn't on the floor, under the bed, or behind the night stand. Now I was on a mission, which took a few minutes. The photo was in the dresser drawer that held those three shirts of Mike's.

Looking down at the drawer I had a sick feeling, before I scanned the perfectly normal room while my blood raced and my heart pounded, searching for what?

There was no shadow from the tree outside.

Could it be that he was here?

"Mike? Please . . ."

Nothing. There had to be some logical answer. I would ask the housekeepers again.

But two days later I walked out of the laundry room with a huge basket full of Mickey's clean clothes and saw Mike sitting at the kitchen table.

I screamed, and the basket tumbled to the floor spilling the piles of folded clothes. When I looked up, he was gone and the chair was empty. I knew then it was impossible for the house-keepers to have had anything to do with what was happening.

I wanted to vomit. The visions were making me sick.

He had been wearing a vee-necked red sweater and plaid shirt. I remembered he'd worn them that last Christmas as he ran around taking photos with a new high tech digital camera Molly and the boys had given him. Every time you turned around Mike was there clicking the camera, and at the time I was annoyed after hours of "smile" and I secretly cursed those big gigabyte photo cards.

Those clothes he wore that day were gone and had been for a long time. I sat down hard in an empty chair and waved my hand in the empty spot where I'd seen him sitting, because these visions were just so real—heart-stoppingly real.

"Mike?" I whispered. "Mike, please . . ." Tears made my throat tight and my eyes burn. I couldn't pull my gaze away and just sat there staring at the empty spot, crying miserably and helplessly, short breaths making it impossible for me to do much else.

I think I might have needed a paper bag to breathe into, but I had never hyperventilated before. So I just sat there panting and crying and panicking, until I could finally manage to take a long, shuddering breath.

And then I knew. I couldn't do this anymore. I had to sell the house.

Chapter Twenty Four

The next morning I was powerwalking up the hill toward home when a familiar long black limo pulled up and the tinted windows powered down.

"Get in. We're going to breakfast," Ellie said imperiously.

I stopped and bent down to look inside. All the girls were in the car, even Harrie, who was the only one who didn't have a mimosa in her hand.

"I look like crap."

"Everyone looks like crap at this ungodly hour," Ellie said, tossing her perfectly-straight, precision bobbed dark hair, her makeup flaw-less, and she was wearing a St. John sports outfit and Prada sneakers I hoped she would later send on to Suki.

I was in hot pink running shoes, black yoga pants and a tee-shirt, with a lime green Cantrell Sports windbreaker tied around my waist, sweaty, red-faced, panting, no makeup, and my hair probably looked like a pineapple.

Ellie opened the limo door. "Come on. Get in, Eugene's double parked. Besides, it took us twenty minutes to find you."

I crawled inside and she poured me a cocktail. I held up my hand. "No. It's seven a.m. I've just been on a walk for my health, which Harrie started."

My doctor and close friend for decades was cupping a large Starbucks' cup in both hands.

"What are you drinking?"

"Venti, double shot, skinny, sugar-free vanilla latte."

"Listen to that," Ellie said. "If all the women in the city lose their ovaries, our Doctor Harrie, here, can have a second career as a barista."

"Nope," Harrie said. "Have you seen those lines in the morning? Too much work for me. I'd rather do a pelvic."

Eugene choked and started coughing, and I laughed at the horrified look on MC's face.

"Here." Ellie shoved a glass of plain, pulpy orange juice into my hands. "You were more fun when you were fat."

"Ellie! March was not fat." MC flushed.

I gulped down half the juice. "She's right. I wasn't skinny."

But the past couple of days had made me unsure about myself again, and I'd eaten a whole pint of Häagen-Dazs pistachio ice cream after I'd seen Mike in the kitchen. That ice cream was one of the reasons I was up and walking this morning.

It made perfect sense that we went to Sears for their divine pancakes and apple sausage because we always ate when we were together; but then I was eating without them, too . . . ice cream.

Later, feeling like Jabba the Hutt, I pushed away my plate while half the meal was still on it. "I'll have to walk again, dammit. But maybe that's better than going home," I admitted.

I looked up at my friends and spilled my troubles. "I've been hallucinating. I see Mike all the time."

"What do you mean you see him?" Ellie asked me.

"I'll walk into a room or casually look up and he's there, for just a second. The visions of him had stopped for a long time, but I saw him again yesterday, sitting in the kitchen."

"Like a ghost? Topper? You've got to be kidding," Ellie said. "Does he talk to you?"

"No. He's not really there. I just think he is. It's my head playing tricks on me."

"The two of you lived together in that house for a long time. I'm not surprised you'd walk in a room and expect to see him." Harrie reached out and grabbed my hand. "I think what you're experiencing is common. Maybe time will make things better."

"I don't think so," I said.

"Do you see him other places you went, like the Tahoe house? Did you see him over the holidays?"

"No," I said, realizing for the first time that I never saw him anywhere but at home. "I only see him in the house. Nowhere else."

"I saw my mother the day she died," MC said quietly. "She was standing in the living room. I don't think I dreamed it all up. I heard her. She said 'Goodbye, my sweet Mariclare.' You all know that's what she called me. And then she was gone."

We all looked at MC.

She was using her fork to stab the leftover pancakes. "I've never told anyone."

"I understand why. You think you're going nuts. At least I do. Mike's dead. I know he's dead." I took a sip of my coffee. "And I must be doing weird things in my sleep again, because our photo keeps disappearing. It'll be on the nightstand and then it's in a drawer. I would never hide that photo."

"Maybe it's your cleaning lady."

"I talked to them when it happened before. I don't think it's them. I have no idea what's going on, but I've made a difficult decision. I'm going to sell the house."

"Are you ready to make that kind of decision, March? It's a major one," Harrie asked.

"My sanity is at risk here."

"But you love that house," MC said. "It was always the only house you ever wanted."

She was right. I *did* love the house. I couldn't imagine anyone else living where I had spent so much of my life, my kids' lives. I was caught between my visions and my memories—one I wanted to stop and one I didn't want to end, or forget.

"That's probably a good idea. Too much is tied to that place for you," Ellie said practically.

"How do you think the kids will react?" Harrie asked.

"The kids? I haven't told them. I just decided yesterday. Honestly? I hadn't thought about them yet. God . . ." I said on a groan and sank my face in my hands. "That's the only home Molly and Mickey have ever known."

"Based on the Molly we all know, I expect she will pitch a damn good fit . . . ." Ellie said.

"Ellie!" MC and Harrie said at once.

"Well it's true," Ellie muttered.

"I don't think Mickey would like it if I sold his home out from under him the minute he's gone off to college. Now I don't know what to do."

"When does he fly back to school?" MC asked.

"I'm taking him to airport this afternoon."

"Talk to him, March," Harrie advised.

"He'd tell me it was okay, even if it wasn't. He'd just agree because he thought that was what I wanted. He's been acting very protective."

"Feel him out a little. Ask him how is it to be in school then come home. Does home feel the same?" Harrie offered. "Something like that and see what he says before you make the decision, or at least until you tell them."

"I just don't think I can live there anymore. It's tearing me up."

"You could redecorate," MC said. "Get rid of everything that was yours together and make the place completely different."

"You think Mike's ghost will stop showing up if she changes the furniture?" Ellie asked facetiously, then she paused and apologized. "I'm cranky today." She watched me for a moment then said, "You know MC's probably right. Every time I get divorced, I redo the whole house. It always makes me feel better." She held up a hand as the others started to speak. "I know divorce is different from losing your husband, but it works. New surroundings can't be a mistake."

"She's got a point, March," Harrie said. "Maybe you will stop seeing him if the rooms don't look like they did when he was living in them."

So my decision to sell the house lasted all of about fourteen hours. Instead, when I got home from breakfast, I called the decorator. I would start with our bedroom.

A room the size of our master bedroom echoed badly when it was empty. My voice seemed to bounce from the stark walls and bare wooden floors as if I were shouting. There wasn't a single stick of furniture, the drapes were gone, the art, even the rug had been rolled up by the movers and added to the truck.

My decorator gathered her tapes and laptop, print outs and portfolio intending to follow the mover out, but she paused in the doorway. "You're certain about this change, March? I remember how much you loved the room."

"I'm absolutely certain," I said and handed her a house key and my contact numbers—I was going back to Tahoe for a while.

We had started only two days ago, when I came home from breakfast with my friends and told her I wanted a whole new room, and that I wanted to do this immediately, then I took Mickey to the airport and by the time I got home, she had booked movers for today and begun her plans, ones that didn't use the same colors we had before.

The master bath would be redone completely, walls, floor, all the fixtures changed, and all the light fixtures replaced with something different, everything was to be changed but the wood floors, the fireplace, which was original, and the windows and doors.

With nothing in the room, my decision seemed easier and felt right, as if I were standing in front of a huge blank canvas, brushes in hand. What I felt was sheer freedom. I could do anything I wanted. As I turned slowly around and looked at the vacant room, there was no way the place felt like our bedroom anymore.

Like a stage set broken down after the last show, what had been there before seemed fake and unreal now that it was only in my memory. I was so overwhelmed with relief that I sat down on the hard wood floor and cried my eyes out.

Maybe it wasn't exactly relief I felt. Maybe this was how I said goodbye.

Chapter Twenty Five

I arrived in Tahoe not knowing if I was running away from something or toward it. My original thought was that being on the mountain would bring me some kind of peace. From the mountains and snow and altitude, a pure closeness to the majesty of life usually settled over me. Riding down a ten thousand foot mountain at a top speed tested my control, my technique and balance. Boarding had always given me joy, and perhaps a sense of power. Now I pushed myself more and rode faster and harder.

Years back there was slogan—a mind is a terrible thing to waste. Well, my mind must have been wasted, because when I first decided to go up to Tahoe, I had painted a rosy mental image of the new me on the mountain—traversing one of the most important places in our lives, and in doing so, erasing the past. Cathartic. Healing. A how-to on making a fresh start.

At some point on the drive there, I even did the mental math on what portion of my life had been spent on the mountain and figured conservatively, over thirty seven plus years, two thousand five hundred days of my life, I had been riding snowboards at Heavenly Valley.

But now, on the first full day on the slopes, I

didn't find comfort on the mountain. Riding alone was not the same. There was no one to trade stories with at lunch. There was no one to share the thrills and spills. There was just no one.

Stubbornly, I kept trying to use the mountain to rediscover myself but after riding down every challenge trail or bowl or run on the whole mountain, both California and Nevada sides, after pulling tricks that would test the skill of someone half my age, all I discovered was I was hauntingly alone, and everything I did was uncomfortably different.

I felt trapped in another dimension—standing at a clear glass wall, hands pressed to the glass and watching the whole world go by. I was the fly caught between a screen and a window. All around me were lovers kissing on the chairs or at lunch, wives and mothers, teens and kids. I had been all those things once upon a time. My fairytale life was gone.

A depressing thought, and here I thought I had made some progress. I did know for certain I was bone tired of lapsing backwards, and tired of letting myself fall back into feeling lost and pitiable.

Perhaps I had set myself up, because I had been too anxious to find a new life, or maybe because I was alone after a lifetime of never being alone. But what I discovered was that I actually didn't know what to do with myself.

One of the good things about age was I had experience to nibble at my thoughts and guide me. I knew that life worked out best when you took charge yourself rather than letting life take charge of you—no getting sucked into the whirlpool of poor me.

I was alone. Okay. Mike wasn't coming back. So now what? I had to find my new path.

At the top of the mountain I knew so well, paths snaked down in every direction—so many possibilities to my future, so I closed my eyes and touched the trail map with a finger, trusting that the Grand Scheme of Things would lead me where I needed to go.

Methodically I rode every trail on the mountain, and when I was done, I had a plan: each day I would ask something new of myself—a test I had to do alone, completely alone.

My first self-test was the easiest. I went to the movies the next night. Sitting alone in a dark theatre seemed doable, and it was. I ate a small bag of buttered popcorn and watched a charming film about a young teenaged girl who bravely chooses to give her baby up for adoption. As I observed the family and friends' fictionalized acceptance of this girl's situation and her choice, I found it fascinating how much times had changed over the past decades.

The movie took me back in time, when I was so

obviously pregnant at my wedding, which pushed the morality boundaries, more so than nowadays when stars and celebrities proudly announced their pregnancies on the tabloid shows, and the ones with big souls sold photos of their children for charity before a wedding ever took place.

Even Rio Paxton and his model didn't marry, but then I had no idea what their circumstances were, except that he must have been around twenty at the time, which was young, and no birth of a son made the news then that she could recall.

My parents would have preferred that Mike and I had done things in the right order, like the old jump rope rhyme:

First comes love, then comes marriage,
then comes March with a baby carriage.

Even after so many years had passed, I can still remember being so shaken when I left the clinic that first day I found out I was pregnant. My knees were weak and my head swam. Other than sheer fear, I hadn't known what else I was feeling, so I took some time for myself to get used to the idea and sort out my conflicting thoughts before I told Mike.

I sat under that same tree in Golden Gate Park, which was why I wanted so badly to be married there. Beneath that tree was where I came to terms with the birth of my first child and the knowledge that Mike was going to want to get married. My whole future took root under that tree.

Before the wedding, there were times when I was made to feel uncomfortable about my pregnancy, not by my parents, who seemed to accept the situation, my father taking a lot longer to come around than my mom. I chose to ignore those other responses: shock, embarrassment, censure, and lived my life with bravado I didn't feel deep inside. It took a lot for me to pretend I didn't care when people treated me badly, and to pretend I wasn't scared.

In the park that day, I had a made a decision: the baby was a gift to us, not a moral thermometer, or visual proof that I had done something to be ashamed of. I had loved Mike long before there was life growing inside of me. I refused to let people's opinion color all that was good about Mike and me and our baby.

At twenty, my dreams were big, real, and in my mind, absolutely attainable. Everything I wanted was just waiting for me to reach out and grab it. With all that assurance of youth, marriage and kids sounded so romantic. Not in the traditional sense, like some housewife from the 1940s or 50s. I was from a generation who shook their fist at tradition. I thought we would do it our way. A new way.

Just the two of us and our babies in our own

place, with all the freedom and uniqueness that was San Francisco laying out before us like some board game from my childhood. I trusted we would roll the dice, choose our paths like we chose the colored game pieces when we were kids, and then we would draw our cards and collect our winnings along the way.

Considering that was how I went into marriage and motherhood, pretty much with blinders on, I was lucky, not like so many other women, women like Suki. Mike and I had weathered the years and come out winners, had picked ourselves up at those times when the game was over and our world seemed to be coming down around us. Both of us ran on the belief that no matter how dire things appeared, everything would work out.

Mike and I just meshed, almost from that first night we met at the Fillmore, we formed some kind of rare and unflappable partnership. Our challenges were not based in testing our love and respect for each other, but in tackling the world together, raising our kids and starting a business—one that was based on something no one but Mike and I believed in. The business was our struggle.

So those early years were on my mind when I came home from the movies, stood on the front porch and stomped off the snow—which had started falling while I was inside the theatre—and once in the house I hung my coat, tossed aside my gloves, and immediately called Scott.

"Mom, is everything okay?" Scott said when he answered. Coloring his voice was the edge of panic that had become so familiar in the past year.

"I'm just calling to talk to my firstborn," I said, a little annoyed because he always felt he had to protect me nowadays, and knowing if I explained that the movie took me back in time and made me want to call him, he would think I was being silly and emotional. "No arrests, I swear."

He laughed on the other end, and I asked about his family and the business, and we talked about both for a few minutes.

"You doing okay up there by yourself?"

"Of course," I said brightly. "It's snowing right now and the mountain has been great, the runs are good. If it snows for a couple of days, the runs will be even better. You should come up."

"So many of the employees wanted to be at that meet next month, we moved the roving week to the end of the month, closer to the meet. But maybe Phil and I can come up. Molly can't. She's flying out Friday to meet Spider at an event in Vermont."

The silence hung between us.

"I spoke the unspeakable, right? He-who-shall-not-be-named?"

"I've lost my sense of humor where Spider

and your sister are concerned," I admitted grimly.

"It's Molly, Mom. The harder you try to get her away from Spider Olsen, the more she's going to want to be with him."

"She's not seventeen anymore. I thought she'd outgrown that stage." I paused and took a long breath. "I hate this."

"We know. She knows. Spider knows. You don't hide your feelings all that well. Look, if it'll make you feel any better, it seems to me that he cares about her."

"I'm certain at some point he cared about all the women he's dumped. What am I supposed to do? Stand around and wait for the fall?"

"She's an adult, Mom. We all screw up. She gets to make some bad choices, too."

"But she thinks she's in love with him, Scott."

"She also thinks for herself. We need to respect that."

"I can't help myself. I want to follow her around, arms out, waiting to catch her when he dumps her."

"What makes you so sure he's going to dump her?"

"His track record. Three divorces. Breakups with young starlets and models covered on entertainment TV. Wasn't he on that stupid dating show with those girls barking like dogs and clamoring after him?"

My son laughed at me. "That was the football

quarterback, who turned announcer, not Spider. You're being unfair. He's a great guy."

"I'm sure he is, but I don't want him with your sister, Scott. Your father would have never condoned this."

"You know as well as I do that Dad had a soft spot where Molly was concerned. I don't think he would have hassled her."

"He would have had a talk with Spider. Have *you* talked to him about her?"

"I'm not Dad," Scott said in a voice that made me turn my worry towards my son.

"What's wrong?" I asked.

"Nothing."

The silence dragged out between us and he said, "It's just work and I worry I'm not making the right decisions."

"Has something happened I should know about?"

"No. I try to think like Dad would, you know? To make the decisions he would have, but some days I just feel lost about what to do. Dad always knew what to do." He paused, then added, "I'm sorry, Mom. I'm just frustrated."

"Believe me, your father did not always know what to do. He lay awake nights wondering if he had made the right decision. But long before he had experience to help him, he had great instincts. Trust your own instincts, son."

Something more was bothering him and I

thought perhaps this might not have been the best time for me to leave the city. But I'd seen the sales and order numbers, the financials. Things were good there.

Perhaps I needed to get Scott alone when he came up. He had been forced to take over everything so quickly, and while all of us were still grieving. In his mind, stepping into a role as head of the family was how he coped with losing his dad, but he was young and had a family of his own. He didn't have Mike's experience to balance his decisions. He had too much to cope with and it bothered me that I hadn't noticed.

"Don't worry about Spider and Molly, Mom," Scott said, changing the subject.

"He's going to hurt her."

"If that happens, she'll survive it. Molly's strong. I'm not worried about her." He hesitated, then said, "I'm more worried about you."

I bit back the urge to tell him he was worrying about the wrong Cantrell, but he had sounded so down I didn't want to add to his troubles.

Neither he nor Phil would budge when it came to Molly. They weren't going to talk to their sister, and with Spider's endorsement on the line, they were not going to keep him in check no matter how much I wished them to. Perhaps it wasn't fair of me to expect them to step in for Mike.

"I'm keeping myself busy," I told him, which

was true. "I went to the movies tonight, and I'm going out to dinner this week, and to a show at the casino." Those actually were on my list of things I needed to do alone, along with stacking wood, going to Mike's favorite breakfast restaurant, and dancing—although how I would go dancing alone and outside the privacy of my own home and not feel self-conscious I didn't really know.

"I'm riding during the day," I continued. "But if the snow keeps up tomorrow, I'll just hunker down here. There's plenty to do in the house. I might go downstairs and practice on the Wii and beat you all when we get together next. And I can always raid the wine cellar, pour myself a glass of wine, and top it off with Seven Up."

He laughed. We used to tease Mike and threaten to make wine coolers out of his prized wines.

Before long we hung up, and I thought about that old photo I'd seen on his desk—my son as a toddler walking in his father's shoes—and I realized now he was trying to fill them, an impossible task for him. The reason he watched out for me was because I had let him down. Maybe I'd let all my children down, mired in my widowhood.

All those changes that had thrown me for a loop had also happened to my son, except Scott had the responsibility for the whole company on his shoulders as well. And though he was smart and worked closely with Mike, he hadn't had a lot of years to watch and learn from his father. Mike had still been running referee between the boys and the two divisions of the company when he was killed.

No wonder my son was feeling lost.

I paced for a while, then went to bed determined to continue with my plan to learn to live my life alone. By taking responsibility for my own life, I would relieve some of the onus I believed my children felt. I needed to find a way to be happy again.

Clearly my happiness was not my children's duty. But learning to find some peace and contentment could only help show them I was okay, and perhaps allow them to let go.

Chapter Twenty Six

I went to breakfast the next morning at a Belgian waffle place we all loved and sat down at a table for two. I always ordered tomato juice and a vegetable and avocado omelet.

The waitress walked toward me from the kitchen with her tray and set my juice down in front of me. I put down the newspaper and said, "I'm sorry, I forgot to order the sour cream and salsa on the side."

Her expression was quizzical as she placed a

plate of peanut butter and banana nut waffles in front of me. I stared at the plate. I had ordered Mike's favorite.

"Is something wrong?"

"No," I said. "I'm sorry. I just forgot what I'd ordered. Can I get some more coffee?" *And a new brain with no memory.*

As the waitress disappeared into the back kitchen, I laughed quietly, shaking my head at what I'd done. Somewhere up there, Mike would have been laughing, too.

By the time I left the restaurant, overly full with the sweet taste of maple syrup and peanut butter, it was snowing heavily again and the plowed roads were growing plush with fresh snow. Our house was off the Grade, where the snow was usually heavier, but with four-wheel drive, the light weekday traffic, and the storm keeping people off the roads, I made it home before the drifts were bad.

Two cords of haphazardly piled wood, tamarack and live oak delivered before I arrived, met me at the end of the drive.

With a husband and three sons, firewood miraculously wound up in the wood racks in my past life. I hadn't thought about paying the delivery service to stack it until I first drove up from the city and voila! There it was, a huge mound of wood, lonely and confused waiting to be stacked.

Maybe that was part of my problem. I was, like the wood, dumped into a confused stack, in no order and blocking my own way forward. Worse than that I was just sitting around waiting, waiting for my life to change, waiting, waiting, waiting for everything to come to me. I had never been such a passive person.

When did I become so complacent and accepting of the world? Why was every decision I faced so difficult? Life was unsure now. I thought about that as I went inside and changed clothes, while I shoveled off the porch and a path to the wood box and rack.

With the wheelbarrow from the shed, I began to move the wood. Over the next hours I worked hard, my breath frosty and my nose growing numb, while I drank from a thermos of hot coffee and loaded split logs. I began to roll the wheelbarrow across the expanse of soft snow, leaving whimsical tracks and designs in my wake. Sometimes I walked in a useless circle just for the loop effect the wheels made in the snow. Before long I had painted a full landscape in the yard with wheel tracks. I signed my name across the bottom and drew a huge daisy next to it, like I had done when I was thirteen and in junior high art class.

But soon the snow picked up and the yard graffiti was slowly erased, and the wood in the racks stacked up into impressively neat rows, the way I thought my life used to be, or wished it would be now. I played that mental if-then game with myself and fitted each log into its rack like a puzzle piece.

If I line up all the wood into perfect rows, then my life will align perfectly, too.

My face was half frozen and I was sweating under my hat and clothes by the time I had finished, muscles sore, but endorphins flying high. As I stood back and looked at the wood racks, I was feeling great. My rubbery thighs however were not, so I trudged limply inside to take a long sauna and bath. Afterward, I ignored my natural urge to throw on some flannel pj's at four in the afternoon and just eat a bowl of cold cereal by the fire.

Instead I dressed in jeans and a sweater and spent time making myself a full dinner. Just for atmosphere, I put Dean Martin on the stereo, singing along as I cooked, set the table, complete with folded cloth napkin and pewter ring, opened a nice bottle of red wine from a famous Italian director's winery. I plated my meal like a chef from the Food Network and set down at the kitchen table to a spread of antipasto atop freshly chopped romaine, Marsala Bolognese sauce over rigatoni, and double baked garlic cheese bread.

I looked through the wide bay windows

overlooking a great expanse of the Tahoe Basin and the veil of falling snowflakes. All that snow looked like the white dots on my mother's old enameled roasting pan. The lake was only a grainy oval of gray in the distance, the mountains flanking it just saw-like shadows at the edge of the storm.

I hadn't thought about that old roasting pan in years. I hadn't thought about my mom in a while, but those moments when I did, I missed her achingly. I don't know that May felt the same.

My sister had gone off to her great Ivy League college and stayed on the East Coast, a journalist who eventually married a National Geographic photographer and spent her lifetime traveling the world, never stopping long enough to have babies or spend time or holidays with the family.

Before Mike's death, contact from May was rather like a fly-by-fruiting. She called, found out you were okay, talked for five minutes, and was gone again for months.

I should call her. The last I'd heard from her, she was off to South America. They had trains and five-star tours, but I doubt they had cell service near Machu Picchu.

Odd how time changed things, and my perfect round-peg-in-round-hole-*Glamour*-Magazine older sister grew away from mother while I, the misfit and rebel, grew closer. My mother and I found our strongest bond around the time Scott was born, and I understood quickly that it took impending motherhood and my own children to make me appreciate and understand my mother, who I had unfairly seen in my blinded and arrogant youth as hopelessly square and old-fashioned.

The voice of reason and calm in almost any storm, the strong spine of our family, that was my mother. She and I used to play canasta for hours when the kids were young. I haven't played canasta since she died.

Outside it was dark and pretty much invisible by the time I washed up my dishes and went into the living room, where the fire was burning a deep red-orange flame, and I turned down the lights and sank into the sofa, curled up my feet, and settled into a deep downy corner as the logs spat and crackled.

Sitting there with my wine glass, I leaned my head back against the pillows and closed my eyes. The only sound was my own heartbeat.

The storm lasted another two days, with white-out conditions on the mountain and only a short break before another storm hit, so my sons didn't come up that weekend after all. Molly was off with Spider (I was going to work on accepting that situation) and Mickey was happily ensconced back on campus, where he loved his graphic arts class and had plans of his own to go up to the local mountains on a boarding trip.

From the time he'd first gone off to school last fall, he called home regularly, Tuesdays and Fridays. I learned the sunny days in Westwood sent him constantly off doing something fun, especially with the mountains in one direction and the beach in the other.

My Monday dawned cold and clear, and everything was feathery white or bright blue sky. I walked outside into that complete absence of sound that comes after a snowstorm. What was it Rio Paxton had said to me that day we were stuck on the lift? Twenty five percent of sound was absorbed by snow. As I stood there in the snow silence, I realized I felt good. There was some peace around me. Signs were all around that it would be an amazing day on the mountain.

The runs at Heavenly were like riding on goosedown, and not crowded. I even ran into some old friends at the lodge during lunch, a couple Mike and I had known for twenty five years, and we met again at the end of the day for a drink and nachos at the crowded bar nearby.

I came home a couple of hours later, cleaned up and threw on jeans and a soft sweater, and walked out to the kitchen for a bowl of ice cream. The message light on the answering machine was blinking like a railroad crossing. I pressed the PLAY button.

The red digital number twenty two flashed on

the small screen. There were twenty two messages? My heart stopped.

Now what had happened? I pressed PLAY again.

"Hi, March. This is Harrie. I'm just checking to see how you are. Give me a call if you have time to talk. Enjoy the snow!" There was a long pause. "If you need to talk, I'm here."

"Hi Mom. It's Scott. Just checking to see if you're okay today."

Next was Phillip, then Mike's brother from Vancouver, Ellie, MC, May from Peru, even Molly. As I listened, I looked at the calendar and wanted to throw up. I had forgotten, or blocked out the date. Mike's accident was a year ago today.

I sat down on a nearby chair, then called my children, assured them I was fine and talked to each of them about their father, guided them toward some moment or memory I knew had been special, one that made them laugh. Only when I was certain each one of them was okay, did I end the phone call.

By the time I was done, my mind was running in every direction, complete chaos. I stood in the center of the quiet house and knew I couldn't stand there a moment longer.

Peacocks screamed and Aztec gods moaned from the long bays of slot machines lined up like neon dominoes. The jackpots rang while a woman's excited laughter came from a busy corner. Waitresses wove their way across the casino floor shouting "Cocktails! Beverages!" and male shouts and whoops pierced the air like buckshot from the hottest craps tables. All around me was noise, loud, blissful, rowdy, clamorous noise.

In the first hour or so I'd won a couple hundred bucks at blackjack and spent another two hours losing it on a slot machine with singing Elvis piggies, then I became bored.

In the lounge, a band from the Eighties had already wrapped up one show, so I sat just outside at the lounge bar, drinking Tequila Marys with three olives and talking to the chatty bartender who kept me supplied with extra olives.

I had already planned to see a magician whose show was coming to the lounge later that week as my out-alone-at-the-casino-lounge-test, but tonight the music was upbeat and it was an uncrowded Monday, so when the midnight show started, I wandered inside, sat at an empty booth table in the darkest back corner and let them entertain me. This could be a new lesson. Maybe I could learn to drink alone.

By the time the show stopped, I had gone through the three drink minimum and more. I looked down at a colorful pile of plastic olive skewers sitting there like Pick-up Stix on the small table. Taxi time. Around me the lounge had emptied, and I could hear the clatter of the band behind the curtain clearing out their instruments. But I didn't get up right away.

When I did stand, the room swam and so I sat back down hard and closed my eyes to stop the spinning, then leaned my head back against the padded leather booth. Somewhere in my tequila-fogged mind, I had the thought that this had been a bad idea.

How long I stayed like that I didn't know, and I might even have been snoring when I thought I heard my name. I closed my mouth and swallowed dryly. My mouth tasted like a parade ground for an army of green pimento-stuffed olives.

"March?"

I didn't have to open my eyes because I knew that deep silky voice. "Uh-huh."

"Are you okay?"

"Uh-huh."

Silence. *Snap, snap, snap!* Was he was snapping his fingers in front of my face? "I'm here," I said, but I just wanted to stay where I was.

"It's Rio."

"I know."

"Open your eyes."

"Can't."

"Open your eyes."

I put my finger to my lips and said, "Shhhh."

"You can't sleep here. Security will take you out. Come on. Let me help you up."

334

"I'm not sleeping."

"Come on, darlin'. Stand up."

I smiled and opened my eyes. Rio's face was just inches away. He really was too damned good-looking for one man to be. "Hi," I said huskily. Why did I sound like Marilyn Monroe?

"Stand up, darlin'."

"Okay. But only because you called me darlin'."

There was a smile to his voice when he coaxed me up again and slid his arm around me.

"My purse." I turned back around and almost keeled over.

"Whoa. Hang on."

"I'm not a horse," I said indignantly.

"I know. I'm sorry. Slip of the tongue."

"You have a golden tongue." I thought I heard him laughing.

"I meant a golden voice."

"Hold still. I'll get your purse."

"But I forgot about my coat."

"Do you have a claim ticket?"

"In my back pocket." I turned around and his hand patted across my behind. He pulled out the claim check.

He took me by the shoulders and sat me down. "Stay there. Do not move. Do not leave. I'll be right back."

"I'll just take a little nap." I leaned my head back and closed my eyes again.

"March? I have your coat." He was back again.

"Thank you, but I'm asleep," I said and didn't move. "I lied before."

"You need to get up again, darlin'." Now he was laughing.

I took a deep breath and thought I needed to pull myself together, so in one big movement, I stood and started to move toward the entrance.

"Not that way," he said and put his hands on my shoulders and turned me toward the stage.

"But I need a cab. Out there." I turned and pointed toward the casino's front entrance.

"I'm not putting you in a cab by yourself. I'll drive you home."

"Okay," I said on a breathless sigh, frowning at the voice that came from my mouth. "I do sound like Marilyn Monroe." I took a few more steps. "Happy Birthday, Mister President . . . Are you old enough to know what I'm talking about? Probably not," I answered myself. "Do I know what I'm talking about?"

"I'm sure you think you do," he said lightly.

I managed to walk up the stage stairs quite well, but I was steadier when he kept his arm around me. I glanced up at him as we maneuvered through the back stage and down a hallway toward doors with red lit exit signs. Tonight he was wearing a dark blue baseball cap.

"I miss the cowboy hat," I said.

"I dressed for poker. Hides the eyes without drawing attention."

Together we moved toward the back doors, this tall, rugged-looking man with his arm around me, who smelled like coffee beans and sounded like rich and creamy dessert. He had my large red leather Dior purse hanging from his arm.

"Your hat's okay, but I like your purse much better,' I said, and his sweet laughter was the last thing I remembered.

Chapter Twenty Seven

A sharp shaft of bright sunshine woke me, and I took my first conscious breath; I smelled like tequila. I groaned and turned over, pulled a down pillow over my head which rang painfully, as if filled with a thousand church bells. The sheets felt silky against my bare skin—I was in my bra and panties—and I vaguely remembered waking in the middle of the night and stripping off my uncomfortable jeans and sleep-twisted sweater and tossing them somewhere.

Even now in my current groggy and hungover state, I was acutely aware that I was not in my own bed.

Rio Paxton.

Sitting up was an effort, and I rubbed my throbbing eyes before I could actually focus on my surroundings. Across from me, a wall of tall broad windows let in a bit of bright yellow sunlight cracking through a dark sky roiling in with an approaching snowstorm. Outside the house, thick mounds of too-white fresh snow went part way up the glass.

I shifted and the view was amazing. My breath caught at the southern panorama spread out before me: those clouds; the towering white Sierras; the round, rolling Nevada foothills; and seemingly miles and miles of the flat, snow-drift covered prairie that was Northern Nevada, broken only by distant tracks of fencing and an occasional barren tree.

The golden shaft of sunlight was the only color; everything else was like looking through the lens of Ansel Adams: black, gray and white.

From the distinctive terrain, I figured I was at the ranch Rio spoke of that day in the chairlift. The wood overhang of the roofline above the sharp point of windows was natural cedar, edged with deep green trim. I could see a glimpse of lodge wood siding, and if I shifted to the right, a flat stone wall that was most likely the back of a fireplace in a nearby room. The house was long and seemed to crouch outward, stretching clear to the corner with large posts that held the open roof of a covered patio. My mental image of "a ranch house in Sparks, Nevada," and this wood and stone home of Rio's were polar opposites.

The place had all the appearances of a big, sprawling and magazine worthy home.

Inside my room, on the edge of a long pine dresser, my jeans and sweater were neatly folded, and a white spa robe was strategically accessible at the foot of the huge pine bed with its four thick, rough-hewn bed posts. To my great relief, a wide open door on the opposite wall showed an *en suite* bathroom, so I crawled out of bed and into the robe.

A few minutes later I braced my hands on the marble counter of the bathroom and squinted into the ugly honesty of a big mirror. The whites of my eyes looked like Thomas Guide roadmaps, and the bed sheet had made creases across my cheek. I looked like what I was: a woman of a certain age who'd had too many drinks.

Inside the medicine chest was an over-sized bottle of Excedrin, the kind they sold in those warehouse stores, so I took two and rummaged through a basket filled with small square boxes of hotel shower caps, mini shampoos, soaps, and body lotions, razors and travel-sized blue mouthwash bottles, mini-tubes of toothpaste and a new package of multicolored toothbrushes.

The shower was hot and long and wonderful and by the time I was done, my head had stopped throbbing and I had scrubbed away the tequila sweat and smelled amazingly clean, in that old-fashioned motel soap scent. Camay, I think it was. My makeupless face was less puffy, but pink from the hot shower and moistened from a layer of Nivea cream. After I toweled my few inches of blonde tipped hair and finger-combed it, I looked semi-human again.

A wooden tray had magically appeared and sat on the corner of the bed with a glass of orange juice and a hot mug of coffee with red dancing elk painted on it. There was a lined yellow Post-it note alongside written in a dark masculine scrawl:

> Aspirin's in the medicine cabinet. Meet me in the kitchen. Turn right and down the end of hallway.
> Rio

My heart began to pound and skip in a way I didn't care to examine, and I wondered what I was going to say to him—other than thank you. Of course part of me was deeply embarrassed, getting so drunk, but it was over and done, like the margarita lunch that set Molly off, there was nothing I could do; you can't live backwards.

Common sense, something I'd seemed to have lost lately, still told me I should just get that first awkward moment over with. I chugged down the orange juice and sipped the coffee.

The last time I had worn my panties inside out the airline had lost my luggage. To my amazement, my jeans were washed, soft and clean and folded with neat creases, and it looked as if my cashmere sweater had been freshened and pressed; it smelled like spray fabric softener.

Outside the bedroom I walked down the hallway, snooping my way past two more bedrooms and a large library with dark wood bookcases and a huge rock fireplace.

Rich and masculine and beautifully decorated, the room had huge hammered copper table lamps with square burlap shades and hanging copper and wrought iron light fixtures, inlaid wood tables and oversized saddle leather furniture arranged in the room's center on an imported rug in shades of gold and green and red.

I cast a quick furtive glance down the hall and went inside the room.

The only wall without custom bookcases was wood-paneled and in its center hung an original Remington, and an antique wood and glass gun case holding a set of very old pistols was displayed above the fireplace.

As I glanced around the room, I liked what I saw. The books on the shelves weren't those classic, identically-bound leather and gilt books that people put in their bookcases to impress.

On Rio's shelves were real books, well-read books with cracked spines, torn jackets and white chips in the paperback covers, by authors you actually read—a timeline of popular writers:

Ludlum, Shaw and Michener, Wilbur Smith, Patterson and McMurtry, Grisham and Cussler. McCarthy, Vonnegut, and Phillip Roth next to long shelves filled with old paperback Louie L'Amour westerns, mysteries, and thick historical fiction. Lined up together were every one of the Harry Potter books, and there was a section of poetry, both classic and contemporary.

"Harry Potter and Keats," I murmured as I left the room.

At the end of the hallway, I could see the kitchen entrance, but to get there I had to walk through a small portion of what turned out to be a huge great room, probably thirty by forty with vaulted beamed ceilings, a bar and more floor to ceiling windows. The slate floors were heated.

I could hear Rio talking in the kitchen when I was just steps away, so I plastered a smile on my face before I walked in.

Rio was leaning casually against a stone counter in the kitchen, his hair looked wet and he was wearing faded jeans, his long legs crossed at the ankles. He was barefooted. Suddenly I felt less uncomfortable.

He was drinking coffee from another red dancing elk mug as he talked on the phone, that rich voice of his a little serious, but he looked up and smiled as he casually waved me in and pointed over at a plank trestle table with comfortable, high-backed tapestry chairs and spread with serving dishes, more juice, and a metal coffee carafe. The table was set for two with plaid placemats the same colors of the tapestry chairs and red and marigold damask cloth napkins. Even the juice glasses were tinted amber.

Rio Paxton evidently had a great decorator and an efficient housekeeper. I lifted the ceramic lid on a pinecone serving dish.

Scrambled eggs with spinach, fresh tomatoes and cheese.

Rio also had a cook.

I sat at the long end of the table, away from another rock fireplace burning bright with wood that snapped and popped and made the kitchen feel too warm, and I poured myself another orange juice.

He finished his business—something about a glitch in some recording equipment—and he set down the phone.

I could hear the beat of my blood throbbing in my ears, and the moment of heavy silence in the kitchen proved it wasn't exactly a race between us to see who spoke first.

I set down my mug. "I need to thank you for what you did for me last night. I'm really terribly embarrassed. I was so drunk." I looked away. "I guess I haven't much to say for myself except it was the anniversary of a very bad day."

He gave me a speculative look, then walked

over to the table and refilled his coffee and topped mine.

"There are some things you don't want to remember," I said in a voice I didn't like.

"You're apologizing to the wrong person, darlin'. My past makes last night look like a sweet little tea party."

I cupped the mug. "You're just trying to make me feel better."

He laughed, then said, "I have the press documentation to prove it, and the sad thing is they don't even know the half of it."

I remembered the old reports of carousing, that he was out of control and breaking up hotel rooms. There were fights in bars and an unfortunate mug shot of him on the news. But that was a long, long time ago. The man I was looking at appeared nothing like that out of control young man. Quite the opposite, in fact.

I poured myself more coffee, while he ate a piece of bacon. "Did I actually sing 'Happy Birthday, Mr. President?'"

"You did. All the way across the casino's back parking lot to my truck," he said, laughing. "And sang it very well."

"You should have put me in a cab."

"Darlin' you couldn't tell me where you lived, except turn right off the Grade, so I doubt you could have told a cab driver. The good news is, now I know there are at least twenty five private roads and driveways off 207. We tried them all."

I groaned. "Our road's just past the two mile post marker. On the right. But it's hard to find when the snow's this bad. We usually put a small blue flag on one of the trees but I forgot." I paused. "I'm really sorry to have put you out."

"You didn't put me out. Hell, you slept all the way home."

"Really?"

"Really," he assured me.

"Well, at least I wasn't singing," I said.

"I know you think you drank a lot, but you should know the bartender was pouring you doubles. I know Nick. When I spotted you, I asked him what you had been drinking."

I looked up at him, surprised. "No wonder I was so blitzed."

"Twice as much booze for your money. I expect he thought he was doing you a favor."

"Well, Lord knows he wasn't doing you one. How did I have such lucky timing?"

"I was playing poker with some buddies and went out through the lounge. I always park in one of the private spots in back of the stage. And there you were, sound asleep in the back corner."

"I'm lucky you saw me."

His long silence made me wince.

"Oh, God . . ." I hung my head in my hand. "I was snoring, wasn't I?"

"No one will ever hear it from me," he said, holding up his hand and he was having trouble keeping a straight face. "Scout's honor."

I laughed. "Were you a Boy Scout?"

"No. Four H. I raised some calves—who could outsnore you—"

I groaned.

"—and entered them in a few fairs and shows. At least for a couple of years before the music and partying became my life goals. And it was better that I found you than security."

"That's true. I've already been arrested once in the past year. My kids would have a fit," I admitted and looked up, then waved a hand. "It's a long story."

He sat down across from me and stretched his long legs out in front of him, took a sip of coffee and said, "Well, we've got all day and tonight and probably tomorrow for comparing stories. The roads are closed and another storm's coming in, so make yourself comfortable."

The moment his words registered my weak stomach sank and my heart raced. I realized I was sweating. My hair felt damp at the temples, and my face was flushed and hot.

I blamed the burning fire and my hangover, but I looked into those clear blue eyes of his and felt that same melting feeling I had that night when he was sitting a foot away from me and singing.

• • •

"Checkmate."

Rio soundly cleaned my clock at chess three times, but I beat him at checkers. "Okay, that's it. I give in. Now I have absolutely no ego left."

Grinning, he stood and stretched, then hunkered down in front of a raised stone hearth to poke at the fire. Outside the snow fell hard, a white landscape with a few shadows in the distance, big flakes, as if there were a pillow fight in Heaven.

I looked back at him. "You could have let me win once."

He glanced at me over his shoulder. "I thought you liked challenges."

"I do but I like to win more," I said and put the chess pieces away in a drawer. We played at a lovely antique rosewood game table taking up a corner of the great room, opposite a gorgeous grand piano and between the windows and fireplace, and near the bar.

One look at the table and I had furniture envy, from the claw and ball feet to the oxblood leather chairs that rolled on roll wheels and swiveled and rocked backwards. When I commented on it he told me it came from a men's club in New England and probably from England before that. I suspected he hosted many a poker game there, with his bar only a few steps away.

"You've seen me drunk and snoring. You had a laugh. I want one. You owe me something, salve for my crushed pride. Tell me your best story no one knows."

"So that press comment I bragged about this morning is coming back to bite me in the butt."

"Tell me something funny."

"Well, let's see . . . I think my best story is my ex-wife's doing."

He had an ex-wife, an ex-model girlfriend and son.

He was smiling, but he looked down and I could tell he was thinking back. "I had just come home from four months on the road and had been used to partying hard, coked up, and ignoring her. We'd had a fight and I left and didn't come home for three days. When I did come home, I passed out on the bed.

"Krista was so fed up she spent hours with a needle and thread sewing together the top and bottom sheet around me. I woke up late the next day sewed between the sheets."

I burst out laughing. "Now that *is* funny. How long did it take you to get out?"

"Between my muffled shouts?"

I laughed again. "That's about the best payback story I've heard in a while. I have a friend, Ellie, who caught her first husband with another woman. She sold his yacht, his sports car, and her wedding ring and bought the most lovely canary diamond the size of a strawberry."

"She had sewed me so tightly I could hardly

flex my hand," he said. And I could see the humor in his eyes as he remembered, which said something about the kind of man he was now.

"She must have been really angry."

"She was, but she was a good woman and she deserved better from me." He looked so sad, and shook his head. "Beautiful, with a great voice. Krista sang backup for Reba McEntire. Getting mixed up with me was a bad deal for her. She married me wanting more than I was able to give back then. My mama had just died, and I was lost. I married her for all the wrong reasons."

"I'm sorry."

"Things work out for the best. After two years of marriage to me, she wanted to get as far away from the entertainment business as she could. She's been married for fifteen years to an attorney, has a passel of kids, boys, and I expect she'll raise them to be better husband material than I was."

"I have three boys and a girl. And I came from a family of girls, just my older sister and I. Raising boys was more about harnessing all that energy. I swear those boys of mine came out of the womb ready to jump on furniture and bounce off walls, to climb up to the ceilings and scare the hell out of me. Mike had a brother so he understood the boys and the fights. My boys were explorers, and they played really dirty tricks on each other. For a few years, it seemed like we were always at the ER for stitches and broken bones."

I told him some of the funnier stories about my sons and my family, and he seemed to want to hear more about the chaos and dynamics of a larger family, especially one of such individual personalities and the closeness in age between the elder two.

"And now?"

"Mickey is in his first year at UCLA. He seems happy, but he always was my social animal. My mother used to say he never met a stranger. The older two are married. They run the company, and sometimes try to run my life." I grew quiet then, not certain why I admitted that last part to him.

He seemed to soak in my comment. "I guess I could be that way with my mama sometimes. Men are taught to take care of their mothers. Maybe with their dad gone, they take that responsibility all the more seriously."

"I know." I stared down at my hands. "We all seem to worry more about each other now."

"So tell me about your daughter."

"Oh, Molly, Molly. Where do I start?"

I chose my words carefully. "Molly was her daddy's girl, from the time she was a baby."

"I expect she wrapped him around her little finger."

"I suppose. He was good with all the kids. Her

brothers claim she terrorizes them into submission."

He laughed. "I was an only kid. Just my mama and me. I thought I wanted a sister, but maybe not."

"Molly is brilliant and talented. She took to photography, graduated from UCLA, has a great eye, even as a child, and is an amazing photographer." I smiled as I remembered her reaction and the day I took her to Golden Gate Park and taught her how to work the lens and light meter.

"Her eye always went to the most subtle things, things the rest of the world might not even see. Everyone thought I was crazy to spend so much money on a Nikon for a ten year old. But I knew it was right for her, and she never gave me a single reason to regret that gift. She works at Stone-Morgan, the advertising agency that handles the marketing for the company. And that was how she met Spider Olsen. She was the photographer for the print ads."

"Your daughter was the redhead sitting with Olsen."

"You noticed her."

"You were trying to set me up with her earlier that day, before you knew who I was. And darlin' except for her hair color, she looks just like you."

"So everyone tells us. I love that she has my mother's hair."

"When you said your daughter was dating someone older, you left out the fact that he was Spider Olsen."

"I know, I know. That's because since the man's been dating my daughter, I like to pretend he doesn't exist."

"How's that working for you?"

"Not well," I said and had to laugh. "I suppose I need to let go of it."

"How old is she?"

"Twenty four, almost twenty five. Are you interested now?"

"Would you want me to be now that you know my past?" He smiled and we both knew the answer.

"No." I laughed. "But I live to annoy and protect my children. Just ask her. She'll tell you."

"Like I said before, she's too young and she looked already taken to me."

I groaned and rested my head on the heel of my hand. "That's what I'm afraid of. That she's taken."

He stood up and held out his hand. "Come on. The snow's stopped. I'll show you around the place."

I was thankful to get off the subject of Molly and Spider Olsen and put my hand in his and he pulled me up, then through the kitchen to a hallway at the back of the house ending in a large mud room with tumbled stone floors, a separate bath and laundry room and a door that led outside.

"You'll need these. The snow's deep," he said and handed me some heavy duty snow boots. My coat and hat and cashmere scarf hung from nearby hooks.

Just outside was a covered area that faced a wide open plain of fresh snow broken only by an occasional glimpse of rock and split wood fence and beyond that, a huge multistory barn-like structure flanked on each side by two other long buildings.

The snow was deep and we trudged through together, our breath frosting into white wisps in the cold air and our gloved fingers laced together as he guided me.

Opening the barn door he said, "In addition to the barn, my recording studio and offices are here." He gestured to one of the side buildings. It was a smaller version of the house and barn made of stone, wood, and glass. "That's a full guest house. Artists and musicians can stay in either of the houses here."

We went upstairs to where there were three offices, the last and largest one with a wide custom desk of glossy dark wood and cowhide leather furniture near a round conference table and a long glass wall that looked out toward the northern plains and towering Sierra mountain range, completely white with snow.

"This is your office," I said with a sense of awe, walking to the broad window and looking out at that incredible view for a moment. Smiling to myself, I turned and leaned casually against the credenza. "When you said ranch, I was thinking clapboard house with a porch, a fenced pasture, and a small barn," I admitted.

"Better than the image of a double wide trailer?" he said, and I laughed. "I didn't blow all the money, only my reputation and singing career."

"Only blew those, huh?"

He laughed and I realized I was relaxed and this was easy. I was enjoying myself. It felt good not to be me, the mother, me, the March I saw day in and day out, that wounded woman who stared back at me from the mirror, and who I was damned tired of seeing.

On the walls were displays of the music awards and plaques, records and framed parchments; it was obvious he was an extremely successful and award winning music producer. I had no idea the number of multi gold- and platinum-selling albums he was responsible for, but I owned a number of them. In a game of "what's on your iPod?" at least two of the albums would be at the top of the list for most people.

He took me down into the studio, which looked like the NASA Command Center, and then he playfully shoved me in a recording booth.

"Sit," he said. "This'll be fun."

"Oh, yeah . . . fun like a root canal fun. You haven't heard me sing."

"Yes I have," he said closing the door.

"You haven't heard me sing into a microphone," I yelled out to him. "My kids won't let me near the karaoke machine."

He was in the control room. Through the glass I saw him flicking switches and his low, sweet voice came in over a sound system. "Sing something."

"You'll be sorry," I said and I could hear my voice in the depths of the mike system.

"Come on, darlin'."

Sitting on a stool with a professional microphone hanging in front of me, I took a deep breath and launched into a breathy, a cappella vocal of Happy Birthday, Mister President and made him laugh. After I butchered the song as Phillip claimed I butchered all songs, Rio called me inside the control room so I could watch as he added background, manipulated and mixed the tracks until when he played the cut, and I didn't recognize my own voice.

"Now that's what I need for karaoke," I said, spinning happily around in a large leather chair and examining the bells and whistles of all the dizzying amounts of electronic and digital equipment in the room. "I need something like this to keep me from embarrassing my kids and myself."

We left and went down into the barn itself, a

full working barn with stalls and tack rooms and its own equine veterinary medical and dental facility in the back. The pride in his voice as he showed me his place was something I recognized. After years of living with men, with Mike and my sons, and of being a large part of our family business and the understanding of it, I got it that most men defined themselves by their work, measured their success and failure in terms of their jobs and professions, very differently from how most women defined success.

I didn't know if I was intimidated or impressed, but I think I was a little of both. There was no boastfulness or self-glorification in Rio's attitude. More over, he was sharing his enthusiasm for his love of what he did, allowing me to look inside to the real Rio Paxton. That he was sharing all this, and himself, with me gave me a warm feeling I couldn't explain, and frankly, didn't want to think about for too long. I was merely lonely.

Ten minutes later, laughing like I hadn't in so very long, I was on the back of a snowmobile, hat pulled down tightly on my head, my arms around Rio's waist and my hands stuffed into his fleece-lined jacket pockets, as we sped across the wide open fields of untouched snow. He gave me the ride of my life, spinning and making tight circles and figure eights, revving up the engine and taking off so fast I had to bury my head in his shoulder and hang on for dear life.

We rode like crazy over a series of low hills, whoop-de-dos, he called them, up then down and down and skidding sideways down the steeper ones, before he turned around and took me back the way we had come, only faster, finally speeding toward the last hill so fast we crested it at full speed.

Without slowing at all we flew over the top, me shrieking and laughing and half frightened, not knowing what he was going to do next. I never knew a snowmobile could be so much fun: all the highs and lows and fast, unexpected spins of an amusement ride.

Coming nearer the house, he stopped where a wooden bench almost covered in snow had been built under a sprawling, lone heritage oak, on a rise, so land and hills and mountains were all there before my eyes. "This is amazingly lovely," I said quietly.

"I built the bench exactly here, because this is my favorite spot. Before I ever built the buildings, this bench was here. When things get to me or I forget who I am, I can come here, to the last best place I can think of, the place where I can see all of the land and mountains and skies, the enormity of it all, and just sitting here reminds me how small I am in the whole scheme of the world, and that my problems, whatever they are, are even smaller."

I absorbed what he said and the view around

me, understanding. "I could see how this could be inspiring. Does your music come to you here?"

He shook his head and said quietly, "The words come to me here."

Neither of us said anything. I had the thought that we could both sit there for hours and never say a word to each other. It was one of those places where two people could just be together, a place you could share something beautiful in complete, companionable silence.

That same silence spilled over us on the ride back toward the barn. I felt wonderful, and I had nothing to say, nothing to be spoken aloud.

About a hundred feet from the barn, we stopped abruptly. The snowmobile had become stuck as he was trying to ride through a deeper snowdrift. He swore under his breath and put his foot down, as he was playing with the motor, and then it started moving again. Way too fast. Rio and the snowmobile flew forward.

I didn't.

I was flat on my back sprawled in the snow, staring up at the thick gray snow clouds in the sky above me and the beginnings of snowflakes that were starting to fall and stick to my face.

"March!"

I could hear the crunch of his boots in the snow, running towards me. I blinked as his face came into my line of vision.

"Are you okay?" He was sincerely worried, and

didn't see the handful of snow I threw right in his face.

Laughing, I rolled away, but he was on me, shouting he was "gonna get me and make me pay", laughing and rubbing my face in the snow, me shoveling handfuls of it anywhere I could, mostly his face and ears, and we rolled around like two Labrador puppies until I cried "Uncle!" and gave up, pinned to the snowy ground by his long body on mine.

Our laughter faded, and I was in deep trouble, looking up at him, feeling things I didn't think I should be feeling for him as our breathing beat the same fast tattoo. My gaze went from his eyes to his mouth and then I completely forgot to breathe. The silence was fast changing to something else altogether, a powerful emotion, taut as a guitar string there between the two of us.

I had forgotten how things passed between a man and a woman, how a man could look at you, making it clear he wanted you, and you melt away like snow under a warm body. I wanted this. I wanted him to look at me like he was, but something inside of me kept saying I was in trouble and this was wrong.

When he was looking at me that way, I couldn't seem to think. I wanted to make a joke to break the moment, but I opened my mouth and all that came out was his name.

Chapter Twenty Eight

Rio all but dragged me into the house with him, through the front door, slamming it closed, pressing me back against it with his body. He cupped my face with his hands, turning it up toward his mouth, then he stopped, frozen, and his look changed, his eyes aware of what was happening and looking intently into mine.

"March . . . I'm sorry." His hands fell away and he took a deep breath and stepped back, shaking his head slightly.

He was apologizing. I didn't want an apology. I wanted him. Suddenly nothing else mattered, not age or time or anything. My breathing was fast and I felt this horrific emptiness without him close to me.

"I shouldn't have done that," he said. "I brought you here to keep you safe. Not for this. I'm not . . ." he paused, searching awkwardly for words. "Look. I don't want to scare you off."

I reached out and grabbed two handfuls of his sheepskin jacket and pulled him back to me. "Who's scared?"

He groaned my name and lowered his head until our mouths touched, his tongue licked my lips and he tasted like coffee and man and I was so terribly hungry for that taste.

"I wanted this. I wanted you so much I ache over you," he said against my mouth, his hand cupping the back of my head possessively.

"Me, too," I whispered on a sigh. "Me, too . . ." My words drifted away.

To be touched again. To be held. To have this. It had been so long. I thought I could never feel again, a passion that was so powerful I wanted nothing else but for him to go on, a ride that was more than any snowmobile or amusement park, as if all the stars in the whole universe were dancing in me and around me, and I was flying, and flying and clearly aware I was not with the man I had loved this way for so long. It was Rio Paxton who was taking me there.

It snowed all night and all the next day, then the storm moved on, the snowplows came out, and the roads were cleared. But I hadn't gone home to Tahoe for three days. I was as comfortable in Rio's house as I was in his arms and in his bed, in his spa tub and in his shower, and on the rug in front of the fireplace and against the kitchen counter.

I was not comfortable lying to my kids, my worrisome sons in particular, who I called from my cell phone regularly after calling the house to check the message machine and voicemail. I checked in with them, chatting casually to keep them unaware that my mountain life was really ranch life, and a newly active sex life, and to keep them from worrying about me, since Tahoe snowstorms were all over the Bay Area news.

So far, so good.

On the other side of Rio's master bedroom was his music room, the place where he worked on his songs. There was no place in his house I wasn't welcome, he'd made that clear. He had gone to his barn office earlier and I was bored and wandered into the music room. There were a couple of soft overstuffed chairs, a huge imported Oriental rug and a line of guitars in metal guitar stands and stacks of notebooks along with a beautiful ebony piano.

I sat at the keys, playing the notes scribbled in pencil across a music sheet. There was a note-book open on the bench. I picked it up and read the words written there, the verses of another song about souls broken and love lost and found, and the kind of man who had trouble finding love. Rio's songs were like reading poetry, the depth and the fear in those words he had written.

Sometimes when I read a line, I had to stop and take a deep breath. My heart ached deeply for a man who knew that kind of pain, and understood it so clearly he could put his feelings into words, the dark emotions and sheer joys of falling in love.

I sensed he was there with me and looked up. He stood in the shadow of the doorway, leaning on the jamb, arms crossed, just watching me. I wasn't certain how long he'd been there, and what I read in his eyes troubled me on some level.

This was all so new. I was caught up in all these feelings. I did not want to love a man again, and yet I was full of emotion. I had been here before. I knew he was beginning to fall in love with me and he wasn't hiding it. He said it openly.

But what I felt wasn't at stake. I read his lyrics and I thought about where I was a year ago—I was in a different place—and I knew I didn't want to hurt this man who had been hurt before.

Could I really start all over again? Was it possible that therewas a new beginning for me? Now, only a year later, a year that felt like ten.

For his sanity, part of me wantcd to run away as fast as I could, because I didn't know if what was left of me was enough for someone to love. But I didn't move. I couldn't run when I looked at him and he was looking at me like he was. There was a glimmer of joy in me. I hadn't felt anything close to joy and happiness for so long.

All I wanted was to run into his arms, not away from them.

Something as powerful as God's hands held me there, that and a cowboy's look. I put down the music book. "The words are amazing, luminous. Tell me about the song."

"It's about a woman who heals a broken man's soul with her love." He joined me on the piano bench, and began to play, singing the words he had written on the tablet from memory. When he was done and played the final note, I was leaning my head against his shoulder, unable to look at him for a minute because I was crying. My name was in the song.

He tilted my chin up so he could see my face.

"This is all happening so fast," I said.

"Because life's that way. Things that are meant to be just sort of click into place. Don't over-think this thing between us. Don't question it, darlin'. Just go with it and let me love you."

I tried not to think about how I would explain Rio Paxton to my children. I hadn't thought about how I could explain that I was even dating to them. I kept both sides of my life separate, and it was easy since I was at the Tahoe house. Deception was my friend. Hiding out from my children gave me the freedom to be with Rio and explore the two of us and give my heart another chance.

We went out together, twice to dinner and once to the movies and I found myself absorbing who he was, how he thought, the big things about him and the little ones, too. He liked to dump a box of chocolate covered raisins in his popcorn rather than butter, and to sit smack dab in the center of the theatre, and he didn't drink soft drinks.

He took me snowmobiling again, something I had taken to and loved almost as much as boarding. This time we each rode our own snowmobile and raced across the white fields together. He promised me we would do the same thing on horseback, when the snow melted.

So I casually broke the news to him that I didn't ride.

"You will. You're a natural, March. From what I've seen you'll ride well. And I've felt your sweet thighs tighten," he said, winked at me and then took off ahead of me, laughing.

Okay, I thought, any man who used the words "sweet thighs" together with the word "tight" when referring to my body was the man for me.

But the truth about my feelings had nothing to do with sweet thighs and a lot to do with the things he said to me, what I was learning about him, and just the sheer joy I felt when I was with him, the passion between us that seemed to grow stronger and better, and when he held me in his arms, the wonderful way I felt loved and safe, healed, and as if nothing could ever hurt me again. I was afraid that it wasn't true, but more frightened not to stay within that soft aura—real or imagined.

The next day the snow was perfect on the mountain so we spent the day at the Nevada side of Heavenly, boarding the mountain together. It was about four o'clock when we went into the lodge for a glass of wine, and were sitting at a table for two talking when a shadow caught my attention.

"March?"

Old friends of the family, the Baileys, were standing there.

I quickly pulled my hand out of Rio's. "Linda, Jeff. It's good to see you." I stood and we hugged. There was an awkward heartbeat of silence.

How did I introduce Rio? Would they know his name? Thoughts swirled like snowflakes through my head.

Rio reached out to shake Jeff's hand. "I'm Rio Paxton," he said smoothly.

Jeff recognized him, before he heard his name, and we all talked for a few awkward minutes. I asked about their kids, their son had been a friend of Scott's in high school and their daughter still knew Molly pretty well.

Soon the conversation waned and the Baileys left, but not before I had a good idea that they understood Rio and I were not merely acquaintances.

I sipped my wine thoughtfully as I watched them walk away.

"Okay," Rio said, setting his wine glass down. "That was not easy for you."

I thought it was perhaps worse for him. "I didn't know what to say," I admitted, feeling sick to my stomach with shame. Was I embarrassed?

He leaned back in his chair and gave me a direct look. "We need to figure out how we're going to deal with your friends."

"I'm sorry. You have every right to be angry with me. I was horrid."

He laughed. "You were caught off guard."

"You think?" I said, disgusted with myself, so I swilled down some more wine.

"Must have been that deer in the headlights look that gave you away."

"Don't make excuses for me. You should be angry with me."

"Why? I get it, March. I know this won't be easy for you. You were married to Mike for three decades."

"Three decades?" That got my hackles up. I looked at his face and realized he was teasing me. I laughed then because what else could I do?

He didn't say anything for a minute. He was staring into his wine glass with a look I couldn't read. "Is what's bothering you me, who I was? Or is it our age difference?"

"Rio, I love who you are and I don't care that you had a rough past. All that is long gone."

"No. It's still there in people's memories."

"And I don't care. What you went through made you the good man you are. I love that about you and wish you could learn to forgive yourself." I paused, choosing my words care- fully. I didn't want him to misunderstand. "I don't think about our ages when I'm with you. But honestly? I did just then."

"Are you having second thoughts?"

What I heard in his voice told me I couldn't hold back anymore. He was as vulnerable as I felt. I was crying when I looked at him again and shook my head. The words spilled from heart, my broken, aching, lost heart. "I love you."

"Oh, darlin' . . ." He smiled indulgently and looked a little relieved. He stood up and pulled me into his arms. "Let's get out of here."

Chapter Twenty Nine

Four days later Rio and I went back up to the lake after another couple of days at the ranch and went out to dinner at a casino steakhouse, then drove to my place afterward. He pulled his truck into the driveway and two of my kids' cars were parked there. Scott's white Land Rover and Molly's silver BMW SUV. My stomach dropped and I took a long breath. This was not good. "They didn't call first," I said.

"Is that a problem?"

"I think so," I said. It looked as if all the lights in the house were on. "I think I'd better go in alone."

"I don't think that's a good idea," he said protectively. "I have to meet them at some point."

"Let me talk to them first."

He studied me for a long time, and then nodded. "Call me if you need me."

I squeezed his hand and got out of the truck, grabbed my weekender with my stomach already in knots and praying this was only a surprise visit. I waited until he drove away, before I went inside.

Scott, Phillip, and Molly were all sitting in the great room. The boys looked worried and angry. I wondered if they were still on the outs. But Molly was chomping at the bit and ready for a fight. She shot up from her chair, her face red and tight when she looked at me. "We're giving you this opportunity to tell us where you've been."

I dropped my weekender on the floor and my purse on the table. "Excuse me?"

Phil wisely grabbed her arm. "Now Molly . . ."

She whirled on Phil. "Don't now Molly me. She's been lying to us."

"I chose to not involve you in a part of my life that's new and private," I said as I walked into the room. "Frankly, I don't have to tell you anything."

"So you admit it."

"Admit what, Molly?"

"That you're involved with that singer. Rio Paxton. The Baileys saw you two out together. When I called you on your cell phone, you pretended you were here, right here in this house. But you weren't here, Mother. I know because I was standing right there when I called you." She pointed to the kitchen counter.

So I was guilty of lying and had been caught. "You're right. I wasn't here. I haven't been here for a few days. And yes, you might as well hear it from me, I was with Rio. I've been seeing him."

"Oh God . . ." Molly put her head in her hands. "Our mother is a cougar."

"What?" I said.

"A cougar, one of those older—" Phillip started to explain.

"I know what a cougar is, and I am not! I do not prowl around for younger men. Rio and I met accidentally."

None of them said a word.

"All of you were at the casino lounge that night when he sang to me." I looked at my sons. "Remember how you both thought him singing to me was so very funny, and safe? What you didn't know was we had already met. And just so you know, a relationship with anyone, let alone him, was the farthest thing from my mind at the time." I wanted to tell Molly that I was originally checking Rio out for her, but she was already thoroughly annoyed with me. I paused and looked at them. They seemed to be soaking in my words and searching for their own. "I'm getting a glass of wine."

I walked into the kitchen, poured the wine, and saw my hand was shaking. I took a long swallow and stood there for a second, getting myself together before I went back into the other room. I tried to appear calmer than I felt and sat down in a chair by the fire.

When no one said anything, I spoke up. "You must have realized that at some point in the future, I was going to start dating somebody. I'm not dead."

"Mom," Scott said kindly. That he looked so worried bothered me, until I remembered he was more than willing to stay out of Molly's relationship. I wanted him out of mine, too, especially when it was so new and fragile and I was already confused and clinging to the deep connection I felt for Rio. "This is not about you dating," he said.

"Isn't it?"

"He is a lot younger than you." Phillip leaned forward, his elbows on his knees and his hands clasped in front of him. Phillip was so serious when he looked at me. "Don't you think that's a problem?"

"Rio's age? I supposed it could be. I certainly would not have picked a younger man."

"You've been so messed up since Dad died. You can't trust your judgment."

Did Phillip really think I was so screwed up? The past year scrolled through my mind, and I remembered all the bad moments, the sleeplessness, the incident that had gotten me thrown in jail. He must remember them, too.

Even if I had actually been that much of a mess, what he said made me angry. "Thank you, Dr. Phil," I sniped at him with all the rancor I felt at my situation and the guilt I felt over my own mistakes.

I hated this. I hated my reaction. I hated their reaction. I hated sharing what I was feeling. It was new and I felt alive again. I wanted to run back down the driveway and into Rio's arms for some small bit of peace and contentment that had been so rare in my life for the last year. I waited a moment, then said, "Look, I loved your father and this has nothing to do with what we had together for all those years, or with what I felt for him.

"Yes, I've been struggling this past year. Yes, I've felt alone. Yes, I've made mistakes. But this is not a mistake. And even if it is, it's my mistake to make. Not yours."

"But Rio Paxton, Mother?" Molly clearly wanted a fight.

"It's perfectly understandable that you kids would have trouble with anyone I dated."

"That's not true," Scott said too reasonably, which told me it was true.

"Well, whether it is or not doesn't matter. I guess we'll never know now, will we? Because I'm seeing Rio," I said firmly.

"See?" Molly said to her brothers. "I told you I couldn't do this alone. She's so stubborn."

"Molly. *She* is right here. Don't talk about me as if I'm not."

"Okay, then, Mother. What do you have to say? There's a huge age difference between you."

"Aren't you the black pot talking to the kettle? Spider is twenty five years older than you are."

"And you're old enough to be that cowboy's mother."

"Not quite," I said through gritted teeth.

"What could you possibly have in common?" she asked me.

"What could you possibly have in common with Spider?"

"Sex, Mother," she said to shock me. "Spider is great in bed."

"So is Rio," I shot back.

"Oh, God . . ." She made a face and held up her hands.

Scott groaned and Phil said, "Too much information, Ma."

"Well, where the hell did you think I was for the last two days? Holding hands with him? Your generation did not invent sex."

"But you hardly know him, and you slept with him?" Molly looked appalled.

"I slept with your father the first night I met him."

They all looked at me stunned, part horror in

my daughter's case, and shock or awe or a mix of the two, I wasn't sure which, with the boys.

"That was back in the Sixties," I said, slightly embarrassed because I didn't exactly mean to admit that to them. "You had to have been there. And frankly, who I sleep with really isn't your concern, especially now that you're adults. I would consider it Mickey's concern since he still lives at home, but it's too early in my opinion for us to all play meet the family."

"Who you date is our concern, Mom," Scott said. "You're a wealthy woman."

"Who can make decisions for herself," I said.

"Like getting drunk and cracking her head open or getting herself thrown in jail," Molly muttered.

I turned to her. "Or dating the wrong man."

"Exactly," she said.

"I meant you."

"If the shoe fits," was her response. "And Spider and I are not dating."

"He broke up with you?" I glanced from her to her brothers.

"We're engaged." Molly held out her hand and twisted a band ring around. A large oversized pink diamond surrounded in more stones sparkled from her ring finger.

I wanted to throw up. "But he's already been married three times." I looked to her brothers with the hope they would at least acknowledge some risk in this. They weren't listening to

374

anything I said about her, just like before. "What is wrong with you two?" I was getting so angry with them. "Can't you see the problem in this?"

"Right now we're only worried about you," Scott said.

"Look Ma, we know who Spider is." Phil's voice was calm. "But we don't know much about this . . . Rio guy."

"Well, you don't need to. Back off of me and try to talk some sense into your sister. This is her whole life. It's a huge decision. I'm dating Rio, not marrying him."

The longer I looked at them, the more I could tell nothing I had said eased their already-made-up-minds.

"I looked him up on the internet," Scott admitted.

"You Googled Rio?"

"Yes," all three of my kids said at once.

I stepped back, a little surprised.

"He's had a pretty wild life, Ma." Phil gave me a concerned look and Scott nodded. That might have been the first thing the two of them agreed on since Mike died, I thought miserably.

"And a bad marriage," Molly added.

"One failed marriage, not three," I said, and she at least had the good sense to look down.

"There's a huge gap in his history," Phillip said.

"Yeah," Scott agreed. "There's been nothing about him for years."

"Perhaps because of the life he lives now. Did that cross your mind? Rio was young when he became famous way too fast. He let the limelight go to his head. My God, he was just a kid when he hit it big. Think about Mickey. Think about yourselves at that age. It didn't take that long for his life to fall completely apart, and he's worked hard to turn everything around. If there's one thing I'm certain of, he's a good man."

I hated being forced to defend Rio, who didn't need defending, and if he did, he could do so himself. He never verbally apologized for the mistakes he had made, although he had come close the afternoon at the ski lodge. But his jokes about them always carried edges of regret.

His humility was real and not just something coy bred from the polite South; it came from having been in the lowest places, and from understanding how easily you could make the wrong choice and ruin a life. I believed he carried with him self-condemnation and dark memories in a place deep in his heart. I also believed his occasional go-to-hell look was instinctive; a defense against a past he regretted so greatly, but knew he could never change.

"At least Rio has a learning curve," I said. "I don't see that Spider Olsen has changed, or even tried to." I faced my sons. "And neither of you had any trouble at all with Spider and Molly, but you question me about Rio? I didn't raise you to practice that kind of a double standard."

"You're our mother," Scott said.

"She's your sister," I shot back.

The doorbell rang before any of us could say another word, and I looked up startled. Though I hadn't expected him, I knew who was standing on the other side of the door. "I'll get it." I walked over and let Rio inside.

He leaned into me and took my hand. "You're not going to face them alone, darlin'."

"This isn't going to be fun or easy," I said quietly.

"I didn't expect it would be," he said and gave my hand a squeeze.

We walked into the great room together. "Scott, Phil, Molly, this is Rio."

Rio moved toward my sons, who stood and shook his hand, and I saw that he kept eye contact with each of them, said their name with a nod of acknowledgment, before he turned to my daughter, who hadn't budged from the sofa. "Molly," he said kindly, and she was stubbornly silent.

With Molly, this wasn't about him, not really. This was about her father, and about me, and my choices which she worked very hard at not agreeing with. She, of my children in that room, I realized all too late, honestly felt betrayed by me, and I was sorry I snapped at her.

"Careful," I said to cut the tension. "She's already called me a cougar."

"You?" Rio burst out laughing, then looked at me, slid his arm around my waist and his face turned serious as he looked at my children. "The truth is she met me at the back door of the stage with her panties in her hand."

For just an instant, the look on my kids' faces was priceless. "He's kidding," I said. "I told him what you boys said New Year's Eve."

"Sorry," Rio said, not looking the least bit apologetic. "Too good a moment to pass up. The truth is that I chased after your mother. It wasn't the other way around."

"That's exactly why we're here," Scott said, giving Rio a direct look that reminded me so much of his dad. "For our mother." Scott had just drawn a line in the sand, a deep line.

"Okay," Rio said easily, sitting down next to me on the sofa. "Fire away. Ask me whatever you want, whatever you need to know about me. I'll tell you the truth." He leaned forward, resting his elbows on his knees.

I sipped wine as my children grilled him on every subject, questions I hadn't asked and answers I hadn't known. They wanted to know his roots and background, about those days as a country star; questions about everything from cocaine to his net worth, a figure which made Molly gasp, Phil choke on his beer, and Scott ask even more pointed questions, like why the hell he sang in a casino lounge.

If there was a sure thing to bet on in this world, it was that Rio loved to sing, and he said as much. Performing wasn't about show business and limelight. "Music needs to be heard, and the stories the songs tell should be shared with as many people who want to hear them," he told my son. "I have something to say in my songs."

Every time someone played a recording of one of Rio Paxton's long list of songs on the radio, every time someone sang his lyrics on TV, Rio was paid. He had been active behind the scenes in recent years, recording and producing some of the biggest groups to come into country music and some top albums, for which he was paid a whole hell of a lot of money. But his work was important to him, not as a claim to fame, but simply how he felt about the music.

It was late when my kids were done with him, and we left them sitting uncomfortably quiet and pensive and perhaps a little more accepting. I wasn't really sure.

Outside, I walked with him over to the driver's side of his truck. He leaned against it and pulled me into his arms, then wrapped me inside his heavy fleece coat and slid his hands into the back pockets of my jeans.

I felt his lips on my forehead and we stood like that for an immeasurable amount of time, hearts beating against each other, and I felt so incredibly good. It was probably twenty degrees out and the moon was big and white and almost full; it was hazy around the edges, as if it were rimmed in dry ice, as if it would burn you if you touched it.

I took a deep breath of frozen air and watched the frost cloud float upward when I exhaled. "I wonder if you have any idea how much I adore you for what you just went through for me."

"I'm selfish, darlin'. I want you, so I did it for me."

"Yeah . . . yeah . . . yeah . . . ," I said and he tilted my chin up with his knuckle and kissed me so tenderly I almost wanted to cry. I couldn't stop the way my body fit against his or the passion that flared so hot and fast between us, passion and something more than that, something I just felt, and still had trouble accepting and being comfortable with. This was all so unexpected and new and fresh and wonderful. And I was scared.

He pulled back after a minute and ran his thumb back and forth across my lip. "I'll miss you tonight."

"I know. Me, too."

Once inside, he rolled down the window and started the truck.

"Call me when you get home. I want to know you're okay." The words came without thought, and at that moment I understood exactly where my heart was. I was afraid I would lose another man I loved.

I walked back toward the house and I could hear my sons' raised voices inside. When I opened the door, the two of them were like bulldogs facing off nose to nose. They both had the same expressions. Molly wasn't in the room.

"You've lost the company more money this year with your crappy choices than I ever did with SkiStar," Phillip shouted.

"Well, it's damned easy for you to stand here and criticize me, Phil. You didn't have to make those decisions. Do you know what Dad would have done? Is it all just so easy for you?"

"Oh yeah, I've got it so easy. You and your wife pop out kids like rabbits . . . in the damned dining room. You don't even need a goddamned hospital, while I almost lost my wife just trying to carry one baby. She cries every night because she can't get pregnant. Yeah, my life is so easy. What can I do right? I can't drive, and apparently I can't screw right either."

Scott fired back. "And isn't it all too easy to look back now and say I should have taken the American Express endorsement deal, or worked out the new insurance contract for the company. Or to say that we could have made more money if I expanded the clothing lines. The list of what

I should have done is as long as my arm!" Scott drove his hand through his thick hair and spun around and faced his brother. "And who the hell are you to call me a coward, to say that I'm afraid of risk? That's ridiculous. You are supposed to be the wild one, the risk taker, the gambler. You are the hip, cool brother, not the square conservative one. I'm a coward? So tell me Joe Cool, why is it that you won't drive a car since Dad died?"

Molly came down the stairs, clearly stunned by her brothers' fight.

"Screw you, Scott." Phillip shouted.

"You brought it up."

"Stop it! Both of you!" I walked into the fray. "Is that true, Phillip?" My mind scrolled backwards over time and I tried to remember if I could remember Phillip driving. What I could remember were two instances when he weaseled out of driving, one of them at Christmas and Keely was driving her car at Thanksgiving. "Do you not drive?"

"He doesn't drive anymore?" Molly asked, as surprised as I was.

Scott was still fuming but he nodded.

"You don't drive anymore because of your dad's accident?"

"It started then," Scott volunteered.

That Phillip was stonily quiet pretty much told me it was true. Molly was eyeing him curiously and she seemed to have dropped her animosity a little.

I felt like a failure, standing there with my three oldest children all of whom were having deep troubles. I hadn't been paying attention. Scott knew what was going on with Phillip but I hadn't noticed. Phillip had been deeply traumatized by his father's accident and I didn't notice.

My son who stopped by to check on me, teased me and watched out for me. The most sensitive of my four, the one who covered all of his tragedies by joking his way around them. I had no Pledge cans for him. I hadn't even noticed what was going on. I grasped my middle son's hand. "It's okay Phil. It's okay."

He raised his head and looked at me. His eyes were moist and his lips thin as a needle. My son was lost, deep in those eyes I knew so well, my son was lost and afraid and alone. He broke eye contact and said, "Drop it, Ma."

I took a deep breath and said firmly, "You both have to stop fighting. You two are the company now. It's both of you, profits and loss, mistakes and brilliant new ideas. But you stop this, now. Neither of you are leaving until you work things out."

"Come on, Molly." I took her gently by her stiff shoulders and led her toward my room. "You and I are going to talk. In my bedroom." I stopped and turned around. I looked at my sons.

"I mean it. You two work out this horrible dark thing between you."

In the bedroom I said to Molly, "Okay. Sit down."

She did.

"So you want to marry Spider?"

She nodded, twisting the engagement ring on her finger.

"You know how I feel about him."

"But you aren't marrying him. I am."

"That's true," I said, refusing to rise to the bait. "Molly, marriage is not easy. Believe me. You're going into this with the deck stacked against you. Even if the age difference weren't a problem, his marriages have been. He has failed three times. What makes you think this time with you will be different?"

She shrugged but wouldn't look me in the eye. "No one can predict the future. I could marry someone who has never been married and we would have a thirty three percent chance of getting a divorce."

She was right. But Spider? I took a deep breath and knew it was time for me to back down. "Are you sure this is what you want?" I asked.

"Yes," she said firmly. "We're getting married in three months."

"Three months? Why so soon?"

"We made the decision. I don't want a long engagement." She looked at me squarely. "Are you refusing to help me with the wedding?"

My mind went back to another time, another place, in a white kitchen with ivy wallpaper and another question *Are we really arguing about my wedding?*

I closed the distance between us, just a mere couple of feet, I sat down next to her and wrapped my arms around her. "Never."

And I sat there holding her for a long time, my hand cupping her head like I had when she was colicky and crying in the middle of the night. Only now, my baby stood on her own two feet. I forced back the tears I could feel rising in my throat. "I'm not certain we can get the dress ordered in three months."

"I know you, Mom. You can work miracles. You can get anything done." Molly stepped back out of my arms and looked at me with a look I hadn't seen in a long time. She needed me. "I thought if you would come home right away we can start planning everything."

My only daughter was determined to marry the wrong man, for what I was certain were the wrong reasons. Mike could have talked some sense into her. But he wasn't here and she needed me. Planning a wedding was important, a rare mother daughter moment. Our fragile, unraveling relationship needed all the mother–daughter bonding it could get.

"I thought that we could go home tomorrow," she said.

Tomorrow. I thought about Rio, but that was only that new part of me who loved the peace I had with him. My kids needed me.

Maybe this would be good for us. Some distance might make me less confused about how quickly my heart had become so tangled with his.

My sons were still yelling in the other room and Molly looked at me. "I brought some bride magazines. Will you look at them with me?"

Did she think I would refuse? I slipped my arm around her shoulders and smiled. "Sure."

She leaned her head against my shoulder. We sat there, my chin resting on my prickly daughter's head. She pulled away after a few minutes and hugged me, something she hadn't done in a very long time and stood up. "I'll run and get them."

I watched her walk away, fully aware that she was not certain about this marriage. Underneath all that attitude she was scared.

"Molly?"

"Yeah, Mom?"

"It will be okay. Everything will be okay." But in my heart, as I listened to the shouting and cursing and name-calling by my sons in the other room, I was certain I was wrong.

Chapter Thirty

The next day was too quiet. All through the morning. No shouting. No raised voices. Apparently for my sons working things out meant utter silence and one word answers. There was a strategy known to larger families—avoidance tactics when you didn't want to be confronted by those who knew when you were lying. With two stories and a large house, Phillip and Scott stayed a step ahead of me and Molly was the distraction, talking to me about nothing while her brothers disappeared separately on some trumped up task, like changing the heater filter or checking the propane tank.

We closed up the house, and I had thought we were to leave at the same time, but when I walked outside, only Scott was standing by my car, his car next to mine, his collar pulled up tightly as a light snow drifted down. Molly's car was gone, the tracks in the drive still deep.

Scott looked up as I locked the front door and walked down the steps. He opened the door for me. "I have a plan."

What I had planned was to be alone with Phillip.

"Molly and Phillip already left," he said in a rush.

"I can see that." I climbed inside. They knew me too well.

"The snow might be bad on 50. I thought I should follow you back."

No, you all cooked this up so Phillip wouldn't have to be alone in a car with me for two hours.

I buckled up. "I've been driving in snow since before you were born, Scott." I faced him. "Afraid I'll make a run for it, rob a Seven Eleven, and end up in the slammer again? Or maybe I'll go throw my panties at Justin Bieber."

"Now that I'd pay to see, Mom."

"Don't hold your breath. He's probably too old for me." I started the car and drove home, with two hours alone to think about my crazy feelings and my life for the last year.

Molly was waiting in the driveway when I pulled in and parked. I grabbed my small suitcase and she met me at the inside door.

"I called the wedding planner and we have an appointment tomorrow morning at ten. I was afraid you wouldn't check your messages."

I chose not to remind her that I was an adult and knew how voicemail worked. Then I remembered how I had been pretending to be at home instead of with Rio. She followed me chattering and I went upstairs toward the master bedroom. I opened the double doors and dropped my luggage inside.

"My God, Mom," Molly said, hovering at my back. "The room is completely different!"

"That was the point. If I was going to change it, I was going to really change it. It was difficult to live here the way it had always been. For my sanity I had to start over completely." My voice was odd, a little strident, and I was sorry.

"I hate change," she said, but her tone wasn't angry. "Truthfully? I thought I would hate it," she said quietly.

"You don't?"

"No." She smiled and squeezed my hand. "I don't. It's lovely. And it looks like you."

That surprised me.

She turned away for a second and I heard her breath catch.

I turned. "What is it?"

She bent down and picked up something off the floor. There in the palm of her hand was a white feather.

"A white feather." She stared at it.

"That must have come from the bedding or pillows," I said, walking toward the bed to touch the new bedding; it was thick and creamy looking, the pillows plump and lined up along a damask covered headboard with nailhead trim. A cashmere throw lay on the end of the bed. "Everything is new. New down pillows and comforters, new sheets, new mattress, new room." I turned slowly.

My master bedroom was finished, except for a chair in the sitting area that had been delayed at the upholsterer's. Mike's chair, of all things.

"I have to run." Molly gave me a quick kiss. Her mood was suddenly light and too cheery and I looked at her oddly for a minute. "We start our appointment schedule tomorrow," she said. "I'll pick you up at quarter to ten." And she rushed out the door. I stared at the empty spot where she just stood and felt as if I had been fly-by fruited.

My mercurial daughter.

I turned back. I was standing in the middle of the room. I closed my eyes and imagined what it had been like for years, the rugs, the chairs, the clothes lined up in the closet, his side, my side. The bed, his side, my side. Then I opened my eyes.

The room was every shade of white, crisp and clean, like a new sheet of paper. The crown molding, the door and window frames, all had been repainted in white, and the fireplace surround was painted in a creamy off white, antique washed, and hand rubbed to match some of the furniture pieces. On either side of the bed hung long beveled mirrors that reflected the light from the tall hand painted lamps on each nightstand—one was a round table from France with delicate curved legs and a mirrored top and the other a mirrored chest with a marble top.

Tall palms and trees and other deep green plants filled cold corners and each accessory was placed perfectly, many of them with mirror bases, so the light reflected everywhere. The master bath was all white with silver tiles and more large mirrors, hand painted cabinetry and clear vessel sinks. Two sides. Both mine.

White, white, white.

I had the screwiest thought and laughed and asked the room, "Where is Saint Peter? Where are the Pearly Gates?" I paused, my hand pressed to my stomach and asked quietly, "Where is my life?"

I walked over to the French doors and looked out at the tree. The limbs had been trimmed neatly and they could no longer rub against the house. I wondered if they could still cast shadows shaped like my husband.

So I turned back, quickly, suddenly, expecting to see him in our room.

The room wasn't us and he wasn't there.

As I stood there, I had a feeling the room could be me, and then I had the strangest warm and odd feeling of peace come over me. Peace.

I loved my husband more than anything. I wanted to grow old with him, holding our gnarled hands in wheelchairs side by side, and leaving this world together. The perfect lifetime.

But only in dreams was life perfect. I didn't ask to have him torn from me, to have our life together ended so horrifically. I didn't ask to live without him.

Without him, I didn't want to live in our life anymore. I needed to live my own.

I walked back to the bathroom and started a bath. It was another test: all the times I had seen visions of Mike when I was walking out of the bathroom in a towel.

Tonight there was no Mike. And I paused in my towel and waited, and my heart broke all over again, like that night over a year ago when the policeman stood at my door and told me my life as I had known it was over. Mike was gone.

I was no longer a wife. I was a widow. God in Heaven but I hated being defined by loss. I'd rather be defined by all the years we had together—a real gift of my lifetime. I hugged myself as I looked at the new bed. I didn't see Mike's spot. I didn't see him missing. And I lay down and I cried like before, but this time over what I couldn't see anymore. I just cried and cried, because this was goodbye.

For the next seven nights, I slept like the dead. And I never saw Mike again, not even in the rooms downstairs that I had yet to change. I didn't cry again, which was something. The tree never cast a shadow. There was no size 17/35 shirt for me to sleep in. There was no more haunting.

After a full two days of looking at venues for Molly's reception, I climbed into bed early, snuggled down under the covers. As I turned to set the alarm, I paused to look at our picture sitting on the nightstand in a new sleek sterling silver frame. It wasn't hidden in a drawer or stuffed under the bed. It wasn't hidden from me at all; it had been there from the moment I stepped into this new room. Our faces stared back at me, and I smiled.

I paused, then threw back the covers and got out of bed. Picture in hand, I walked over to the custom bookshelves and moved some things around, then set the photo there, angled it right, then left, then right again. Then I moved it up one shelf. I crawled back into bed and looked at it from across the room. It belonged in the bookcase with beloved family photos scattered on shelves, between stacks of books, those glimpses of our lives captured so we could never forget.

Mike would always be my blood and bone, so much a part of who I am and the woman I have become. He is my history. He is love defined by my decades of life with him. I did not and do not walk away easily from him. I never could. Ours was a separation forced by fate, and I fought the reality of it with everything I had. I resisted, I imagined, I fell apart. I did not want to go on in a world without Mike.

But I am here and he is gone. To not live my life to its fullest every hour, every minute and second would mean death has more meaning for us than life, than love, than all we were.

He is not here to finish my journey beside me. But he is with me . . . in my mind and my heart, and my children's heartbeats.

The morning we were supposed to look at wedding dresses, I got a frantic call from Molly as I sat drinking coffee and waiting for her. "I'm late, Mom. I'll have to meet you there."

She was panicked and I tried to remember as I drove to Union Square, if I had been that high strung the day I chose my dress. I didn't think so. I bought the first one I tried on. How easy decisions were when I was young. My mistakes didn't influence me, or make me tentative. But back then in those days I didn't think I made any mistakes, which reminded me of Molly.

Two hours later my pale daughter was standing on a pedestal surrounded by mirrors and sales people, silk organza and satin and seed pearls and lace and netting seemingly everywhere.

"I look like a marshmallow," Molly said, turning and glancing over her shoulder festooned with a large bow. "Everything is puffy." She grabbed a puffed sleeve, frowning. "What do you think?"

She did look like a marshmallow and I had to laugh. She and that dress would be at war just walking or flouncing down the aisle. "I think all we're missing are the singing bluebirds and a mouse named Gus."

And Molly laughed then, but not with her usual energy. She had been running late all week and came into the bridal department looking like hell in a UCLA sweatshirt and jeans, flip flops, no makeup and her hair pulled up in a ponytail. The wedding must have made her off, because I couldn't ever remember seeing her so unkempt.

She grabbed the silk and tulle skirts, pulled them up and trudged back to the dressing room. Soon the marshmallow dress came out carried by a sales associate. A moment later I heard a commotion back behind the dressing room wall.

The saleswoman came rushing out. "Mrs. Cantrell? Quick. Come here." I followed her.

Inside the large dressing room, Molly was lying on a damask sofa, her face so pale she matched the dresses.

"Honey, what's wrong?"

She moaned, looked at me as if she wanted to say something, and then stood and ran to the bathroom. I followed her inside, feeling as ill as she looked. She was vomiting in one of the stalls. It went on for a long time and when she stopped, I said, "Do you need some help?"

She was crying when she came out, wiping her mouth and her tears. "I'm pregnant."

Chapter Thirty One

We sat at a red light close to home. Molly was in the seat next to me, still crying. We'd left her car at the parking garage. She was too queasy to drive.

"I'm so embarrassed," she said, her hands covering her face.

"Why?" The light changed and I drove on, and then turned onto our street.

"You saw what happened," Molly said. "I almost threw up on a two thousand dollar dress."

"A two thousand dollar marshmallow," I said, hoping to get a smile out of her. "And you made it to the bathroom."

"I'm still embarrassed."

I stopped in the driveway, pressed the garage opener and sat waiting for the door to open. I looked at my daughter, who now looked more than unkempt; she looked pitiful, with her bright red blotchy face and nose. "You're embarrassed because of the people in the bridal salon?"

She nodded.

I tried not to laugh when she looked so upset. "Sweetheart, believe me, you are not the first pregnant bride they've had in there with an attack of morning sickness. Come on," I reached across the seat and rubbed her arm. "Let's go inside and we can talk."

"Okay," she said wanly.

We walked into the kitchen and I stopped. "Your room or mine or the living room?"

"Your room," she said, and then stopped looking like someone had slapped her. "It's all new and what if I get sick?"

I popped open a can of ginger ale, poured it over some crushed ice, and grabbed some saltines out of the pantry. "This will help. And don't worry about my room." I led her up the staircase and into my bedroom, and tucked her into the bed. I set the ginger ale down. "Ginger ale and saltine crackers. Still the best remedy in the world for morning sickness. Sip the ginger ale and eat small bits of the crackers. You'll feel better before you know it." I climbed in with her, both of us lounging against the huge downy pillows.

She tilted her head back against the pillow and took a shallow breath. "I feel so awful all the time."

"During the first trimester I used to throw up every morning if I brushed my teeth past my cuspids."

"Really?"

"Really. You're normal, dear. My gag reflex was always touchy when I was pregnant. And I got sick at night, too, more often than in the morning. Around dinner time, about six thirty, I'd go to bed to lay down and sleep all the way through until the next morning." I paused as she sipped the ginger ale, then asked her the big question. "How long have you known?"

She started crying all over again.

I put my arms around her, and she curled into me like a toddler. I rested my chin on the top of her head and just held her. "It's okay. Everything's going to be okay." Yet inside I hated that it was something so difficult that gave me my daughter back.

Time and the years disappeared and I remembered sitting like this. Molly was maybe two and I was holding her, rocking her to sleep almost every night. She was the daughter I wanted so badly in a house full of boys, born with my mother's glorious red hair.

When did all that change? When did she leave me?

"Spider didn't ask me to marry him until I told him I was pregnant."

What a loser, I thought, wishing I could throttle him. "What exactly did he say?"

"That we should get married for the baby's sake."

"No, I love you, Molly? No, I want to marry you?"

She shook her head again.

"I see," I said tightly. "Okay, tell me again why you want to marry Spider. Are you in love with him?"

Molly took her time, which in itself was pretty

telling. "I think I could be," she said finally.

"That's not exactly the most reassuring answer, Shortcake. Marriage is difficult enough if you love each other madly. If you don't have that going for you, I'm not certain what will keep you together, much less keep all of you happy. The baby is involved, too."

"Why don't you like him? He says it's because you're jealous."

"What?" Oh, God . . . Mike, Mike, Mike. I wish you were alive to punch his lights out again.

"He told me that you flirted with him in Calgary."

I'll wrap my hands around his throat and squeeze and squeeze and squeeze. . . . What I said was, "He said that, huh?"

"And that Daddy blamed him."

"We were in a bar in Calgary. Your father punched him out cold."

She ate a saltine and took another sip of the ginger ale. "You're not denying it."

"Do I really need to? Have you ever known your father to be unfair?"

"God no." Molly almost laughed. "He worried his head off about being fair and equal to everyone, especially us. Remember how he used to measure and weigh the birthday cake and divide our Halloween candy evenly? I remember when you got so frustrated with him and called him Karl Marx." Now she did laugh, and I did too.

"Spider was drunk and put his hands all over me, more than once."

"That sounds more like the truth," she admitted.

"There doesn't have be this huge rush to the altar," I said evenly. "I was married in June and Scott was born in October."

"You were pregnant when you got married?"

"My stomach was already huge. I walked across the grass to your father with your brother kicking my ribs all the way."

"But then you chose to get married, too."

"We did. But your father and I loved each other. To everyone who knew us we were March and Mike, Mike and March and we were already planning on getting married. Your brother was just an extra surprise. We were mad about each other and inseparable from the moment we met."

"The night you first slept with him."

I laughed softly. "I am going to regret that outburst, aren't I?"

"I goaded you into it. I was upset because of Daddy," she admitted with her head down.

I took an action from Rio and tilted her chin up so she was looking at me. "I understand, more than you probably know."

"The Baileys were really supportive of you, Mom. They thought I knew you were seeing some-one. I should tell you that. Jeff said he liked Rio."

"I like Rio. You're probably going to have to get used to having him around, because I don't think I want to give him up. He is a really good man and good men are not easy to find. Like your dad."

She was quietly thinking. I could see the wheels turning. My daughter was smart. She could put two and two together and get four. She faced me. "So what do you think I should do?"

Don't marry him! My mind screamed.

But instead I chose my words carefully. "It's your decision, not mine. Just like keeping and raising your baby is your decision. I will tell you this. You do not need a man to raise that child growing inside of you, and you do not have to marry its father. You have a whole family of men and women who will love you and love your child. I will do anything for you. We can raise your child together, and we, your family, will be there to catch you if you fall or your child falls. If you don't love Spider, then I would say to you think long and hard about what kind of marriage you want, what kind of marriage environment you want your child, or children, growing up in."

Molly was leaning back against the pillow and her eyes were heavy. She was exhausted and this was weighing heavily on her.

I patted her arm and said, "Take some time and think about it. But right now I think you need some sleep." I started to get up, but I looked at her and knew I didn't want to leave her, so I lay back down and slept by her side.

‧ ‧ ‧

The next day I walked into Scott's office at Cantrell Sports unannounced.

"Mom," he said and stood up. "What are you doing here?"

I closed his office door behind me and said, "I need to talk to you, or maybe I should say you need me to talk to you. Sit." I waved my hand at him and sat down on a corner of his desk.

Next to my hip was a photograph taken years ago, in the loft apartment we first lived in. Scott was probably a year and a half and he was shuffling along in his father's huge shoes. I picked it up and laughed slightly. "I remember this. Your dad kept it on his desk for years. I stared down at it for long time, and then looked up at him, turning the photograph so he could see it. "See this?"

He nodded.

"You sit here and you look at it every day. I think this is what's wrong. This is what's creating all those doubts in your mind. The idea that you cannot run this company unless you think like your dad did."

Scott frowned. "What do you mean?"

"Scott, son, you are not your father. He was a wonderful man but he made mistakes, big ones. Remember the year he used that factory in China for the clothing line?"

"And more than half the embroidery for the

logos on the winter jackets were spelled wrong."
Scott smiled.

"And sized wrong. I believe that was a costly mistake that took us into the red."

"I had forgotten about that."

"That's why I'm here. To remind you. You do not have to be your father to be successful, Scott." I pointed to the photo. "Put it away or interpret it differently. Use it to guide you in the right direction, not the wrong one. I talked to Renee. She says you're not sleeping. Seems to me that you worry so much about how to fill his shoes that you aren't making your decisions for the right reasons.

"He wouldn't want you to try to be him. He would want you to be yourself. He used to come home, proud as a peacock, and tell me about something you did that was great for the company, something he said he hadn't looked at before."

"He did?"

"Yes. For example: the expansion of our own retail outlets into the larger ski areas. You came up with the idea of opening our own shops in all those mountain villages."

"Yes. I did." Scott looked like her old son. There was something about him that said she had him thinking, and perhaps moving toward believing in himself again.

"Remember that. You know what to do. And

you're not half as conservative as Phillip makes you think you are." I stood and walked around the desk, settling my hands on his shoulders. "You boys should make this company yours. Your dad started it, with a lot of harping and begging and convincing on my part. He had doubts and worried about his decisions. But you are the future. You and Phillip and maybe Mickey. His sons are who can take this company in new directions."

He looked at her as if he finally understood.

"So what if you passed on the American Express endorsement and Burton took it. It's Burton in the commercial, not his son. What were you going to say? 'My dad Mike Cantrell did this and my dad did that? "Come on. My hunch is they would have dropped you for Burton anyway."

He laughed. "You're probably right."

"Now, I have something else to talk to you about." I handed him a check.

"One hundred thousand dollars? What's this for?"

"It's from my personal account."

"I see that. What are you doing giving me this?"

"I'm making things fair and even, the way your dad would have wanted." I paused then told him. "I'm going to give Phil your dad's Porsche." I nodded at the check. "That's enough money for you to go out and buy one for yourself."

"So what are you going to do about Molly and Mickey?"

"Nothing, for now. They won't care. Phil needs to heal. This is the only thing I can think of that might work."

He looked up at her. "You don't have to give me this." He handed the check back to her.

"You take it. It's your money and you know as well as I that your dad would do the same thing. Fair and equal."

Scott nodded, folded the check, and put it in his wallet. I bent down and kissed him on the cheek. "Be yourself. There's no one better."

He laughed.

"Now I'm off to make your brother's day . . . or scare the hell out of him."

"Good luck," Scott said.

I left my eldest son's office and went to the SkiStar wing and knocked on Phillip's door.

"Come on in, Ma!"

I walked inside and looked at him.

"I saw you coming down the hall," he admitted.

"Can you take some time away, maybe an hour? I need your help."

He checked his watch. "Sure, I was just waiting on a call from London but it's too late now. They won't call until tomorrow. I'll check in with Rachel and let her know when I'll be back."

A few minutes later we were in the parking lot. "You drove dad's Porsche?"

"I did. Here. I have something for you." I handed him a paper grocery sack and he pulled out the can of Pledge. His shoulders dropped and he gave me a small smile, grim, but a smile.

I walked up to passenger door and tossed him the keys. "I need you to take me somewhere."

"But Ma—"

"Drive. You always loved this car." I sat inside and closed my door, waiting.

Eventually Phillip opened the door and got into the driver's seat. He sat there a moment, both his hands on the steering wheel, flexing his fingers. He put the car in gear and started it, shifted forward and popped the clutch.

"Your dad would have loved that. Are you going to roll backwards down the hills, too?"

"Shut up, Ma." His hands on the wheel were bloodless and white.

"Is that any way to talk to your mother?"

"I hate this," he said through tight teeth.

"I know you do. Drive, son."

He followed my directions to the letter and we pulled onto a street not far from the house.

"Pull over here and park," I told him.

We were just sitting there in complete silence. I turned and I pointed at the skid marks on the road. "This is where it happened."

Phillip stared at the street and slowly closed his eyes.

"I have not had the courage to come here before

now, to even drive down this street, Phillip." My voice cracked and I took a deep breath.

The next minute he was sobbing, loud and harsh sounds that came from deep in his chest. I grabbed him and he fell against me, his shiny shaved head red and hot from spilling his grief, his arms around me, clinging to me, and we cried together.

Chapter Thirty Two

I looked up from my game of Solitaire when Molly came through the back door. "Are you okay?"

"I'm fine." She dropped her purse on the granite counter and crossed to the refrigerator, pulling out a diet cola and pouring it into a tall glass of ice.

"So what did he say when you gave him the ring back?"

She turned around, her free hand resting on the edge of the counter, Spider's pink diamond engagement ring was gone. "He asked if I was sure. He didn't seem surprised." She took another sip of cola. "Or maybe he just didn't care very much one way or the other."

I got up from the game table near the fireplace, where the night before Molly had walked in and promptly handed my delighted friend Ellie a pile of rush ordered wedding invitations, and I walked over and put my arms around Molly. "I'm sorry, sweetheart. I wish for you and your tender heart that I would have been wrong. If I could trade places with you and take all your fears and doubts away, I would."

"I know you would, Mom. I wish I could be less selfish. Like you. I resented you for being right. You are, you know . . . right. It's very annoying and difficult to keep up with. Some days I hated that you knew the right choice when I made the wrong one."

"Blind luck and the experience of making the wrong choices," I said.

"We talked about the baby and he wants to make certain his attorney draws up a support contract, with me having main custody. He will be in the picture, when he can, but not obtrusively. I think he's going to be easy about it."

"Our attorneys can work it all out." I wasn't that trusting and had talked to a good family law attorney. I wanted Molly and her child protected and safe and never to be part of a custody battle.

"Is there any ice cream?"

"Rocky Road, Peppermint, French Vanilla, Caramel Fudge Swirl and Neapolitan. Oh, and Dove bars."

"Did you get lost in the frozen food section?" Molly laughed. "I think I'll have a scoop of each."

"Want some pickles?"

"Not yet."

I joined her and we took out the ice cream cartons. "I craved black-eyed peas and ham with Scott, shepherd's pie with Phillip, root beer floats and pizza with you, and chili cheese omelets with Mickey. There's a lot ahead of you. A lifetime, really. Kids are forever."

"I told Keely today."

I groaned. "That poor girl."

"I know. Everyone around her is having babies."

"She and Phillip have options. I expect they will be okay."

"Phillip is back driving to work again. The Porsche must have done the trick. Good idea, Mom, giving him Dad's car."

Only Phillip and I knew the real story, and it was our secret. It wasn't the car. The car only got us both to the place we needed to be.

Molly and I sat down at the game table, bowls in hands. "Hmmm. This is so good."

"So how do you feel?" I asked.

"I'm not as tired. I'm so glad we called off the wedding. So glad."

"Yes, well, Ellie can't wait to burn things from someone else's marriage mistakes for a change. She claims she has eventually burned every dress she ever wore to get married in as a sacrifice to the divorce gods."

"She would," Molly said. "You old broads are a pushy lot."

"Ah. I've graduated from cougar to old broad. How sweet."

"Speaking of sweet, how is your boy candy?" Then Molly laughed.

"I talked to him last night. He said hi and to tell you that you can only marry a man you give your panties to." I took a bite of ice cream and then added, "Did I ever tell you that I tried to set him up with you when I met him on the chairlift?"

She stared at me and I saw when she realized it was true.

I shrugged and said, "Yes, well, we mothers are a pushy lot. You'll see."

"Why *is* that exactly?"

"I can only speak for me. I think it's because I feel like I want you to have everything. I want you to have it all. Although there have been times when I've felt as if I had turned into this obnoxious, overbearing mother who thinks she knows what's best for you." I paused.

Molly merely took another spoonful of ice cream.

"Okay, here's the part where you're supposed to say, 'Oh no, no, no! Mother, you could never be that horrible person.'"

We laughed together and she took my hands in hers. "I know you're coming from a good place, and I love you for it."

"Well," I admitted. "I didn't listen to my mom

either. I remember sitting in the kitchen and thinking she was so out of touch. She couldn't possibly understand what it was like to get married. I was certain she had forgotten all the things I thought were important."

"I miss Grandma."

"Me, too." I smiled, opened the game table drawer and took out a different set of cards. "Set the bowl down, Shortcake, and I'll teach you Canasta."

"So pour me another Cosmo, March." Ellie held her martini glass up in the air and I leaned over my trio of dearest friends and refilled their glasses.

"Me, too. I need another drink before we throw away a small fortune in engraved wedding invitations."

"Harrie? You're the doctor," Ellie asked. "With my body fat, how much alcohol can I consume before I'm legally drunk?"

"What body fat would that be Ellie? You lipo'd most of it out when you were married to the plastic surgeon."

"So how big should we make this fire?" MC took a poker to the fireplace and stoked the flames, then threw on some more wood. She stood back, eyeing the fire for much longer than necessary. She was stalling.

Four large white boxes stamped with Crane

were stacked in the center of the family room floor and MC, Harrie, and Ellie had come over ostensibly to help me get rid of them. But that was three and a half hours ago and not a single invite was yet burned. But we were on our third pitcher of cocktails.

Rio was coming tonight.

"Hand me a box. Let's burn them," Ellie sipped her drink. "I should have burned the invitations to all my marriages and cancelled the ceremonies, too."

"Maybe if you stand close to the fire, Ellie, you can get a faux peel," Harrie said. "Cheaper than divorce from the city's top plastic surgeon."

"Jerk. What medical school did you graduate from?"

"Screw U."

"Harrie!" MC shrieked. But the rest of us were laughing.

"That was good, Harrie. Let me pour you another," Ellie took the cocktail shaker and dumped it into Harrie's glass. "The more you drink, the funnier you are."

"That's because she drinks so seldom," MC said. "Would you want your doctor to be a drunk?"

"That's why I divorced the plastic surgeon," Ellie said, and she tossed half of a box of invitations in the fire and they flared and snapped and the heat in the room swelled more than I thought was smart.

MC jumped back. "Maybe this isn't such a good idea. Let's recycle."

I picked up the boxes and carried them out toward the garage. Recycling was my original idea. Ellie and the others just used the ceremonial burning as an excuse to meet Rio.

Just as I kicked the back door closed, I heard the doorbell. As I walked past the family room, my friends were tiptoeing (like the Pink Panther) into the living room, closer and closer to the front door. I was laughing when I opened it.

"Hey darlin'." That voice, that voice. . . .

I heard Ellie suck in a breath.

Rio pulled me into his arms and kissed me senseless.

MC was giggling.

He pulled back and looked into my eyes. "We're not alone."

I shook my head.

Rio looked over my shoulder, where a few yards away my best friends were lined up like foot soldiers in the living room.

Ellie stepped away first, her Cosmo in her hand. She walked closer and eyed him up and down. "So you're the singing cowboy?"

I laughed because it was so Ellie.

"I'm the singing cowboy," he said. "And you must be the infamous Ellie." He went down on one knee before she could blink and he began singing with a forced, off note twang about an old cowhand on the Rio Grande only he changed the words to encompass his downfall from a bad woman named Ellie.

I had not seen Ellie blush and laugh so hard in thirty years.

He met the others and we talked for a while. Every so often one of my friends would give me the okay sign.

Finally he went into the bathroom and I stood up. "Okay. You need to leave now. Go. Go. He's mine."

"Okay, okay! You're no fun at all, March."

"Is Eugene outside?"

"Of course. We're drinking aren't we?"

I waited for Rio. "My friends have to leave," I said pointedly and he walked with us outside.

He'd left his bag and a guitar case by the door and he picked them up as he came inside. A few minutes later we were in the house with the doors closed.

"I've missed you," he said.

My arms were around his neck in an instant, his arms were around me, and I was in a world of his scent and taste, and it wasn't long before we went upstairs.

About eleven that night, after we had messed up the sheets and taken a shower, I came out from blowing my hair dry and Rio was on the bed, leaning against the huge pillows wearing only jeans and his guitar. His hair was still damp from the shower and I just took in the view. He was picking out a tune.

It was okay, seeing him there. He belonged in my bed, wherever that was. He was deep inside my heart, and my head. I loved him, madly, deeply loved him.

"I have a present for you," he said. "Come sit." He patted the bed. I crawled on top and sat cross-legged.

"It's called *Because He Loved You*."

The title registered and I put my hand on his thigh. I smiled at him, looking at me and wearing that familiar tender look I knew was for me alone, and his face grew fuzzy through my teary eyes, and Rio began to sing:

> You met him too young with stars in your
> eyes,
> He taught you truths and never told lies.
> His love was honest and not for show
> He had a dream to fly upon snow.
> Together you made his dreams come true
> Because he loved you . . .
> Because he loved you . . .
>
> The years of my youth were wild and free,
> I searched for someone who could see the
> real me.

And you were in another place and time,
A place where you could never be mine.
You learned what it meant—a heart that
  was true,
Because he loved you . . .
Because he loved you . . .

The world said my love was a sin
I loved and lost again and again.
And I paid the price with my name
No one could ever forget my fame.
But you and he knew what to do,
Because he loved you . . .
Because he loved you . . .

I thought I could never love again
But then, but then, but then . . .
There you were sittin' next to me
Willing to see me for what I could be.
And soon, together, our hearts are true
Because he loved you . . .
Because he loved you . . .

Epilogue

Spring in Sparks, Nevada is a mercurial thing. You can get frosted by snow, or blown by wind, pelted with rain, or turned bright red from the hot rays of high altitude sunshine. Today is a celebration, of three generations of families, brought together because of mistakes and tragedy, kept together by a simple but sometimes elusive thing called love.

As I sit on a bench under a sprawling oak tree and watch my family with the Sierra Mountains behind them and a great blue bowl of Nevada sky over us, a year from the day I stood here and married a forty five year old singing cowboy, before all our children and their families, Scott and Renee, Phil and Keely, pregnant again with another set of twins, Molly, Mickey and Rio's son Duncan, and the grandchildren Miranda, Tyler and Trey (Turkey), Phillip's twin girls Lola and Eva, Molly's flame haired daughter Bea, named after my mother, all forming a happy, warm circle around us, our friends watching nearby. I didn't know I could find that kind of joy again.

How lucky am I? I am March Randolph Cantrell Paxton, and I was named for the time of year I came into the world. My heart was crushed one night on a one-way street in San Francisco, and in its place was left a black stone so hard and so painful, I could hardly live with it inside me, let alone carry it around; I did not know how to go on. So I limped and trudged and fell my way through the days, never thinking, never believing, I could find my heart again.

Unexpectedly, unbelievably, I found there is room in a single lifetime to love again, and I know this because of the great luck that brought me two good men. I had always thought love was a once in a lifetime thing. Just once. Just him. Never anyone else. That we would grow old together, just as we had been young together.

And though my love then was for him alone, I learned the most wonderful thing: you can recreate love with someone else. It's different. My new love is not the same as my old love had been. Though no less stronger. No less deeper.

I felt Rio walk up beside me. He placed his arm around me and kissed my ear, whispering something he loves about me. Together we stare out at the hills, the pastures, speckled yellow with mustard, and the fences, at our families, and beyond.

The breeze picked up, and a single white feather floated down from overhead. I looked up into the tree branches, where sunshine came through and touched my face.

Readers Group Questions

1. What makes our first real love so special?

2. Relationships between women are the most complex. *Bridge To Happiness* explores those relationships. How did March's relationship with her mother relate to her own relationship with Molly? Whose judgment is stronger, mother or daughter?

3. March forms lifelong relationships. Her friends were her sanity. How have your friends saved your sanity over the years?

4. March and Mike had a strong marriage for a long time. What is it about these two that makes for a lasting marriage? What are the most important aspects of a good marriage?

5. Do you believe March was a good mother? Why? Why not?

6. Do you believe raising daughters is harder than raising sons? Different? Why? Why not?

7. March's life was turned upside down in a single moment. Was her grief selfish at times? When? Was it honest? Why or why not?

8. What is the one thing you would have March do differently? Why?

9. How are Scott and Phillip, Mickey and Molly alike? How are they different? Who are they most like, March or Mike?

10. Do you believe competition in a family and between siblings is healthy? Should a mother get involved when adult siblings fight?

11. Mike died because he was in the wrong place at the wrong time. Yet Spider told March he tried to get Mike to stay the night he was killed, which opened a haunting and painful "if only" for her. Rio chose not to tell March he took Mike to the airport. Do you believe Rio should have told her? Is the truth worth the deep wound it would make? What do you believe were Spider's motives? Rio's motives? Valiant or selfish? Can love exist with a secret like this?

12. March believed Molly was with Spider for the wrong reasons. Do you believe it? Should Molly have married him for the baby?

13. Do you believe March should have walked away from Rio? Would you?

14. The age difference between Rio and March was a problem for her kids. Is it a problem for you? Why? Interestingly, age was not a problem for her sons when it came to Spider and Molly. Do you believe men see age in a woman differently?

15. How were Mike and Rio alike? How were they different? Does March have a "type"? Do you believe it's possible to have more than one great love?

About Jill Barnett

Jill Barnett was born and raised in Southern California, in the kind of idyllic coastal town the Beach Boys made famous. But as a young girl she spent plenty of summers on her grandparents' farm in Texas. Among her Southern family she was the lone native Californian. "My dad used to tease me and say I was the only prune picker in a family of cotton pickers."

A gap in jobs in her mid-thirties sent Jill back to college and working toward her Master's degree. "I intended to finish school and teach, perhaps write college textbooks that wouldn't bore all the enjoyment of history out of the average nineteen year old." But the gift of a baby daughter (something Jill had been told she could never have) changed everything.

Soon she was juggling childcare and classes, motherhood, marriage and home, and found herself in the shoes of so many women, trying to be everything to everyone. "It was October and I took my daughter to a local pumpkin farm to pick a pumpkin. I stood there watching the absolute, pure delight on her two-year-old face as she ran through the rows, finding each pumpkin more wonderful than the last. It was a seminal moment in my life. The ordinary world from your child's eyes is a magical place. You see that joy in something you take for granted—if you notice at all—and suddenly you remember to stop and pay attention to life around you, to not pant through every day but pause to really take deep breaths. You find wonder all over again."

Four days later Jill quit school to rethink her choices and concentrate on family, something she has never regretted. She was asked once if sacrificing her goals for her daughter and husband wasn't traveling backwards. "It was never a sacrifice. It was and is enrichment. I am more of a woman for the experience."

And Jill's goals had only changed, "not evaporated." Always an avid reader, she had been dabbling with a novel. "Writing is very intimidating. To dabble with an idea was safer, but was also how I found my way into my first book." Soon she was writing during downtime and almost two years to the day she quit school, she sold her first book to Pocket Books, a division of Simon and Schuster.

"We women walk such a fine line in our lives, often straddling motherhood and career, and feeling the push-pull between the two, when the truth is: we need both to be fulfilled and each one enriches the other. I discovered I had to redefine happiness away from my own expectations and guilt and especially my demands on myself. Family, love and relationships all feed my writing. My emotional response and experiences, the grittiness in life, give my work a sense of humanity.

In the years since, Jill has written thirteen novels and six short stories. There are nearly 7 million of her books in print. Her work has been published in 22 languages, audio, national and international book clubs, and large print editions, and has earned her a place on such national bestseller lists as the *New York Times*, *USA Today*, *Washington Post*, *Publishers Weekly*, Barnes and Noble and Waldenbooks—who presented Jill with the National Waldenbook Award.

Center Point Large Print
600 Brooks Road / PO Box 1
Thorndike ME 04986-0001 USA

(207) 568-3717

US & Canada:
1 800 929-9108
www.centerpointlargeprint.com